WHATEVER HAPPENED TO REAL MEN?

"I can take care of myself," said C.J. "You may think women are helpless, Mr. Hackett, but let me tell you that you're wrong. I don't need some redneck, macho idiot jumping in to save me every time I turn around . . ."

"Could'a fooled me," Sam murmured. He went on, "And what's wrong with being macho? I speak a little Spanish, I know what that means. It means bein' a man. What's wrong with that?"

"Yeah," Lucy chimed in, her blue eyes twinkling mischievously, "what's wrong with that?"

"We're getting off-track here," C.J. said with a massive effort at controlling her temper. "Mr. Hackett, you had a very bad blow to the head yesterday. That can cause disorientation and hallucinations."

At Sam's look of confusion, Lucy explained succinctly, "She doesn't believe you're from 1882."

He stood up and faced C.J. "You sayin' I'm one brick shy of a full load?"

"I'm saying you need to see a doctor."

"Huh-uh."

Lucy stepped between them. "C.J., *look* at him. The way he's dressed, the way he talks, the way he walks. This isn't the kind of guy you run into at happy hour at Hamburger Hamlet!"

She went on, "He's different. He's . . ." Her voice softened. "A real man. . . ."

PARTNERS
IN
TIME

Pamela Simpson

BANTAM BOOKS
NEW YORK · TORONTO · LONDON · SYDNEY · AUCKLAND

PARTNERS IN TIME

A Bantam Book / May 1990

ISBN 0-553-28472-X

Published simultaneously in the United States and Canada

Bantam Books are published by Bantam Books, a division of Bantam
Doubleday Dell Publishing Group, Inc. Its trademark, consisting of
the words "Bantam Books" and the portrayal of a rooster, is
Registered in U.S. Patent and Trademark Office and in other
countries. Marca Registrada. Bantam Books, 666 Fifth Avenue, New
York, New York 10103.

PRINTED IN THE UNITED STATES OF AMERICA

OPM   0 9 8 7 6 5 4 3 2 1

"*All love is a species of time travel. In order to love we transcend the boundaries of sex, of selfishness, of ego, so why not the boundary of time?*"

ERICA JONG

Prologue

Los Angeles
June 27, 1882

Sam Hackett sensed death as he stepped up to the broad front porch of the small clapboard house.

It was evident in the subdued quiet of several small children who watched him wide-eyed from the corner of the house . . . in the softly muffled weeping that came from the deep shadows within . . . and in the bedroom beyond the small front parlor, where a single lantern sputtered feebly on a bedside table.

The trail Sam had been following for months ended this evening in a house set at the end of a dusty street, hundreds of miles and countless cold camps since it all began.

As Sam crossed the parlor toward the bedroom, the light from the lantern glinted dully off the U. S. Federal Marshal's badge he wore. His eyes took in the house—the meager furnishings, the haggard young woman who stared at the gaunt man in the bed.

On this hot summer evening the man was covered only by a sheet pulled up to his waist. He lay on his side. The stain of blood across the wide bandage at his back was a badge of death. Rollie Prescott, outlaw, was dying.

His young wife clung to him, burying her face in his shoulder. Another man, slightly older, stood behind her, his hands resting on her shoulders as he tried to offer comfort. There was a family resemblance in the wheat-

1

colored hair and light blue eyes—possibly they were brother and sister.

The man whispered something to the woman, and her weeping grew louder. Shaking his head, he turned away. One sweeping glance took in Sam's badge, several days growth of beard, and the layer of trail dust on his clothes. The man's eyes narrowed in anger, and he stepped forward as if to shield the woman. "What do you want here?"

Under normal circumstances Sam would have offered sympathy, but he was no hypocrite. The truth was if he'd found Rollie sooner, he would have arrested him. Now Rollie lay dying, but that wasn't the end of it. It wouldn't end until Sam had the man he *really* wanted, the man Rollie used to ride with and whose trail Sam had followed to Los Angeles.

Emmett Traeger.

Facing the angry young man, Sam responded, "I need to talk to him."

"Can't you see he's dyin'! He can't tell you nothin'."

"Hackett?" The whisper was faint, a short, rasping breath filled with pain and the telltale rattle of blood in Rollie's lungs.

His wife looked up, her startled gaze fastening on Sam as he rounded the end of the bed.

"Hackett?" Rollie repeated. The opaque haze of death disappeared and there was recognition in eyes glittering with fever and pain.

Sam leaned forward until his face was only inches from Rollie's. "Was it Traeger?"

There was a brief nod as Rollie closed his eyes, gathering what little strength he had left. Then his eyes opened and his fingers grasped the front of Sam's shirt with clawlike desperation.

"Tell Addie . . ." he began, his breath coming in jerking gasps through parched gray lips. But it was too much. His eyelids slowly closed. They were almost translucent, shot through with blue veins vivid against ashen skin. His grip on Sam's shirt loosened, and as his hand fell to the sheet, he finished with his dying breath, "*Matthew . . .*"

"No! Dear God, no!" Addie Prescott shouted, throwing herself across her husband's lifeless body.

The sound of her weeping followed Sam as he left the bedroom, crossed the parlor, and stepped out onto the porch.

He rolled a cigarette and lit it. Leaning against the front porch post, he stared out across the small yard bounded by a white picket fence. He watched the ragtag bunch of children who were playing quietly now.

Behind him, Sam heard the front door open and close as Rollie's brother-in-law came out.

"How'd it happen?" Sam asked, still looking at the children.

"Why should I tell you anything?"

Sam faced him. "Because Rollie's dead and Traeger shot him. You've got no reason to protect Traeger."

Sam saw indecision in the subtle shift of the man's body. Then his shoulders slumped wearily and he leaned against the opposite post.

"The last few months were good for my sis and Rollie. She thought they'd put the past behind them. Rollie bought this place and all the empty land out back. He sunk every penny he had in it. He was farmin' it, makin' a go of it."

Sam didn't need to ask where Rollie had gotten the money to buy so much land. He knew where it must have come from.

"Go on," he urged.

"Traeger showed up two days ago. He and Rollie argued about somethin', scared Sis real bad. Rollie wouldn't say what it was all about, but he started wearin' his gun again and made Sis and their little boy come an' stay with my family. Then this morning Sis came back and found Rollie in the barn—shot in the back. I went to the sheriff, but it was no good. We got no proof."

"Is Traeger still around?"

"Far as I know. He's been stayin' down at Peterson's boardin'house on Wilshire."

Sam took a long drag on the cigarette. "Who's Matthew?"

"What?"

"The last thing Rollie said was *Matthew*."

The man gestured toward the children playing in the yard. "Matthew is Rollie's boy." He pointed out the child, no more than three or four years old. Matthew tumbled with another boy about the same age, the two of them squealing with delight.

It didn't make sense, Sam decided. A dying man *might* speak of the son he would never live to see grow to manhood. But why did Rollie sound so urgent as he whispered his son's name? And what did he want Sam to tell Addie?

Sam flicked the cigarette down into the dirt of the small flower bed that surrounded the porch and stared into the distance. Scattered houses lined this street, giving way to stores and businesses farther along. But Sam was not interested in the view. Instead, he saw only Traeger, finally within his grasp after the long miles of trail.

Without saying another word Sam stepped off the porch and jerked his hat low over his eyes as he started toward his horse, tied near the front gate. As he passed the children, he felt a stab of regret. Not for Rollie, who'd waited until it was too late to change his life, but for Rollie's son, Matthew, and for Matthew's mother.

They were like too many other widowed wives and fatherless children Traeger had left behind over the last few years. Their faces had begun to haunt Sam.

It was long past time for Traeger to die.

Sam watched and waited. He lit another cigarette, letting the heat sear into his lungs. A curl of smoke spiraled slowly upward, then hung suspended in the still morning air.

The air was cool and dry. The sky was cloudless, intense blue like over the high desert just after a storm. The sun rose over the rooftops of the low buildings, cutting shadows into the dirt on the street. There wasn't a breath of wind.

The arrest warrant he'd carried for months said that Traeger could be brought in dead or alive. It didn't matter much to Sam how it ended, just that it finally end. Traeger had cut a bloody path across the Outlet in the Cimarron Strip and then down into the Arizona and New Mexico territories.

Now Sam's eyes narrowed as he watched the dining room of the boardinghouse across the street. Shadows moved behind the curtained windows. One of them was Traeger.

Sam was alone now, but in the beginning he'd had a partner, Tom Hagen. He'd been with Tom when the boy earned his badge. Tom was young, fast with a gun, even faster with his temper. He was cocky about being a Federal Marshal. He thought it impressed the ladies. Sam thought he'd read too many of those dime novels.

Sam liked Tom—the kid was tough and never complained. Neither one of them paid much attention to the old shaman when they stopped that last night outside of Nogales. They'd practically ridden right into the middle of a Navajo Indian village. The Navajos were a handsome, peaceful people. There were mostly old people and women in the village, for the warriors were off hunting.

Sam respected the Indians, their ways, and their territory. Besides, it wasn't wise to make enemies. A man never knew where his trail might lead.

The old shaman sat before a roaring fire with his young grandson.

Yes, a man fitting Traeger's description, riding a lame buckskin, had passed this way.

Sam and Tom were eager to move on, but Sam knew it would have been an insult to refuse the old man when he offered to share his fire with them. The night was bitterly cold on the high desert. The old man looked at them, seeming to see straight through them. Then his gaze fixed on Sam, and he stared intently, as if he'd never seen a white man before.

"What is it?" Sam asked the boy. "Why's he lookin' at me like that?"

The boy explained in broken English that the shaman could see into tomorrow.

Still staring at Sam, the shaman's eyes slowly closed as

if he were dozing off. He startled both Sam and Tom when he began to speak.

"You will travel far to find the man you seek," the boy translated. "A journey unlike any you have ever known."

Tom hooted with laughter. Then he said, "Hey, old man, what about me?"

For a moment the shaman was silent. Then he spoke a few terse words.

The boy translated matter-of-factly, "You will die."

"Now, wait a damn minute!" Tom exploded. Catching Sam's warning look, he shrugged. "Hell, it ain't like it really means anything. Right?"

The shaman motioned to his grandson to help him stand, then he walked with painstaking slowness into his hogan.

The next day Tom died—shot in the back by Traeger in Nogales. Sam stared at the boardinghouse restaurant. Anytime now Traeger would step into the street and Sam would make his move. Months of tracking, worthless leads, sleeping on the hard ground or in some fleabag hotel, were finally going to pay off.

Sam shoved all that to the back of his mind. Instead, he looked forward to what was to come after he dealt with Traeger. He wanted a shave, a long soak in a hot bath, and a hot meal—a rare steak, fried potatoes, and fresh apple pie with a thick slice of cheese on top. He was particular about the cheese.

And he wanted a woman. He wasn't particular about her so long as she didn't do a lot of talking. He didn't like gabby women. After all, he'd been on the trail a long time and had become accustomed to silence.

He gazed down the length of the dirt street to a whitewashed building with a clock in the tower. The clock sounded the half hour. It was ten-thirty and unusually quiet. Not a breath of air stirred. There wasn't a bird in the sky.

Sam tossed down his cigarette and crushed it under his boot heel, at the same time flexing his fingers in response to a faint tingling sensation. Once more he sensed death. But this time it would be Traeger's.

A shopkeeper sweeping the boardwalk in front of his store nodded to a woman pushing a baby carriage. A water wagon creaked slowly down the street, the driver slapping the reins over the rumps of dusty mules.

A little boy, no older than Rollie Prescott's son, walked past Sam, dragging a stick in the dirt, teasing a black and white kitten.

"Is that your kitten?" Sam asked, smiling down at the boy.

The boy looked up at him with round dark eyes, bright with mischief. "No, sir. But I'm gonna tell my ma he followed me home an' ask can I keep him."

"He probably wouldn't follow you if you didn't drag that stick in front of him."

The boy put a finger to his lips. "Shh—don't tell my ma. Okay?"

Sam assumed a serious conspiratorial expression. "Okay."

The boy continued across the street, the kitten following the thin trail the stick made in the dust.

Out of the corner of his eye Sam caught a movement. Traeger ambled casually out of the boardinghouse, relaxed, unguarded, as if he hadn't a care in the world.

Sam's gaze quickly swept the street. The woman had gone inside the store with the shopkeeper, leaving the baby carriage by the open doorway. The waterhauler had stopped and gone into a laundry after loosely tying the mules to a post. The boy with the kitten was out of sight.

Sam stepped off the boardwalk, flexing his fingers once more. He wanted this done quiet and peaceful, but he wasn't a fool and knew it wouldn't happen that easily. With men like Traeger, fools ended up dead. He ran his fingers down over the smooth handle of the Colt pistol on his left hip. It was a reassuring feeling, sometimes the only one he could count on.

"Far enough, Traeger!" he called out with deadly calm.

Twenty feet away Traeger stopped abruptly. Sam took note of the sudden tension in Traeger's shoulders, the hiss of a quick, indrawn breath. His gaze fixed on Traeger's gun hand.

"Hello, Hackett. Been wonderin' how long it would take you to catch up." He spat a long stream of tobacco juice into the dirt. "You're right on my tail. I just got in day before yesterday. You must not've taken time to bury the kid."

There was no denial that he'd shot Tom. Just that wide, lethal grin.

"I buried him. I called on Rollie Prescott too. They'll be buryin' him shortly." His voice lowered. "Now it's your turn."

The grin widened. "Maybe. Then again, maybe you're not fast enough. The kid was fast, and he's dead."

"Shot in the back, just like Rollie." Sam's jaw tightened. He knew exactly what Traeger was trying to do, to make him lose his concentration and get a crucial split-second edge. "No one's fast enough to beat a backshooter. But you know that, don't you?"

Traeger's shrug was almost indifferent. "Front or back, what difference does it make?" Then he went on in a harder voice. "I don't like bein' followed."

"That's all right, 'cause the trail just ended. You're under arrest."

"There's just one problem, Hackett," Traeger replied, his hand shifting almost imperceptibly toward his gun.

Sam tensed. *Do it!* he thought. Make this fast and simple.

Traeger went on. "I don't much fancy hangin'."

Sam nodded slowly. "It doesn't have to be hanging. I can be accommodating."

Traeger's smile dissolved in an instant.

Sam saw in Traeger's eyes, in the subtle shift of his right shoulder, what was coming. Traeger's fingers flexed as his hand jerked toward the gun on his hip.

At the same time he noticed something else—a flash of black and white as the kitten shot into the street. The little boy ran after it, stopping in the middle of the street to scoop it up.

Damn! Sam cursed as he saw Traeger's attention shift to the boy, that lethal smile widening once more. But the smile didn't reach Traeger's eyes. They were cold and hard, and held the kind of expression that looked straight through a man just before shooting him. It was a cold-blooded expression no man ever forgot—if he lived to recall it.

Overhead a flock of birds burst into frenzied flight from the rooftop of a nearby building. The mules hitched across the street jerked as though startled.

Then Sam heard it: a low rumbling sound like distant thunder that seemed to come from far below the street. It rolled on, intensifying, sending Sam staggering off balance.

"What the hell!" he shouted.

He saw Traeger go down as the ground buckled beneath them. The mules fought the restraining harness, eyes rolling wildly as they bucked, broke free, then bolted forward into the center of the street.

Buildings shifted and groaned. Wooden siding popped and splintered off the buildings as windows shattered, raining glass onto the ground. The boardwalk in front of the mercantile twisted and collapsed. The two-story building with the clock tower swayed crazily. People were screaming and running around madly in confusion.

Sam looked for Traeger, but he'd disappeared. Then he saw the little boy desperately clutching the clawing kitten. The boy had fallen to his knees in the path of the frantic mules.

As the child screamed in terror, Sam had only a fraction of a second to react. In less than a heartbeat he made his choice. Forgetting Traeger, he went for the boy. And as he stumbled across the shifting ground, he wondered what the hell was happening. And where the hell was Traeger?

Chapter 1

Los Angeles
June 27, 1989

The look in his blue-green eyes was brooding, sensual, tinged with a dangerously erotic edge. As Mel Gibson slowly walked toward her, his lithe body exuded an animal intensity.

C.J. gave him a long, cool look. She appeared utterly calm, but inside she fought for control. "What are you doing here?"

"I had to come back. You knew I would."

She tilted her chin defiantly. "We said our good-byes."

He took one last step, breaking the invisible barrier between them. He was close now, so close.

"You know we'll never say good-bye."

C.J. drew in a sharp breath as he brought his hands up, cradling her face for the kiss that sent tremors of desire coursing through her. His breath was warm against her cheek as he kissed away every last ounce of resistance, silenced all her protests until they were soft whimpers of desire.

He began to undress her slowly, peeling off layer upon silken layer, pressing her down onto the bed. His breath blew warm and sweet across her cheek, his lips moved toward hers as he . . . licked her face?

C.J. came up out of the dark depths of sleep to stare into the furry face of Redford, a one-eyed yellow tabby, sitting in the middle of her chest, his loud purr roaring in her ear.

She groaned, fighting off consciousness, trying to recapture the dream of dreams. Dislodging Redford, she turned and buried her face in her pillow.

It all came back . . . Mel's hands moving over her body with a practiced ease that curled her toes. There was no stopping him now, he meant to have her. No more good-byes, no more . . .

The loud knocking jarred her finally and irrevocably out of sleep and out of Mel's arms.

She swore a muffled oath into her pillow. Then, raising her head slightly, she mumbled, "Go away!"

Her bedroom door flew open and the same familiar voice that she'd heard on countless mornings all her thirty years called, "Good morning, pumpkin!" The voice was disgustingly cheerful for so early in the day.

Peeling open one tired eye, C.J. stared at her mother.

Lucy Grant Kleinfeldt Ferrer was a petite redhead with vivid blue eyes. An amused expression continually shone in those eyes and curved the corners of her full lips. She was dressed in typical fashion this morning—a bright magenta silk shirt and equally bright crimson skirt, pulled together, so to speak, by a neon-yellow belt. A matching magenta scarf fit snugly around her head, tied behind one ear, pinning back her unruly hair.

A gold chain with a large, clear crystal pendant hung from her neck. Each finger of both hands was covered in an odd assortment of rings, and a series of tiny gold bells hung suspended from one ear. Multicolored dime-store gems winked in the other earlobe.

"How can you be so damn happy so early in the morning?" C.J. grumbled as she pulled herself to a sitting position against the hard brass headboard.

"It's a gorgeous day," Lucy said with a huge grin. As she slipped around the door, countless gold bangle bracelets covering the length of her arms jangled loudly. "I've brought you the paper and a nice hot cup of tea."

She set both on the scarred oak nightstand next to the bed, shoving aside a half-empty can of Diet Coke, a yellow legal-size notepad and pen, a box of tissues, a small enamel box that contained condoms, and the latest Danielle Steel novel.

Just then Newman, a pint-sized, shaggy, blue-eyed mutt raced in, jumped on the bed, and began chasing Redford back and forth across C.J.

She sat up straighter and stared suspiciously at the tea. "What kind is it?"

Lucy's grin widened. "Fresh herb tea with mint, lightened with just a hint of goat's milk."

C.J. fell back onto the pillow and shuddered. God, from Mel Gibson to tea with goat's milk, and a dog and cat chasing each other in a blur of yellow and gray across her bed.

I have lost control of my life, she thought.

"What time is it?" she asked Lucy, who was busily picking up clothes from the floor and hanging them in the narrow closet.

"Quarter to nine. Better hustle your buns, sweetie, or you'll be late. I'll be downstairs."

With that, she swept from the room.

Ignoring the tea, C.J. stretched tiredly, yawned, then reluctantly got up. She decided she was going to have to talk to her mother about walking in on her like this. It could be embarrassing under certain circumstances. Although, she admitted to herself ruefully, it had been a long time since that particular circumstance had occurred.

C.J. padded across the cold hardwood floor in stocking feet, heading toward the bathroom. The worn, oversize T-shirt that she used as a nightshirt had twisted around her hips, and she tugged at it, pulling it down around her thighs. It seemed to fit more snugly than usual, and she realized with a sinking heart that it was diet time again.

In the bathroom, with its thirties-era pink and burgundy tile, she took one quick, critical glance at herself in the narrow mirror over the medicine cabinet, wincing at the circles under her eyes. That wasn't the worst of it. Her auburn hair—the same deep shade of copper Lucy's had been before she turned to l'Oréal Light Auburn—was a mess, plastered flat against one side of her head and sticking out on the other side. Her brown eyes were bleary, her complexion pale.

No more late nights with the girls, prowling West Side singles bars, C.J. vowed as she turned on the shower. She was getting too old to come crawling in at two A.M. when she had to be at work by eight. Besides, it was such a waste. She met the same kinds of men over and over again—married ones looking for a no-strings-attached fling, single ones looking for a no-strings-attached fling, neurotic ones looking for commitment.

Why is it, she wondered as she savored the delicious feeling of hot water beating against her body, *that the only men who are willing to make definite plans for, next New Year's Eve, let alone the rest of their lives, have severely damaged psyches?*

The question, C.J. was certain, ranked right up there with the big ones—the meaning of life and why people continued to give money to Jim and Tammy Bakker.

Whatever happened to real men anyway? The kind of men who were honest and sincere, who said what they meant and meant what they said, who had no hangups about their masculinity and weren't threatened by strong women, who could be both tough and tender, who didn't take sex lightly . . .

Where can you find a man like that nowadays, C.J. wondered as she turned off the shower and stepped out onto a furry bathmat that had once been white but was now beige. She knew she wasn't going to come up with the answer to that one. Because the hard truth was that men like that, if they ever existed, certainly didn't exist anymore.

In five minutes she had moussed her hair into a semblance of order and put on just enough makeup to look California casual-chic. In her days as a struggling actress, she had learned how to use makeup skillfully and quickly. That was one of the residual benefits of training as an actress—along with an ability to lie extremely well (a real benefit in her current profession) and a sense of how to carry her five-foot-eight-inch body with grace.

Eight years earlier, when she was fresh out of

U.C.L.A. film school, she had big dreams of stardom. But she discovered that her "young Shirley MacLaine" type was out of fashion. In one cattle call after another, she found herself passed over for buxom blondes.

In those days she lived next door in a studio apartment that, like this narrow, two-story house, faced Venice Beach. Harry Carlucci lived here and operated the Continental Detective Agency out of the office below. At thirteen Harry had met Dashiell Hammett, author of *The Maltese Falcon* and a former private detective. Harry immediately decided to become a detective too. By the time he hired C.J. to do undercover work for him, he'd been a self-described "gumshoe" for over thirty years.

C.J. discovered she was good at the work, and she certainly needed the money. She earned almost nothing as an actress, and spent most of her time at the unemployment office in Santa Monica, standing in line with a lot of other out-of-work actors. Rumor had it that Groucho Marx had once showed up there to collect his check. She was in good, if generally impoverished, company.

Though they were as different as a ditsy young actress and a tough-talking private eye could be, somehow C.J. and Harry meshed. As she did more and more work for him, he taught her everything he knew. When he died, he left her the Continental Detective Agency simply because there wasn't anyone else.

C.J. liked to believe that the roles she played in undercover work kept her in touch, somehow, with her acting. Actually, they paid the rent and kept food on the table for the assorted strays, both animals and people, she was always taking in. She never could resist a sad, imploring look, whether it was on a furry face or a human one. That accounted for Redford and Newman, not to mention various men who came and went.

Over the years a succession of unemployed actors, artists, writers, and less creative but equally needy types had slept on her sofa and occasionally in her bed.

On her way to her closet she stepped over Redford, and took a wet, bedraggled sock out of Newman's tightly clenched jaws. Grabbing a white gauze blouse and faded jeans, she dressed quickly. As she tugged the zipper to get it up, she thought once more, *Yup, diet time*. It would be rice cakes with tuna for dinner over the next week or so.

Picking up the paper that still lay on the nightstand, she quickly scanned the morning headlines—the usual graft, corruption, murder, mayhem, and smog. It was going to be a typical L.A. day.

Leaving the tea untasted, she went into the kitchen and grabbed a Diet Coke from the refrigerator. She sipped it as she went outside, down the cement stairs to the office below. The Spanish-style beige-colored stucco building dated from the thirties and had been one of the first homes on the beach. Originally designed as a duplex, with one apartment upstairs and another downstairs, it was now both home and office to C.J. As she went around to the front door of the office, she glanced in the huge, arched window and saw Lucy sitting at the receptionist's desk. Lucy, who had recently started working part-time for C.J. as a secretary-receptionist, glanced up at her and frowned as she noticed the Coke.

"Do you know what you're doing to your body? That stuff is full of all kinds of preservatives, not to mention caffeine."

C.J. ignored the criticism. "Pay the power and phone bills. There's just enough in the checking account. And type the Levkowitz report. I should be back by noon."

She glanced longingly out the window at the waves that beckoned. It would feel great to go bodysurfing. But there was no time now. She had a brand-new Mercedes 560 SL to repossess for a client.

As she left, Lucy asked, "How'd you like the tea?"

"Delicious," C.J. threw back over her shoulder. Actually, she thought it would make a great mudpack, but she wouldn't dare tell her mother that.

At the rear of the building she backed her white '66 Mustang convertible out of the garage. She had bought the car ten years earlier when she was in college, using student loan money. Even then the paint was peeling and the top had holes in it. Now it looked like the cars the Rent-a-Wreck agency advertised for ten dollars a day. But C.J.

loved it, just as she loved all quirky, slightly defective but charming things—and people.

As she pulled away, she waved to her neighbor, a grandmother in her seventies who loved to roller-skate down the walkway that ran along Venice Beach. At five feet two inches tall, she was definitely one of the more colorful residents. She wore bright purple boxer shorts and a lime-green tank top. Headphones rested around her wrinkled neck and she sported a baseball cap with the words "Born to Boogie," emblazoned like a welcome sign across the front.

Farther along the narrow road, C.J. passed a local artist making life-size sand sculptures on the beach. The figures looked as if they were participating in an orgy, and C.J. had no doubt that the artist intended just that.

She continued on down the length of Venice, a mile and a half along the Pacific Ocean between staid Santa Monica to the north and Marina del Rey, ghetto of affluent singles, to the south. While the rest of L.A. was gearing up for heat and smog, the air at the beach was clear, freshened by a cool ocean breeze.

She passed Westminster Beach, where the boys met the boys and the girls met the girls, and Muscle Beach, where musclemen and musclewomen pumped iron. Street musicians and improvisational theater groups performed on the walkway that ran the length of the beach. Strolling past them were Sikhs, healers, skateboarders, elderly Jews, burnt-out hippies and a variety of young men and women on the loose.

Three- and four-story buildings with murals on the once-blank walls passed in a colorful blur. Leaning against them were panhandlers, both traditional big-city middle-aged winos and young drug addicts.

On Ocean Front Walk peddlers and street artists had set up their stands in the vacant lots among the small apartment buildings, shops, and restaurants. They sold everything from paratrooper pants to baskets, and a bewildering variety of food. The aroma of grilled hot dogs and hamburgers, tacos and burritos, soul food and chili already filled the air.

Venice was a mecca for the health-and-fitness conscious, from vegetarians who shopped at organic food shops to professional male and female bodybuilders who worked out at Gold's Gym.

It was raunchy, sometimes dangerous, never boring. C.J. couldn't imagine living anywhere else.

She turned her car onto the Santa Monica Freeway, east, and headed toward downtown L.A., leaving behind the "anything goes" atmosphere of Venice for bumper-to-bumper freeway traffic. She felt great. Bruce Springsteen played on the tape deck, there wasn't a cloud in the sky, and the case she was working on was highly lucrative. A wealthy Beverly Hills socialite who'd married her much-younger hairdresser, then divorced him when she caught him sleeping with her gardener, had hired C.J. to repossess the Mercedes 560 SL that *wasn't* part of the divorce settlement.

She had given C.J. the keys to the car and told her where it was likely to be found. All C.J. had to do was pick up the car and return it to her client. For that she would collect a thousand dollars and the rent would be paid for another month.

All in all, it looked like it was going to be a terrific day.

Shortly before ten-thirty C.J. pulled into a parking lot in the heart of Century City. The errant ex-husband worked in the building next door and always parked his car—actually, C.J.'s client's car—in this lot.

Century City was a niche of high-rise office buildings and high-priced condos surrounded by Beverly Hills, West L.A., and West Hollywood. It was some of the priciest real estate in L.A. Attorneys, money managers, and independent movie production companies all had offices there. The address definitely carried a certain cache.

Originally it had all been part of the old United Film Studios back lot, where countless movies, especially westerns, had been shot from the silent movie era up to the sixties. Then the owners of the studio had started selling off the land to developers, bit by bit, until now the studio itself occupied a mere five hundred acres out of what had once been five thousand. It sat at the edge of Century City, the old two-story buildings and sound stages looking incongruous next to the skyscrapers.

One of the first acting jobs C.J. had when she was in the business had taken place on the United lot. Now, as she stepped out of her car, she could still remember the excitement she'd felt on driving onto the lot and entering a world of make-believe. She rarely felt regret over the acting career that had never quite taken off, but now she knew a twinge of something—perhaps wistfulness—because she knew she had been good. Really good. She'd just never been given the chance to show it.

She had just slammed shut her car door when she heard a low rumble that sounded as if it came from deep within the bowels of the earth. At first it seemed distant, but it quickly grew louder, like a freight train coming at her. The ground beneath her feet buckled, the sidewalk cracked, and the tall buildings began to sway back and forth.

"Oh, my God!" C.J. whispered.

Cars on the street bounced jerkily around, banging into each other. On the sidewalk, people screamed in panic and pushed crazily past each other. A young mother picked up her small son, then looked around desperately.

C.J. was knocked to the sidewalk by a falling piece of plaster molding from a nearby building. As she struggled to get up, she felt blood streaming down one side of her face, pain pulsing through the back of her head.

A large piece of molding fell on the panic-stricken mother, knocking her and the child to the ground. As they lay there, the child crying in terror, an out-of-control car careened wildly in their direction.

Stunned, feeling as though she were moving in slow motion, C.J. ran on shaky legs toward the mother and child. "Come on, you've got to move!" she shouted.

Pulling the woman to her feet, she looked back to see the car heading straight toward them. There was no way she could get all of them out of the way. She was going to die, she just knew it.

A crazy thought flashed through her mind—her mother's admonition to wear clean underwear because you never knew when you might be in an accident and wind up in the hospital.

What happened next was like something out of a movie. A man came from out of nowhere, scooping up the boy, and pushing C.J. and the woman out of the car's path. The front fender struck him a glancing blow, knocking him to the ground. But as he fell, he kept his arms wrapped protectively around the little boy.

It all happened in no more than a split second, yet it seemed like a freeze frame in a movie—the car, the terror-stricken mother, the hysterical child, and the man, dressed like a cowboy in a B western. He was big and tall, with dark hair and a mustache. He wore a long overcoat, and strapped to his left thigh was a holster holding a pistol. Slung over his shoulder was a long rifle.

"I'm in the middle of a movie, and I didn't even know it," C.J. thought before everything went out of focus and she lost consciousness.

She came to slowly. First she heard sounds—the loud wail of a siren, voices shouting, crying. Then her vision cleared and she saw medical equipment, including a respirator. After a moment she realized she was inside an ambulance that was just beginning to move.

When she tried to sit up, she discovered she was strapped to a gurney. Good God, what happened? It all came back to her as her gaze fastened on the man lying on the gurney beside her. He had saved her life—as well as the lives of the mother and child. He was still unconscious, and there was a bandage on his head, another on his arm.

Seeing him so close now, C.J. caught details of his appearance—a tiny white scar on his chin, crow's feet at the corners of his eyes, the deep bronze of his skin. He had the rough, weathered look of someone who spent a great deal of time outdoors.

But why was he dressed that way, she wondered. The last time she saw an outfit like that, it was on a movie set extra.

Then her nose caught his pungent scent. No extra, she

decided, but a wrangler. What was a wrangler who'd obviously just been around horses doing in Century City?

C.J.'s gaze focused on a paramedic sitting at the foot of the gurney. "Will he be all right?" she asked anxiously.

He flashed a knowing smile. "Sure. His arm isn't too bad. That cut on his head will need a few stitches and he may have a concussion, but that should be all."

She felt a surge of relief. Somehow, it mattered very much to her that this rather odd-looking stranger be okay.

The paramedic hesitated, then asked, "Do you know this guy?"

C.J. shook her head and immediately regretted the movement as a sharp pain surged through her.

"I was just wondering," the paramedic continued, "because of the way he's dressed. I thought maybe he was an actor, somebody I should recognize."

C.J. had forgotten about the gun and rifle. She wondered if they were real, or merely props. They certainly looked real. Maybe he was an actor after all, and not a mere wrangler. But they wouldn't be shooting a western in Century City. They'd do that on what was left of the back lot at United Film Studios, or maybe at Universal.

Besides, she knew for a fact that all props were carefully checked in and out with the prop department. They wouldn't let someone just walk off the lot with them, especially if the weapons were real.

Her thoughts were jumbled, nothing made sense. Whatever the explanation, this man certainly didn't belong with the dark-suited executives bustling around Century City.

Staring at him, C.J. wondered where on earth he did belong.

The emergency room at the hospital was pure bedlam. There had been a lot of injuries in the quake, though apparently no deaths. The examining rooms, the waiting room, the hallway, were all filled with injured people. Doctors and nurses hurried from patient to patient, seeing to the most serious cases first. It was hours before C.J.'s relatively minor cut was taken care of with five stitches and a small bandage, and she was told she could leave.

She called Lucy to make sure she was okay. It took an hour of trying. The lines were either down or busy because of all the emergency calls being placed. When she finally got through, she heard the immense relief in Lucy's voice. Lucy went on to tell her that there had been little damage in Venice.

Several people were lined up behind C.J., waiting to use the pay phone, so there was no time for a lengthy talk. She told Lucy she'd be home as soon as possible, and hung up.

At one point she saw the mother and child whose lives the man had saved. They, too, were treated and released. The woman looked exhausted and high-strung, and left without attempting to thank their rescuer. That was typical of L.A., C.J. thought as she watched the man lying on a gurney, still unconscious.

She thought about leaving, too, but somehow she was reluctant to simply walk away without making sure he was all right. He looked so alone. The least she could do was stay with him until he regained consciousness and thank him.

All the chairs were taken, so C.J. curled up in a corner on the floor and waited. Around her the noise, confusion, and tension gradually abated as people were admitted to the hospital or released. She watched the man lying on the gurney. His arm had been bandaged by a doctor, the cut on his head stitched. He lay still, his eyes closed. She wondered what color they were—dark, like his hair? Or blue. Maybe even green.

She had no idea how long she'd been sitting there when his eyelids finally flickered. Rising quickly, she went over to him. Instinctively, she reached out to place her hand over his rough, strong one in a simple gesture meant to soothe and comfort.

Immediately, his eyes flew open and his fingers closed around her wrist in a viselike grip.

Startled, C.J. stared down into intense blue-green

eyes. The expression in them was confused, almost disoriented. It touched her profoundly.

"Who the hell are you!" he demanded. At the same time he started up off the gurney. Wincing at the pain from the sudden movement, he fell back onto the stiff white sheets and closed his eyes for a moment. He was pale, his breath shallow and rapid.

"It's okay," C.J. reassured him. "You're all right."

But his grip didn't relax. Opening his eyes, he asked, "Where's Traeger?"

She managed to pull her wrist from his grasp. "I'm sorry. I don't know who you're talking about. Did you lose track of someone in the quake?"

"Yeah," he whispered, his voice weak with exhaustion.

"Maybe you could ask a nurse to see if your friend was brought here," C.J. suggested helpfully.

But the man wasn't paying attention now. His eyes slowly scanned the emergency room. "Where the hell am I?"

"Century City Hospital."

"Why is everyone dressed like that?"

C.J. followed his gaze. She didn't understand what he was getting at. "They're doctors and nurses," she explained slowly, wondering if the blow to his head had seriously affected the man.

"You've got a concussion," she went on, "but you'll be okay. By the way, I'm C.J. Grant. I want to thank you for what you did. It was very brave, Mr.—uh . . ."

Her voice trailed off questioningly.

For a long moment he was silent. Then he answered slowly, as if he weren't sure. "Sam . . . Sam Hackett."

"Mr. Hackett, you saved my life. I'll forever be in your debt."

He focused on her. "You always look like this?"

Her smile dissolved in an instant. "What do you mean?"

"Your hair's all chopped off. And you're wearin' Levi's."

C.J.'s temper flared. "They're Pierre Cardin," she snapped. "And I happen to like my hair short. Not that it's any business of yours. You know, you don't exactly look like you just stepped out of José Eber's salon."

"Who?" he asked with a blank look.

"José Eber," she repeated in a tight voice. She would have gone on to comment on his lack of a shave, not to mention the pungent odor his clothes gave off, but just then an officious-looking woman with a clipboard and a sheaf of forms stepped up to them.

"Name?" she asked tersely, looking down at Sam.

"Why?" he demanded.

"For insurance forms, of course."

"I don't have insurance," he answered.

The woman grimaced. "I knew it." She immediately moved on to another patient.

C.J. decided that even if Sam Hackett had just saved her life and the lives of two other people, he had a major attitude problem. And she didn't need to put up with it. She had better things to do than stand around the emergency room being insulted.

"Good-bye, Mr. Hackett," she finished, biting off the words, then turned and headed toward the pay phone.

The line had dwindled, and in a few minutes she was able to call for a cab. But she still fumed over her conversation with her irritating rescuer.

Jerk, she muttered under her breath. Where did he get off, criticising her short hair. Men were all alike—they liked the Barbie-doll look—long hair, huge breasts, no thighs, no brain.

Who was he to talk anyway? He wasn't exactly the perfect candidate for *GQ*. Although, she admitted reluctantly, he was attractive in a rugged kind of way. A throwback to the old days, when women liked men who would grab them by the hair and drag them off to a cave.

A few of her friends still went for that kind of man. Donna, for instance, would take one look at those blue-green eyes, and that broad chest covered with a soft mat of dark, curling hair, and just melt. Not that C.J. had been looking at his chest, but a doctor had unbuttoned his shirt and she couldn't help noticing.

C.J. was outside the emergency room entrance now,

waiting for the cab. Glancing back over her shoulder, she found Sam Hackett standing there, holstered gun slung over one shoulder, the rifle cradled in his bandaged arm.

She couldn't believe they'd released him already with that head injury. If he'd had insurance, they probably would have admitted him to the hospital.

He stood staring at a newspaper rack just outside the door. He seemed totally oblivious of everything and everyone around him as he stared at the front page of the paper, visible through the glass front of the rack. The expression on his face was unlike anything C.J. had ever seen before—stark disbelief.

His insults were forgotten as her heart went out to him. For all his size and tough demeanor, at that moment he looked as vulnerable and helpless as the child he had saved only hours earlier.

She walked up to him. "Are you all right?" she asked, her voice soft with concern.

He stared at her with an intensity that would have been flattering under different circumstances. Now it merely seemed desperate.

"The date on the paper says June 27, 1989," he responded slowly.

"Well . . . yeah." She wondered why the date should be so significant.

An ambulance pulled up to the entrance, siren blaring, red lights flashing.

Sam jumped as if he'd been hit. "What the hell is that!" he shouted over the loud wailing.

C.J. thought, *Poor guy, that head injury must be more serious than it appeared*.

Just then a cab pulled up. The cabbie leaned out the open window and asked, "You the lady who called for a cab?"

"Yes," C.J. answered quickly. She looked back at Sam, who stood there, rigid, tense, staring out at the world as if it posed an immediate and terrifying threat.

"C'mon, lady," the cabbie protested irritably, "the meter's running. Where ya' goin'?"

"Venice." She opened the door and started to get in.

But she couldn't resist one last look at Sam. He looked so utterly lost.

"Just a minute," C.J. told the cabbie.

"What?"

"Just wait a minute," she called back over her shoulder.

Walking up to Sam, she asked, "Are you okay?"

He didn't respond. He simply stood there, staring past her at cars rushing by on the busy boulevard.

"Where do you live?"

"I—" He stopped, then shook his head. His eyes, filled with a troubled expression, stared around him in bewilderment as if he couldn't quite grasp anything.

She frowned. "They shouldn't have released you yet. With that concussion you're not thinking clearly."

"Lady!" the cabbie shouted impatiently.

"All right!" C.J. responded.

She turned back to Sam, and as her eyes met his she came to a reluctant decision. "C'mon," she said, taking his elbow and leading him toward the cab.

"What are you doing?"

"It's late, you can stay at my place tonight. In the morning we'll get you home. It's the least I can do, seeing as how you saved my life."

But as she got into the backseat of the cab ahead of him, he hesitated. "It's okay," she reassured him, "I can afford the cab." He certainly didn't look as if he could afford so much as a cup of coffee.

"What is this?" he asked.

The cabbie yelled at him, "Get in, buddy. I'm backin' up traffic."

C.J. tugged at Sam's arm. Finally he allowed himself to be pulled into the cab. As they took off, he was thrown back against the seat.

"My God," he whispered in an awed voice, his hands braced on either side of him on the seat. "I'll be damned—a horseless carriage!"

Chapter 2

"Where . . . did . . . you . . . get . . . this . . . guy?" Lucy asked between gasps.

"Just . . . pull . . . the . . . damn . . . boot . . . off," C.J. responded, bracing her foot against the sofa in her small living room and holding Sam's leg while Lucy pulled the boot. Sam lay sprawled on the sofa, not just asleep but unconscious.

It was after midnight, she'd been through an earthquake, and she hadn't repossessed the damn Mercedes. She was dead tired and her head was beginning to pound. In the morning she'd have to calm down her impatient client and try again. And the stranger she'd brought home had passed out as soon as he'd crossed her threshold.

Lucy straightened for a moment to take a deep breath. "This boot is not coming off." Wrinkling her nose fastidiously, she went on. "Judging by the smell, it hasn't been off in weeks."

"Look, he saved my life, okay? So quit bitching and pull the boot off."

After several more tries the boot finally came off. Five minutes later the other followed. Lucy held them at arm's length before dropping them on the floor. Newman sniffed at them curiously, then backed away.

Sam's shirt and pants followed, leaving him in dirty white cotton longjohns.

C.J. hesitated.

Lucy grinned. "Do you believe this guy? Longjohns in the middle of summer! He must be a tourist." Then, taking

27

in his wide shoulders and long legs, she murmured, "My, he is a big one, isn't he?"

"Mother! Just help me get the damn things off."

Lucy's blue eyes twinkled mischievously. "Whatever you say."

As they tugged at the longjohns, Lucy went on. "Lord, the man has terrible taste in clothes. I've seen skid-row bums who are better dressed."

Ignoring her mother, C.J. finished pulling off the longjohns and dropped them in the pile of other clothes destined for her washing machine. She tried very hard not to look at Sam, especially certain parts of Sam, but her eyes seemed to have a will of their own. They focused first on hard, muscled calves, then narrow hips . . .

"C.J."

. . . broad chest . . .

"C.J.!"

She jerked to attention. "What?"

"Would you look at those guns!"

"I've already seen them. Put them where I don't have to look at them anymore. They make me nervous."

In spite of the fact that C.J. had a license to carry a gun, and had been well trained in how to use one, she felt extremely uncomfortable around them. She rarely carried one when she was working, because most of the time there was no need. On the rare occasions when she found herself in trouble, she relied on her wits to get out of it.

Lucy insisted, "Did you *really* look at them?"

C.J. threw a blanket over Sam. She blew a strand of hair out of her eyes as she grabbed one well-muscled leg and tried to rearrange him in a more comfortable position. "You know how I feel about guns," she responded.

Lucy shook her head. "I'm no expert, but these look old. Really old." There was a note of awe in her voice as she ran her fingers over the chiseled handle of the revolver.

She looked at Sam stretched out on the sofa. "Where do you suppose a guy like that would get authentic period pieces like a Colt revolver and a Winchester rifle? They must cost a fortune. He looks like he doesn't have a cent to his name."

"Oh, here, give them to me," C.J. said testily. She put both guns on the coffee table. "I'll put them away later."

Lucy went on. "What's he doing, armed to the teeth, anyway? You don't suppose he's a robber or a drug dealer, do you?"

C.J. gave her a long look. "Don't be ridiculous. Drug dealers dress better than this. At least they do on *Miami Vice*." She sighed. "It's been a long day. I'm going to bed." She pointed Lucy toward the door. "Good night, Mother. I'll see you in the morning."

"Why don't I stay here, just for tonight. I could push a couple of chairs together . . ."

C.J. gave Lucy a firm push in the direction of the door. "Good night, Mother."

As she closed the door on Lucy, C.J. turned back to look at Sam for a long moment. Lying there, dead to the world, he looked surprisingly vulnerable. His tough expression had softened, the lines easing around his mouth and eyes. She remembered the expression she'd seen in his eyes earlier, outside the emergency room—confused, wary, like a wounded animal brought to bay.

Sam wasn't as easy to read as most of the people she came into contact with. Acting had taught her to see through people, to their underlying feelings and motivations. Usually she could characterize anyone as to type, but Sam Hackett defied being typed.

On the surface he was simply a stranger who had been in the right place at the right time, as far as C.J. was concerned. Even now she shuddered, remembering what might have happened if he hadn't been there.

But she couldn't accept that superficial evaluation of Sam. For one thing, he was dressed so strangely that she couldn't help being intrigued by him. Even in a city like L.A., where the bizarre was commonplace, Sam didn't seem to fit in.

He might be a wrangler, or a movie extra, as she had first assumed, but somehow that didn't sound quite right. Then there was his odd reaction when he awoke in the hospital. He actually acted as if C.J. and everyone else looked strange. The obvious explanation—that he was on something—was quickly dismissed. The hospital wouldn't have released him if that had been the case. They wouldn't have released him if he was crazy either, so that couldn't be the explanation.

She shook her head in frustration. There was no point in this speculation. The guy must have a home somewhere. In the morning maybe his concussion would be better, he'd be less disoriented, and could tell her where he lived. She'd give him a ride home, and that would be that.

It was the least she could do for someone who'd just saved her life. Then she could put him out of her mind.

C.J. went into her bedroom, got ready for bed, and turned off the light. As she slipped between the sheets, the thought occurred to her that he might have a wife or girlfriend waiting for him at home. A man as attractive as Sam was bound to have someone.

Somehow the thought wasn't as comforting as it should have been.

Early the next morning—too early after the kind of day and night she'd just had—C.J. sat in her office downstairs, listening to a new client. Julie Prescott was no more than twenty, rail-thin, and outrageously punk. She made Lucy look positively demure by comparison, with her orange and blue hair moussed into a pretty fair imitation of the Bride of Frankenstein, blue eyes heavily lined with kohl, and black T-shirt and worn jeans, both of which were artistically torn in interesting places.

Despite her determined effort to look as radical as possible, there was something sweet and fragile about her. She was polite and soft-spoken, her slightly breathless voice catching occasionally and leaving her momentarily speechless. C.J. found herself battling an almost irresistible urge to clean Julie up, then feed her very well.

"Dee Dee Conrad recommended you to me," Julie began in her tentative, little-girl voice.

C.J. smiled, remembering the case, one of her more eccentric ones. When Dee Dee separated from her immensely wealthy, much older husband of only a year it was very messy in spite of a premarital agreement. Dee Dee had been wife number four, and at Ruxton Conrad's age, more of a highly paid caretaker/companion than a wife in the true biblical sense.

Ruxton had lavished Dee Dee with every extravagance during their twelve months of wedded bliss. But Dee Dee, who at twenty-two had a very healthy libido, decided she needed a few extracurricular activities—racquetball, tennis, the tennis pro. When Ruxton discovered his wife's enthusiasm for sports both on and off the courts, he promptly kicked her out of their Holmby Hills mansion and sued for divorce.

Both sides haggled over the property settlement. Of particular concern was a fully functional bidet with one-quarter-inch solid eighteen-carat-gold plating and ornate dolphins in strategic places.

Ruxton argued that the bidet was a household fixture and Dee Dee had no right to it. Dee Dee argued that since her soon-to-be-ex-husband was incapable of using it, and had purchased it expressly for her during their honeymoon in Venice, Italy, it clearly belonged to her. When negotiations broke down, Ruxton simply had the bidet removed, gold floor bolts and all, leaving a gaping hole in the master bathroom's tiles.

Dee Dee hired C.J. to find the bidet. After C.J. located it, she made the mistake of telling Dee Dee's attorney the location in front of Dee Dee. At four o'clock the next morning Dee Dee was pulled over by a cop for doing seventy in a thirty-five zone in her fire-engine-red Lamborghini Countach (a twenty-first-birthday present from Ruxton). She wore a black turtleneck sweater with a hood, skin-tight black pants, boots, and gloves. The police cruiser's red lights gleamed off the gold bidet in the passenger seat beside her.

She promptly went to jail for grand theft.

Now, looking at Julie Prescott, C.J. smiled broadly. "How is Dee Dee?"

"She's out on bail. They're nowhere near a settlement on the divorce. Actually," Julie admitted, "I think Ruxton is having second thoughts."

Somehow C.J. wasn't surprised. "How did you meet Dee Dee?"

"We took an acting class together before she got married. Principles of Method Acting. It was great, I learned how to really dig deep and pull up all kinds of stuff from my psyche." Julie finished confidently, "My teacher said I could be the Marilyn Monroe of the nineties."

C.J.'s heart sank—she didn't need another client who was a would-be actress. That meant getting her fee up front, or writing it off entirely.

"What can I do to help you?" she asked, a slight wariness in her tone.

Julie's smile dissolved in an instant. "I want you to find the person who murdered my grandfather."

Whatever C.J. had expected, it wasn't this. With a young woman like Julie, she was prepared for a heartbreaking story regarding an itinerant actor or rock musician who disappeared from her life. A murdered grandfather was something else again.

"Perhaps you'd better tell me exactly what happened."

Julie launched into a long, rambling story about her grandfather, Dan Prescott, a stuntman and extra on western movies. He'd started out in the '30s in movies with everyone from John Wayne to Roy Rogers, and according to his granddaughter he was just about the greatest person who ever lived.

"He raised me," Julie explained, "after my mom and dad died in a car accident when I was eight. He was my whole family, there wasn't anyone else."

She stopped and stared down at her hands twisting in her lap.

"How did he die?" C.J. asked gently.

Julie looked up at her and her soft voice hardened. "The police said it was an accident, but it wasn't. It was murder."

Julie emphasized the word with dramatic effect.

"What exactly happened?"

"He hadn't worked in a while. Well, you know, they haven't made too many westerns lately. But then he was hired to do this new one and he was so excited. Everything went fine until his last scene, where he was supposed to be killed by the hero." Julie's voice caught as she finished. "Only instead of blanks, there was live ammunition in the gun."

C.J. didn't know what to say. Accidents during filming weren't exactly rare. Egomaniacal directors who wanted a dramatic effect at any price, careless crew members, actors who didn't know how to deal with firearms and explosives, all contributed to serious, sometimes fatal accidents.

Julie's accusation of murder sounded more emotional than rational. Obviously, she'd cared deeply for her grandfather and wasn't handling her loss well.

C.J. began carefully, "You know, accidents do happen, unfortunately, when people aren't being as careful as they should be—"

"That's just it," Julie interrupted. "Grandpa grew up using guns. He knew a lot about them and he was very careful around them. He always told me that he saw too many mistakes happen and would never put his life in the hands of the property master. He always checked the guns himself just to make sure. If there had been a mistake, he would have caught it."

"Julie, you're saying that someone deliberately put live ammunition in the gun just before the scene was shot."

"Exactly."

"But why would someone do that? Did your grandfather have any enemies?"

"No, everyone loved him. I told you, he was the best, the kindest . . ."

Her voice trailed off helplessly.

Trying not to sound unsympathetic, C.J. said, "I know it must be terrible, losing your grandfather like that, but—"

"But you think the police are right."

C.J. nodded reluctantly.

Julie leveled a stubborn look at her. "All I know is that someone on that set murdered my grandfather. I don't know who or why. I need you to find out."

C.J. sighed. She felt tremendously sorry for Julie and wanted to be kind, but at the same time she knew it was best to face the truth, however harsh. "I'm afraid I have to agree with the police. It was probably a tragic mistake. All you have to go on is a *feeling.*"

"It's more than a feeling! The day before he died, Grandpa told me that something really big was about to happen. We were going to be where we belonged, on top. Those were his exact words, 'We're finally gonna be where we belong, Julie, on top, instead of working for men like Emmett Traeger.' He wouldn't tell me any more just then, but he said if everything worked out, then he'd have something important to tell me real soon. The next day he died! That can't just be a coincidence."

What could C.J. possibly say? It was obvious Julie was extremely emotional about this and grasping at straws.

Julie went on. "There's something else. The night after he was killed, someone ransacked my apartment. They didn't take anything. There isn't anything worth taking, anyway. Do you think that's a coincidence too?"

C.J. was quiet for a moment. Choosing her words carefully, she explained. "I have a rule about taking cases where I don't honestly believe I can do anything. I don't want to take your money if I seriously doubt that I can help you."

Julie asked abruptly, "Do you have any family?"

C.J. thought of her mother . . . her handsome, charming father who came in and out of her life like a fresh but fickle breeze . . . her numerous aunts and uncles and cousins . . . and her two widowed grandmothers who adored her.

Meeting Julie's look, she answered, "Yes."

Julie went on. "I'll make a deal with you. If you can prove to me that I'm wrong and it *was* an accident, I'll accept it and . . . and get on with my life." Her full lower lip trembled faintly as she added, "But if you can't prove it was an accident, then I want to hire you to find out who killed my grandfather."

C.J. frowned. She knew she should send Julie away. It was a pointless case. It was all too clear what was going on here—Julie worshipped her grandfather and felt utterly alone and abandoned by his death.

It would be best if Julie could simply accept the

obvious—her grandfather died in a tragic accident that was probably due to someone's carelessness. But looking at the stubborn set of her small, round chin, and the tension in the stiff way she held herself, it was clear Julie wasn't about to do that. If C.J. turned her down, she would probably find another investigator, one who would charge a great deal more and come up with the same result—accident, not murder.

"I charge thirty dollars an hour plus expenses," she said, hoping that would discourage Julie.

Julie looked dismayed by the figure, but she insisted. "I'll pay you. Somehow."

C.J. sighed. There was simply no way to get out of this. "All right," she said slowly. Pulling a yellow legal pad closer, she picked up a pen. "I'll need some information."

Sam slowly opened his eyes. Brilliant sunlight streamed in through a huge window. He immediately sensed he wasn't alone. Turning his head quickly, he saw a woman sitting in a nearby chair. The sudden movement sent a flash of white-hot pain through his head. With one hand he reached up to a bandage on the side of his forehead.

"Looks like you got quite a bump on the head," the woman said in a friendly tone.

As his eyes slowly focused, Sam stared at her. She was petite, with long, flaming red hair and vivid deep blue eyes. She looked to be several years older than he, and was utterly unlike any woman he'd ever seen before in his life—even in a dance hall.

He closed his eyes, thinking he'd better start over.

"Where am I?" he asked in a raspy voice.

"Don't you remember?"

He slowly shook his head.

She laughed, and as she did so, tiny crystal bells hanging from one ear tinkled merrily. "I've awakened in some strange places in my time, but I've always remembered where I was. By the way, I'm Lucy, C.J.'s mom. I know it's hard to believe. People always think we're sisters," she said with a flirtatious smile.

Sam replied politely, "Pleased to meet you, ma'am."

Her eyes widened with a mixture of surprise and approval. "A hunk with manners. C.J.'s taste is definitely improving. Not like that heavy-metal guitarist she brought home last time. Say, I'll bet you could use some coffee."

His mouth was dry as a bone and things still weren't coming together real well in his head. Coffee sounded great. Sam nodded carefully. "Yeah . . . thanks, ma'am."

"You don't have to call me ma'am even if I am old enough to be your—" She paused, then added with a wink, "Older sister. Call me Lucy. Everyone does."

As she rose and crossed the small parlor, she went on. "You know, you're definitely not the kind of guy C.J. usually brings home. What's your sign?"

He gave her a confused look. "Sign?"

"You know, your astrological sign." When he still looked blank, she asked, "When's your birthday?"

"July twenty-fourth," Sam answered, tenderly probing the bandage on his head.

"Ah, Leo the Lion." Lucy smiled broadly. "That explains it. C.J.'s a Gemini. You two should have a very interesting relationship. Why don't you hop in the shower? The coffee will be ready by the time you get out."

She gestured toward a door across the room. "Bathroom's in there. I hope C.J. remembered to pick up her underwear and put out fresh towels. Just yell if you need something."

When Lucy disappeared into the kitchen, Sam sat up. At that point he realized he was buck naked under the blanket. Then he saw his clothes folded in a neat pile on a nearby table. Reaching for them, he found that they had a funny odor, unlike the usual lye soap smell when they were freshly washed.

Taking in the entire room in one sweeping glance, he called to Lucy, "Where are my guns?"

Lucy thrust her head around the corner of the door. "Don't know. You'll have to ask C.J." Then she was gone again, in a whirl of bright colors.

C.J.? A vague image, dimly remembered from the night before, came into Sam's head. A young woman with short hair dressed in Levi's. There was something else, something disturbing, but it wouldn't quite come to him.

Sam forced himself to stand. His head felt like it might come off his shoulders. He wasn't about to let that stop him. He had to get dressed, get his guns, and get the hell out of there. Something strange was going on, but he didn't have time to figure it out. He had to get back on Traeger's trail.

Still, the thought of a bath and a cup of hot coffee was tempting. He couldn't rightly remember the last time he'd had either. Traeger already had a good start on him. Ten minutes more to get himself together wouldn't make much difference.

Wrapping the blanket around the lower half of his body, Sam grabbed his clothes and went into the room Lucy had indicated. Damn, but it was a strange-looking place, just like the parlor had been. Instead of the usual brass or metal hip bath in the middle of the floor, there was a small tub, pushed up against the far wall. Instead of handles at the edge of the tub, they were located halfway up the wall. The spout was even farther up the wall, just about level with his chin.

It took him a minute to figure out how everything worked, and he nearly scalded himself with hot water that sprayed out of the spout.

A shower, by God. He'd seen one in a fancy hotel in Denver once, but it was nothing like this. Still, as Sam stepped under the water, he had to admit it felt good. He picked up the bar of soap and lathered himself real good. The accumulated dirt, dust, and mud of weeks washed from his body and hair.

It was tempting to just stand there for a long while, letting the hot water beat against him. But he had to get a move on. Time was wasting. And Traeger was out there somewhere.

As he quickly dressed, he glanced at the array of bottles on a shelf below the mirror over the sink—powders and scents and things he couldn't identify. Picking up a small bottle of perfume, he sniffed it tentatively. A vivid memory of the woman he'd met the night before washed over him, catching him off guard with its intensity.

Women, he thought with amusement. They didn't seem to understand that a man didn't care about these things. What mattered was what was inside a woman—her character and strength. Someone who would stick by a man, in bad times and good.

Looking closer at the bottles, Sam frowned. He didn't understand any of this. Nail hardener—why would a woman want to make nails harder? Eye makeup remover. Something called deodorant. It smelled funny, all flowery. Then there were little pills called vitamin E capsules, and something called Instant Body Groomer and Conditioning Spray with Sunscreen Factors. What the hell were sunscreen factors?

Shaking his head, he opened the door and immediately caught the aroma of fresh coffee. Lucy sat at a low table in the front parlor, pouring coffee from a strange-looking pot into a cup.

"How do you take it?" she asked.

"Black, ma'am. Er, Miss Lucy."

She smiled. "Just Lucy will do. Here." She held out a cup to him.

Sam took a long drink, not caring that it was steaming hot.

Lucy watched in amazement. "Looks like you needed that. Last night must have really been something."

He wiped his mouth on his sleeve. "Yes, ma'am. I mean, Lucy."

"Did that happen in the quake?" she asked, pointing to his bandage.

"Quake?"

"The earthquake."

"Is that what that was?"

Lucy smiled wryly. "Sure was. Good old rock and roll. You must be new to L.A. if you didn't recognize the signs."

"Yeah, I just got in a couple of days ago."

"Looks like it," Lucy said in something of an understatement. Taking in his well-worn jeans, cambric shirt, and scuffed cowboy boots, she went on. "Where are you from? Bakersfield?"

"Bakersfield?" He'd never heard of it. "No. The last place I can rightly call home was Santa Fe."

"A cowboy, huh? I thought so. That explains your clothes and the drawl. Are you a rodeo rider? I knew one once for four unforgettable days—and nights."

"I'm a U.S. Federal Marshal."

Lucy's blue eyes grew wide. "You're kidding! How interesting. That explains the guns."

Sam rose abruptly, trying to ignore the sharp pain slicing between his eyes. "I've got to be goin' now. Thanks for the coffee. If you'll just ask your daughter where she put my guns, I'll be on my way, ma'am."

"*Lucy*. C.J.'s in the office downstairs, talking to a client. She's a private detective, you know."

A lady Pinkerton? Sam thought in surprise. Boy, Los Angeles was some different kind of town, all right.

Lucy went on. "You don't have to go running off yet. That looks like a nasty bump on your head."

"Sorry—Lucy. Best be on my way. If you'll just show me where that office is . . ."

"It's downstairs, on the right. You're welcome to stay. If not here, I've got plenty of room at my place."

If his head didn't hurt so bad, and things weren't confused enough already, Sam might actually think she was making him some kind of offer. But despite her funny clothes, she was obviously a lady. It couldn't be that.

"Thanks anyway, ma'am, " he said in polite refusal.

"Well, nice meeting you, Mr. . . . er . . ."

"Hackett. Sam Hackett."

"Well, Mr. Hackett, if you're ever in Los Angeles again, look me up. I'm listed in the Yellow Pages under Mystics and Clairvoyants. Actually, I'm into channeling, but the phone company wasn't sure how to classify us New Age professionals."

Sam wasn't following much of this, but he wasn't about to start asking questions. Instead, he quietly followed Lucy out of the apartment.

On the small landing outside, he froze in his tracks. As far as he could see was a broad stretch of sand, and beyond it the Pacific Ocean. But it wasn't his first view of the Pacific that stopped Sam. It was the people, wearing what looked like skimpy underdrawers, lying on the sand and splashing in the water.

In his childhood Sam had spent lazy summer days frolicking in the altogether down at the swimming hole. But he'd never seen grown-up people behave with such abandon, and it surprised him. Even more surprising was the sound of music, a strange, raucous sound that seemed to come from out of nowhere. As far as Sam could see, there wasn't a band, or even a Victrola, in sight.

He heard the faint rumble of an engine in the distance. He remembered the loud, rather frightening sound from the night before, but this time it seemed to be coming from overhead. Looking up, he saw a terrifying sight—a machine with huge blades whirling overhead, sweeping in low over the rooftops, heading for the beach.

Instinctively, Sam reached for his gun, then realized he didn't have it.

In front of him Lucy cupped her hand over her eyes to shade them, and stared up at the strange machine. "Those damn L.A. beach patrol copters fly lower all the time," she muttered.

Immediately, Sam's ears were assaulted by another sound—a horseless carriage moving down the beach on four fat wheels. Totally different from the contraption Sam had ridden in the night before, it looked like a steel box. Two men rode in it. They wore caps with "L.A. Beach Patrol" emblazoned across the brims. The same words were written on the side of the horseless carriage.

As Sam's eyes and ears were assaulted by these new sights and sounds, it all came back to him—waking up in the hospital, everyone wearing strange clothes, and the newspaper with the date—1989.

Grabbing Lucy by the shoulders, Sam shouted over the noise of the air machine, "What date is this?"

Lucy looked at him in bewilderment. "June 28th."

"No, the year!"

She hesitated. "You really did get a bump on the noggin, didn't you? It's 1989, and, I might add, an excellent year for cosmic transmigration. That is, if California doesn't fall into the ocean first."

"You're sure it's *1989*?"

"Sure I'm sure. I turn the big five oh this year. Not that it matters. You're as young as you feel, you know."

"It's 1989," Sam murmured. He fought back the pain in his head and a sense of growing desperation. It had to be some kind of trick.

Lucy took hold of his arm. "Say, do you remember who you are?"

He nodded. "Sam Hackett."

Lucy brightened. "Good. Do you, by any chance, remember if you're married?"

"No . . . no, I'm not married."

Lucy grinned. "Good. Then you haven't forgotten anything important."

But Sam wasn't listening. Christ, *1989*. What the hell was going on? Horseless carriages in every size and description, flying machines, people wearing odd clothes . . .

You will go on a journey unlike any you have ever traveled before.

The old shaman's words came back to Sam, reverberating over and over in his head. Suddenly he remembered everything—Traeger, the boardinghouse, the street, the boy and the kitten. He remembered the ground moving beneath him and the panic that followed.

Lucy went on in obvious concern. "You've got a nasty head wound. I think you'd better go back inside and lie down."

Sam frowned. "No. I've got to see C.J."

"Well, just take those stairs real carefully."

Sam slowly descended the stairs leading down the side of the building, trying to absorb what was happening around him. His legs felt wobbly, and he was in a daze, but he knew it wasn't from his injury.

It must be some kind of dream, he thought, staring at the beach, waiting for everything to change back to something familiar.

It didn't.

He wasn't dreaming. This was all real. Somehow he'd

gone on the journey the shaman predicted—a journey unlike any he'd taken before.

Downstairs, he found C.J.'s office and heard voices coming through the open doorway to an inner office. He didn't understand what was going on, but he knew one thing for certain—he wanted his guns. He felt vulnerable without them.

As he entered the office he heard a young woman saying, "Emmett Traeger was on the set too."

That name focused everything in Sam's bewildered mind, blocking the pain and confusion. In a few furious strides he crossed the room, entered the inner office, and faced C.J. across a desk.

"Where's Traeger?" he demanded. "And where the hell are my guns!"

Chapter 3

"What are you doing in my office?" C.J. responded angrily.

Sam placed both hands on her desk and leaned across it to face her. His expression was dangerous. "Where are my guns?" he repeated.

C.J. shot an apologetic look at Julie Prescott, who was staring in wide-eyed wonder at Sam. Then she got up, rounded the desk, and took Sam by the arm. "They're upstairs. I'll get them for you when I finish with my client. Now, if you'll excuse us . . ."

Sam pulled his arm from her grasp. "I want them *now*." Turning to Julie, he said, "And I want to know what you know about Traeger."

Julie looked from Sam to C.J., her expression bewildered. She began hesitantly. "He's taking the position that my grandfather's death was a tragic accident, and the studio isn't responsible."

C.J. took Sam's arm again and pulled insistently. "This is a confidential matter, Mr. Hackett. If you'll just wait upstairs, I'll be with you in a few minutes."

Sam wasn't about to be gotten rid of so easily. "Studio?" he asked, once more pulling his arm from C.J.'s grasp.

"Mr. Traeger's the head of the studio," Julie explained slowly. She flashed a confused look at C.J. that clearly said, Who is this guy and has he lost all his marbles?

C.J. began to explain. "Mr. Hackett was injured in the earthquake. A *head* injury," she emphasized.

Turning back to Sam, she said in a no-nonsense tone, "Mr. Hackett, this is a private, confidential meeting be-

43

tween me and my client. It doesn't concern you, and I would appreciate it if you would leave until we are through."

Ignoring her, Sam walked over to Julie and stood towering over her. "If it concerns Traeger, it concerns me. What did Traeger have to do with your grandfather?"

Of all the nerve, C.J. thought through clenched teeth. Questioning *my* client.

C.J. planted herself between Sam and Julie. Her self-control slipped another notch as she crossed her arms on her chest and glared at him. She looked up the full length of Sam Hackett, all six-feet-something of him, from those scarred boots and faded jeans molded to lean hips, right up to the broad expanse of chest, partially revealed by the buttons left open at the neck of his shirt. At her height, she was used to looking most men in the eye, especially when she wore heels. Somehow, Sam made her feel small and vulnerable, almost like a little girl.

Her voice wasn't quite as tough as she would have liked, when she went on. "None of this concerns you."

"It does if it's about Traeger. I've been after him for six months."

"What do you mean, you've been after him?"

"I'm a United States Federal Marshal."

"Wow," Julie breathed.

C.J. wasn't so gullible. "You actually expect me to believe that?"

Sam shrugged. "I don't rightly care what you believe. The only thing I'm interested in is findin' Traeger."

C.J. didn't buy any of it. Obviously, the man was even more loony tunes than she'd first suspected. "Look, this is *my* investigation—"

"*You're* investigating Traeger?" Sam's expression was a combination of amusement and disbelief.

"I'm investigating the death of Dan Prescott."

"Prescott?" Sam asked quickly. "Any relation to Rollie Prescott?"

"He was my great-great-grandfather," Julie answered with a surprised note in her voice. "Grandpa used to tell me stories about him being an outlaw."

C.J. tried to act as if she still had some semblance of control over this situation. "Mr. Hackett, this is *my* office, *my* client, and *my* case."

"Not exactly, ma'am. You see, I'm the authority here."

"Authority!" C.J. exploded. The nerve of the man, the gall, the absolute balls! After all she'd done for him too! She was so furious she couldn't see straight. And he just stood there, looking like the Marlboro man, so calm, so cool, so sure of himself. She wanted to wipe that smug expression of superiority right off his face.

He went on in that slow drawl. "Yes, ma'am. As Federal Marshal, I outrank every other peace officer. I can go anywhere, ask any questions, arrest anyone who gets in my way."

"Are you threatening me?"

"No, ma'am. Just trying to set the record straight."

C.J. stiffened. "Fine. I suppose you have some ID."

"ID?" The expression on Sam's face was blank.

"I thought not," she concluded. "Now, if you'll excuse us . . ."

"I do have this," he went on, pulling a badge from his pants pocket. He handed it to C.J.

It was heavy. It had the look and the feel of the real thing. How on earth could she have missed it when she washed his clothes the night before? Of course, it *was* very late, and she was exhausted.

Well, this certainly explained the guns, though she would have expected him to carry something more impressive, like a Magnum. Maybe the guns and the odd clothes were all part of an undercover operation. She'd worn some strange outfits herself when she had to go undercover.

But this beat anything she'd tried. Usually when she went undercover it was done in an unobtrusive manner, the idea being to direct attention away from herself. In his getup, Sam Hackett was hardly unobtrusive.

She felt Sam's gaze on her. Damn, she hated admitting she was wrong.

As if sensing her discomfiture, Sam turned away from C.J. and concentrated on Julie. "What's this about a"—he hesitated, then finished—"*movie* studio?"

"United Film Studios in West L.A.," Julie answered promptly, clearly awed by Sam.

"Is that close to here?" Sam asked.

C.J. couldn't believe it. For a Federal Marshal, he sure didn't know much. "It isn't far. About a ten-minute drive."

Julie suddenly brightened. "Miss Grant, if a Federal Marshal is after Mr. Traeger, then maybe he had something to do with Grandfather's murder!"

"Emmett Traeger is the head of a studio and heir to a fortune. I doubt very much that he would be involved in a murder."

"But you'll still take the case?"

C.J. hesitated. This case was getting more complicated by the minute. She looked hard at Sam, then said, "Maybe Mr. Hackett doesn't want me butting in on *his* case."

For a moment their eyes locked. She couldn't read his expression, but it was clear he was involved in some tremendous inner struggle. Silence stretched between them until the tension could be cut with a knife.

When he finally spoke, his words weren't at all what she would have expected, considering what his attitude had been so far. "I guess I could use your help."

Well, that was real big of him, she thought dryly.

"Okay," she snapped, "let's go."

"Where are you going?" Julie asked as C.J. grabbed her purse and headed for the door.

"The police. I want to go over the report on your grandfather's death."

Sam followed on C.J.'s heels. As they left the office, he asked in an oddly hesitant tone, "Uh . . . just how are we getting there?"

"My Mustang's out back," she replied. "I picked it up earlier this morning."

Behind her, she heard Sam breathe a sigh of relief. "Thank God," he muttered under his breath.

They climbed the stairs to her apartment, and C.J. took Sam's guns out of the closet where she'd put them the night before.

As Sam took them, she asked, "Why do you want to

work on this case with me? That isn't exactly the usual procedure, is it?"

To her surprise, Sam's mouth softened in the barest hint of a smile. "Nothin's exactly usual just now." Then he went on. "Besides, you know this town and I don't. You have transportation and I don't. It's as simple as that."

"Wait a minute, I'm not a chauffeur service for the U.S. government!"

"Chauffeur?" he asked.

She couldn't believe it. That knock on the head had really affected his memory. He couldn't seem to remember the most mundane things. But she didn't push the chauffeur issue. If she irritated him too much, he might turn her over to the I.R.S., and there was the matter of those questionable business entertainment deductions on last year's tax return.

Sam checked his pistol and rifle with a brisk efficiency that was somehow unsettling. He was obviously comfortable with guns.

As he started to strap the pistol and holster to his thigh, C.J. asked in surprise, "You're actually going to wear that in plain sight?"

Sam hesitated. "You mean people don't do that nowadays?"

"Not in L.A. Anyway, I thought you guys wore shoulder holsters."

"*Shoulder* holsters?"

"Yeah. Don't you have one?"

He shook his head.

"I really don't think you're going to need them where we're going," C.J. insisted.

"I'll just carry 'em," Sam replied.

Clearly, he wasn't going to give in on this. "Okay," she said with a sigh of frustration.

"Let's go," Sam said impatiently.

C.J. was beginning to understand that Sam was a man of few words, and moved quickly. Now he was out the door ahead of her and down the stairs before she'd closed the door behind her. As she watched him, she realized there was a lean, animal intensity to his every movement. Now, what did that remind her of?

She followed Sam to the back of the building where her car was parked in the open garage. The top was down, and on this crystal-clear sunny day she didn't bother putting it up. Getting into the driver's seat, C.J. turned the key. As usual, the engine sputtered briefly before finally kicking in. She told herself she really should take it in for a tune-up. Of course, she'd been saying that for two years.

Suddenly she realized Sam was standing away from the car, staring at it.

"You said you had a mustang."

C.J. gave him an offended look. "All right, so it needs a little work. It's a classic. And it runs. So get in."

Sam just stood there. His expression was almost comic as he seemed to be struggling with some inner dilemma. Finally, in a surprisingly agile movement, he swung himself over the door and into the seat beside her. Depositing his guns on the floorboard, he gripped the edge of the seat with both hands and sat there looking as nervous as he had the night before in the cab.

C.J. buckled her seat belt and waited for Sam to do the same. When he made no move to do so, she said, "Aren't you going to buckle up? It's the law, you know," she added pointedly.

He looked at her seat belt, then at his lying on the seat beside him. He fumbled with it for a minute, until, in exasperation, she reached over. As she buckled him in, she felt his body tense. Looking up at him, she thought, as she had the night before, *He's scared.*

He must have been in a bad accident at one time, she decided. She wanted to reassure him that it was all right, she was actually a very careful driver. He was so intimidating and downright overbearing one minute, and lost as a child the next. It was totally confusing.

They drove in silence through Venice, toward the West L.A. police station. The whole time Sam's hand gripped the door handle so tightly his knuckles were white, and his left one curled over the edge of the seat.

When they reached the police station, and she parked in the visitor's parking lot, he relaxed visibly.

"If you're nervous about my driving," C.J. began tightly, "you're welcome to drive."

Sam looked chagrined. "No . . . no, that's okay, you're doin' just fine."

Inside, C.J. got a copy of the police report from the desk sergeant, and she and Sam read it through quickly. There was no new or surprising information in it. Dan Prescott, 66, had died instantly from a single gunshot wound during filming of an otherwise routine scene from the movie *Hard Country*. There were no other bullets in the murder weapon. Someone had put one real bullet in it instead of the blanks that were supposed to be used.

The report concluded that Prescott's death was an accident due to carelessness on the part of someone connected with the production, but there wasn't enough evidence to charge anyone.

Case closed.

C.J. shook her head. "It doesn't make sense. Why would anyone want to kill an elderly, unimportant bit player?"

Sam looked at her intently. "You've never trailed a murderer before, have you?"

She was reluctant to admit she hadn't. Up to this point she'd dealt exclusively with divorce cases, insurance fraud, industrial espionage—cases where using a computer got her further than using a gun. "Maybe it was an accident after all," she insisted.

Sam's gaze narrowed. "If Prescott crossed Traeger's trail, it was murder. You can count on it."

"Gut instinct?" she asked with barely disguised sarcasm.

He nodded. "Something like that."

"Then let's talk to him. We'll need his okay to get on the lot and talk to the people who were on the set that day."

"I'll face Traeger alone," Sam responded, his expression one of stubborn determination.

"How are you going to get to the studio?"

That stopped him. Finally, he answered, "All right, you can come along. But I'll do the talking."

A half hour later they drove up to the front gate of United Film Studios.

"Who are you seeing?" the guard in the tiny cubicle asked perfunctorily.

"Emmett Traeger," she answered. "C.J. Grant and Sam Hackett to see him."

She had called Traeger from the police station. At first he refused to cooperate. When she said her client was considering a wrongful death suit against the studio, he reluctantly agreed to meet them on the set.

After checking his list of drive-on passes, the guard handed one to C.J. and said, "Follow that yellow line to the back of the lot. *Hard Country*'s shooting there."

He pushed the button that raised the bar blocking the lane, and C.J. drove onto the lot.

Almost immediately a flashing red warning light caused traffic to halt. She stopped her car, waiting for the light to go off.

"What are we stopping for?" Sam asked impatiently.

"They're shooting a scene," C.J. explained, motioning to a group of people and cameras in the distance. "We have to wait here until the red light goes off."

A second assistant director stood near the red light, talking into a two-way radio. In the distance the shoot was in progress. There were actors in police uniforms, the director riding with a Panaflex camera mounted on a crane, and assorted crew members.

With a rueful smile C.J. remembered her last acting job. She'd played a corpse and had, of course, no lines.

The scene was completed and the red light went off. Traffic moved ahead. They drove past rows of old two-story, dull gray office buildings, massive sound stages, and the permanent sets—city blocks, small-town neighborhoods. As always, C.J. thought how the studio was just like any other factory, only it was a dream factory, creating the stuff audiences' fantasies were made of.

She was dismayed to see so much of the studio being dismantled. She'd heard the Traeger family, who owned the studio, had decided the land it sat on, in the heart of some of the most expensive real estate in L.A., was worth more than the studio itself. So they were gradually tearing down the studio buildings to make way for development of office and condominium skyscrapers, like the rest of Century City. In a couple of years all that would be left of United Film Studios would be one tall office building with the U.F.S. logo emblazoned across the front of it, across the street from the old lot.

It had happened to MGM and was happening to Twentieth Century Fox. C.J. knew it was inevitable, but it saddened her to think a studio that had been turning out movies for nearly seventy years would soon be just a memory.

When they reached the set where Traeger was to meet them, C.J. parked the car. She and Sam walked to the end of the set, where a scene was about to be shot.

It was like stepping back in time, to another world—people in costume walking down a dusty street, clapboard buildings, horses tied to a hitching post in front of a saloon. There were buckboard wagons and carriages. Women wore sunbonnets and long gingham dresses over high-topped boots. Men wore dusty denim pants, chambray shirts, an occasional leather vest, and guns on their hips.

C.J. knew it was all a fake—mere illusion. The dirt that covered the street had been hauled in by truck and spread by tractor. The buildings were nothing more than props, false fronts nailed to an empty frame. If anyone stepped through the saloon doors, they would find a lunch truck on the other side. The men and women were actors, extras, and stuntmen. Beneath all the historically accurate costumes were zippers and Velcro fasteners.

But a movie set had a magic all its own, and C.J. felt a familiar rush of excitement just being there.

Then she noticed Sam. He simply stood there, staring down the length of the dusty street, his gaze focused on some point only he could see. The rigid, defensive set of his shoulders relaxed as tension eased from him. It was as if he'd seen someone or something reassuringly familiar.

"Hey, buddy," the first assistant director called out to

Sam, "you wanna get on down there with the rest of the extras."

C.J. started to say, "Oh, he's not one of—" but Sam cut her off.

"This is all wrong. Those men shouldn't be comin' from that end of town."

The second assistant director glared at Sam. "What the hell are you talkin' about?"

Before Sam could answer, the director, a short, slight man in his early thirties with lank blond hair and watery blue eyes, confronted the assistant director. "What the bloody hell is going on here! We need to get this gunfight in the can *today*."

"This guy says the setup's all wrong."

The director turned on Sam. "An *extra* is trying to tell me how to shoot this picture?"

Sam answered quietly, "I don't know anything about any picture. I'm just tryin' to tell you no man worth his salt would come from that end of town to face a gunfight. He'd be lookin' right into the sun. Can't aim real accurately when the sun's in your eyes. You should know that if you're tryin' to tell all these people what to do."

The director looked as if he were about to have some kind of fit. His pale face reddened and his eyes bulged. "This is *my* film, *my* artistic vision . . ."

An older man with salt and pepper hair and a luxuriant white mustache, dressed like a wrangler, or an extra, unfolded his arms from across his broad chest and slowly sauntered forward. His rolling gait suggested he spent a great deal of time in the saddle.

"The fella's right," he said matter-of-factly. "If you want it authentic, you bring the outlaws from this end of town with the sun at their backs. It's an old outlaw trick. Most lawmen never learned about it till it was too late."

"Ah, Cody, what do you know about it?" the second A.D. grumbled.

"I don't have time for this," the director muttered as he walked away. He yelled back over his shoulder, "Get the scene set up *now*!"

Cody rested his hands on his hips. His skin was dark,

weathered. He looked like the real thing—an honest-to-God cowboy—from the tip of his battered Stetson right down to his scuffed boots. He extended a hand to Sam.

"Name's Cody Wilkerson. I used to do stunt ridin' when I was younger. Now they say my face has character, so they give me work as an extra."

"Sam Hackett. Pleased to make your acquaintance."

"Funny you knowin' that trick about the sun."

"Nothin' funny about it if you've ever been drawn on that way," Sam remarked easily.

C.J. watched in amazement. This man who had been so difficult with her was easygoing and friendly with the old cowboy.

"My grandaddy told me about it," Cody went on. "He saw Wyatt Earp and his brothers in action. He used to bust broncs for a livin', and was a big influence on me. Because of him, I've spent my life sittin' on a horse or scramblin' to get out from under one." He squinted thoughtfully. "What did you say your name was, son?"

"Hackett."

"Hackett? Now, there's a name to remember. My grandaddy used to talk about a fella . . ."

C.J. couldn't stand there quietly any longer. This was her case and Sam was acting like he'd completely forgotten about her. "Mr. Wilkerson, did you know Dan Prescott?"

He stopped and gave her a long look. Finally, he said quietly, "Yes, I did. Dan and me went back nearly fifty years in this business. Started out workin' for a dollar a day plus meals and glad to get it."

"Were you on the set the day he died?"

He nodded.

"Do you have any idea how a real bullet got into the gun?"

"There's only one way it could have, isn't there?"

Before C.J. could go any further, the assistant director called, "Places, everyone! Quiet on the set!"

Wilkerson nodded to Sam and C.J., then moved to take his place with some other extras.

The scene went without a hitch. When it was over, the assistant director called, "That's a wrap, break for lunch."

As everyone dispersed, Sam walked across the dusty street toward the row of storefronts. Hesitating in front of a door, he opened it slowly. When he saw there was nothing on the other side, he looked stunned.

"It's something, isn't it?" C.J. said behind him. "Like stepping into another world."

"It's not real," Sam murmured as he stood in the shadows of the plywood frame that braced the false store-front.

"Nothing on a movie set is," C.J. replied. Then she added thoughtfully, "Except the bullet that killed Dan Prescott."

"Miss Grant?"

C.J. turned at the sound of her name. She'd seen photos of Emmett Traeger in the trade papers, *Variety* and *The Hollywood Reporter*, and recognized him instantly. He was young, barely into his thirties, and widely regarded as a boy wonder filmmaker, much as Irving Thalberg had been in the 1930s. He'd taken over control of the studio five years earlier when his father died of a heart attack, and had produced a string of hit movies. Tall and slim, with dark hair and eyes, he looked as if he'd just walked off a tennis court and quickly changed. His clothes were casual chic, his hair slightly disheveled, his tan utterly perfect.

He was New Hollywood personified, bright, well-educated, young, and fiercely ambitious.

C.J. had been prepared for the dark good looks, but she wasn't expecting his easy charm.

He said, "I'm Emmett Traeger. You know, Miss Grant, you're the first private detective I've ever met. And a female one at that."

"You're the first studio chief I've met—male or female."

He flashed a devastating smile. "Yes, well, you sounded so competent, one might even say tough, over the phone, I didn't expect you to be attractive. I suppose that's hopelessly chauvinistic. Forgive me."

"You're forgiven."

She remembered Sam standing just behind her. Turning to introduce him, she was taken aback by the expression on his face as he stared at Traeger. Disbelief warred with some other, stronger emotion.

She said, "This is Federal Marshal Sam Hackett. He's investigating Mr. Prescott's death also."

Traeger's dark eyes narrowed. "Federal Marshal? I didn't know anyone besides the police were investigating the accident."

"Is that the studio's official line—that it was an accident?" C.J. asked.

"Of course. What else could it be?"

"His granddaughter doesn't think it was an accident."

Traeger shook his head in dismay. "Poor thing. I understand she's all alone in the world now. It's very sad. I can certainly appreciate how upset she must be. Though the studio lawyers would be furious with me for saying this, I must tell you I feel that the studio bears some responsibility. We'll certainly do all we can to help the girl."

"That's very kind of you, Mr. Traeger. But, if you don't mind, I'd like to complete my investigation before accepting your conclusion that it's an accident."

Traeger's look was amused. "Miss Grant, do you really believe that anyone could have conceivably wanted to murder a minor bit player who was, by all accounts, a harmless, likable old man?"

"Probably not. But I won't know for certain until I talk to everyone who was here that day. Do I have your approval to question people?"

"If I said no, would that stop you?"

C.J.'s lips curved in a wry smile. "No."

"I thought not. Very well. Pursue your investigation. Just don't let it get in the way of this picture. Prescott's death upset everyone and put us behind schedule. I hope I don't sound too heartless in saying that, but I do have a business to run here."

"The show must go on," C.J. commented.

"Exactly. And there's another thing. I can't have you interrupting filming. I have to ask you to leave now and come back at the end of the day, when shooting's over. That way you can question people on *their* time, not the studio's."

"Fair enough."

"Good. Now, if you'll excuse me, I'll leave you to your job and get back to mine."

He nodded to Sam, exchanged a polite smile with C.J., and strode away.

As soon as he was out of earshot, she turned on Sam. "You weren't much help. I thought you couldn't wait to get to Emmett Traeger."

For the first time in ten minutes, Sam spoke. "That's not Emmett Traeger."

"That *is* Emmett Traeger," C.J. replied. "He was named after his great-grandfather, who founded the studio. Which Emmett Traeger were you looking for?"

"One I'll never find," Sam replied slowly.

On the way back to Venice Beach, C.J. stopped at an ATM to get some cash. Sam sat in the car, utterly quiet, as he had been since they'd left the studio. From the moment they'd met Traeger, Sam had seemed at a total loss, just as he had been the previous night. C.J. was concerned, but had no idea what to do. While Sam had remembered some things—like the fact that he was a Federal Marshal—he didn't seem to remember much of anything else, including his address.

She decided to let him stay with her one more night. But the next morning she was taking him straight to the Federal Building in West L.A. and let someone there deal with him.

She had just taken a handful of twenties out of the machine and was getting her card when she felt something sharp thrust against her ribs.

"Give me the money, lady!"

Whirling around, she faced a young derelict. His hair was long and filthy, his clothes disheveled, and by his wild-eyed expression C.J. knew he was high on something. All that was beside the point. What mattered was the vicious-looking long-bladed knife he pointed at her.

"Okay," she said, trying not to sound as terrified as she felt, "you can have the money, just don't hurt me."

"Drop the knife!"

C.J. looked past the young man to see Sam standing behind him. In an instant she went from fear to panic as she realized that Sam could easily scare the guy into doing something rash. "Are you crazy?" she shouted. "He's got a knife."

Sam pulled his Colt .44 from the deep pocket of his coat. "And I've got a gun."

At sight of the gun the young man's face went white. "Drop the gun, man, or I'll cut the bitch."

"Touch her, and you're a dead man," Sam responded.

C.J. couldn't believe it. She didn't know who scared her more—the would-be thief, or Sam, for putting her at such risk. The thief hesitated, glancing from Sam to C.J. in desperate confusion. That moment—when she couldn't tell if he was going to give up or attack her—seemed to stretch out for an eternity. She held her breath, unable to speak, unable to move.

In what almost seemed like an anticlimax, it was over. The young man dropped the knife and ran like hell.

Sam aimed low, at the young man's heels, and fired one shot that must have missed by a hair.

C.J. was consumed with fury. "What the hell do you think you're doing?"

"Teachin' him a lesson," Sam replied laconically.

Turning her back on Sam, C.J. hurried to the car and got in. Her heart was racing; her adrenaline was still pumping. When Sam joined her, she yelled at him, partly out of reaction to the fear she'd just felt. "You could have gotten me killed!"

"I wouldn't have let him hurt you."

The simple statement, uttered with such quiet conviction, unnerved her. "This is Los Angeles, not the Old West." She gunned the motor as she backed out of the parking place, then took off. "You can't just go around shooting at people, even punks like that."

"If I'd been shooting at him, I'd have hit him. I was just making a point."

"That's not how things are done around here."

"Maybe not, but that's the way we do things where I come from."

"Just where *do* you come from?" she snapped.

"1882."

C.J. slammed on the brakes.

Chapter 4

"*Wow!*" Lucy breathed in awe as she stared at Sam. "A real honest-to-God time traveler. I knew it as soon as I saw you. There was something different about your aura. It was completely turquoise, which is a color of higher consciousness—"

"Mother!" C.J. snapped. "Don't encourage him."

She and Sam had returned to the office only a few minutes earlier, arguing furiously. When Lucy asked what the argument was about, Sam told his amazing story of traveling through time.

Turning to Sam now, C.J went on in a voice that was frayed at the edges. "Do you really expect anybody—any *normal* person—to believe such a crazy story?"

Sam couldn't help smiling inwardly as he watched her pacing back and forth in front of him. She looked fit to be tied, and he couldn't say he blamed her. After all, it was a pretty tall tale. Unfortunately, it was a true one.

C.J. went on. "Mr. Hackett . . ."

"Might as well call me Sam, seein' as how we're workin' on this case together."

"We are *not!*"

Sam shifted his long legs, lifting one booted foot to rest it against his knee. "I'm not any happier about it than you are. I never expected to have to put up with a woman. 'Course, a lot of things have happened that I never expected."

"Put up with a woman!" C.J. nearly screamed.

Sam shook his head, bemused. "Don't it beat all. Somehow or other, even though it's a hundred years later,

I'm still dealin' with the Traegers an' the Prescotts. Only now I'm saddled with a woman. But I don't see any way around it. I don't know the territory, and you do."

He leaned forward and looked C.J. straight in the eye. "So, if you're willin', I guess I am—just until this business with Traeger is finished."

Her huge gold hoop earrings jangling, Lucy interjected. "Can you imagine what a sensation this would make in the newspaper? 'Wild West Marshal Travels Forward in Time to Get His Man.' The *National Enquirer* would pay a fortune for an exclusive."

"Hold it!" C.J. cut off her mother curtly. She turned to Sam, her voice straining to sound calm and patient. "Obviously, Mr. Hackett, that head injury is more serious than the doctors thought. I think perhaps you should go back to the hospital for further tests. And as for working together, well, I work alone. I do my job pretty damn well."

Sam gave her a long look. "You weren't doin' too well a little while ago. You didn't even have enough sense to carry a gun."

"I don't need a gun."

Sam snorted. "Sure looked like it to me. What would you have done if I hadn't been there when that no-good pulled a knife on you?"

"I would have been just fine, thank you. I can take care of myself. You may think women are helpless, Mr. Hackett, but let me tell you that you're wrong. I've been trained in self-defense. I don't need some redneck, macho idiot jumping in to save me every time I turn around."

"Coulda fooled me," Sam murmured.

C.J. stopped short and glared at him.

He went on. "And what's wrong with being macho? I speak a little Spanish, I know what that means. It means bein' a man. What's wrong with that?"

"Yeah," Lucy chimed in, her blue eyes twinkling mischievously, "what's wrong with that?"

"We're getting off track here," C.J. said with a massive effort at controlling her temper. "Mr. Hackett . . ."

"Sam. By the way, what do I call you?"

"Ms. Grant," she answered coolly.

Sam raised one eyebrow quizzically. "Mzzzz?" he asked, drawing out the syllable awkwardly.

"It's the feminine equivalent of mister," Lucy explained.

Sam frowned. "What's wrong with Miss or Mrs.?"

"They're sexist," C.J. answered.

"What's that?"

"That's an attitude that men like you have about women like me."

"Now, how the hell would you know what kind of attitude I have about women? I respect 'em, all kinds of 'em, from whores to schoolteachers."

He turned to Lucy. "She always this touchy?"

Lucy grinned. "If you think this is bad, you should see her when she has PMS."

"Does that have anything to do with Mzzzz?"

"You're catching on." She turned to C.J. "He may be a hundred years older than us, but he's quick."

C.J. gave her a withering look. "Getting back to the point, Mr. Hackett, you had a very bad blow to the head yesterday. That can cause disorientation and hallucinations."

At Sam's look of confusion, Lucy explained succinc* y, "She doesn't believe you're from 1882."

He stood up and faced C.J. "You sayin' I'm one brick shy of a full load?"

"I'm saying you need to see a doctor."

"Unh-unh."

Lucy stepped between them. "C.J., *look* at him. The way he's dressed, the way he talks, the way he walks. This isn't the kind of guy you run into at Happy Hour at Hamburger Hamlet!"

She went on. "He's different. He's . . ." Her voice softened. "A real man."

There was a moment of absolute silence.

Sam rose, picked up the rifle he'd leaned against the wall, and headed for the door.

"Where do you think you're going?" C.J. demanded.

"Lady, I don't know how the hell I got here, and I don't understand much about the way things work in your time, but I do know one thing. I've got a job to do and I'm gonna do it."

"How?"

"By goin' back to that studio and talk to those people. It should be just about quittin' time now, and Emmett Traeger said we could question 'em then. 'Course, I'm only a Federal Marshal, and you're a private detective, so maybe you have a better idea."

She tried to come up with a withering response, but she couldn't. He might be crazy, but he was right. It was time to go back to the studio and start asking some hard questions.

"I just don't see how it could've happened," Harry Jones, the portly, gray-haired prop master, said for the third time. He sat in a sagging, ancient leather chair in the prop trailer, opposite Sam and C.J., shaking his head morosely. The huge trailer was outfitted with cupboards, shelves, and closets, all filled to overflowing with a staggering array of props.

Noticing a locked cabinet labeled "ammunition," C.J. asked, "Do you keep live ammunition here?"

"Sure. There are times when we need it. The police really hammered at me about that. They seemed to think I might've used the real thing by mistake."

Harry was clearly insulted. "As if after forty years at this job I don't know what I'm doin'. Like I told 'em, the live ammo is kept completely separate from the blanks. There's no way the two could've gotten mixed up accidentally."

"And you checked the guns before the scene?"

"Of course. I checked all the guns that morning, just an hour or so before they shot the scene, and everything was fine. They all had blanks in them."

He shook his head sadly. "Poor old Dan. He was a great old guy. We used to get together for a drink after work and tell each other stories about the old days." He frowned. "I just don't see how it could've happened."

"Could someone else have gotten hold of the gun and switched the blanks to the real thing?" Sam asked.

"I s'pose so," Harry answered, scratching his chin

thoughtfully. "I mean, I don't lock up the trailer during the day, and I'm in and out of it constantly."

"Did you see anyone come in here that day?" C.J. asked.

"Nobody unusual, if that's what you mean. The crew, the actors, the director—they're all in here at one time or another."

"Just how did it work?" Sam asked with a puzzled frown. "How could someone know which gun would be fired at Prescott?"

"The extras just take any old gun, but the actors are assigned a particular one. In the scene where Dan was shot, the actor, Lance Ford, used the same Colt .44 he was supposed to use through the whole movie. Except, the police took it as evidence, so I had to round up another gun that looked just like it."

"Did other people know which gun Ford was using?" C.J. asked.

"Probably. I mean, it wasn't a secret. But, look, if you're sayin' someone deliberately killed Dan, well, that's hard to believe. Why would someone want to kill a harmless old extra?"

"Why indeed?" C.J. murmured. "Did Dan Prescott have any enemies?"

"Not what you'd call real enemies. He rubbed some people the wrong way, that's all."

"Who?" C.J. asked quickly.

"Well, the director, for one. Walks around sayin' he's gonna 'redefine the American West.' Don't know nothin', if you ask me. Dan tried to tell him a thing or two, to help him out, like, but the guy wouldn't listen. He's one of these auteurs who thinks he should get all the credit for a movie." Harry snorted disdainfully. "I'd like to see him try to make a movie by himself, without a script or actors or a crew."

"Did he and Prescott have words?" Sam asked.

"Sort of. The day before Dan died, the director told him he was 'compromising his authority,' as he put it, and he told Dan to stop questioning his decisions in front of the crew. He said if he wanted the opinion of a washed-up nobody, he'd ask for it. Can you believe it? Dan knew more about the Old West than this guy could learn in a month of Sundays."

"How did Prescott take it?"

Harry shrugged. "Water off a duck's back. He knew what directors are. Neurotic, if you ask me."

"Was there anyone else who didn't get along with Prescott?"

"Well, that young ass, Lance Ford, had a couple of run-ins with Dan. If you ask me, Ford's mama should've spanked him more often. He's a real pain in the backside. Somehow, he got the idea that he's special. Believe me, he ain't."

C.J. interjected, "When you say 'run-ins,' do you mean they argued or they actually fought?"

"They mostly argued, but earlier that morning they actually had a scuffle. Dan put the kid in his place, and Ford didn't like it one bit. Told the director to fire Dan. But they were shooting Dan's last scene that day, so the director wouldn't do it. It would've meant reshooting some other scenes, and that costs money. This picture's already way over budget as it is."

C.J. asked quickly, "Is the picture in trouble?"

"Yup. Mr. Traeger's been down to the set several times to talk to the director and generally make it clear that the studio isn't happy."

Sam frowned. "*Traeger.*" He drew out the name slowly. Then he asked Harry, "What do you think of Traeger?"

"Real smart guy. Knows his business. 'Course, his family's been in the movie business since the days of the nickelodeon."

"How did his family come to own this studio?"

"His great-granddaddy had the land. He built the studio around the turn of the century. The Traegers have always been shrewd operators."

Sam nodded. "Yeah," he said darkly.

C.J. didn't know what Sam was getting at, but it was time to move on. It was dusk and nearly everyone had left the set. "We've got to be going now. Thanks for your help."

"Not at all, ma'am. If there's anything I can do to help

you find out who killed Dan, I'd be happy to do it. He was a good friend. I miss him. I'd like to get the guy who killed him."

"You're convinced it was murder?"

Harry gave C.J. a no-nonsense look. "Sure wasn't no accident."

"Thanks, Mr. Jones. We'll get back to you."

Later, as they drove off the lot, Sam said, "We'd best talk to Traeger again, first thing in the morning."

"First thing in the morning, you're going back to the hospital for another check-up."

"Nope."

C.J. took her eyes off the street for a moment to glare at him. "Why are you so fixated on Emmett Traeger?"

"I knew his great-granddaddy, and they're both the same—no good. Now, if you'll just let me handle this case, and stop horning in—"

"Horning in! Wait a minute—*you're* the one who's horning in! This is *my* case. Julie Prescott is *my* client. Even if you are a Federal Marshal, I'm not sure you have any business—"

"Traeger's my business," Sam cut in. "He's involved in this, I know it."

C.J.'s mouth tightened in irritation. "Studio chiefs occasionally commit embezzlement, but not murder."

"His great-grandfather was wanted for murder. *And* robbery. That's how the Traegers got the money to buy this land. I'm tellin' you, Traeger had somethin' to do with Prescott's murder."

"You don't have the slightest shred of evidence for that."

"Evidence! Hell, lady, I've got my gut instinct, and that's better than any proof. Sometimes it's all you've got. It's saved my hide more than once."

C.J. said witheringly, "You sound like my mother. She doesn't like looking at reality either."

"Your mother may look kinda funny, and maybe she does have some strange notions, but she's all right. She knows the difference between the truth and a lie. Which is more than I can say for you. You know what your problem is?"

C.J. sighed heavily. "Yes. *You.*"

Sam went on. "Your problem is you can't see past the surface of things. This guy looks okay, so you think he's okay. Hasn't anybody ever taught you that you've gotta get past the outside and see what people are like on the inside?"

C.J. was furious. "You push your way into my life, acting so damn superior, trying to tell me how to do my job—"

"That's another thing. You're tryin' to do a man's job. It's not right."

Her mouth dropped open, then snapped shut. "I don't have to listen to this bullshit."

"It's not ladylike to swear. It makes you cheap."

C.J. slowly counted to ten. But it didn't do any good. She still wanted to kill Sam. "You pea-brained Neanderthal! You belong in another time!"

He leaned back in the seat and stared straight ahead. Under his breath he murmured, "You're right about that."

"I can't deal with this." C.J.'s tone clearly indicated that she was dangerously near the edge. "I've been through an earthquake, lost a thousand-dollar fee because the car I was supposed to pick up was totaled in the quake, befriended a bozo who's ready for the Twinkiemobile, accepted a case that probably isn't even a case, and been mugged. And I haven't eaten in hours."

Without looking at her, Sam said laconically, "I could do with something to eat myself. I'll buy you supper."

"*Fine.* And immediately afterward, you're going back to the hospital."

Ignoring that, Sam asked, "So where are we gonna eat?"

"A place near here called The Saloon."

Sam smiled, and for instant C.J. realized how really handsome he was.

"A saloon? Good." Then a disturbing thought occurred to him. "Say, people still eat steaks nowadays, don't they?"

"Some people do."

He breathed a sigh of relief. "Considerin' the way everything else has changed, nothin' would surprise me."

The Saloon was a small, casual restaurant in an old building with wood siding. Swinging half-doors led into the dimly lit interior. As they walked inside, Sam stopped dead in his tracks. This was reassuringly familiar. There was sawdust on the floor, and a long, curving bar with a brass footrail. In the corner a player piano played an old tune. The waitresses were dressed just like all the saloon girls he'd ever known—in low-cut, full-skirted satin dresses, with lots of paint on their pretty faces.

Of course the other people there looked strange, but Sam ignored them. All that mattered was that he felt at home.

When he tore into a thick, juicy steak a few minutes later, he felt even better. He hadn't realized how hungry he was. He wolfed down the steak and fried potatoes.

He watched curiously as C.J. munched on a salad. "That all you're havin'?"

"I'm on a diet."

"Does that mean you don't eat, you just graze?"

C.J. couldn't help smiling. "Yeah," she admitted, "I guess it does."

"Why would you want to do that?"

"To lose weight, of course."

Sam eyed her critically. "I'd say you're skinny enough as it is. You could stand to put on a few pounds."

C.J.'s eyes opened wide. "Are you making fun of me?"

"Why would I want to do that? You know, men don't like skinny women. Nothin' to hold on to."

Their waitress had returned. "Would you like some dessert? We have homemade apple pie."

Sam's face lit up. "With cheese?"

"Sure. Any way you like it."

The waitress turned to C.J.. "How about you?"

"No, I shouldn't."

"Aw, come on," Sam insisted. "That green stuff can't have filled you up."

"Well . . ."

He turned to the waitress. "Bring her a piece too."

"With cheese, or à la mode?"

"À la mode," C.J. said quickly.

Later, when they had finished the last bites of pie, she said with feeling, "God that was good. It's been so long since I allowed myself the luxury of dessert. I don't regret a single calorie."

"What's a calorie?" Sam asked.

C.J. looked at him in amazement. "You really don't know?"

"I wouldn't ask if I did."

Staring at him, she asked, "Where are you from?"

"You mean, where was I raised?"

She nodded.

"Abilene, Kansas. My folks are dead, but I've got a couple of brothers and a sister back there." He frowned. "At least, I did."

"What do they do?"

"My brothers work the farm. My sister lives nearby."

"What does she do?"

Sam raised an eyebrow. "Do? You mean, is she married?"

C.J. gave him a wry look. "I mean, does she have a career—a job?"

"She's married and has five kids. That's enough of a job for a woman."

She grimaced. "You really need your consciousness raised."

"What?"

She shook her head. "Never mind. Why didn't you stay on the farm with your brothers?"

"It just wasn't for me. I wanted to see more of the country than a dirt farm outside Abilene." He shook his head ruefully. "I guess I've seen a helluva lot more than I bargained for."

"How did you get into law enforcement?"

"When you're good with a gun, like I always was, there was only two ways to go—with the law or against it."

C.J. was surprised by his answer. Most of the policemen she knew had a rigid sense of right and wrong. Sam's casual attitude seemed to indicate that he might just as easily have gone the other way. "Why didn't you go against it?" she asked curiously.

"My folks raised me right, I guess. Anyway, it seemed more fun to chase people than to be chased. I could stop and rest when I wanted. When you're bein' hunted, you're always on the run, always lookin' back over your shoulder. I didn't think I'd much care for that."

C.J. couldn't tell if he was serious or actually showing a little humor.

He paused, then asked, "What about you?"

She met his look. "What about me?"

"Tell me about your family."

C.J. took a sip of coffee. "Well, you've met my mother. And yes, she's always been a little off key. She's been married three times. She's still trying to get it right."

"And your father?"

This was a harder question, one she would prefer not to answer. But she knew by now how persistent Sam was. Better just get it over with, she decided. She answered with as little emotion as possible. "He's handsome, endearing, not the best provider, and like so many men, only passing through. In spite of all his shortcomings, I don't think my mother ever really got over him."

"Did you?"

She looked at him, startled. "I've come to terms with it. I've learned that most men are just passing through." Determined to change the subject, she went on. "Anyway, it was just Mom and me for a long time. She worked hard to put me through film school."

"Film school?"

"I wanted to be an actress."

"Then why are you a private detective?"

C.J. smiled. "At first I told myself I would just do it on the side to support my acting career. Getting started is tough. Then I discovered I was good at it, and I could even use my acting talent occasionally. I like what I do."

"You got any brothers or sisters?"

"Nope." She laughed. "You've got me doing it now. No, there's just me. Mom said if she'd had more children, she would have run away from home. Besides, my dad didn't stick around long enough, and neither of her other husbands were the father types."

Sam leaned across the table, his long fingers easily surrounding the coffee cup. "What's a father type?"

"You know—the kind of man who makes a good father."

He shrugged. "Can't be much to it. You feed 'em, put clothes on their backs, teach 'em right from wrong, and love 'em a lot."

C.J. eyed him thoughtfully. He had a way of making things seem so simple. "You surprise me, Marshal."

"Why?"

"I wouldn't have thought a man like you, in your line of work, would want to be tied down to a family."

"Well, that just shows you don't know everything now, doesn't it?" Sam responded with a wry smile. "A family, roots, that's the only thing that counts when all's said and done."

Before she could ask another question, he said, "C.J. isn't a proper name for a woman. Why do you go by that?"

She couldn't believe it. Every time they actually started communicating, he said something that made her furious. "Because I prefer it," she answered through clenched teeth.

"What do the initials stand for?"

"Caitlin and Jane."

"Those are both real pretty. They're strong names— names to be proud of. They shouldn't be hidden behind initials."

"Look, it's easier with my work. People take me more seriously, especially in correspondence, when they don't know I'm a woman," C.J. explained, then immediately hated herself for bothering to defend her choice.

The waitress returned to their table. "You folks need anything else?"

C.J. shook her head. "Just the bill, please."

As the waitress laid it on the table, C.J. reached for it but Sam got it first. "I said I would buy supper," he reminded her.

Taking a silver dollar from his pocket, he placed it on top of the bill.

The waitress picked up the coin and eyed it curiously. "Look at this—an 1882 silver dollar. I've never seen one that old before. What a neat tip. Thanks."

C.J. stared at the coin as the waitress tucked it in her pocket. She was no expert on coins, but she knew that an old one like that must be worth a great deal. Looking at Sam, she wondered where on earth he'd gotten it. And why he was giving it away as a tip.

Noticing the expectant, slightly impatient look on the waitress's face, C.J. took the bill from Sam, scanned it quickly, then pulled a credit card out of her wallet and handed it to the waitress.

"Be right back," she responded with a smile.

"Wait a minute," Sam said to C.J., "what are you doing?"

"I'm putting it on my credit card. Don't worry, it was only forty-five dollars."

"Forty-five dollars!" Sam shouted.

People at nearby tables turned to stare.

"That's robbery, pure and simple. Forty-five dollars for a steak and potatoes and a piece of pie! Why, at any respectable restaurant that should only cost a dollar."

"Forget it," C.J. insisted. "I didn't think you'd be able to pay for lunch."

The waitress returned with the credit card. C.J. signed the receipt, then led Sam out of the restaurant before he could make more of a scene. As they got into her car, he shook his head and muttered, "Forty-five dollars . . . maybe I shouldn't have had the pie."

"Looks like Mother's here," C.J. said as she pulled into the driveway of her apartment a half hour later. "You go on up, I'll be back in a little while."

Sam looked at her curiously. "You goin' to let me sleep on that davenport again, Katy?"

"Katy?"

"Sounds better than C.J., don't you think?"

She sighed. "Look, I've got to get some groceries. I'll be back shortly."

"All right. Try not to get into any trouble when I'm not around to help you."

She thought about explaining to him that she'd never once been in any real danger until she met him. Instead, she merely peeled out on a screech of burning rubber.

At the main branch of the Santa Monica Public Library, C.J. went straight to the reference section.

"Do you have any books on lawmen of the Old West?" she asked a young librarian.

"Certainly. But the real old ones are for reference only, they can't be checked out."

"That's all right, I just want to look up something."

"If you'll fill out this card with your name and address, I'll get one of the more comprehensive reference books for you. If you don't find what you're looking for there, bring it to the counter and I'll get more."

For the next two hours C.J. skimmed through book after book on the Old West. She began to get caught up in the history of outlaws and lawmen, settlers and cowboys. What a life, she thought. It was harsh, sometimes cruel, always challenging. A time when men were men and women were schoolmarms or "sportin' women."

This is ridiculous, she finally told herself, closing yet another book. She wasn't sure what she was doing there. It wasn't as if she believed his crazy story. It was just that he walked, talked, and acted like someone straight out of the Old West. He was so convincing. Most loonies were, she supposed.

Then there was that silver dollar . . .

She didn't know if Sam had been this way before the blow to his head. She only knew that while he was undoubtedly crazy and often infuriating, he was also fascinating. There was something, well, heroic about him. He had a way of being there when she really needed him, unlike most of the other men who'd come in and out of her life.

Still, he was clearly some poor dumb guy who'd lost track of the difference between fantasy and reality. He probably read books about the Old West, and watched movies, and decided he'd rather live in that world than the modern one. The best thing she could do for him was take him back to the hospital.

C.J. carried the book back to the reference desk and handed it to the librarian.

"Thanks," she said. "That'll do it."

"There's one more book," the librarian said. "It took me a while to find it. Would you like to see it?"

C.J. hesitated. It was late, she was tired, she still had to buy groceries, and she had a lot of thinking to do—about Sam and about the Prescott case. She felt uncomfortable with her decision to take him back to the hospital when he clearly didn't want to go. But, all things considered, that was probably the wisest thing to do, even if he had saved her life. Twice.

The problem was that Sam Hackett had a way of getting under her skin. Especially when he called her Katy. The way he said it with that deep voice, and faint, lazy drawl, made it seem special, almost like an endearment. Nobody had called her that since grammar school. It made her feel like a beloved little girl instead of the tough, self-sufficient woman she'd become out of necessity.

She looked up at the librarian, who waited expectantly. "Okay. Let me see it."

This book was even older than the others. The leather binding was faded and cracked, the spine barely held together. The title *Lawmen of the Old West*, was barely legible.

Quickly, C.J. flicked through the pages. There were photos of lawmen and the outlaws they'd killed—or the outlaws who'd killed them. Wyatt Earp was there, along with Doc Holliday, Bat Masterson, and a lot of others C.J. had never heard of. The photos were reproductions of old tintypes. They were faded but the details were remarkably clear—right down to the bullet holes peppered across the bodies of some of the corpses.

She shuddered as she skimmed through the pages.

Then she stopped and all the breath went out of her.

A photo showed the bullet-riddled body of an outlaw

named Flatnose Pete. Just below it was a sepia-tone photo of a strikingly handsome man. A man with dark brown hair and a full mustache. From the photo it was impossible to tell the color of his eyes, but C.J. knew they were blue-green.

"Oh, my God," she whispered as she read the caption below the photo.

U.S. Federal Marshal Sam Hackett.

Chapter 5

Sam leaned forward on the edge of the chair, his elbows propped on his knees, his chin resting on steepled fingers. He stared with a mixture of concentration and wonder at images flickering across the glass front of a box on a shelf a few feet away.

Television, Lucy called it. Holding a strange little object, she made the images stop, then move one by one so that Sam could grasp that it was nothing more than a series of photographs strung end to end in a continuous flow. And, even more unbelievable, they spoke!

She explained that they were watching movies. Finally, Sam understood what went on at United Film Studio, and what Dan Prescott had been involved in when he died.

Lucy had taken Sam to a store unlike any he'd ever seen before. Huge posters hung on the walls, sort of like the wanted posters he was used to, only these were in color. More amazing were these things called movies. Lucy said it was the quickest way to fill him in on the past hundred years. As they watched bits and pieces of each movie, Lucy explained what was happening in them. And so he was brought up-to-date—fast-forward style.

More than once Sam closed his eyes, gingerly pressing the bandaged lump on his head, certain that when he opened his eyes again, everything would be the way it should be—back in 1882.

Only it wasn't.

Lucy took another movie from a stack of small containers, each one identical except for the label. This movie was called *The Outlaw*, with an actress named Jane Russell.

Lucy called it a "western," but Sam couldn't quite figure out what she meant by that. Although the men carried guns and rode horses, it hardly resembled life as Sam knew it.

Then Sam's eyes widened appreciatively at the generous display of Jane Russell's breasts. These movies might not bear much resemblance to reality, but they sure were entertaining.

"What do you think?" Lucy asked as she turned off *The Outlaw* and stacked it on top of *All Quiet on the Western Front*, *The Sands of Iwo Jima*, *A Hard Day's Night*, and *The Right Stuff*.

"It's sorta like seeing a play at the Opera House," Sam answered slowly. Then he asked haltingly, "Did we *really* go to the moon?"

Lucy grinned. "Yup. But we haven't made all that much progress. We still haven't cured the common cold."

Inserting the last movie, she went on. "As a Federal Marshal, you'll appreciate this one. It's called *Lethal Weapon*, with an actor named Mel Gibson. It's about policemen. Want some more popcorn?"

"No, thank you, ma'am."

She sighed. "I wish you'd stop calling me that. Just remember, I'm young enough to be your great-granddaughter."

A smile lifted the corners of Sam's mouth. He liked Lucy. She was colorful, open, and warm. She reminded him of Rose Moffatt at the Bella Donna in Tucson. Rose was a lusty, good-natured woman who ran the girls in the upstairs rooms, and didn't mind working once in a while herself. She always had a hot meal for a man's stomach, good whiskey for his soul, and clean girls for everything else in between. He could see a lot of Rose in Lucy's bawdy humor and genuine warmth.

Watching *Lethal Weapon*, he was fascinated by the language, the automobiles, and the actors. He couldn't figure out what angel dust was, however. But he knew if he asked Lucy, she'd explain it, just as she had explained about popcorn and Coca-Cola. The drink reminded him of champagne with its bubbles, but it was much sweeter.

When Lucy turned off the movie, he asked, "Is that how policemen do their job nowadays?"

Lucy's bracelets jangled as she scooped up a handful of popcorn. "It's still the white hats against the black hats."

At Sam's look of confusion, she continued. "In the first movies about the West, they always used to dress the good guys in white hats and the bad guys in black hats, so people could tell them apart."

Sam glanced at his battered brown Stetson. When he looked back at Lucy, they both burst out laughing.

"I know," she said. "Talk about culture shock. But you'll get the hang of it. E.T. did."

"E.T.?"

Lucy got up and put another movie on. "This is *E.T.* It's great, Spielberg's best. It's all about this extraterrestrial who comes to earth from another planet and gets stranded." Lucy's heavily mascaraed eyes narrowed thoughtfully. "Sorta like being in 1882 one minute and 1989 the next."

As he watched the movie, Sam began to feel that maybe he was an alien too. He felt a lump in his throat, though he never would have admitted it to Lucy. He wondered if he would ever return to his own time again, to all the familiar people, places, and things. He missed his family, especially his brothers, who teased him about his footloose life as a lawman . . . his friends, mainly the other marshals, but also a preacher he played chess with and a doctor who'd saved his life more than once. . . .

And the room he rented from the Widow Purdy. It wasn't much, but it held all his worldly possessions—a photograph of his parents, a small silver crucifix given him by a girl he'd loved once who ended up marrying someone else, books by Mark Twain and Bret Harte.

He remembered Twain's story, "A Connecticut Yankee in King Arthur's Court." He'd thought it an entertaining but very far-fetched yarn. Now, in a way, he was living the same story.

He wondered if he would ever manage to find his way back home again, or if he would be stranded here, out of his own time, forever.

* * *

C.J. took the Pacific Coast Highway north and just kept driving—beyond Malibu and Trancas, through small communities with single-light intersections, along winding stretches of state beaches. Finally she pulled into a parking lot next to a beach and turned off her car. For several minutes she simply sat there, trying to come to terms with what she'd discovered at the library versus what common sense told her.

It kept coming back to one thing—Sam Hackett had traveled forward through time from 1882 to the present.

The photograph proved it. It wasn't simply a matter of someone who looked a great deal like U.S. Federal Marshal Sam Hackett. It *was* him—right down to the double-breasted black shirt, the stained brown hat with the braided leather hatband, and the rifle with the intricate, decorative carving on the handle, including the initials—*S.H.*

"He must be over a hundred and thirty years old," C.J. whispered out loud to the cool ocean breeze that tangled her short hair.

Amazing as that was, it wasn't the most critical issue. The real problem was what to do with him. She'd told him they'd find out where he lived and get him back there. But how could she do that when his home was probably a boardinghouse in a time and place that no longer existed?

There was no answer to that question, or to the others that filled her mind. After an hour of fruitless conjecture, she turned the key in the ignition and headed south again, back toward Venice. She couldn't avoid Sam any longer. But the closer she got to seeing him again, the more confused she felt.

"What am I going to do with him?" she wondered over and over again.

She hadn't the faintest idea how to help him. She wasn't qualified to deal with this sort of thing—whatever this sort of thing was. He needed the help of experts, people who were authorities on the subject of the paranormal.

Suddenly it hit her—U.C.L.A. Medical Center. *Of course,* she thought with relief. It was one of the foremost research facilities in the world, and there were people there who did research into the paranormal. When she was a student at U.C.L.A., she had earned extra cash by participating in experiments.

As she pulled into the garage, she breathed a sigh of relief. She could turn Sam over to those people. They would know how to deal with him. And she could get back to her life and her work, without Sam constantly butting in.

As C.J. put the key in the lock and opened the front door, she felt that she'd finally regained some control over her chaotic life.

Because the volume was turned up on the TV, Lucy and Sam didn't hear her enter at first. C.J. saw Lucy sitting in the huge, overstuffed chair in the corner, her feet tucked under her voluminous skirt, a bowl of popcorn nestled in her lap. Sam sat across from her on the sofa, leaning forward, intently watching the TV. It was all strangely ordinary—she might have walked in on any two people in the world, quietly watching television and munching on popcorn.

Then Lucy looked up. "Hi, sweetie. Where did you disappear to?"

"I . . . had some things to do."

Sam gave her an intent look. "Katy."

The greeting was warm and guileless. The expression in those blue-green eyes was equally warm and trusting. Somehow she felt like a worm.

As Lucy got up to turn down the volume, she gave C.J. an amused look. "I haven't heard anyone call you Katy since you were in kindergarten."

Before C.J. could respond, Lucy gestured toward the coffee table, cluttered with an assortment of video cassettes, magazines, and books. "I decided we'd better start Sam's education right away. Oh, and I took him out for pizza. He doesn't like anchovies either."

She gave Sam a conspiratorial wink. "He likes Jane Russell."

"Jane Russell?"

"Never mind. I'll go make some more popcorn."

When she left the room, C.J. deposited her purse on

the end table by the sofa and sat down next to Sam. Taking a deep breath, she began, "Look, I've come to a decision about all this."

"Oh?"

"You see, you need to be with people who can help you."

Distracted by the television, C.J. glanced at the screen. It was toward the end of *E.T.*, when the feds had captured him. She loved the movie and never tired of watching it. It touched something deep within her, an overwhelming affection and concern for a being so far from home, lost and frightened.

Now she watched E.T. strapped to a table, hooked up to tubes and electrodes, being monitored, poked, and prodded by physicians and scientists who cared nothing for his feelings. It was cold, clinical, brutal. As always when she watched this scene, C.J. felt heartsick and outraged, just as the little boy, Elliot, did.

"*Stop! Stop! You're killing him! You're killing him!*"

Elliot's words tore at her heart. Suddenly the image of Elliot and E.T. seemed to freeze as the reality of it sank in. Slowly, C.J. turned back to Sam, staring at him as if seeing him for the first time.

He was out of his time, out of his place, out of his world. Just like E.T. Sam was a phenomenon any scientist would give his soul to get his hands on. And then what? Tubes and electrodes . . . machines, tests, poking, prodding.

Dear God, what had she been thinking of when she decided to turn Sam over to the scientists at U.C.L.A.? He saved her life—how could she repay him this way?

"C.J.?"

She looked up. Lucy had returned with a bowl brimming with popcorn. For once Lucy wasn't her usual crazy self. As she met C.J.'s look, there was something quiet and thoughtful about her.

She knows, C.J. thought in surprise. Her mother knew what she had contemplated, and knew also that she couldn't go through with it.

Dear Lucy, so sweet, so scatterbrained, believing in

extraterrestrials, reincarnation, channeling to the spirits, and, without question, time travel. Even with all her ditziness, her goat's milk and crystal power, at this moment C.J. thought Lucy had a better grip on some truths than she did.

She turned back to Sam. "As I was saying, you need people who can help you, and I think Lucy and I can do just that. Now, in the morning we'll get you some new clothes. And maybe a trip to the drugstore for a few personal things."

Lucy grinned. "Oh, Sam's up on all that sort of thing. We watched some network television, mainly for the commercials. He knows all about Spuds MacKenzie and Bud Lite, Close-Up Toothpaste, Arrid Extra Dry, L'Eggs Pantyhose—"

"Good," C.J. interrupted. "But I think we can forget about the pantyhose."

Turning to Sam, she found him studying her with that slow, measured watchfulness she'd already come to recognize after only one day with him.

"I think we'd better talk," she said, crossing the room to turn off the television.

He nodded.

C.J. smiled faintly. He could certainly never be accused of being overly talkative. Even in the restaurant earlier, when he'd answered her questions, he had given away little of his emotions or deepest thoughts. Once more she had to remind herself that he was from another time, a simpler time, when people's thoughts were less complex.

What kind of man was Sam Hackett anyway? Everything she'd ever learned about men didn't apply to him.

Lucy said, "I put Redford and Newman out." She gathered up glasses and half-empty bowls of popcorn. Glancing quickly from Sam to C.J., she went on. "I guess I'd better be going."

She took the dishes into the kitchen, then returned, scooping up the cassettes and snapping them into their cases. "I'll return these and pick up some more tomorrow." Standing on tiptoe, she gave Sam a kiss on the cheek.

"Hang in there, Marshal. It may be a cockeyed world, but for now it's the only one you've got."

C.J. followed Lucy to the door. As she stepped outside, Lucy pulled one cassette out of the bunch. "I saved this one for last. Sam hasn't seen it yet."

Opening the case, C.J. read the title—*Body Heat*. She looked up at Lucy. "You think Sam needs to see *this*?"

"No, *you* do. You could use some pointers."

"What's that supposed to mean?"

"It means your choice of men over the past few years leaves a lot to be desired. They're outta luck, outta work, or out to lunch. For the first time in a long time you have a real man under your roof. Don't blow it."

C.J. glared at her mother. "Shall we discuss your choice of husbands?"

"Precisely my point. I've put a lot of time and effort into the search for the right man. Now I know why I was doomed to failure. The last good one lived a hundred years ago." She let out a long sigh. "What a time that must have been . . . when men were men and women were put up on a pedestal. You know, I could really get into that." Her eyes lit up. "What an adventure that would be!" Suddenly she turned serious. "About Sam . . ."

"What about him?"

Lucy twisted her mouth thoughtfully, looking rather like a child contemplating something beyond her comprehension. "I know how you feel about some of my more avant garde ideas. But Sam is *real*. I don't know why we've been chosen to help him, but we have. We have a sacred obligation toward him. Do you have any idea what would happen to him if other people found out about him?"

C.J. nodded. She had a very good idea what would happen.

Lucy went on. "We have to keep him our little secret, until I can figure out a way to get him back to his own time."

"Get him back?"

"Of course. If he came forward in time, there's no reason why he couldn't go back. Somehow he slipped through a door in time, so to speak. I've read up a little on time travel—you know, other dimensions—and there has to be a way to get back. I just have to find it for him. I'm going to talk to Ravi, to see if he knows anything about it."

Ravi was Lucy's psychic mentor. He was young and darkly handsome. C.J. had always assumed that explained Lucy's interest in him, rather than his supposed psychic powers.

As Lucy started down the stairs, she flung over her shoulder, "'Night, Katy."

C.J. grimaced. Back in the living room, Sam sat on the sofa, looking through the books and magazines Lucy had bought for him. Now that it was just her and Sam, C.J. felt awkward somehow, especially when she remembered she was holding the *Body Heat* cassette. Setting it down on the television, she asked, "Would you like a cup of coffee?"

"Sure."

"I'll be right back."

In the kitchen she started the coffeemaker, then sat down at the tiny table to think. Without even realizing what she was doing, she absentmindedly pulled a cigarette from a pack in a drawer and lit it. During her days as a struggling actress, she'd started smoking. Then the antismoking campaign got into high gear, with vivid color photos of cross-sections of diseased lungs and statistics on cancer.

C.J. had quit cold turkey. No cutting back, no pills, no visits to Schick Centers. It amazed her friends, who tried to quit but failed miserably. Now she sat there, smoking her second cigarette in the span of five minutes, thinking intently.

When Sam came into the kitchen, he frowned.

Catching his look, C.J. said, "Does smoking bother you?"

"No. I'm just not used to seeing a lady smoke."

A lady? It was the second time he'd said that, and it gave her a strange feeling. Not bad, but strange.

Without even thinking she stubbed out the cigarette. Then she realized what she'd done—she'd let Sam's opinion of her affect her behavior. The realization brought a tiny jolt of surprise. She'd made it a point never to care what anyone else thought of her. Maybe it came from being raised by an unconventional mother who was always out of step with the mothers of C.J.'s friends.

She remembered her sixth-grade geography class in particular. They were studying the Mayan ruins. The teacher went into great detail to explain possible theories regarding the disappearance of an entire civilization. Lucy was helping out in the class that day as a volunteer room mother. When the teacher was called to the office, leaving Lucy briefly in charge, she promptly told the kids to close their textbooks. Then she began a fascinating discourse on an entire culture traveling to another dimension, where they undoubtedly existed simultaneously with these very kids.

The kids were fascinated, the teacher appalled, and the parents outraged. So, C.J. had learned early to march to the beat of a different drummer.

Or maybe it came from the rejection she experienced as an actress. If she'd listened to all the casting directors who said she was too tall, not pretty enough, not what they were looking for, she would have lost all sense of self-esteem.

So now, as she stubbed out her cigarette, she couldn't understand why Sam's opinion should be so important.

She got up and poured two cups of coffee, then sat down opposite Sam.

"Let's begin at the beginning. You said you were following someone named Traeger?"

"Emmett Traeger. The *first*," he added with a wry twist to his mouth. "I was on his trail for six months, from the New Mexico Territory to Los Angeles."

"New Mexico is a state now."

"I know—Lucy showed me a map of the states." He shook his head. "I've never even heard of these Hawaiian Islands."

"What did Traeger do?"

Sam reached inside his shirt pocket and pulled out the wanted poster he'd carried in the pocket of his coat all these months. Unfolding it, he handed it to C.J. The bold lettering spelled it out—robbery and murder. And a five thousand dollar reward.

"Five thousand—he must have been pretty bad to have that kind of price on his head." Looking up from the wanted poster, she said curiously, "Tell me about Traeger."

Sam said thoughtfully, "I suppose it reads like a story in one of the dime novels those eastern writers made sound so romantic—a fine, upstanding young man turning to a life of crime and violence to avenge some misdeed. Only in this case the misdeed was Traeger's. He was sixteen when he was caught gutting out one of his neighbor's steers."

"That doesn't sound so bad."

"Cattle stealing was a hanging offense. Traeger didn't want to be hung, so he shot his neighbor dead."

C.J. was stunned. It was like something out of a Sam Peckinpah western, only what Sam was describing so matter-of-factly was real. "What happened to Traeger after that?"

"By the time he was twenty, he could've supplied those writers with a lot of stories for their novels, if they were willing to print the truth. There was the old man he horsewhipped to death outside Oklahoma City, and a dead whore in Las Cruces who'd tried to collect for services rendered."

"Is that when you went after him?"

"Yeah. He started riding with an outlaw named Dawson. They had a lot in common—fast guns, fast women, and trains. By the time they hit the Flyer out of Junction City, there were four others riding with them. Black-eyed Charley got his name from a gun misfiring at close range, burning him with gunpowder. Dawson's brother, Clancy. Flatnose Pete—"

C.J. interrupted. "I saw your picture with him in a book. You killed him."

Something in her tone made Sam frown. "He liked to fight with his fists rather than guns. Beat a couple of people to death before I got him. Rollie Prescott rode with them briefly before deciding the outlaw life wasn't for him."

"Prescott?" C.J. exclaimed.

"Julie Prescott's great-great-grandfather. He didn't stay with the gang for long. From what I heard, he was just hard up for money to take care of his wife and kid. He couldn't stomach the killing, and quit."

"What happened to Traeger?"

"He took over the gang when Dawson died. They hit more than a dozen trains and banks throughout the territories, until the railroad called in the Pinkertons. One by one the gang members died, until only Traeger was left. He hit the Territorial National Bank in Santa Fe alone. We thought for sure we'd get him after that."

"We?"

"Me and my partner, Tom."

C.J. looked at Sam in surprise. "You had a partner?"

"Yeah. Young guy. Fast with a gun." Sam's expression softened in a barely perceptible smile. "Thought being a marshal would impress the ladies. I remember how disappointed Tom was those first weeks on Traeger's trail. We spent long days in the saddle, hard nights sleeping on the ground or atop a horse, following leads that usually disappeared into thin air. We ate beans, hardtack, and teeth-bustin' corn dodgers, washed down with cold coffee. Sometimes we stopped to eat, but usually we ate in the saddle. We froze over the winter and damned near died of thirst in the heat of early summer. All for three dollars a day plus expenses. So long as expenses didn't exceed two dollars a day."

C.J. shook her head in amazement. "I don't believe it."

"It wasn't that bad," Sam insisted. "Besides, I knew what I was getting into when I signed up. Tom was kind of inexperienced, though. He thought it would be a few weeks work followed by a fat reward and a long recuperation with a girl by the name of Cherry he liked to visit at the House of Mirrors in Denver. I didn't disillusion him until we were far enough along on the trail that there was no turning back."

"Was Tom with you when you found Traeger in L.A.?"

Sam's expression hardened. "No. Traeger shot him in the back in Nogales. Just like he shot Rollie Prescott in the back."

"How did you find Prescott?"

"I'd heard that Rollie had a family in Los Angeles, that

he'd gone straight. So when Traeger's trail led to L.A., then disappeared, I looked up Rollie. I thought Traeger just might have turned to his old sidekick."

"But why would Traeger kill Prescott?"

"Maybe there was bad blood between them. Maybe Prescott had something Traeger wanted. Anyway, I went after Traeger and caught up with him outside the boardinghouse where he was stayin'."

"What happened?"

Sam grimaced. "The earthquake. I'd heard of 'em before, but I'd never been through one." He shook his head. "That was really somethin'."

C.J. smiled. "You get used to them if you live in L.A."

He looked at her curiously. "What were you doin' there when that earthquake hit?"

"Repossessing a car." At his confused expression, she explained. "Sometimes, in my line of work, a client pays me to pick up something of theirs that someone else has taken. In this case it was a car—an expensive one. I would have made a cool thousand."

"*Dollars?*" Sam asked in amazement.

C.J. laughed. "A thousand dollars doesn't go as far as it used to. Remember the cost of lunch?"

He nodded. "Yeah. But a thousand dollars for a day's work. That's pretty good wages."

"Donald Trump wouldn't think so, but I'm satisfied."

"Is that what Julie Prescott is paying you?"

"Julie is probably going to be one of those clients who can't pay at all," C.J. said with a long sigh.

"Doesn't matter. I'm not interested in her money."

"What is that supposed to mean?"

Sam's eyes narrowed and his voice was hard. "It means that I'm going to find out who killed her grandfather. And I'll just bet it has something to do with Emmett Traeger."

C.J. didn't know whether to feel amused or angry. "Look, this is ridiculous. First of all, Dan Prescott may have died because of someone's carelessness. It may not even be a case of murder. And *if* it is murder, it probably has nothing to do with Traeger. You're confusing him with his great-grandfather, for heaven's sake."

He gave her that long, speculative look that slipped right under all her defenses. "Doesn't it seem a little strange to you that the man I was after, Emmett Traeger, killed Rollie Prescott in 1882. Now, in 1989, another Prescott has died and another Traeger is involved?"

"It's a coincidence. Fate. Karma," C.J. answered. *My God*, she thought, *I'm beginning to sound like my mother*.

"I don't know what those other two things are, but I don't believe in coincidence."

"What exactly do you believe in, then?"

"Gut instinct."

She threw up her hands. "Here we go again. Now, look, Marshal—"

"No, you look, Katy. I may not understand a lot of things, but I have a real strong feeling that Dan Prescott's death is somehow tied up with the Traegers. And I'm going to prove it."

C.J. glared at him. "Listen, Marshal, this is *my* case, if it even is a case."

"I was involved with the Prescotts and the Traegers first. It's my case too." He finished in a tone that brooked no argument. "You just took on a partner."

Chapter 6

385 Melrose was one of a row of chic, trendy boutiques lining Melrose Avenue in West Hollywood. Known simply by its address, it carried an exclusive line of men's wear by European designers, and was frequented mainly by up and coming young actors and rock stars.

Last year C.J. had investigated a shoplifting case for the owner. The routine case escalated to something more complex when the stolen designer apparel was traced to a regular customer, a prominent Beverly Hills bank executive. It made no sense at first. The banker was conservative, highly respected, and could easily afford to pay for the clothes. They weren't even his size.

Further investigation uncovered the fact that the apparently happily married banker had given the clothes as gifts to his young male lover. He was afraid to buy them, for fear someone might guess his guilty secret.

Neither C.J. nor her client wanted to ruin the man's reputation. An arrangement was made for the banker to pay for the stolen clothes, and in the future purchase whatever he wished with the utmost privacy and discretion.

C.J. collected a substantial fee, the eternal gratitude of the owner, and a lifetime discount on purchases from his shop. Occasionally, she bought something for herself. She loved comfortable, oversized men's shirts. And men's jeans were a better fit on her long-limbed, slender frame than women's jeans.

But this time when she entered the store, she wasn't shopping for herself. Sam followed hesitantly, eyeing the merchandise critically. As far as C.J. was concerned, the

situation was desperate. If she had to look at those worn
Levi's and faded chambray shirt, not to mention that torn,
filthy coat, for one more day, she was going to scream. The
longjohns were another story altogether. In L.A., in the
middle of summer, they were a ridiculous anachronism.

Barry, the young salesclerk whom C.J. knew well,
beamed when he saw her. He was shorter than C.J. and
stocky, with thinning blond hair and huge, dark eyes with
perpetual bags under them. To her he looked like a basset
hound puppy, and had the amiable, not overly bright
disposition to match.

"C.J., precious!" Barry exclaimed, kissing the air near
her right cheek. "It's been too, too long." He eyed Sam with
undisguised interest. "And *who* is this?"

As Barry's gaze went from the tips of Sam's boots to his
broad shoulders and down again, C.J. answered, "This is
Mr. Hackett. He needs a little of everything—shirts, pants,
socks, et cetera."

"Did you have a particular look in mind?"

C.J. glanced briefly at Sam. Somehow, she couldn't see
him in the Armani wardrobe Emmett Traeger wore. Nor
was he the leather-jacket type either. It occurred to her
that he wasn't any type at all—he was uniquely and
refreshingly himself.

Looking back at Barry, she replied without cracking a
smile, "Something a bit more contemporary, I think."

Barry's eyes narrowed as he contemplated Sam. "Ah,
yes, I see what you mean. Though, I must say, this look—so
earthy, so masculine, has a certain je ne sais quoi."

Sam had stood there quietly while she and Barry
talked about him. Clearly growing irritated with being
treated like a dressmaker's dummy, he said tersely, "Let's
get on with this, Katy, we've got work to do."

"So sorry," Barry apologized. "We'll have you out of
those clothes in no time." At Sam's startled look, he added,
"And into something marvelous, of course."

At Barry's mention of getting Sam out of his clothes,
C.J.'s thoughts went back to the first night she'd met Sam,
when he was unconscious and she undressed him. With
Lucy standing over her shoulder, she'd been reluctant to

stare too pointedly at Sam, but she'd seen enough to realize that Sam would look wonderful in something lean and tight in all the right places. The typical clientele at 385 went through hell working out at a gym or with their own private body builder, trying to get the lean, hard look that came naturally to Sam.

Barry lifted his delicate brows. "We have some absolutely stunning things that just came in a few days ago. Italian—leather. Need I say more?"

C.J. bit back a giggle as Barry winked suggestively at Sam.

"Just bring me another pair of Levi's and a shirt," Sam responded. "And maybe some longjohns."

"Longjohns?" Barry's eyebrows shot up in delicious excitement. "Silk, of course. I think I have something you'd like. Now, what size?"

C.J. stepped forward. Spreading her small hands thumb to thumb, she wrapped them around Sam's waist. "I'd say probably about a thirty-four waist, Barry, and maybe a thirty-six inseam."

"My, you are a big boy." Barry sighed sweetly. "I'll bring several things."

As Barry left, Sam looked at C.J. "Is that some new way of measuring?"

Color flooded her cheeks. "Um . . ." she stammered, trying furiously to think of something to say.

"Something wrong, Katy?" he asked with a faintly bemused expression.

"You're what's wrong," she snapped, irritated with herself.

"Come again?"

"You don't fit. You've come out of 1882 into 1989. The whole world has changed, nothing is the way it used to be for you. And yet you're not crazy. You're taking it all in stride."

"Does that bother you?"

Ignoring the question, she fumbled in her purse for the cigarettes that only last night she'd sworn she would give up—again. This was something else in her life she couldn't seem to control lately, along with clients, her investigations, and Sam.

Inhaling deeply on it, she blew out the smoke slowly, trying very hard to ignore Sam's critical look.

The irony of it—she'd given up trying to find a serious relationship with a man. She told herself she didn't need the hassle of waiting for a phone call that never came, of worrying about whether she was coming on too strong or not strong enough, of wondering if she liked a particular man more than he liked her.

Yet here was a man she hadn't asked for, didn't know what to do with, and couldn't get rid of.

Finally, she looked at Sam. "Yes, it does bother me. I'd be absolutely bonkers if something like that happened to me."

"I don't know what bonkers means, but I can make a pretty good guess. Actually, I think you'd handle it just fine."

"How?" she asked simply.

His mouth softened in one of the sudden, unexpected smiles she was never prepared for. "Adapt and overcome, Katy." He went on slowly. "Life is hard, no matter when you live. There's always somethin' to deal with. Right now it's that fella, Barry, who prefers men to women."

C.J. stared at Sam. She had no idea he understood that Barry was flirting with him. Sam was always doing this to her—just when she thought she had him all figured out, he surprised her. He might have simple values, but he wasn't a simple man.

She laughed ruefully. "I didn't think you noticed."

"I noticed. And I noticed something else."

"What?"

"I noticed that when you laugh, it's a real pretty sound, like it's comin' from way deep inside you. I like your laugh, Katy."

She blushed down to the roots of her hair. She hadn't blushed since the eighth grade, when a boy she had a dreadful crush on overheard her telling her best friend that she wondered if he was a good kisser.

Determined to steer the conversation to safer waters, she asked, "What else do you adapt to and overcome?"

"Sometimes it's a Mustang that isn't a horse. The ride's more comfortable, and a helluva lot faster, but I think I prefer a horse."

"And?"

"A forty-five-dollar meal."

"Go on."

"Legs."

"Legs?"

"Yup." Sam's gaze fastened on her miniskirt.

"Go on."

His expression sobered. "Outlaws that wear a suit and look like a banker."

She frowned. "Emmett Traeger."

"It may be another time and another Traeger, but I'm tellin' you, there's somethin' about that man. I'm not sayin' he killed Prescott, but he can't be trusted. That, I'm sure of."

C.J. put her hands on her hips and glared at Sam. "You're not going to let go of the notion Prescott was murdered, are you, no matter how crazy it is!"

He didn't back down one bit. "No, I'm not. A lot of things may have changed, but I'm not gonna change the rules I follow."

"Rules! You mean, some antiquated code of the West."

"Call it what you want. There are rules men live by. Men who break those rules have to be stopped."

C.J. made an effort to control her rising temper and inject a note of reason into the argument. "But we have almost nothing to go on."

"We have Julie Prescott. She doesn't believe her grandfather's death was an accident. Neither did that propman, Harry Jones."

"He didn't say it was murder," C.J. pointed out.

"He didn't say the word, but that's what he was gettin' at."

"Fine, if it was murder, what was the motive?"

Sam looked blank. "Motive?"

C.J. explained, "A reason for someone wanting Dan

Prescott dead." When he didn't respond, she added, "See, there isn't one."

"There's a motive. We just haven't found it yet."

That did it. "Dammit, Sam," she exploded, "I'll bet you wouldn't push this if Traeger weren't involved."

He didn't raise his voice. He simply said in a quiet voice, "You're wrong."

"Oh, I am, am I?"

"Yes, you are."

"I'm afraid to ask why." C.J.'s tone was scathing.

"Instinct. Gut instinct."

At that moment Barry returned, his arms laden with pants, shirts, and men's briefs. He deposited them in a nearby dressing room, then said, "Shall we get started? Why don't you try the briefs first?"

He held up a pair of silky, very *brief* briefs. The designer label was nearly as big as the garment itself.

C.J. couldn't help grinning at Sam's discomfiture.

"What are those?"

"You need them."

"For what?"

"To replace those longjohns. It's much too warm in L.A. to wear them."

Sam's eyes narrowed. "Is this some kind of joke?"

C.J.'s tone was perfectly innocent. "Of course not."

Sam looked skeptically at Barry. "You really think I need these?"

Barry nodded enthusiastically. "Oh, my, yes."

Still, he hesitated.

"Trust me," C.J. said pointedly. "Gut instinct."

For a moment she thought Sam was going to laugh. Instead, he said, "I think I'll just try the pants first."

Barry held open the door of the dressing room as Sam stepped inside. He started to go in with him, until Sam said, "I can manage just fine by myself."

"Right," C.J. said, "just let Barry know if you need any help with the zipper."

"What's a zipper?" Sam asked.

"You'll figure it out. Adapt and overcome, Marshal."

* * *

They ended up compromising on Sam's clothes. He picked out a few pair of jeans, some plain shirts, and a jacket, but kept his boots and hat. He couldn't bring himself to try on the underwear, and when C.J. insisted on buying some, he told her he'd never wear them. Warm or not, he'd stick with his longjohns.

When they returned to C.J.'s house, she said, "Looks like I've got a client," pointing to a battered old pickup truck parked behind Lucy's MG.

As she got out of the car, she said, "They'll just have to wait. I have some calls to make."

She didn't add that one of the calls was to Julie Prescott, telling her that she just couldn't see any reason to pursue the case.

While C.J. talked, Sam struggled with the door handle. Finally, he swung open the door and stepped out of it, instead of climbing over it the way he had been doing. The look he gave C.J. was full of such delight in his accomplishment that it took her breath away. At that moment there was something boyishly endearing about him.

"Finally got the hang of that thing," he announced.

She smiled. "Yup." She laughed at herself. Now he had *her* doing it.

While Sam set the bag with his new clothes on a chair in the outer office, C.J. stopped by Lucy's desk to check for messages. Lucy's voice drifted from the inner office.

C.J. and Sam walked inside to find Lucy sitting behind the desk. She greeted them with a broad smile. "Hi, kids. I was about to give you up for lost." Eyeing the new clothes Sam wore, Lucy said, "I can see you were busy. They say clothes make the man, but in this case I think it's the other way around."

C.J. looked past Lucy to the figure slouching in a chair opposite the desk. Cody, the old wrangler from the *Hard Country* set, pulled his lanky frame out of the chair. Holding his wide-brimmed hat in one hand, he came forward and extended his hand. "Afternoon, Miss." He nodded at Sam. "Hope you don't mind me comin' by."

"Of course not." C.J. found a comfortable place to lean

against on one side of the desk since Lucy didn't look as if she were going to give back her chair.

"I had a devil of a time findin' this place," Cody went on, grinning good-naturedly. "You got some real colorful neighbors. Then Lucy here found me drivin' back and forth, and had me come in. We've been havin' a real nice conversation."

Lucy smiled like a Cheshire cat. "We're going to get together tonight. I'm going to show Cody my crystal collection and he's going to give me some pointers on wild-bull riding."

C.J. cast a quick, desperate glance heavenward. God save her, there were moments when she wished she'd been an orphan.

Sam said, "Well, that should be real interestin' for both of you."

As he spoke, he rounded the desk and leaned against a corner beside C.J. It was a simple gesture, but it emphasized his determination not to be shut out of the Prescott case. He intended to be C.J.'s partner whether she wanted one or not.

Lucy rose. "Well, I'll get back to my work and let you people get down to business." She winked at Cody. "See you later."

As Lucy left the room, C.J. asked Cody, "What brings you out to the beach?"

"I wanted to talk to you about Dan's death. I understand you came back to the studio yesterday. I had to leave early to go out to the ranch and must've just missed you."

The ranch. C.J. smiled. Cody was a real cowboy, through and through. He walked, talked and, apparently, lived the part. No wonder he and Sam hit it off immediately. Here, at least, was one person Sam could feel comfortable around, someone who belonged more to the last century than the present one.

C.J. had loved cowboys as a child. She never missed a John Wayne western. The good guys were heroes she could look up to. They might get shot, but they never died. They simply rode off into the sunset to face another bad guy in another town.

She glanced at Sam. No, they didn't make them like that anymore.

Cody explained, "It's not really my ranch, of course. It was Dan's old place out in Canyon Country. Belongs to Julie now."

"Dan Prescott had a ranch?" C.J. was surprised. Somehow, she hadn't envisioned him as owning any property, at least not any that amounted to anything.

"It was the old family homestead handed down from Dan's grandmother. There's only about a hundred acres, just enough to run a couple of horses and a few head of cattle. The ranch house itself ain't much to speak of, doesn't even have electricity or indoor plumbing. Julie worried about him, usin' kerosene lanterns and that old wood stove to cook on."

"Did he live out there and commute to the studio?"

"Yeah, up until a few months ago. It got to be too much for him, livin' out there alone, and drivin' all that way every day. After his heart attack Julie made him move into her place in the city, so she could keep an eye on him, and he just went out to the ranch on weekends."

"Julie didn't mention anything about a ranch."

"Dan raised her out there after her folks died. But it was kinda boring for her, and she couldn't wait to grow up and move into the city."

Julie hadn't mentioned anything about her grandfather having a serious heart condition either. C.J. immediately wondered if Prescott might have chosen a dramatic way of committing suicide as a result of bad health. He certainly wouldn't be the first person to do so.

But Cody went on. "Don't get the wrong idea, though. The heart attack wasn't nothin' serious. Angina, I think the doctor called it. He just told Dan to slow down, take it easy. But Julie was real worried, 'cause her grandpa was all she had, and she wanted him to be with her. I've been goin' out to the place ever since Dan died to take care of the animals."

"Is the property valuable?"

Cody shook his head. "Naw. It ain't in a place where they're buildin' houses and you can't farm it. If Julie decides to sell it, I doubt that she'll get more than a few thousand for it."

He gave C.J. a shrewd look. "If you're thinkin' someone might've killed Dan to get their hands on his land, forget it. It wasn't worth it."

"No, I wasn't thinking that," she replied.

"I heard you're askin' questions about Dan's death."

"I spoke to the propman, Harry Jones," C.J. saïd.

Cody nodded. "Harry's a good man. I've known him for years. Some people in this business get sloppy about details, but not Harry. That's why Dan liked workin' with him. If Harry said the guns were all right, then I believe him."

"He also said several people could have gone into the prop trailer without him noticing," Sam said.

C.J. knew perfectly well what he was getting at, and she was determined to put a stop to it immediately. "The point is, there was no motive for anyone to kill Dan Prescott."

"Maybe. Maybe not," Cody responded. "Truth is, I don't buy the story that it was an accident."

"Accidents do happen on film sets. Just a few years ago a young actor was killed when he played around with a gun that was supposedly loaded with harmless blanks."

"Dan didn't play around with guns, Miss Grant. He'd been around 'em most of his life, got his first .22 when he was just a kid, and his daddy taught him to respect 'em."

C.J. returned to something Cody had said earlier. "What about his health? You didn't think there was a serious problem, but Dan might have been more depressed about it than you realized."

"A man who's worried about dyin' doesn't go around making big plans for the future."

"What do you mean?" Sam asked. "What kind of plans?"

"Big plans," Cody repeated. "You see, Dan's big regret was that he never had very much to give Julie. Like me, he went to work for the studio back in its heyday, when it was makin' a lot of westerns. He didn't make a lot of money, but it was steady work up until about fifteen years ago. They stopped makin' so many westerns then, and work sorta dried up."

C.J. could well imagine how Prescott felt, seeing his livelihood slipping away just as he was getting older and had an orphaned granddaughter to support. As she well knew, acting was an insecure profession at best. Most actors could never hope to earn even a modest living at it. She asked gently, "What happened to Dan then?"

"Some of the old boys got outta the business, others like me and Dan took whatever work we could get, mainly on television shows, and stuck it out. But it was hard. He didn't have money to send Julie to college or get her a nice apartment. Then this movie came along, and he was real excited."

"It must have been special for him to work on a movie like that again."

"Special? Hell, yes, it was special to him. 'Course, he didn't have a leading role or anything, but he sorta figured it would be a good way to go out."

"Go out?" Sam asked.

"That's what I was tellin' you about the big plans Dan had. This movie was gonna be his last one. He was gonna retire after this. Said he was gonna fix up the ranch, set up Julie in a nice place, maybe send her to that fancy acting school in London she's always wanted to go to. He was real excited about bringing in some purebred stock to the ranch and building up a herd of horses."

"But you said he didn't have any money?"

"Not a window, nor a pot," Cody quipped. "He could barely keep up the taxes on the property and buy feed for the stock."

"Then how was he going to pay for all these grandiose plans?" C.J. asked.

"He had somethin' goin' on. Somethin' real big. He told me so."

Suddenly C.J. remembered something Julie had said in passing. Something about her grandfather telling her that everything was going to be different. Then, three days later, he was dead.

She looked up to find Sam watching her carefully.

Sitting down at her desk, she picked up a pen and pulled a yellow legal tablet in front of her. "I know who was on the set the day Dan died. I need to know everything you can tell me about those people."

Sam looked at her intently. "Does this mean you think it was murder after all?"

She hated to admit he might be right, but there was more here than she had originally suspected. Based on everything she'd learned so far, Dan's death didn't look like an accident or suicide. That left only one possibility—murder.

She had resisted that possibility because it simply didn't make any sense. Now, meeting Sam's look, she admitted, "Yes, I do."

She was prepared for a smug I-told-you-so from him. Instead, he asked slowly, "What changed your mind?"

"Gut instinct," C.J. answered without hesitation.

Chapter 7

C.J. parked her car in an empty space marked "Visitor" near the brand-new thirty-story United Film Studios Enterprises building. In a couple of years, when the original lot and soundstages were demolished to make way for condos and office buildings, this would be all that was left of the historic studio. Movies made by United Film would be shot on soundstages rented from other studios, or shot in Canada and other countries where production costs were cheaper.

She sat staring up at the glass and granite facade of the building, saddened by the tremendous changes taking place. Moviemakers who once made decisions by gut instinct had given way to bottom-line number crunchers. It was the end of an era that began with the nickleodeon and the notion that dreams could be put on film.

"You comin'?" Sam asked as he got out of the car.

"Yeah, I'm coming." She swung out of the car, mentally trying to shift gears from nostalgia to current problems.

"Somethin' wrong?" he asked in that surprisingly intuitive way of his that always caught her slightly off guard.

"Oh, I was just thinking how sad it is that the movie industry is changing. It's all P and L statements, shareholder reports, and investor audits now."

Sam fastened her with a vaguely perplexed expression that said he hadn't the least idea what she was talking about. "Come again?"

"An end of an era," she explained with a sweeping gesture at the cold, stark office building that loomed in front

of them. "The creative genius of filmmaking has been
reduced to year-end reports and profit statements. Accoun-
tants decide which films get made, not dream merchants."

"End of an era," Sam echoed thoughtfully. "Sorta like
a U.S. Federal Marshal out of his place and time."

At that moment C.J. saw a long black limousine pull
out of a parking space directly in front of the building. The
name on the space was Charles Traeger. Talk about dream
merchants, she thought. Traeger had been making movies
since the twenties, and must be well over eighty, maybe
even ninety.

As the limo passed them, an open window in the rear
slowly, silently, rolled up. C.J. couldn't see the occupant
through the black-tinted glass, but she had the oddest
sensation that whoever it was had been watching her and
Sam.

Telling herself she was being ridiculous, she took Sam's
arm and led him toward the building. They passed a space
with Emmett Traeger's name on it. A shiny black four-
wheel-drive Range Rover was parked there. Of course, she
thought with a wry grin. Range Rovers were the new "in"
car in L.A. for those who could afford them. Even Tom
Cruise drove one. It was the logical choice for a man like
Traeger. A BMW, Mercedes, or Jag would be hopelessly
out of sync, out of chic, out of the question.

Inside the lobby C.J. punched the button for the
elevator and the doors whispered open. There were only a
few scenes left to be shot on the movie. Most of the cast had
been dismissed. From here on it would be difficult to reach
members of the cast and crew who were on the set the day
Dan Prescott died. She needed addresses and phone
numbers for everyone she hadn't yet spoken to. As she and
Sam stepped into the polished steel and marble cab, she
wondered if Traeger would cooperate in giving her the
information she needed. She suspected he was the kind of
man who was accommodating only when it was in his best
interest.

Just as the elevator started to close, two young men
hurried inside. The doors closed silently behind them, and
the elevator began to ascend to the top floor. While the two

men talked in low tones about an upcoming movie, C.J. watched Sam. He braced himself against the rear of the elevator, standing absolutely still with his fingers locked around the interior railing.

"You feel about elevators the same way you do about taxis?" C.J. couldn't resist asking in a whisper. It was meant as a joke, but she immediately saw that Sam didn't think there was anything funny about the question. She thought she caught the brief flicker of something that resembled fear in those blue-green eyes. Then it was quickly hidden away behind a hard expression. It was the same fear she'd seen that first night at the hospital. It caught at her heart as it had then.

When the elevator doors finally opened and the two men hurried out, C.J. took Sam's hand and pulled him into the hallway. The doors quickly snapped shut behind them.

"Are you okay?" she asked as they walked down the hall.

"Sure. I've been in one of those things before, in a hotel in Denver." Then he laughed, in a small, self-deprecating way. "It just didn't leave your stomach down at your feet like this one."

She understood. Elevators always made her equilibrium turn over a couple of times. She glanced at Sam as they walked down the hallway. He had been unnerved by the elevator, maybe even a bit frightened, but he'd handled it, just as he'd handled the taxi, a ride in her car, and everything else foreign to him in this century. With growing insight C.J. realized how balanced Sam was—more so than anyone she had ever known. He might be afraid of something, but he faced it head on, he might not understand something, but he didn't turn away from it. He examined it, thought things through, and then came up with a solution.

"We can take the stairs when we leave," she offered, even though it made her feet ache just to think about it.

"I'm not afraid of it, Katy," Sam said quietly in that way of his that suggested she had overstepped some undefined boundary.

"I didn't say that. But it's all right to be scared. Everybody has something that sets them off."

"I'm not scared."

"Look"—C.J. turned on him in the middle of the hallway—"you don't have to pull this macho stuff. Women don't find it attractive anymore. Men have changed since your time, they can show their feelings, they can cry . . . they can be afraid of elevators."

"Look, Katy, I know what the word *macho* means. You talk like it's something bad."

"Not bad, just passé. Men have learned to get in touch with their feelings, they're not afraid to express them in front of a woman. In fact, most women like men who can be vulnerable and open. It helps them connect."

"Connect what?" Sam flung back at her.

For an instant she wondered if Sam had any idea what he'd said. "Connect on an *emotional* level," she explained. "In the past men haven't been very good at expressing their emotions. Today there's a whole new consciousness about emotions."

"Hogwash, Katy!"

"What?"

"I said *hogwash*. Do you really expect me to believe that a woman would rather have a man whine about every little thing instead of a man who takes care of business without gripin' about it?"

Images of Arnold Schwarzenegger and Sylvester Stallone flashed through her mind. They didn't appeal to her, but most of her friends found them irresistible. And she had to admit she was bored stiff with men like Phil Donahue and Alan Alda, who wore their sensitivity on their sleeves. Besides, she never believed that in real life they actually helped with dirty dishes or garbage.

If she was really going to be honest with herself, she would have to admit that she found it tiring to deal with men's emotional needs as well as her own. Just last month she'd had to choose between dating two men—one was sweet, talked frankly about his fears and insecurities, and the other was an immensely egotistical but charming male slut who would never admit that he knew the meaning of the word *insecurity*.

She had gone out with the male slut simply because she couldn't deal with analyzing one more fragile ego.

Now, as she faced Sam, her righteous indignation dissolved. He aggravated her, but at the same time he made her acutely aware he could take care of himself. He didn't whine, analyze, or endlessly dissect his feelings. Considering what he'd been through, he certainly had more right to do so than any man she knew.

Sam simply got on with the business of things, even if that had a tendency to make her a little crazy once in a while. Like it or not, she had to admit that Sam Hackett was one helluva desirable male precisely because of his strength and the quiet resolve with which he faced everything. He might be in a strange new world, but he wasn't about to let it get the better of him. If the tables had been turned, C.J. would have been a basket case by now.

"All right," she gave in grudgingly. "Can we go meet Traeger now?"

"I was just waitin' for you, Katy. You seemed to be content to stand there all afternoon jawin' about things nobody understands anyway."

C.J.'s mouth fell open. She wasn't too certain, but she had the impression she'd just been had. She followed Sam down the hallway.

In the reception area outside Traeger's office, a stunning red-haired secretary asked them to wait for a moment. She eyed Sam with thinly disguised interest. But Sam was oblivious to it as he stood staring at the portrait gallery on the far wall. Every Traeger from the founder of the company, the original Emmett Traeger, to his son Charles, his grandson David, and his great-grandson and namesake had his portrait on the wall. Sam's gaze was fixed on the portrait of the original Traeger.

The middle-aged man in the painting was fierce-looking. His thick hair, mustache, and beard were gray, and his pale eyes seemed to burn with a disquieting intensity.

Noticing Sam's interest, the secretary explained, "That's the founder of the studio."

"I'd know him anywhere," Sam murmured.

"I beg your pardon?" the secretary asked.

"Never mind," C.J. replied. She could see a strong resemblance between the founder and his great-grandson. The young Emmett Traeger was charming, but there was something of his forebear's toughness about him. The thought occurred to her that he simply wore that toughness more easily under an Armani suit.

Traeger's voice through the intercom jarred her back to the present.

"Send them in."

Gesturing toward a set of elaborately carved double doors that looked as if they might have once adorned the entrance to a Chinese palace, the secretary said, "Mr. Traeger is expecting you."

Sam was silent as they entered Traeger's private office. C.J. could only wonder what thoughts were going through his mind as he faced the great-grandson of his old nemesis. Now she understood why he'd reacted so strongly when they'd first met Traeger. Did Sam accept that this was a different time and a different man? Given the unpredictability of his moods and reactions, she certainly hoped so. She pushed back mental images of Sam drawing on Traeger and demanding blood retribution for something that happened over a hundred years ago.

Traeger's office was just what she had expected, and more. The polished granite top of his desk was oblong, cut straight on the sides, left jagged on the ends, like the huge rock it had been cut from. It was mounted on a polished steel pedestal and behind it stood a black leather Gunlocke chair. Both sat on a raised carpeted platform that heightened Traeger's aura of power.

The carpet was a shade of soft pewter, bordered with a wide strip of deep burgundy. One wall contained an elaborate entertainment center and a door that undoubtedly led to a private suite. It was covered with slabs of black marble shot through with white veins. Another wall was floor-to-ceiling glass and opened onto an indoor atrium with a skylight.

The third wall was reinforced plate glass, curved in

panels for a breathtaking view of L.A. It was like stepping into the throne room high atop a castle that looked down on everything below. Traeger stood behind his desk on that raised platform, looking like a king. In spite of herself, C.J. responded to the feeling of power. Careers were made—and broken—here. Movies were created. All decisions became final *here*. It was a little unnerving.

Traeger stepped down off the platform. "What a pleasant surprise, Miss Grant. Somehow I hadn't expected to see you again."

She might have been mistaken, but C.J. sensed something more behind the casual remark. She resisted feeling flattered. He couldn't mean that he was disappointed at the thought that he might never see her again. Still, there was that disarming smile and the flash of warmth in those grey eyes.

He nodded politely to Sam, his expression shifting to bemused speculation. "Mr. Hackett."

C.J. was curious. "Why didn't you expect to see me again, Mr. Traeger?"

"Emmett, please," he insisted as he escorted them to a low table with several chairs around it.

"This is much more comfortable for conversations." He made an offhand gesture to the elaborate desk and chair he had abandoned. "That's a little intimidating. I use it only for whipping wayward producers back into line."

He chuckled softly but C.J. had the impression no joke was intended. That, too, heightened the sense of power. She studied Emmett Traeger as she hadn't had a chance to earlier. He was lean, tall, and slim, with an ease of movement that appeared too casual to be practiced. His eyes were watchful and conveyed no emotion. He was movie-star handsome. His deep tanned skin suggested sailing or tennis. Probably sailing, C.J. decided, on a sleek mahogany-decked fifty-footer that he moored weekends at Catalina or various points south.

"I thought your preliminary investigation would lead to the same conclusion the police are rapidly reaching—that Dan Prescott's death was a tragic accident. Someone, probably the prop master, was lax. Unfortunately, accidents happen."

"The propman seems to know his job," Sam spoke up, his thoughtful gaze fixed on Traeger. "Not likely to make a big mistake like that, especially when someone's life depended on it."

Traeger's gaze met Sam's and never wavered. "As I said, accidents do happen. C.J. can tell you we have them in this industry, no matter how careful we are."

C.J. felt a dry taste in her mouth as she was forced to contradict him. "That is true, but I'm afraid in this case I can't agree. I believe Dan Prescott's death may have been intentional. And I intend to follow it up."

"You're talking murder, Miss Grant," Traeger stated without hesitation in that cool way of his. "That is a serious accusation. Do you have someone in mind?"

"Not yet," she admitted. "According to the prop master, there were several people who could have entered the prop trailer without arousing any suspicion. It could be any one of a half-dozen people who were on the set that day and knew which gun was going to be fired at Prescott."

"Including myself," Traeger volunteered, catching her off guard.

Before she could respond, Sam spoke up. "That's right."

Again Traeger had that faintly bemused expression, as if this were all very entertaining but hardly credible.

"Why on earth would anyone want to kill an elderly extra who was harmless? Prescott was well liked by everybody."

C.J. was forced to admit, "I'm not saying I'm convinced it was murder. I simply want to investigate further."

She saw Traeger's expression change in a subtle way. Gone was the wry quirk at the corner of his mouth as well as the slightly amused light in his eyes. It had all shifted to something closed, almost cold. His smile was tight.

"You are tenacious, aren't you, Miss Grant? You do realize what sort of an effect this kind of thing can have on a production?"

"Yes, I'm aware. And you have my guarantee I'll keep everything as quiet as possible."

Traeger turned to Sam. "Is this the official government position too?"

Sam met Traeger's gaze evenly. "It is."

Traeger's voice matched the cold expression in his eyes. "I suppose I can't convince you this is all ridiculous." He looked directly at C.J.

"It's my responsibility to find out what happened," she answered flatly. But she felt her stomach turn over at the thought she was standing up to one of the most powerful men in Hollywood.

"What do you want from me?" he asked, getting right to the point.

"I need the addresses and phone numbers of the people on this list."

She pulled the list from her purse and handed it to him. "They were seen either in or near the prop trailer, and knew which gun would be fired at Prescott."

Traeger glanced quickly at the list, then looked back at C.J. The amusement was back as he said, "I notice that my name isn't here."

"You're on *my* list," Sam interjected. Traeger's amused expression immediately dissolved.

C.J. cut in before Traeger could respond. "You weren't part of the cast or crew on the movie. And, besides, from what I can tell, no one saw you near the prop trailer."

His gaze bore into Sam a moment longer, then returned to her. "Ah, I see. You checked me out as well. Or, perhaps, Mr. Hackett checked me out."

"It's all part of a routine investigation," C.J. insisted.

"And if I don't cooperate?" Traeger asked with a faint smile, giving her the impression he was deliberately testing her. Before she could respond, Sam answered, "We'll talk to these people anyway. It'll just take longer if we have to dig up the addresses ourselves."

C.J. added quickly, "With your cooperation, we can get this over with quickly and everyone can get on with making the movie. And, of course, there's still the question of Julie Prescott's potential lawsuit against the studio. If my investigation shows Dan Prescott's death was an accident, then she will undoubtedly forget about a lawsuit."

She was dangling bait by reminding him of the lawsuit—something no studio head liked. It brought too much unwanted publicity.

His eyes held hers for a long moment. Finally, he said slowly, "If I ever find myself in need of a private investigator, I'll definitely hire you, Miss Grant. You seem to know exactly how to get results."

She smiled. "Like I said, I try to do a good job."

He handed the list back to her. "I'll tell my secretary to give you the information. But you realize I can't guarantee that any of these people will cooperate with you."

He rose by way of dismissal, and looked at C.J. with a slightly puzzled expression. "Ever since we met I've had the feeling I've seen you somewhere before. Were you ever on the lot?"

C.J. was surprised—and gratified—that he would remember her. "I used to be an actress. I had a small role in a movie made by this studio—*Licence to Kill.*"

His face lit with sudden understanding. "Of course! It was at the back of my mind, but I couldn't quite place you."

"It wasn't much of a role. I didn't even have any lines."

"In spite of that, you made quite an impression."

C.J. was torn by mixed emotions. On the one hand, she was sure Traeger was merely handing out empty flattery. On the other hand, an actor's ego knows no bounds. She said hesitantly, "That's remarkable that you would remember something so minor."

"Oh, I remember. I was working in the business affairs office then, but if I'd been at all involved in casting, I would have seen to it that you were cast in other roles."

Sam said abruptly, "We'd better be going. We've got a lot of work to do."

"Oh—right. Well, good-bye, Mr. Traeger."

"Emmett."

"Emmett. Thank you for your help."

"I'm giving a wrap party for this picture on Friday night, here at the studio. Why don't you come?" Glancing at Sam, he added, "Of course, you're welcome also, Mr. Hackett."

C.J. hesitated. "I don't know . . ."

Traeger went on. "Everyone connected to the movie will be there. It might be a good opportunity to see everyone together. And, frankly, I'd like you to come."

"Well, I . . ." C.J. glanced at Sam and saw the muscles harden in his jaw. She could just imagine what he was thinking with all his preconceived ideas about Emmett Traeger. But the idea of a wrap party was exciting. Frankly, she wouldn't have missed it for the world, in spite of the anger she saw in Sam's blue-green eyes.

"I'd love to come."

"Great." Traeger walked out into the reception area with them and instructed his secretary to give her the information she needed. As he turned to go back into his office, he called over his shoulder, "See you Friday."

"Right," C.J. responded, ignoring Sam's irritated expression.

While the secretary flipped through the Rolodex on her desk and wrote down the information, C.J. watched Sam. She could tell he was angry with her.

Sam didn't seem to have any reservations about the elevator this time. As the doors closed, he stared rigidly ahead, pointedly ignoring her.

"What is this all about?" she demanded as she stuffed the list into her purse and punched the lobby button.

"Damn fool women!" Sam muttered under his breath.

"Do you mind explaining that remark?"

Sam was standing with his back to her. She saw the struggle for control in his slow, even intake of breath, the subtle shift of his shoulders, and the frustration as he jammed his hands into his pockets. It was several more seconds before he spoke. Then he turned around and pinned her with those hard aqua eyes.

"It means that guy is a snake-oil salesman, and you bought a barrel of the stuff," he flung at her, his eyes glittering with suppressed anger.

C.J. wasn't about to be intimidated by him. "And I

suppose you think we would have gotten further if I'd let you handle that situation back there."

Sam nodded without the least hesitation. "I think we'd get a whole lot further if you'd start thinkin' more like a man instead of a woman about this whole thing. He's pullin' the wool over your eyes, Katy." And then he went on without taking time to draw a breath. "This is exactly why a woman shouldn't try to do a man's job."

"What!" So they were back to that again. C.J. couldn't believe the Neanderthal stupidity of his attitude. She took a deep breath, trying to decide just which scathing remark to make first, but Sam wasn't about to give her that opportunity.

"You heard me. Unless, of course, your hearing is going, along with your common sense."

She didn't know whether to laugh or scream. "Just because Emmett happens to appreciate talent when he sees it . . ."

"*Emmett*," Sam responded, his voice dripping sarcasm. "So it's Emmett now. A few minutes ago it was Mr. Traeger. He really did a job on you, Katy."

"Of all the . . ." Now cold fury tripped her up.

"That's right. And that's exactly what I mean about a woman doin' a man's job. No man would fall for that story he was feedin' you. But you just stand there and go all warm and buttery right in his hands. The man is slick, Katy, just like his great-grandfather. You can't even see what's right in front of your eyes."

She was too furious to speak. It occurred to her that he sounded like a jealous boyfriend. Except they didn't have that kind of relationship. Ever since they first met, all he'd done was criticize her—her hair, her clothes, her job. He certainly hadn't given any sign that he found her attractive.

No, the problem was his single-minded determination that Emmett Traeger was his man. It obviously didn't matter that this wasn't even the same Emmett Traeger.

The elevator gently bumped to a stop two floors from the lobby. C.J. was about to tell Sam Hackett exactly what she thought of him, when two young women stepped inside the elevator and began a lively discussion about some producer who'd promised them both parts in his next film. It was just more of the nauseating rhetoric that went on constantly in the film business, and C.J. recognized it for what it was. Unfortunately, it underscored exactly what Sam had been saying about women being swayed by a man's charm.

The elevator settled on the ground floor and the doors whispered open.

"Thank God," Sam muttered, practically throwing himself out into the lobby.

C.J. struggled to bring her churning emotions back under control. If anyone else had said those things to her, she would have stuffed their opinions right down their throat. Long ago she'd stopped explaining herself or defending her actions.

But Sam wasn't just anyone else.

She caught up with him in the parking lot and grabbed him gently by the arm.

"Hey, wait up."

Without turning around, Sam muttered, "I think we should talk to that director person first. He seems to be in charge." Then, as he gathered momentum, he went on, still without looking at her. "Then maybe that other guy—what did you call him? A production manager? And then—"

"Look at me, dammit!" she demanded, forcing him to turn around and face her. His eyes had darkened with a troubled expression.

Somehow, all her anger drained away, and she said slowly, "I sometimes get a little pushy about things and I expect you to understand everything, when I forget that you can't possibly because . . ."

"I'm sorry, Katy," he said softly. "I know things are different and I've seen the way you can handle yourself. You do real fine at it too. Maybe that's why it gets my back up to see you buying what that fella's sellin'."

"Let's call a truce, okay? How about dinner? It's almost six and I'm starving. Afterward we'll decide who to talk to first."

"You're trying to bushwhack me, Katy," he said with a hint of a smile.

She insisted, "I'm really hungry. Honest."

"How about you let me make dinner?" Sam suggested. "We could go by that store near your place and buy some steaks. I'm pretty fair in the kitchen."

C.J. shuddered at the thought of another steak. She wouldn't have to worry about anemia for the next fifty years on the kind of diet Sam was used to. Of course, what she was about to suggest was pure diet suicide, but necessary.

"Actually, I have something else in mind," she replied as they got into her car.

"Not another forty-five-dollar meal. I can't let you do that. It just isn't right, you paying my way."

C.J. laughed as she backed the car out. "Don't worry, this will be real cheap. It's a chance to experience a major cultural phenomenon of the late twentieth century. Look upon it as part of your continuing education."

Sam raised one eyebrow quizzically. She grinned back at him and said, "A Big Mac."

A half hour later they sat in McDonald's, having something actually called a Big Mac, french fries, and Cokes. Sam glanced around curiously as he ate. This was really something. He wasn't exactly sure what, but it was really something. C.J. had explained it was called fast food, and all he could say was that it was fast all right, if not very good.

It wasn't much better than the hardtack and corn dodgers he was used to eating on the trail, but he wasn't in a position to be choosy. All he had with him were three silver dollars and some small change. That wouldn't even pay for this meal, let alone pay Katy back for everything she'd done. He hated being beholden to her like that, but for the time being he'd just have to swallow his pride.

Looking at Katy sitting across the narrow table from him, Sam knew she didn't agree with his notions about men and women. She'd spout some nonsense about women being equal to men. He couldn't get over that. For someone who was pretty damn smart in a lot of ways, she sure had some wrong-headed notions. You'd think she'd realize that women were better than men, not equal to them.

He watched her fiddle nervously with her soda straw. It was the one thing in this entire place that was familiar. Funny how the simplest things never changed.

She looked up at him and began hesitantly, "So tell me about your life . . . you know, back in 1882. Have men and women really changed all that much?"

He shrugged. "It's hard to say."

"What did people do together in your time?" she asked.

"I imagine it's the same things they do *together* now," and then he added with a wry twist of his mouth, "unless that's something else that's changed."

C.J.'s cheeks flooded with color. "I don't mean *that*! I mean, going out together for fun, to be together. Did they go out to dinner, or dances?"

"Oh," Sam replied with sudden enlightenment, "you mean courtin' and sparkin'."

She practically choked as she laughed. "Courtin' and sparkin'? Yeah, I guess that's what I meant."

"Sure, we do all those things." Then he corrected himself. "Or at least we *did* those things back in my time. A fella might take his girl out to dinner at the local boardin'-house, or maybe to a dance if there was one. Usually they have dances on holiday celebrations or special occasions, like a church bazaar. Sometimes we might go on picnics. They still have those, don't they?"

"Oh, yeah," C.J. reassured him, "we still go on picnics. They're great on the beach. What else did you used to do?"

Sam was thoughtful. "Well, sometimes on a warm summer night you might go for a buggy ride to a special place."

C.J.'s eyes lit up. "That hasn't changed. Necking in a convertible."

"I beg your pardon?"

"Never mind. Just a new term for an old game."

Sam was incredulous. "You mean people still go for buggy rides?"

C.J. nodded. "The buggies are a little different, but we

still use them for *courtin' and sparkin'*." She chuckled softly.

Sam liked her laugh. He liked so many things about her, especially the way she constantly surprised him. Just when he thought he had her figured out, she changed on him again.

"Was there someone you were close to? You know, a special girl?"

Her question caught him off guard. Sam answered slowly. "There wasn't anyone in particular—not lately anyway."

It wasn't any kind of answer, at least not the kind she wanted and he knew it. But for some reason he didn't want to tell her about Maria, the girl who had given him the crucifix. It still hurt to think about her, and he didn't want to dig up all the old feelings—no matter what Katy said about it being all right for men to show their feelings. It was a private and personal thing and better left that way.

But C.J. was nothing if not stubborn. She persisted. "Was there someone special once?"

Sam nodded but didn't say anything. He wasn't going to talk about Maria. But he couldn't help thinking about her . . . remembering how beautiful she'd looked the first time he saw her . . . the softness of her body when they made love . . . how her dark eyes glistened with unshed tears the last time they were together . . .

But it was all part of the past now, and Sam forced himself to concentrate instead on the present—the bright, almost harsh light of the restaurant, the workers in their funny uniforms, the strange texture of the tables and chairs.

"What did you say this stuff is called?" he asked, running his palm along the smooth tabletop.

"Plastic," she replied.

She picked up her pocketbook. "We'd better be getting home. It's going to be a long day tomorrow."

Sam breathed a sigh of relief. As he rose, he took her hand. Looking down at her slender fingers in the palm of his hand, he said simply, "Thanks, Katy."

It might have been for the Big Mac, but both of them knew it wasn't.

"Hey," she said softly, "everyone is entitled to their own space."

"I beg your pardon?"

She said slowly, "You're welcome."

They found Lucy waiting for them when they got back to the house.

"Where have you two been?" she demanded. "I've been waiting for hours!"

"What is it? Has something happened?" C.J. asked anxiously.

"No, but it's going to." Facing Sam, Lucy announced, "I've figured out a way to get you back!"

"Oh, for heaven's sake, Mother!" C.J. threw her purse and keys down onto her desktop with a loud clatter that suggested she had little patience for such nonsense.

"I'm serious," Lucy insisted. "Ravi and I figured it out."

"You told Ravi about Sam?" C.J. asked angrily.

Lucy waved her hand through the air. "Oh, don't worry, he won't tell anyone. And even if he did, no one would believe him. He's tremendously unappreciated, you know."

C.J. rolled her eyes heavenward. "I can't imagine why," she said with thinly disguised sarcasm.

"Who's Ravi?" Sam asked with more than a little confusion. He was still trying to get a grasp on Lucy's first announcement.

"No one," C.J. said in a tight voice.

But Lucy wasn't about to be put off. "He's only the most brilliant trance medium clairvoyant of our time."

"Clairvoyant?" Sam asked, stumbling over the unfamiliar word.

"Never mind that," Lucy rushed on, "the important thing is that we spent the entire day researching your situation and we've come up with some simply amazing answers."

C.J. gave in. When Lucy was on a roll like this, it was impossible to stop her or dampen her enthusiasm. Sitting down on the sofa and tucking her feet under her, C.J.

prepared to hear her mother out. She looked up and was surprised to find Sam listening intently to Lucy. She would have to explain to him just how flaky Lucy's theories were. It could be downright dangerous if he actually thought Lucy knew what she was talking about.

Lucy sat down in the chair facing them. "You see, it's like this. We combined the theory of quantum mechanics, particularly relating to imaginary time and time dilation . . ."

C.J. buried her face in her hands. It was worse than she thought. "Oh, God."

Ignoring her and focusing on Sam, Lucy went on. "And combining this with what we learned about time travel from Atlantis, the answer was obvious."

"Oh?" C.J. asked with mock innocence.

"Of course!" Lucy went on enthusiastically as if a mere child should be able to understand it all. "Sam was in the middle of an earthquake in 1882 when he was thrown forward to 1989, where there was another earthquake happening." Staring wide-eyed at both Sam and C.J., Lucy finished eagerly, "Well, don't you see?"

Sam said slowly, "Well, no, not exactly . . ."

"The earthquake opened a door in time and Sam walked right through it. Or ran, apparently." Lucy stopped and screwed her face up in a thoughtful expression. "Now, what was it that Ravi said about a black hole possibly having something to do with it?"

C.J. had heard enough. "Mother, this is ridiculous."

Lucy merely smiled in an infuriatingly superior way. "Oh? And how do you explain Sam's travel through time, then?"

She couldn't come up with an explanation and Lucy knew it. Lucy went on explaining to Sam with a smug expression. "But the really important thing is that we figured out how to get you back again."

Sam's gaze sharpened when she said that. If he hadn't understood much of anything else she was saying, he understood this part.

"Okay—how?"

"Go back to the same spot, wait for another earthquake, and repeat what you did before. The door in time works both ways, according to Ravi."

Sam looked skeptical. "How do I know when another earthquake will happen?"

Before C.J. could respond that no one could answer that question, Lucy said, "Ravi is working on that right now. He says that he should be able to predict the next quake. He predicted this one."

C.J. looked at Sam. He seemed to be accepting all this and giving it serious consideration.

"Look," she insisted in her best no-nonsense tone, "Mother doesn't know what she's talking about." She gave Lucy a withering glare as she said, "No one can predict earthquakes."

"Ravi can," Lucy said in an offhand way, pretending to study her brightly polished nails.

Sam turned to C.J. "Maybe she's right. After all, I got here somehow."

They were back to that. And the damnedest part about it was that he was right. She could argue about Lucy's crazy ideas all she wanted, but the fact was that Sam was real and somehow he'd come forward in time.

Lucy went on brightly. "So you see, there's a chance you could go back to your own time. We just have to know when the next earthquake will hit."

She looked from Sam to C.J. and back again. "That is what you want, isn't it?"

It was a simple enough question. Yet for a long moment Sam didn't say anything at all. He simply looked at C.J. as if searching her expression for the key to the answer. Finally he looked away and said, "Yeah . . . that's what I want."

Chapter 8

"This is the way Hollywood used to be in its heyday," effused an elderly woman dripping with diamonds, her gray hair tinted with just a hint of pink.

"Ah, yes," her equally elderly male companion agreed with a sigh of obvious nostalgia. Gesturing toward the huge windows that offered a breathtaking view of the city, he said, "Just look at that—those hills, the ocean. It's the same view we had from the Trocadero."

"But the Troc is long gone," the woman said sadly.

Her companion brightened. "Still, we have the St. James again, and it has quite the same old Hollywood glamour."

Sam and C.J. stood behind the couple, who were waiting to be seated in the restaurant. Sam stared in awe at the unabashed luxury of the recently remodeled St. James Club. Housed in the lavishly restored Sunset Tower, a 1929 landmark on Sunset Boulevard, the St. James was an exclusive private club/hotel decorated appropriately with Art Deco pieces.

C.J. had been to the club when it first opened. Her date, a stereotypical yuppie attorney with the requisite Porsche and upscale condo on the West Side, had thoughtfully booked a room for après dinner. He hadn't bothered to consult her beforehand, and his presumption that she was interested in sleeping with him on their first date cost him the relationship and the nonrefundable price of a room he didn't use.

The maître d', who carried himself with all the savoir faire of Cary Grant, and had an English accent to match, seated the elderly couple. Then he returned to greet Sam and C.J.

"Welcome to the St. James." He pronounced it "sin James."

"We don't need a table," C.J. explained, "we're joining Mr. Denny."

The maître d' nodded with raised eyebrow, then led them through the Terrace Restaurant, all wicker, stylized palm trees and live flowers, to a corner table where Alan Denny, the director of *Hard Country*, sat alone. A waiter finished clearing away the remnants of his dinner while Denny sipped what appeared to be cognac.

Denny gave them both a less-than-friendly look, a subtle reminder of his original refusal to meet with them when C.J. had called him earlier. Only after Sam got on the phone and made certain things very clear, such as the fact that he was a Federal Marshal, had Denny finally relented and agreed to this meeting. He refused to let them come to the beach house at Malibu he was renting while making the movie, but he reluctantly agreed to give them a few minutes of his time after dinner.

Now, as Sam and C.J. sat down, Denny said in his very English accent, "Let's get on with this, shall we? I have to get back to the studio to watch dailies."

At Sam's questioning look, C.J. explained briefly. "Dailies are the footage of film from the movie shot each day." Then she turned back to Denny and smiled her most polite but no-nonsense smile that had but one message—if time was brief, she wanted answers. She knew from experience that directors could be real prima donnas. Denny hadn't disappointed her. The expression on his face suggested he didn't have time for this and had even less interest.

"I appreciate your time, Mr. Denny. I'd like to know exactly what happened the day Dan Prescott was killed."

He gave her a cool look. "I've already explained everything to the police. There's nothing more I can add."

C.J. lightly drummed her fingers on the damask linen tablecloth. She'd known this wouldn't be easy.

"I realize that," she replied evenly, "but I want to go

over it again. Perhaps there's some minor detail you forgot to tell the police."

Denny's thin mouth thinned even further as he frowned. "Oh, very well. As I explained to the police, everything went pretty much as usual that day. We shot one scene with no problem, and were on the first take of the second scene when Dan was shot. I thought he was overacting scandalously when he went down, then someone said he was really hurt."

C.J. knew that wasn't exactly all that had happened. "I understand Dan had a fight with Lance Ford earlier."

"Oh, *that*." Denny shrugged his thin shoulders. "It wasn't what you would actually call a fight. It was just a small scuffle, a minor altercation."

"What led up to it?" Sam interjected, obviously not satisfied that it was something minor.

Denny made a gesture with his hand, as if he were swatting at a bothersome insect. "Prescott said something to Lance and the boy didn't take kindly to it. There was a bit of shoving back and forth. But before anything came of it, one of the crewmen stepped in and ended it. Lance went to his dressing room for a few minutes to cool off, then came back in a perfectly equable mood and we finished shooting the scene. That's all there was to the matter."

Sam obviously still wasn't satisfied. "What did Prescott say to Ford?"

"Good God, I really don't remember." Denny's voice was clipped with irritation.

"Try to remember," Sam encouraged him in a tone of voice that suggested it might be wiser if he did.

Denny stiffened. "I said I don't remember," he repeated in that clipped British accent. "Now, if that's all, I really do have to be going." And without waiting for consent from either of them, he asked a passing waiter for his dinner check.

As an actress C.J. had often dealt with men like Denny. Most of them took great pleasure in dismissing her out of hand. But the roles were a little different now. She wanted some answers and she intended to have them. She leaned forward in her chair. "That isn't quite all, Mr.

Denny," she informed him coolly. "What about Lance Ford? Was he alone in his dressing room?"

"How would I know? I don't keep track of such things. You really should ask him that."

"Oh, I intend to, Mr. Denny. But right now I would like you to answer a few more questions for me."

"I've told you everything I know. I'm not willing to waste any more time on this pointless discussion."

Sam leaned across the table in a gesture that was clearly threatening. "I suggest you cooperate with the lady."

"It's all right, Sam," C.J. assured him as she saw Denny's face blanch to the same shade as the tablecloth. She bit back a smile of satisfaction. Actually she and Sam worked quite well together in their good-cop/bad-cop roles. Taking advantage of Denny's suddenly cooperative attitude, she asked, "How long was Lance away from the set?"

"About fifteen or twenty minutes. No longer." He laid his napkin down on the table as his waiter reappeared with his dinner tab. "Now, if that's all, I really must go."

Before he could get up, C.J. asked, "Is it true the production is over budget and the studio is unhappy with you?" It was a direct hit. She saw it in his eyes as Denny flinched.

"We are only *slightly* over budget, not that it's important," he informed her coldly. "All that really matters is the integrity of the film. One can't put a price on art, Miss Grant."

C.J.'s mouth curved into a wry smile. "Oh, I think the studio could put a price on it. After all, it's their money."

With a delicious sense of satisfaction she said with cool dismissal, "That will be all for now, Mr. Denny. Thank you for your time. It's been very . . . enlightening."

Without saying another word Denny rose, turned on his heel, and walked away, his back stiff and his hands clenched tightly at his sides.

"What was that all about?" Sam asked in frustration. "Did I miss something in the conversation? I didn't find it very enlightening at all."

"You're right." C.J. agreed as she stared after Denny.

"He didn't tell us anything. Which is why it's so enlightening."

"This must be one of those twentieth-century things I'm not quite up on," Sam muttered.

C.J. was thoughtful. "Directors are usually very astute people, even the ones who are a royal pain in the ass, like Denny. It's their business to pay attention to details, and they usually know everything that's going on with everyone on a movie set."

"You think he's hiding something?"

"Maybe. I can see why Dan Prescott didn't get along with him. He's obviously lying about how serious the fight was between Prescott and Ford. As a director, he doesn't want any bad publicity about his precious movie."

Sam had become very thoughtful. He was obviously turning possibilities over in his own mind. "Do you think Denny might have killed Prescott because Prescott criticized him?"

C.J. shook her head, her delicate brows knitting together as she thought long and hard. After being treated like dirt by so many directors, she would love to get a revenge of sorts by nailing Denny for this murder. However, much as she disliked the egotistical little man, she didn't believe he had the guts to commit murder.

"I doubt it. Directors have immense egos. I don't think he'd care about Dan Prescott's opinion." She twisted her mouth thoughtfully. "What I'd really like to know is what Dan said to Lance Ford."

"Then you think it might have been Ford?" The doubt in Sam's voice suggested he found that unlikely.

"He could have slipped into the prop trailer without any suspicion and put live ammunition in the gun. He had more opportunity than anyone else." She looked up and caught the critical look from the maître d' as he passed their table for the second time.

"I think we've outstayed our welcome," she said to Sam. "We'd better go."

Outside, it was a clear, warm summer night, with the whisper of a breeze off the ocean a few miles away. Standing there next to Sam, C.J. realized they'd quickly settled into a surprisingly smooth teamwork of sorts. It was amazing, all things considered.

"That was really something, the way you handled Denny," Sam complimented her as they stepped out into the parking lot.

She fixed him with a smug Cheshire-cat grin. Maybe there really was hope for Sam Hackett after all.

"Like I tried to tell you, Marshal. A lady can take care of herself nowadays."

Sam gazed thoughtfully over her right shoulder. "Does a lady also know east from west?"

She stared at Sam. "Of course. I was a Girl Scout."

"I don't know what that is, but unless I'm mistaken, Denny's headed in the wrong direction—away from the studio."

"What?"

Sam pointed across the parking lot where a white Lincoln Town Car pulled out onto the boulevard and entered the maze of traffic. It had a rental sticker on it and Denny was driving—in the opposite direction from the studio.

The parking attendant arrived with C.J.'s car. He gave her a deprecating look that suggested she better give him a large tip for being seen in such a rundown car. But she didn't have time for tips or egos. Hurriedly getting into the car as Sam got in the opposite side, she jammed the gearshift into first and spun the Mustang out of the lot in pursuit of Denny.

She followed at a discreet distance, keeping another car between her and Denny. When he turned north onto a road that led up into the Hollywood Hills, she waited for a moment, then followed.

The narrow, twisting, poorly lit road wasn't easy to maneuver, and she had to slow down. After about a half mile, Denny pulled into the driveway of a two-story Spanish-style house.

Pulling over to the side of the road, C.J. turned off her headlights and watched as Denny got out of the car and hurried to the front door. As he pressed the doorbell, he was clearly visible in the overhead porch light.

The door was opened almost immediately by a young woman wearing a white silk robe, who gave Denny a long, passionate kiss, then took him by the hand and pulled him inside.

Sam grinned from the seat beside C.J. "Looks like he had better things to do than work late tonight. I wonder why he bothered to lie to us about it?"

C.J. didn't wonder at all. "Perhaps because that girl is Lisa Kennedy, the lead actress in *Hard Country*." She drummed her fingertips on the steering wheel, her thoughts racing.

"Why keep it a secret?" Sam asked.

C.J.'s gaze narrowed as she stared across the street. "Because she's engaged to marry Lance Ford." She saw Sam's blue-green eyes glitter in the light of the instrument panel of her car.

"You mean betrothed?"

"That's exactly what I mean. It was in all the trades." Realizing that Sam didn't know what "the trades" were, she explained. "It was in *Variety* and *The Hollywood Reporter*—film industry newspapers. There was a big, splashy party celebrating their engagement. The question is," she went on, thinking out loud, "is this simply a case of an actress with limited talent but limitless ambition sleeping her way to the top, or does it have something to do with our case?"

Sam was silent for a moment. It was impossible to read his expression in the muted light inside the car. Finally, he said with studied casualness, "Do you know that's the first time you called it *our* case?"

There was something in his voice that pulled at her—something uncharacteristically tender and deeply moving, as if this meant a great deal to him. She was both embarrassed and pleased. It was a very disconcerting feeling, and she couldn't quite meet Sam's gaze. For the first time in a long time, C.J. was at a loss for something to say.

Sam went on. "I guess that means we better talk to Lisa Kennedy next. Don't you think?"

"Yeah, first thing tomorrow morning."

"You mean you don't want to question her tonight?" Sam asked in a tone tinged with wry humor.

"Somehow," she said as she let the car roll back a short distance down the street before starting it, "I think the timing is wrong tonight."

Sam chuckled beside her. "Right. So what do we do until then, Katy?"

She made a U-turn and they headed back down out of the Hollywood Hills. It was too late to contact any of the other suspects. There was nothing more she and Sam could do that night. But it was too early to go home and go to bed.

She glanced at Sam. The top was down and the slight breeze gently ruffled his dark hair. He watched her with that intense focus she found so disturbing.

Actually, everything about him was disturbing—the way he called her Katy . . . the way he looked at her sometimes, *really* looked at her, as if he were trying very hard to understand her . . . the way he acted as if she constantly needed someone to protect her . . . the way he expected her to live up to his values, old-fashioned and outmoded as they might seem to be.

Don't swear, it isn't ladylike.

Women shouldn't smoke.

There were times when he made her so angry, she wanted to scream at him. But at the same time he made her feel—

"Katy?"

She looked up at him briefly as they merged back into the heavy traffic on Sunset Boulevard. He made her feel all kinds of things she'd never experienced before. And she didn't quite know what to think about that. She smiled to cover the uncertainty.

"I've got an idea. You've been so busy getting used to all the changes around you that you haven't had a chance to sit back and take a look around—you know, people-watch. It's the best education in the world."

"All right. What did you have in mind?"

As she negotiated the twists and turns of Sunset, she answered, "I know just the place for people-watching. It's an area of town called Westwood."

Westwood Village was a small area sandwiched between Beverly Hills, Santa Monica, and Bel Air. Originally farmland, it had grown up with the nearby campus of the University of California at Los Angeles, and was known for its many movie theaters, restaurants including sidewalk cafés, and shops that stayed open until midnight on weekends. It was one of the few areas of Los Angeles where people actually parked their cars and strolled around.

Walking around there now brought back memories to C.J. Pointing to the Bruin Theatre, she said to Sam, "That's where I worked part-time behind the candy counter when I was going to college here."

He looked at her in surprise. "You went to college?"

"Yeah. Why?"

Sam gave her a long, appreciative look. "I've just never met a woman who went to college."

She laughed. "There are a lot of us around nowadays. Get used to it, Marshal."

He shook his head as he glanced at the people they passed. "I've got a *lot* to get used to."

As they walked along, Sam looked with interest in the shop windows that displayed everything from T-shirts with crazy logos to designer clothes. To her surprise, he was especially interested in the bookstores. They spent over an hour browsing in the local Waldenbooks. Sam's face lit up when he saw editions of books by Mark Twain and Bret Harte.

"People still read these?" he asked.

"Sure, they're classics. Twain is one of my favorite authors," C.J. replied, surprised that he knew of them.

"Mine too." He shook his head. "I can't believe it. I was readin' these books a hundred years ago, and you're doin' the same thing in 1989."

C.J. found it amazing too, but for a far different reason. Somehow she'd just never thought of Sam enjoying reading a book.

"What's your favorite story of Twain's?" he asked with a sense of almost childlike wonder.

"*Huckleberry Finn*," she answered without hesitation.

"My mother gave it to me as a Christmas present when I was little, and it made a big impression on me."

"That's the one I like best too. Reverend Porter gave me a copy a couple of years back and it's dog-eared, I've read it so many times." He stopped abruptly when he realized what he'd just said. "I guess it's been more than a couple of years," he finished.

For an instant his eyes clouded. Then a shutter seemed to close over them, and he said, "Anyway, it's good to know I can get another copy sometime."

C.J. took the copy out of his hand and went over to the cashier. When she came back, she handed it to Sam. "Here, this is for you."

He looked completely taken aback. "Wait just a minute, I can't accept this."

"Why not?" She stood toe to toe with him, looking up at him.

"Because you've been payin' for everything since I got here. It just isn't right, Katy," he said in that straight-forward way of his. For Sam, things were right or wrong, no gray in-between.

"You can pay me back when you get some money if it'll make you feel better. In the meantime, I want to do something nice for you, so just accept it and shut up."

For a moment they stood there staring stubbornly at each other. Then Sam burst out laughing. "All right, but I intend to pay you back."

"Agreed."

His voice softened. "Thanks, Katy."

"You're welcome, Sam."

His mouth turned up in such a breathtaking smile that for a moment she completely forgot about everything else around them.

"Do you know that's the first time you've called me by my name? I like that, Katy. I like it a lot."

It was such a simple thing to say, and yet it went straight to her heart.

She realized Sam rarely gave pieces of himself away like that, but when he did it was something to be treasured.

She shoved her hand nervously back through her wind-tousled hair.

"How about some coffee at that sidewalk café across the street?" she suggested, stumbling over her own words. She added because she knew it was important, "You can pay."

"With pleasure."

For an hour they sat in the café, sipping the coffee that the young waitress kept refilling for them. Sam couldn't get over the colorful variety of people who walked past—young, old, rich, poor. Many of the younger ones wore skimpy clothes—shorts, C.J. called them—on this hot summer night. They seemed totally unselfconscious about their bodies. After thinking it over, Sam decided it was a good thing. It sure beat the hypocrisy he had seen in his own time.

After a while he began to sense that the people passing by weren't so very different from the people of his time. Most of them looked fairly happy, some looked worried or tired. The bits and pieces of conversation he overheard were reassuring because they indicated people still talked about pretty much the same things.

"I'm concerned about how he's doing in school. His grades are bad and he's just not interested . . ."

"I miss him so bad, but what could I do? He was sleeping with half the school . . ."

"My parents make me so mad. You wouldn't believe what they did this time . . ."

For the first time since he'd awakened in the hospital and found himself in a strange new world, Sam began to feel that he could get along here. It was still very different and he longed for the reassuring, familiar things of his own time. But at least he no longer felt terrified of what he would encounter next.

Looking at Katy, he realized that she was totally comfortable with all this. Of course she would be. After all, this was her time. He couldn't get over the fact that she'd bought him a book. It was more than generous of her, it was real sweet.

Normally, "sweet" wasn't a word he would apply to

Miss—no Ms.—C. J. Grant. Reckless, maybe. Headstrong, definitely. He was just beginning to realize that there was a great deal more to her than he was used to finding in a woman. She could act as bold as a man one minute, then turn around and show a softness and sensitivity that was pure female.

He'd sure never known a woman like her in his own time. He wondered if all women were like her nowadays, or if she was special.

C.J. yawned, then said. "Had enough people-watching for one night?"

Sam nodded, "Yeah, I guess so." Then he added as they headed back to the car, "It was real interesting."

"I know. I do it myself sometimes. When I was an actress I watched people to copy their mannerisms for a role. Now I just find them fascinating."

On the way back to Venice, she explained how she'd gone from acting to investigating, about Harry Carlucci and the agency, and shared some of the more eccentric cases she'd worked on. In exchange, she learned about the outlaws Sam had tracked down or killed and the towns where he'd been the only law and order for hundreds of miles around.

By the time they got back to the house, they were carrying on a conversation just like any other two people—interested in each other, comfortable with each other, their guards down. As she pulled the car into the driveway, she said, "There's something you haven't done yet, and until you do your education is sorely lacking."

Sam's tone was wary.

"What's that?"

"A swim in the ocean," C.J. announced as she slipped out of the car and closed the door. "I'll bet you've never done it before."

"No, but—" Sam paused, uncertain how to explain that he couldn't quite bring himself to go skinnydipping in such a public place. While the beach was almost deserted this time of the evening, there were still a few people around scattered bonfires, not to mention those who lived in the nearby houses and apartments.

"What's the matter, Marshal? Can't you swim?" C.J. flung at him with a good-natured laugh.

"Of course I can swim," he snapped back at her a little irritably. "That's not what I'm worried about."

He didn't elaborate, but simply stood there with his hands jammed in his pockets. She looked at him for a moment, then understanding dawned.

"Don't worry, I've got some bathing trunks you can borrow. They were left by an ex-boyfriend who never quite got around to clearing out all his stuff."

"Bathing trunks? You mean those skimpy underdrawers I saw other men wearin'?" His expression had gone from skeptical to obstinate.

She grinned. "Everybody wears them. You might as well get used to it. What's the point of wearing some contraption that pulls you down to the bottom of the ocean?" She turned and was about to head up the side stairs when she caught sight of the single lamp at her desk in the back office. It had been left burning.

"Damn! Lucy must have left the lights on before she left. No wonder my electric bill is so high." She headed for the office, searching through the keys on her key ring, but as she got to the door she saw that it stood slightly ajar.

"Great! Every place in the neighborhood is barricaded like the state penitentiary and she leaves the door wide open," C.J. muttered under her breath.

"Need any help?" Sam asked.

"No, I'll be right out." He waited as she felt her way past the desk in the front office to the back. After turning off her desk lamp, she retraced her steps to the front door, locking it securely behind her.

Upstairs, she went into her bedroom then returned a moment later with the trunks.

"He wasn't as tall as you," she explained, "but he was a little heavier, so these should be okay. You can change in the bathroom. I'll meet you downstairs."

Sam took the trunks, and after a moment's hesitation went into the bathroom. He wasn't at all sure about this. But the truth was he loved swimming, and he'd been wanting to take a swim in the ocean ever since he'd first seen it.

After stripping off his clothes and slipping on the trunks, he tried to look at himself in the small mirror over the sink. He couldn't see much, and only hoped the trunks didn't look as odd as they felt. Telling himself he shouldn't feel embarrassed, that Katy wouldn't think anything of the way he looked, he left the bathroom and slowly descended the outside stairs.

C.J. was already in the water. As Sam crossed the warm, soft sand, she walked out of the water toward him. He saw her startled expression as she took in the brief swim trunks that rode low on his hips, concealing very little of his body.

He couldn't help staring at her. Her bathing suit was cut high over her gently rounded hips, and low across her breasts. Her body was wet and glistened darkly in the moonlight that shimmered across sand and water.

The silence was broken only by the gently lapping waves as they broke on the shore, and the distant hum of cars on the adjacent roadway.

C.J. came to a halt a few feet from him, and they stood facing each other, eyes locked.

Sam didn't know what to say. He hadn't felt this way since he was a boy, intensely attracted to girls but painfully shy when he came face-to-face with them. It was a long time since he'd been at a loss as to what to do with a woman on a warm, dark night. It stunned him to realize that he thought of her that way, and stunned him even further to realize that he was reacting to her the way he would in his own time. He supposed it was true—some things just didn't change.

To hide his confused emotions, he asked in a voice much less self assured than usual, "Is the water cold?"

"Just a little." She sounded a bit breathless.

Now that she was so close and there were absolutely no distractions, Sam noticed little things about her he'd missed before—a tiny scar on her shoulder, white against the deeper tan of her skin, the way her short-cropped hair curled when it was wet, the way her small, round breasts rose and fell with each breath.

He pulled his gaze away from her and looked out at the gently rolling ocean with waves frothing at the shoreline. "I guess the best thing to do is just plunge right in."

"I guess so," C.J. agreed.

When Sam hesitated, she went on with a little laugh. "Come on, Marshal, if I can handle it, you can."

She turned and ran back into the water, laughing as she did so. Sam followed, his long legs easily covering the distance between them. They dove into the water together and came up only inches apart. Sam barely noticed the shock of the cold water, he was so intent on watching her.

"So what do you think of the Pacific Ocean?" C.J. asked with a grin.

Sam shook droplets of water from his hair. "It isn't as cold as a Rocky Mountain stream, but it's a damn sight bigger."

She laughed as she treaded water. "You should come out here during the day, when it's hot. It feels wonderful." Then with sudden inspiration she said, "I'll have to teach you to bodysurf."

"Bodysurf?" His voice was dubious as he stroked away from her and then back again.

C.J. backstroked a small distance away, then dove and resurfaced in front of him. "Believe it or not, Marshal, there are a few things you could learn from me."

Sam chuckled and agreed without the slightest hesitation. "Oh, I believe that, Ms. Grant." And with that he thrust away from her in long, powerful strokes, plunged underwater, and then broke the surface where she should be—only she wasn't.

He spun around in the water. "Katy?"

There was only the hiss and sigh of the water as it rolled toward him, then arced away only to erupt approximately twenty yards away along the shoreline in frothing rollers. Inky darkness surrounded him.

"Katy? Where are you?" Sam twisted in the water, listening for her because he couldn't see more than a few feet away. The luminous moon overhead sent a narrow path across the water. The panic began to build and he called again.

She'd been concerned whether he could swim. But because she simply plunged in, unafraid, and lived right next to the water, he assumed something that he shouldn't have—that she was a good swimmer. Now uneasiness churned to real fear. Even the strongest of swimmers could get in trouble. He remembered a young wrangler who'd tried to cross a river, been unseated from his horse and sucked under by the current. The weight of his heavy clothes had been his undoing. They found his body downstream on a snag of tree limbs.

"Dammit, Caitlin! Where the hell are you?" He whirled about once more.

C.J. sputtered as she laughed and choked at the same time. "Why, Marshal, you almost sound worried."

"Where the devil were you?" Sam demanded, his voice slicing through the cool night air.

"Don't you know you have to be careful of monsters from the deep?" she teased, not realizing how angry Sam really was.

"I ought to thrash you for that." He made a lunge for her, but she slipped just beyond his reach.

"Why, Marshal, I do believe you were worried about me." Her tone was somewhere between disbelief and wonder.

"If I get my hands on you, I'll show you just what I feel right about now," he threatened, the iron taste of fear still thick in his throat.

Suddenly, she disappeared again.

"Caitlin?"

"Over here, Marshal," she called from several feet away and much nearer the shore. "Are you always this slow?"

Sam slipped beneath the surface of the water. He'd show her two could play this game.

"Hey, Marshal! Better get a move on or you'll turn blue."

Nothing but silence and the restless murmur of the water answered her. C.J. turned around in the water, cocking her head to listen for the sound of a swimmer. She was about to lunge toward the nearby shore when he resurfaced beside her.

"Are you always this slow, Ms. Grant?" he asked as his big hand came down on her head, shoving her below the surface of the water.

C.J. came up sputtering. Of all the . . . he'd dunked her! But when she looked around, Sam was gone, the sound of his strong, efficient strokes disappearing toward the shoreline.

"I'll get you for that, Sam Hackett," she called after him as she took off toward the shore. He was waiting for her on the beach. With only the meager light from a nearby beach house glowing across the sand, she saw the gloating smile.

"You'll have to learn to cover your tail, Ms. Grant. Never leave yourself open to ambush." He handed her a towel.

She snatched it from his fingers. "I'll try to remember that. And I was actually foolish enough to be concerned for you. Is there anything you can't do, either in 1882 or 1989?"

Sam was thoughtful for a moment. "I can't drive a car—yet. And"—he hesitated and became far more serious—"I haven't got my man yet."

The playful mood of their swim was now gone.

"You may have to give up on that one, Marshal. Emmett Traeger, CEO, isn't Emmett Traeger the outlaw. They're two distinctly different men."

Sam shook droplets of water from his longish hair. When he looked up at her, he said, "I never give up, and I never give in, Katy. I don't know the meaning of those words."

She believed it. Everything she'd discovered about Sam Hackett since he'd first quite literally dropped into her life were defined by those few words. No, a man like Sam Hackett didn't give up and he didn't give in. She'd read stories about the code of the West, and every man's individual code. This was Sam's. In his time a man lived or died by those words.

"This isn't 1882, Sam," she said quietly, shivering

slightly as she pulled the large towel around her shoulders.

"No, it isn't." He brought his hand up and brushed a droplet of water off her nose with his fingers. It was a simple gesture, but his fingers lingered against her skin. "But it's the only way I know."

"Then you'll keep after him," she whispered with a hollow ache in her throat, realizing that everything he'd learned about the twentieth century in the past few days meant nothing.

"I'll keep after him," he said simply, spreading his fingers across the cool skin of her cheek. His thumb traced the sensitive fullness of her lower lip, and then back again. His mouth was so close to hers as he bent forward, she could taste the wild heat of his breath.

"And nothing else matters?"

"It matters, lovely Kate." He answered so softly, it might have been a sigh. "It all matters, but this comes first. It's who I am, Katy."

He wanted her to understand. He wouldn't beg; this was as close as he would come to that.

"All right, Marshal." Her voice was calmer now as she took a small step backward, putting emotional and physical distance once more between them. "I guess I'll have to accept that. If you can accept the same about me."

That heartstopping grin flashed in the darkness. "I already have, Katy. Now, how about if we get back up to the house. I'm freezin' my a—" He caught himself. "It's cold out here with that wind comin' up off the water."

C.J. flashed him a devilish grin. She was more confident now that everything was back on familiar territory and away from unsettling things such as how handsome Sam was, how well those slightly too small trunks molded his body, how his hard muscles worked beneath his glistening skin. She whirled away from him before her thoughts could get her into any more trouble.

"You're right," she called over her shoulder as she headed across the sand, "it is cold out here. I'm freezin' my *ass* off."

"Katy!"

She ran at full speed across the sand. She was breathless when Sam finally caught up with her in the driveway at the agency.

She danced away from him, making a dash past the windows toward the outside stairs.

"It's who I am, Hackett." She threw his own words back at him. Just as she was starting up the steps, she stopped.

"That's strange."

Sam was right behind her. "What's the matter?"

She pointed past him to her office. "I turned that light out before we left for our swim." She cut back past him and started for the door. As she grabbed for the knob, the door slowly swung open.

"I locked this myself," she said uneasily as she stared back through the darkness of the reception area to her private office where the desk lamp glowed. She started to go inside. Sam's fingers bit sharply into her arm as he stepped around her.

"You stay here."

She wasn't about to "stay there." As Sam walked through the deserted front office to her office in the back, C.J. was right behind him. She grabbed at his arm.

"Be careful, someone might still be in there. Maybe we should just call the police."

"Whoever was here is already gone."

"Are you certain?"

"They left by the front door. That's why it was unlocked after you locked it." Sam stepped aside in the doorway to her office, and for the first time she had a full view around his wide shoulders.

Her office was a shambles. Chairs had been turned over, the cushions in the cheap sofa against the wall had been slashed apart, the desk drawers had been jerked out of the desk and emptied onto the floor, but that wasn't the worst of it. The drawers in her three-drawer fireproof locking file gaped open. Every single client file had been pulled from the dividers, their contents strewn across the desktop until they spilled over the edges.

C.J. wasn't fussy about many things, but her client files were sacred ground. Harry Carlucci had taught her that a complete, meticulous file often held the solution to a case. It was just a matter of sorting through the information and arriving at the answer. Her files were the one thing she was fanatical about. On one occasion one small tidbit of information had led to the whereabouts of an abducted child. She kept them up-to-date, complete, and locked away.

"Oh, my God," she breathed out shakily, and then said it again because it was all she could come up with.

She'd been after Lucy to lock the place when she left. Sometimes Lucy remembered, other times not. Besides, C.J. never had anything worth stealing . . . until tonight.

"There's nothing of value. The typewriter and the answering machine are still in the outer office. What could anyone want in here?"

"Information," Sam answered simply as he stood behind her desk, staring down at the mess strewn across it.

C.J. rounded the desk. "What information? There's nothing in any of those files of value to anyone but me."

"Except for this." Sam indicated the one file that remained intact. It was spread open on her desk. Julie Prescott's name was neatly typed on the label. "There's not much here. Where did you keep your notes on the investigation?"

Her thoughts were like fragmented pieces of a jigsaw puzzle that refused to come together.

Sam took hold of her by the shoulders. "Katy, listen to me. Someone came here tonight looking for your information on the investigation into Dan Prescott's death. And they went to a lot of trouble to find it. What did they find?"

C.J.'s dark eyes were stark. The reality of what had happened was only just beginning to sink in. Whoever did this must have been in the office when C.J. came in earlier to turn off the light.

"Oh, God," she whispered, for the first time realizing the danger they had both been in. She blinked twice and the shock receded as she swallowed back her fear and forced herself to think.

"The file . . . I . . . didn't keep it down here." She ran her hand back through her hair. "It's under the seat."

"What seat? What are you talking about?"

"I kept the file in my car because we had so many appointments with the people on the set the day Dan died. I put it under the seat because I had the top down and I didn't want any of the papers to blow away."

"Then they didn't get anything?"

"No, the preliminary workup sheet on Julie was all that was in there. I hadn't even filed the copy of the police report yet."

Gesturing toward the messy office, Sam asked, "What do you normally do in a situation like this?"

C.J. gave him a narrow look. "Believe it or not, this doesn't 'normally' happen." She went on. "I guess I should call the police. They'll want to dust the place for prints, file a report, all the usual stuff."

Sam nodded. "All right, you can call from upstairs. Just leave everything as it is. C'mon."

The police were no help. Whoever had done this had been too smart to leave fingerprints. By the time C.J. finished giving them the necessary information, it was very late and she was physically and emotionally drained. It was frightening to think that someone she knew or had talked to in connection with Dan Prescott's death had been desperate enough to ransack her office looking for information about the case. It proved Dan's death was no accident. Not only that, the person must have been hiding in there when she came in to turn out the light. How close had she come to him, she wondered.

C.J. felt cold clear through even though she had long changed out of her swimsuit, and her head was pounding violently.

As Sam tucked her into bed, she protested, "Nobody's done this since I was a little girl."

Sam ignored her protests in that quiet yet persistent way of his. He had dressed before the police got there. Now he padded across her bedroom in his bare feet, jeans, and shirt.

He straightened the comforter on her bed, pulling it up to her chin, then reached across her to turn out the light. She was acutely aware of the Colt handgun neatly snugged in the waistband of his pants.

"I'll be right on the other side of that door," he said softly.

She made a feeble attempt at humor. "You're taking the first watch?" It was meant as a joke but it failed miserably. She could hear the fear in her voice and hated herself for it. Weakness was not something she tolerated in herself. She bit at her lower lip, trying to disguise the fact that she didn't want to be alone right now. Sam's eyes glittered back at her through the shaft of light from the other room.

"Please stay for a little while, Sam." The words were torn from her reluctantly.

He sat on the edge of the bed beside her.

"Will they be back?" she asked in a small voice.

"Probably not tonight. But I'll stay up just in case."

He eased back against the headboard of her bed, placing the Colt on the nightstand within reach. With his right hand he took hold of hers. Their fingers naturally meshed, hers curling inside his.

"Go to sleep, Katy."

"Be sure to wake me for the next watch," she murmured sleepily as she snuggled against him. In a matter of minutes she was fast asleep.

Sam smiled down at her as her head nestled beneath his chin. She'd started out on her own pillow and somehow wiggled her way into his arms and across his chest.

He turned his face into the soft cap of her hair and breathed in its subtle scent. For the first time since they met, he'd seen her vulnerable. But she hadn't crumbled, whined, or gotten hysterical. She'd simply fallen asleep in his arms. Ms. C. J. Grant was one helluva woman.

Chapter 9

C.J. and Sam sat in her Mustang outside the rented home of Lisa Kennedy. C.J. slumped beside Sam, staring wearily at the house.

"You okay?" Sam asked softly, knowing she hadn't slept well the night before.

"Yeah, I'm okay. Just a little tired." She hadn't gotten much sleep at all. She kept waking up with questions about the case and the ransacking of her office. Someone—perhaps Prescott's killer—had been searching for information on the Prescott case. First Julie's place and now hers. But who, and why? Was it someone she'd already questioned in connection with Dan's death? Someone with something to hide who felt she was getting too close? Or was it someone yet to be questioned?

Sam had stayed with her all night, and paid for it with a stiff back and a crick in his neck. She had chuckled at the old-fashioned term. But she hadn't laughed about his concern and protectiveness toward her. The concern had been deeply touching, the protectiveness something completely new. Surprisingly she had accepted both, simply because what had happened had blind-sided her.

C.J. had always considered herself capable, independent, strong enough to handle any situation. But the realization that someone had been inside her office when she went in to lock up, and undoubtedly watched her from some hiding place, then calmly went about his or her business of ransacking her office, left her feeling vulnerable. Worse, it felt as if she'd been violated in some way.

Sam hadn't lectured and hadn't said "I told you so,"

about all her independent, liberated notions. He simply stayed with her, holding her through the night, asking nothing, giving what she needed most—his understanding, his strength, and his support.

But the long hours when she hadn't slept, when everything about the case kept churning through her mind, made for a short temper, little patience, and eyes that felt as if they were full of ground glass.

To top it off, Lisa Kennedy had been less than cooperative when they questioned her. She had reluctantly agreed to give C.J. and Sam a few minutes of her time before she had to leave for the studio to shoot her final scene on *Hard Country*. If C.J. had known the interview would be conducted in Lisa's exercise room while she worked out on a rowing machine, showing off her magnificent body—complete with body-hugging hot pink leotard—she would have suggested they talk later. She was in no mood for mental comparisons with that personal-trainer-molded body. Lisa's long dark hair was pulled back in a ponytail with a pink ribbon. She wore no makeup—she didn't need any with that perfect complexion and those dark amber eyes fringed with thick lashes. There was no doubt the woman would be successful, at least up to a point. She had the looks and she'd already taken certain critical steps toward that end in her affair with Denny.

But there was little she could or would tell them about what had happened the day Dan Prescott died. She was polite and coolly remote, informing them she hadn't seen a thing that day. According to her, she was in her dressing room, alone, during the shooting of the scene where Dan was tragically killed. She expressed just the right amount of regret over his death—right out of a script as far as C.J. was concerned.

Then C.J. had dropped the bomb, her words sharpened with a certain edge from lack of sleep. She bluntly asked Lisa about her affair with Denny.

C.J. had to give her credit, she was cool under fire. Lisa calmly denied there was anything to it, and proclaimed that the love of her life was Lance Ford. Even now she was planning their wedding for the fall in New England. With a flutter of those thick lashes she had asked them both to leave.

"Do you want to go back to the house and get some sleep?" Sam asked quietly as his fingers gently massaged the taut cords at the back of her neck when they were back in the Mustang. "Lucy could drive me around and I could do some of this questioning on my own—that is if you think I'm capable."

C.J. let out a grateful sigh at the magic in those long fingers. Sam had talents she was only just discovering. She slowly turned her head and opened her eyes, gazing at him beside her.

"I'm finding out just how capable you are," she said softly, remembering last night. She smiled at him. "I couldn't sleep. I'd just think about the case, or listen for the person who broke in, coming back for something they forgot."

"All right, Ms. Grant. Who's next on your list of suspects?" Sam asked, surprising her by giving in so easily. Normally, he would have argued with her about being stubborn and foolish. It seemed they were coming to a little better understanding of each other.

C.J. flipped through the pages of her notebook. "Let's go ahead and go by Gloria Ames's place. She's through shooting her scenes and she'll be home. She and Dan Prescott had an affair years ago. According to Julie they remained close friends, but we should question her anyway. Maybe she saw something that morning that might be helpful."

"You look real tired. Want me to drive?" Sam asked with that lazy drawl of his, giving her a long sideways look. His eyes sparkled with mischief.

C.J. made a face at him. "Not on your best day, Marshal. I'm not *that* tired."

Gloria Ames lived in a small, exquisitely furnished condo in Marina del Rey. The green and yellow chintz-covered furniture, Waterford crystal vases filled with fresh flowers, and lovely watercolor paintings on the pale butter-yellow walls were a flattering backdrop for Gloria. A petite, fading blonde, she would never see fifty again.

C.J. had been more than a little surprised by the address with its stunning view of the bay and sailboats berthed in the marina. She knew what a place like this cost, as well as the pale pink suit Gloria wore bearing the unmistakable cut of Chanel and the long string of pearls shimmering against her silk blouse.

She also knew Gloria's movie career had been less than illustrious.

Gloria was one of dozens of actresses who had been groomed to be successor to Marilyn Monroe. But as the world came to know, there could never be another Marilyn. Gloria, like all the others, had been launched in the role of sex kitten in the late fifties. Her career had descended from there to a series of B movies and second-lead parts that were forgettable at best, and hardly paid the kind of money to finance this kind of life-style.

If Gloria were twenty years younger, C.J. would automatically jump to one logical conclusion—a wealthy lover. But in a town where very beautiful, very young women were plentiful, it was doubtful that Gloria had found a sugar daddy who preferred middle-aged women.

As Gloria gestured to Sam and C.J. to sit down opposite her, she said with feeling, "It's just so awful about Dan. I still have nightmares about it. I saw it happen, you know."

C.J. smiled sympathetically while her mind raced to take in all the details of Gloria's *very* comfortable life. "I'm looking into his death for his granddaughter. Can you tell us what happened that day? Anything you noticed might be helpful."

Gloria shuddered. "I hate to even think about it. It's so painful."

C.J. touched her hand in a reassuring gesture. "I know how difficult it must be. You and Dan had known each other for a long time, hadn't you?"

"Oh, my, yes." She smiled softly. "One of my first features was a western. That was in the late fifties, when they were still doing them on a fairly big budget. That's where I met Dan. Of course, he'd been in the business quite a while." She folded, unfolded, then refolded her hands in her lap. It was obviously difficult for her to talk about Dan. She made a visible effort to pull herself together, then said in a halting voice, "Of course I'll help any way I can. But I didn't realize there was a private investigation."

"I'm just checking out a few details, to satisfy his granddaughter."

"Yes, Julie is such a dear girl. Although I don't know her all that well. I believe she wants to be an actress." Gloria shook her head. "I'd certainly advise her against that."

C.J. made a sweeping gesture that encompassed the room. "You seem to have done well enough."

There was a subtle change in Gloria's expression. "I earned every dime I ever made. It wasn't easy either, not with the way the industry has changed over the last thirty years." There was a bitter edge to her voice, something that came and went almost before C.J. noticed.

Then Gloria was smiling once more. "Anyway, it can be a rough business—a very competitive one."

"Yes, I know," C.J. agreed, tucking that little revealing response of Gloria's away in the back of her mind. "Now, if you can tell us what you remember about the day Dan died?" She gently brought the conversation back to the reason they were there.

"Yes, of course. I'm sorry. I do tend to ramble on a bit." Gloria assumed a thoughtful expression. "We had rehearsed the scene earlier and everything went smoothly. There was absolutely nothing unusual about that."

Then she hesitated, as if suddenly remembering something. "There was that little disagreement between Dan and Lance Ford, but it was over almost before it started." She laughed as if it meant nothing. "You know, probably just letting off a little steam. Actors sometimes get such pent-up emotions before a scene."

Sam leaned forward on the expensive chintz sofa. "What happened?"

Gloria made an offhand gesture. "It was nothing really. Lance is such a talented young man, maybe a little high strung. He and Dan didn't agree about the way the scene should be shot. Of course, Dan had a lot of experience with westerns. On the other hand, Lance is a rising young star and he had his own ideas."

Gloria shrugged. "Like I said, it all blew over and we shot the scene. It was going marvelously and I just knew Alan was going to say it was perfect on the first take. That would have been a relief, because he's the sort of perfectionist who requires take after take."

C.J. frowned. There had to be something more.

Obviously Sam felt the same way. He leaned forward, his arms propped on his knees. "Can you go through the scene for us," he suggested, "exactly the way it happened?"

C.J. felt a ripple of admiration. Sam really was getting the hang of investigating, 1989-style. He was like a cat that always landed on his feet, self-assured, confident.

"Sure," Gloria smiled sweetly, "Lance faced Dan down the middle of the street, typical gunfight fashion."

C.J. found it ironic that Gloria was describing a scene right out of Sam's life.

"I stood off to one side," she said softly, "just behind Dan, and watched. Lance was supposed to say, 'You bastard,' or something like that, then pull his gun and fire."

"How far away was Ford standing?" Sam asked.

Gloria was once more thoughtful. "Oh, only three or four feet. It was a tight shot, so they had to be close together."

"So he couldn't miss," Sam commented in a low voice.

"No." Tears came to Gloria's soft gray eyes and she took a white linen handkerchief from the pocket of her skirt and dabbed at them. "Alan wanted realism, he wanted to be able to focus on both men's expressions." Her lips trembled. "No one was prepared for what happened. It was just so awful."

"How long did it take people to realize that Prescott had actually been shot?" C.J. asked.

"Oh, I realized it immediately. I was close to him, and I could tell by his stunned expression and, well, by the blood. It was on the right side, closest to me. According to the script, Dan was to be shot on the left side. That's how the special effects department had arranged for his wound—you know, fake blood under the shirt and all that. But that was supposed to be in the next shot, where the cameraman shows Dan lying in the street *after* he's been shot. It's all a matter of camera work." She smiled briefly as she explained.

"What did you do when you realized what had happened?" C.J. asked gently, knowing this must be very difficult for her.

"I didn't handle it very well," Gloria admitted with a pale expression. "I fell apart. I screamed something, I don't remember what it was. Someone ran up to Dan, who'd fallen to the ground. Then it was just pandemonium as everyone realized what had happened. Someone sent for the paramedics, but I'm not certain who that was." She stopped, then finished weakly, "I'm afraid I haven't been much help to you."

C.J. spoke kindly. "You're doing just fine. I just need to ask a few more questions."

Gloria said, "It's just so hard, realizing Dan is really gone."

"Do you have any idea how a live bullet could have gotten into that gun?" C.J. asked.

Gloria's eyes opened wide in innocent confusion. "No, I can't imagine how that could have happened. You know, the studios are absolutely fanatical about the weapons used in their productions."

"Yes, I know. What about someone else Dan might have had a run-in with on the set?"

"Someone else?" Gloria asked vaguely, her eyes clouded and uncertain. "No, there were no problems on the set." Then her voice quieted. "Dan was the nicest, sweetest person I've ever met."

C.J. couldn't think of any easy way to approach her next question, but it had to be asked. "In fact, you were closer than just friends, weren't you?"

"I don't see that it's really any of your business." Gloria's innocent expression was instantly transformed to one of irritation. C.J. had the distinct impression that Gloria was a better actress than she'd given her credit for.

Sam diplomatically stepped into the conversation. "It

could be Dan Prescott was murdered, ma'am," he said softly. "If it's true, his granddaughter would like to see the person responsible brought to justice."

"Well, of course," Gloria agreed, the anger immediately defused. "I hadn't realized it was being investigated as a murder. It's just such a shock." She reached for a covered porcelain box on the glass-topped lamp table beside her. As she took a cigarette from the elegant box, Sam struck a wooden match and lit it for her. C.J. noticed her hands shook badly.

"It's just such a *dreadful* shock," Gloria repeated, blowing a trail of smoke through the air. "Of course, if that's the case, I want Dan's murderer caught too. But I just can't imagine who would do such a thing. As I said"—her voice grew more emphatic as she said it—"Dan didn't have any enemies."

The case was going nowhere. C.J. felt as if she were spinning in circles, asking the same questions, coming up with the same answers from everyone. Abruptly changing the subject, she asked, "Did you see anyone go into the prop trailer that morning?" She thought she caught a brief flash of Gloria's earlier uneasiness, then it was gone.

"Well, of course, Harry Jones was in and out of the trailer all morning."

"What about someone other than Jones? Please, try to remember. It's important."

"What about Lance Ford?" Sam suggested. "He would have access to the weapons."

"That's true," Gloria admitted, "but I'm afraid I can't help you there. I don't recall seeing anyone else. Of course, I was there only for my scenes," she reminded them.

C.J. looked at her thoughtfully, and then jotted down a specific note. That was not what Gloria had just explained to them. She had specifically said she stayed to watch Dan's scene with Lance Ford.

She was certain it was pointless to try to get further information out of Gloria. Still, she couldn't shake off the impression she was watching a brilliant performance on Gloria's part.

Rising, C.J. said, "Thank you for your time, Gloria. I hope we haven't upset you too much."

Gloria rose, composing herself perfectly. "Please, don't apologize. I understand that you're just doing your job. It's just so painful remembering that morning."

As they left the condo, she had a final image of Gloria, standing at the door, looking suitably wistful and sad.

"That was one helluva performance," Sam remarked as they got into her car.

"In more ways than one," C.J. remarked thoughtfully.

Sam shook his head. "Something just doesn't fit."

C.J. backed the car out of Gloria's driveway, her gaze once more taking in the expensive view.

"I'll say it doesn't fit. She never even came close to making the kind of money that could support that place."

Sam pushed back his hat and looked at her thoughtfully as they skimmed along Marina Boulevard. "Meanin' what?"

"Meaning either she's frugal as hell and clipped one helluva lot of coupons all her life, or she has a very rich sugar daddy on the side. Or some other source of income."

"So what do we do now?"

C.J. threw him a wicked smile. "We party. The wrap party at the studio is tonight."

Sam groaned.

"It'll be fun," she assured him. Her thoughts shifted to Emmett Traeger. He was a fascinating man.

Sam was quiet beside her. She glanced at him. "Do you know anything about *fun*?"

He said laconically, "I've had my share."

"Well, you'll have some tonight, 1989 Hollywood style." Her fingers drummed along the steering wheel. She felt a tingle of anticipation. Invitations weren't just handed out to this sort of thing. The guest list was limited to privileged company. Heightening her excitement was the fact that Traeger had actually seemed to be coming on to her when he invited them.

As Sam frowned, C.J. teased, "Loosen up, Marshal, you just might enjoy yourself."

* * *

The outdoor western set where *Hard Country* was filmed had been turned into the site of a lavish party with a western theme. Guests had been invited to bring their children, and there were pony rides, along with hayrides and a live band playing country and western music. Waiters dressed as cowboys maneuvered through the crowd, carrying trays of drinks and hors d'oeuvres. A huge side of beef roasted on a slowly rotating spit over an outdoor barbecue. Inside the saloon a long table was covered with delicacies ranging from shrimp to caviar.

"Chasen's is catering this bash, you know," one studio executive said to another.

"Of course. Nothing but the best for Emmett," his companion responded, "he really knows how to do things."

Overhearing their conversation, C.J. had to agree. It was a throwback to the old days, when this kind of party was the norm. Nowadays, with cost-accounting businessmen running the studios, they were rare.

Sam fit right in with his worn Levi's, scuffed boots, chambray shirt, and weathered Stetson. The outfits worn by the guests had come from one of the many costume shops in L.A. Sam's was the real thing.

He stared in amazement around him. "This is some shindig. I've been to a barbecue before, but nothing this big. There must be hundreds of people here." He tucked C.J.'s hand through the curve of his arm. As they walked through the clusters of chatting people, his other hand tightened over hers to keep them from getting separated.

"All the studio employees were invited," C.J. explained, "as well as the cast and crew from the movie. It appears Traeger was determined to take everyone's mind off the negative effect of Dan Prescott's death by throwing one helluva party."

Sam looked shocked. "Does he think people will forget about a man's death that easily?"

"In this business, worse sins than murder are forgotten all the time." She thought of the headlines in recent years about embezzlement and fraud, not to mention crimes from the golden days of Hollywood, when people bought and sold souls to make movies.

"Some business," Sam muttered under his breath.

"Yeah, as they say, there's no business like it." Looking at the western set and the costumed waiters, C.J. asked, "Does this sort of make you feel at home? You know, back in your own time?"

"*This?* No. It's all make-believe. The stores and shops are just pieces of plywood. It's all a mighty pretty face, but there's nothing behind it."

Then he thought for a moment. "About the only authentic thing around here is Cody. I felt right at home talkin' to him. He wouldn've fit right in back in 1882."

C.J. smiled. "I'm sure he would." She looked up as a young man bumped against her. Her fingers tightened over Sam's arm in an obvious signal as she looked up and smiled at the young man. She had hoped for just this kind of opportunity.

"Sam," she said as an introduction, "I'd like you to meet Lance Ford. He's the hottest young actor in town."

She'd used just the right words. No actor worth his weight in ego would pass up the opportunity to respond to a comment like that. And, of course, the young woman on his arm was none other than Lisa Kennedy. C.J. saw the guarded expression on Lisa's face, the subtle message quickly whispered in Lance's ear—obviously some kind of warning. But Lance was too drunk to heed Lisa's warning. He fastened his bleary gaze on C.J.

"Well, hello there," he said congenially as he took another drink from a passing waiter's tray.

She appraised him carefully. He wasn't particularly handsome. His brown hair was dull and already beginning to thin over his forehead. He was short and slender, with a bony, angular face. A perennial sullen expression marred whatever charm he possessed.

His acting ability was confined to an explosive intensity that seemed to impress a lot of people, especially critics. But as someone who had seriously studied acting in college and countless workshops with some of the top professionals in the industry, C.J. knew that Ford's range was extremely limited. She suspected he would end up like so many actors who became successful at an early age—burned out and unemployed by thirty. But at the moment she was the object of that explosive intensity as he assumed that famous sullen expression.

"We were on the set a few days ago," C.J. explained. "Mr. Hackett is somewhat of an expert on the Old West." When Sam started to make some comment of his own about her choice of words, she put her elbow discreetly into his ribs.

"He was very impressed with your work," she went on.

It was then Lisa Kennedy spoke up. "Ms. Grant is investigating Dan's death. Be careful, darling," she hinted to Lance. Her camera-perfect smile suggested it was a joke, but C.J. knew better. "Anything you say can and will be used against you. Isn't that right, Ms. Grant?"

Ford's expression hardened.

"I already told the police everything. I assumed the gun was loaded with blanks like it was supposed to be. Now, if you'll excuse me . . ."

Sam planted himself in front of Ford, making him crane his neck to look up into his face. That cool blue-green gaze had gone to ice and Sam's face was hard. C.J. had a feeling she was seeing an expression that had been turned on more than one outlaw. It was chilling.

"We have reason to believe Prescott's death wasn't an accident, that someone deliberately put that bullet in your gun. Someone who knew you'd be firing at Prescott from real close range. Someone who wanted him dead."

Ford glowered in a way that probably intimidated a lot of paparazzi. "Who the hell would want to kill a nobody like Prescott?"

Sam wasn't the least intimidated as he towered over Lance, his expression as hard as granite. "I hear you had a fight with him earlier that morning."

Ford flushed angrily. "Are you accusing *me* of killing that old son of a bitch?"

The tone of Sam's voice never wavered. "Did you kill him?"

C.J. held her breath. She'd never seen Sam like this, and for a split second she thought Ford was going to slug him. Obviously, Lance wasn't used to people speaking to him like that, he wasn't used to reining in his volatile temper, and he wasn't used to being confronted by someone like Sam Hackett, whose presence alone was enough to make someone think twice. He stood head and shoulders above Ford, and it was clear he would just as soon forget the discussion completely and settle this physically.

Ford backed down. "I didn't kill the old guy," he muttered. "But I don't blame whoever did it. He was a sanctimonious old geezer."

C.J. breathed a sigh of relief. She had no doubt Sam could handle Ford easily, but she didn't want to get in the middle of a public brawl. That would almost certainly infuriate Emmett Traeger, who would instantly stop being cooperative.

"What was the fight all about?" Sam demanded.

Ford didn't quite meet his look. "Nothing in particular. He kept riding me about stuff."

"What kind of stuff?" Sam persisted.

"He jumped on me about not being prepared with my lines, said I was unprofessional. I told him off. That was the end of it. It certainly wasn't anything to kill anyone over. Now, if you don't mind, I've got better things to do." He eyed a passing waiter with a tray full of drinks.

"C'mon, babe." He shouldered his way arrogantly past Lisa Kennedy, on a direct path to the waiter. With an icy look that spoke volumes, Lisa turned and trailed after him.

"I see you met up with the entertainment for the evenin'." A voice behind them brought them both around.

Sam's hard expression immediately dissolved into a smile of genuine warmth. "Cody, how ya doin'?"

"Not bad." Cody grinned widely as he touched the brim of his wide Stetson in greeting to C.J. He glanced after Ford. "Is he as congenial as ever?"

C.J. gave him a rueful smile. "He's everything the press has made him out to be . . . and worse."

"Yeah"—Cody shook his head—"that's our boy Lance. A real pain in the . . . beg pardon."

"That's all right," she assured him. "If you won't say it, I will." She grinned at Sam. "You're right, he's a real pain in the ass. And it looks like he's been drinking pretty heavily."

Cody shrugged. "Could be. More'n likely he's high on somethin' else."

C.J.'s attention fastened on Cody. She'd heard rumors about Ford's problems in the past—brushes with the law, including being caught with a few grams of cocaine in his car. He swore he'd been set up. He was given a suspended sentence and fined six months of community service on weekends. But that was over a year before. Now she wondered if Lance was courting the old demons again.

"High on what?" she asked.

Cody shrugged. "It's a cinch he's not high on life, not with that attitude. Hell, it ain't no secret. He was loaded practically every day he was on the set."

C.J. was stunned. As far as she knew, Emmett Traeger ran a clean operation. In fact, he'd publicly denounced drugs in conjunction with any of his productions.

"How can you be sure of that?"

Cody lowered his voice so that only she and Sam could hear. "He had his very own candy man on the set."

"Candy man?" Sam's expression clearly indicated he didn't have the least idea what Cody was talking about.

She explained to him. "The candy man is the name for a drug supplier on a given production. He's usually a member of the cast or crew and sees to it that those who use drugs have access to them."

Cody said, "Only in this case the candy man was a candy *lady*."

"Lady?" C.J. was stunned. "What are you talking about? Who was dealing drugs on the set of *Hard Country*?"

Cody looked at the crowd that surrounded them. His eyes narrowed as he focused on someone across the way. He obviously found whom he was looking for. Glancing back at C.J., he tipped his high-crowned hat in that direction.

She followed his gaze. Her eyes widened in disbelief. She spun back to Cody. "Are you certain?"

Cody frowned as he nodded. "I'm certain. Dan was the one who found out about it."

C.J. stared in disbelief at Gloria Ames.

Chapter 10

It fit—the designer clothes, the Waterford crystal, the expensive condo in an equally expensive area. Now, C.J. knew how all that was possible. Still, it was hard to believe. Gloria didn't fit the usual sterotype of a drug dealer, but C.J. knew there were those who came along who simply didn't fit the mold. Like the sweet, likable young man who hijacked a bus full of schoolchildren and held them for ransom, or the mild-mannered bank employee who went home and slaughtered his entire family.

Sam obviously found it hard to believe, too, as he stared hard at Gloria. C.J. had given him some background on current drug problems, but he was having just as hard a time as she was with the fact that Gloria was a drug pusher.

"I went out to talk to her earlier today. I thought her life-style was a bit extravagant," C.J. admitted. "I know her career never really took off."

"Nope, it never did," Cody concurred. "Some folks just can't accept that. They keep at it and want all the fancy things that go with success . . . fancy window dressin'."

C.J. asked, "Did Dan ever say anything to Gloria?"

Cody shrugged his shoulders. "Not that I know of. It hurt him when he found out about it though. They went back a long ways. Dan was always a straight shooter as far as something like that was concerned. He just didn't have no use for it."

Then his mood shifted. "Well, folks, I guess I'll mosey on over to the barbecue and get me somethin' to eat, then I'll just slip outta here early. This really isn't my sort of shindig, but the boss wanted everyone to put in an appearance. Besides, I gotta get on out to the ranch."

"C.J." Someone said from behind them.

She stiffened at the sound of that familiar female voice. It was Lynn Delvecchio, probably the hottest female agent in town. She had once represented C.J., but dropped her when she realized she wasn't going to get to the top of the glitzy heap. It was Lynn's policy to take on only those clients who could guarantee furthering her career.

Lynn was somewhere between thirty and forty-five, tall and svelte, with close-cropped platinum hair and shrewd gray eyes. She wore a deceptively simple little black dress that C.J. recognized as a designer original. It put her white silk tank top and slacks to shame. Normally, C.J. didn't spend a lot of time thinking about clothes, but tonight she wished she owned something slinky and expensive.

Lynn had predatory female stamped all over her, but never wasted time with anyone who wasn't at the top or on the fast track in that direction. For an instant C.J. wondered why Lynn, who hadn't spoken to her in years, had bothered to notice her. Then she saw the way Lynn was eyeing Sam—the way a hungry Doberman eyes a thick juicy steak—and she understood perfectly.

"Hello, Lynn." C.J. didn't bother to disguise her irritation, "It's been a long time."

"Too long, sweetie. What on earth have you been up to?" Before C.J. could respond, Lynn went on. "And *who* is this?" She seemed to forget anyone else was around as she focused on Sam.

"I don't believe I've seen you around before. I'm sure I would have noticed you, and once I notice, I don't forget."

Sam smiled politely. "Sam Hackett, ma'am. Pleased to meet you."

Lynn rolled those gray eyes. "What a charming Southern accent. I just adore men from the South, they're such gentlemen."

C.J. felt as if she might throw up. "If you'll excuse us, Lynn, we're actually rather busy."

Lynn flashed her a cool look. "Oh, are you part of the help here tonight, C.J.?"

C.J. opened her mouth to tell Lynn exactly where to go, but Lynn had already turned back to Sam. "Don't try to tell me you're working here, Sam. It's too too obvious what you do."

Sam raised one eyebrow with a faintly bemused expression. "Oh?"

"Of course." Lynn oozed that deadly charm. "Do you mind if I ask who you're with?"

Sam smiled. He was thoroughly enjoying this. C.J. could have joyfully strangled him. "I'm with Katy," he said simply.

Lynn's lips curved upward, but there was absolutely no trace of humor behind that feral smile. "No, I mean who's representing you? Your *agent*?"

C.J. answered for Sam. "He isn't an actor, he's in law enforcement."

Lynn's eyes widened with mock disappointment. "I simply can't believe it. Why, you're a young Tom Selleck. And those eyes—my dear, they're just like Mel Gibson's." Her fingers closed around his arm. "Oh, the camera would love you."

So that's why those eyes looked familiar, C.J. realized with a start.

Lynn's fingers tightened over Sam's arm. "I have clients bringing in seven figures a year who can't hold a candle to you. Now, why don't you and I enjoy this nice, slow dance together, and we'll talk, just the two of us, with no distractions. I'd really like to do things for you, Sam." Her voice was velvet seduction as she pulled him toward the roped-off dance floor.

C.J. glared after Lynn. You mean, you'd really like to do things *to* him, she thought cattily.

"Now, there's a woman with a way about her," Cody remarked, rolling his tongue into his cheek. "Reminds me of a mountain lion toyin' with her next kill, only in this case I'd wager she's caught herself a bear."

"She's got a way about her, all right." C.J. muttered with disgust.

"Well, I think I'll just go on over and get somethin' to eat," Cody announced. "Can I get you anything, Miss Grant?"

A big stick, C.J. thought with a deadly look at Lynn's back. She forced a smile as she answered, "No thanks, Cody. I think I'll just take a tour of the set."

He nodded. "This will be the last anyone will see of it. They start tearin' it down next week. Say," he said with a sudden thought, "you might want to go on up there." He gestured to the facade of the two-story building that formed the nearby backdrop of the set. It had been used as the saloon in *Hard Country*. The second story supposedly housed the upstairs "rooms," where ladies entertained their customers. Heavy red satin drapes were visible at one window with the look-through backdrop of what appeared to be a bordello.

C.J. knew it was all illusion. As Sam had said, there was nothing there, but it would be fun to see it anyway. And besides, that second story gave a spectacular view of the entire set.

"Thanks, I think I will. I always wanted to work on a western movie set. I guess this is as close as I'll ever get."

"There's a set of stairs at the back that leads up to the second-floor scaffolding. The saloon was Dan's favorite place." Cody winked at her. "Probably because it's pretty much intact. He sneaked a real bottle of whiskey behind the bar. We used to go in there for a pull or two when they were shooting elsewhere on the set."

C.J. laughed with him. "Just like the real thing."

"Well, almost." His voice became almost wistful. "Now it's all gone forever." Then he seemed to mentally shake himself. "Well, anyway, that food smells good. Good evenin', Miss Grant."

She accepted a glass of champagne from a passing waiter as she gazed out across the dance floor. Watching Lynn and Sam, she felt an unexpected stab of resentment. Lynn placed her arms around Sam's neck and leaned against him. After a moment's hesitation Sam began to move haltingly. C.J. couldn't help smiling. She was certain it was the first time he'd ever danced to "Delta Dawn."

Actually he didn't do too badly, all things considered. Not that Lynn would care. She wasn't interested in Sam for his grace and coordination—at least, not on the dance floor.

C.J. decided she would simply have to explain to Sam about maneaters like Lynn. Whatever kind of woman he was used to in his own time, she was certain nothing had quite prepared him for Lynn.

She was just trying to figure out exactly how to tell Sam that Lynn was a barracuda, when Emmett Traeger walked up to her.

"Good evening, Miss Grant. I'm glad you could make it. If you hadn't come, the party would have been distinctly disappointing."

He looked even more polished and attractive than usual, as if he'd just stepped off the cover of *GQ*. The combination of those dark good looks and his attention focused intently on her alone affected her in a way she wasn't quite prepared for.

"I hope you're enjoying yourself," he went on to say.

"Let's just say it's been an evening full of surprises," C.J. replied. "I think your party is a success."

"That was the intention. I won't accept anything less than success."

While she talked to Traeger, C.J. never lost track of Lynn and Sam on the dance floor. Reminding herself that she was a woman of the eighties, confident, strong, even bold, she asked, "Would you like to dance, Emmett?"

He smiled. "I'd love to. I never turn down the opportunity to hold a beautiful and fascinating woman in my arms."

This was heady stuff, especially for a girl who hadn't had a date for the senior prom.

As C.J. and Traeger danced together, she looked for Sam in the crowd. When she caught his eye, she grinned broadly as if to say, "Aren't we both having fun?" To her delight, Sam frowned, and seemed to be ignoring Lynn, who was whispering persistently in his ear. Then they were lost once more in the crowd of dancing couples.

"How is the investigation coming?" Traeger asked, his hand resting lightly against the small of her back.

"Not very well," C.J. admitted. "We have only one more person to talk to, and so far we haven't learned anything significant." Despite Traeger's charm, she never discussed details of her cases with anyone. She was sure it would be wise to keep what she'd learned about Gloria Ames to herself until she could find out more. She felt the subtle pressure of Traeger's hand, pulling her just close enough so that their bodies brushed lightly.

He moved to the beat of the music the way he moved in his office—with the assurance of someone who knew just what he wanted and just how to get it. "I don't think there is anything to learn. After all your hard work, and your client's money, you're going to find Dan Prescott's death was a tragic accident. Nothing more."

He pulled her closer. The combination of the champagne and the heat from his body was a little intoxicating.

"But let's not waste time talking about that." He went on, his breath warm against her ear. "You're a smart woman. You'll reach that conclusion on your own."

Just then the music ended. As C.J. stepped back slightly to applaud, she drew in a steadying breath of air. "I have to go mingle. It's one of my official duties," Traeger said as he held on to her hand for a moment longer, stroking the tips of her fingers. His eyes fastened on hers.

"Can I call you sometime? Maybe we could get together somewhere away from all this." He gestured to the set and the crowd of people.

C.J. hadn't expected this. Summoning the considerable poise she'd learned as an actress, she managed to respond without tripping over her tongue, "Of course, I'd like that."

"Good." Traeger smiled as he gently released her hand. "Later, then."

As he left, Sam came up to her. She was relieved to see Lynn wasn't with him.

"What were you doin' with Traeger?" he demanded. His anger was so abrupt and so unexpected, it caught her completely off guard. When she finally recovered, she spoke from between clenched teeth. "The same thing you were doing with Lynn—*dancing*."

"Is that what you call it?"

C.J. felt color burn across her cheeks. "Yes, that's what I call it."

Sam's hands were jammed into his back pockets, as if it were all he could do to keep from strangling her. "Have you forgotten about the case? That man just happens to be a prime suspect."

C.J. was determined to set him straight. "For your information, I haven't forgotten about the case for one moment—*my* case, I might remind you. But it looked as if you might have, the way you were plastered all over Lynn."

That obviously wasn't quite the response he'd expected. "What do you mean by that?"

"I mean, Lynn seems to want to help you make a career switch—from law to acting."

"Me, an actor? That's ridiculous. She was just havin' a good time."

"Oh, she was having a good time all right. The problem is, you don't know Lynn the way I do. She's famous, or perhaps I should say infamous, for grooming the careers of a lot of young actors."

Sam looked perplexed. "You mean like groomin' a horse?"

"Forget it." She whirled around and started to walk away. His voice was deep, dark, subtle, as she'd heard it once before—last night, when he'd comforted her.

"What's wrong, Katy? Why are you upset?"

"I'm not upset," she nearly shouted. Several people standing nearby turned to stare at her curiously. Lowering her voice, she went on. "All right, here it is—Lynn was coming on to you." At Sam's look of confusion, she said, "She was making a pass at you."

When he still looked confused, she added, "Oh, hell, she wants to go to bed with you!" She wasn't at all certain what sort of reaction she expected from him, but the one she got surprised her.

Sam chuckled softly. "I know that, Katy."

She blinked. "You *know?*"

"Of course. Do you think things have changed that much in a hundred years? Or that I'm blind?"

C.J. swallowed back her chagrin. "Well, no . . ."

He put his hands on her shoulders, his fingers gently massaging into the muscles at her back. "It *was* pretty obvious, and I have run across one or two women like that in my time." He gave her an amused smile.

"Well, I just thought you should know . . ." It was a lame response and she knew it. Then she looked up at him and asked, "What did you tell her?"

As soon as she said it, C.J. groaned inwardly. Of all the gauche, unsophisticated things to ask. She sounded like some girl in high school anxious over her first boyfriend.

"About what?"

"About . . . what she . . . *wanted.*"

Sam's expression was completely innocent. "Oh, *that.* I told her I was livin' with you and for some reason that seemed to discourage her. Now, how about gettin' somethin' to eat? That barbecue sure smells good."

As he led her over to the tables, she wasn't sure he understood the full meaning of what he'd told Lynn. Her immediate reaction was no, of course not. But she saw laughter glinting in those blue-green Mel Gibson eyes. And she wondered . . .

Later, as they were standing at the edge of the dance floor, Sam asked, "Want to dance?"

C.J. was completely unprepared for the invitation. "What? You mean here?"

Sam grinned. "Well, this is where the music is."

She hesitated. She wasn't sure why the invitation unnerved her so much. She hadn't been the least bit hesitant about dancing with Emmett Traeger.

"I know you can dance, Katy. You seemed to be doing a pretty good job of it with Traeger. Unless, of course, you don't want to dance with *me.*" There was something in his voice that caught at her. She found herself drawn into those eyes. How could she possibly make him understand why she hesitated when she didn't understand it herself?

He bent his head very close to hers. "So what do you say?" Like Traeger, she could feel the heat from his body, but it had an entirely different effect on her. Whereas it had been faintly provocative before, there was nothing faint about her reaction now.

She tried to sound casual. "Sure."

Sam led her onto the dance floor, then took her gently in his arms. He held her just close enough so that the thin silk of her tank top lightly brushed the heavier chambray of his shirt. Looking at him this close, C.J. noticed the small scar on his chin, an uneven line of white in an otherwise deeply tanned face.

"Where did you get that scar?" she asked curiously.

Sam grinned as he carefully maneuvered her, his thigh brushing against hers, then moving away, only to brush it once more.

"I could tell you I was wounded in a gunfight, but the truth is I fell off my horse and landed facefirst in some sagebrush."

She choked back laughter. "Fell off your horse?"

"It's not as dumb as it sounds," Sam went on to explain, trying to salvage his wounded dignity. "I was chasin' a train robber at the time, and my horse stepped into a gopher hole and threw me. Damn near broke my neck."

C.J. grinned as she imagined Sam Hackett, Federal Marshal, facedown in a clump of brush. She admired anyone who could make fun of himself and laugh about it.

"Did you catch the guy?"

"Of course," he said matter-of-factly.

"*Of course.*" She should have realized it was a foolish question. Sam Hackett *always* got his man.

As they danced she noticed there was a softness about his mouth that wasn't normally there. When he was relaxed, he lost the hardness, the defensiveness that she suspected had always been there, even in his own time.

Yet there was a boyishness about those chiseled features. He was younger than C.J. had first assumed—no more than two or three years older than she was.

As he held her, moving to the strains of an old Patsy Cline ballad, she felt the tensile strength of his body. Beneath the blue shirt and jeans, she knew it was hard and fit and lean. The lithe, sinewy body of a runner or a swimmer—or, in his unique case, a man who was used to living a hard life, always on the edge.

C.J. felt a tingling somewhere below her stomach and abruptly decided she'd better stop focusing on Sam's body.

Just then the music came to an end. For one timeless moment Sam continued to hold her. He looked down at her with an expression of almost wistful longing. He started to say something but was cut off by that soft, sultry voice C.J. recognized with a sharp flash of annoyance.

"Sam, you've deserted me." Lynn flashed her a brief look, then concentrated on Sam. "And you did promise me one more dance."

C.J. stepped back from Sam. "Go right ahead, don't let me stand in the way."

"That's so generous of you, darling." Lynn's voice dripped with honeyed venom. She fastened her eyes on Sam once more. "This song is one of my favorites."

C.J. recognized the song. It was long and slow, a perfect overture for seduction. But at least Sam knew what Lynn was all about. Although for the life of her C.J. couldn't decide whether that was good or bad, or even why it should bother her.

Leaving Sam and Lynn on the dance floor, C.J. mingled with the crowd. She was amused at the conversations that buzzed around her. Even now, high-powered deals were in the making, for new roles, new projects. It was always the same—the come-on. C.J. supposed she had tired of that as much as the cattle calls, and realized she didn't miss it at all. She grabbed another glass of champagne. If she was inclined to drink—which she wasn't—this would be the place to do it. Booze ran like water.

She wandered to the edge of the set, in front of the saloon, and decided to take Cody's advice. The saloon and the fake bordello on the second floor above it were nothing but one huge prop. She found the stairs at the back and slowly climbed to the railed catwalk at the top. This was where the camera crews had worked on long shots of the street and the gunfight below when it was filmed. Another crew on the ground would cut in for the tight shots.

She walked along the catwalk. There was no one else

up there right now, although she had seen other people there earlier. She sipped at her champagne as she walked along behind the facade of what appeared from the other side to be the upstairs bedrooms of the infamous Lucky Lady saloon and brothel.

In the crowd below she caught a brief glimpse of Gloria Ames and pondered what she'd learned about her that night. If Dan had threatened to expose Gloria's drug dealing, would that have been enough motivation for murder?

The night breeze stirred the satin and lace curtains at the windows. It was dark up here, the fake street below illuminated by lights from fake storefronts or the overhead floodlights that had been turned on. In the growing darkness and muted light from the street below, she could almost feel the town transform into what it might have been a hundred years earlier, in Sam's time.

It was an old set and the craftsmen who'd built it had paid painstaking attention to detail. Everything was as authentic as they could get it, right down to the hitching posts in front of the saloon, and the dirt that swirled from the street up onto the worn boardwalks in front of the buildings.

C.J. sighed, letting her imagination take her back to another time and place. She could almost feel it, even with the buzz of freeway traffic in the distant background. With a tug of emotion she remembered what Cody had said—in a matter of weeks it would all be dismantled, another piece of the Hollywood dream factory gone forever.

She caught sight of Sam. He'd left Lynn and his gaze wandered the crowd, finally finding her leaning out of one of those satin-draped windows. She waved. Draining the last sip from her champagne glass, C.J. turned and continued along the catwalk to the far end, which descended into what appeared from the street to be a darkened alley—the very same alley Lance Ford had emerged from in his gunfight with Dan Prescott.

It happened quickly. There was the sound of footsteps behind her on the catwalk, then hands pushing at her back. She was thrown against the wood railing of the catwalk, and heard the sickening splinter of timber as it gave way. Fear constricted her throat as she scrabbled for a handhold, anything that might stop her fall. Her right hand closed over the sagging railing and splinters cut into her hand.

She screamed as she realized she was losing her tenuous grip and was going to fall.

C.J. stared wide-eyed at the ground two stories below her. She focused on the man running toward her.

"Katy!"

"Sam!"

"Hang on, Katy!" he shouted up at her.

"I can't!"

"Hang on, dammit! Don't let go!" Sam yelled as he ran up the steps from the ground below.

"I'm slipping!" she cried out.

"Don't move!" Sam ordered her. When he reached the top of the catwalk where the railing had broken away, he wasn't more than three feet away from her. He reached out to her, bracing his own weight against the solid siderail that descended the steps.

"Take my hand, Katy."

"I can't." Her eyes were clamped shut now. She refused to open them.

His voice was gentle, soothing, coaxing. "If that was going to give way, it already would have. You can do it. Just open your eyes and look straight ahead. I'm right here."

She was afraid even to breathe, but she clung to the sound of his voice as it broke through the fear. Slowly she opened her eyes.

"That's right, darlin'. Now look at me." When she started to look down, he said with amazing tenderness, "Right here, Katy. Look at *me*. I'm not goin' to let anythin' happen to you. But you have to help me."

C.J. swallowed convulsively as she kept her eyes fastened on him. She breathed out slowly. "All right."

Sam inched his way closer to her, still keeping his weight and leverage on the stairs. "I want you to slowly let go with your left hand and reach out to me. No sudden moves."

She looked at him as if she thought he'd lost his mind,

and her double-handed grasp tightened. It succeeded only in bringing another groan from the splintered railing above.

"Katy, you have to do this! There's no other way. And you have to do it now." When she still hesitated, his voice changed once more, growing insistent.

"C'mon, Katy, you can do it." He extended his hand to her. "I won't let you fall, darlin'."

C.J. focused on his voice and hand as he reached out to her.

She took another deep breath, tightened her grasp with her right hand even though her fingers ached, and slowly released her grasp with her left hand. Her hand was level with his, their fingertips only inches apart.

Above her the wood groaned as the railing finally broke away with her weight. At that instant Sam's fingers locked around hers. C.J. felt the steel grasp of his hand around her wrist as he pulled her to the stairs. As she crawled under the broken railing and onto the stairs, he gathered her into his arms. She collapsed against the hard wall of his chest. The tears she'd been too afraid to cry until now flooded her eyes.

"It's all right," he soothed as he cradled her, his big hand at the back of her head. He whispered against the silken cap of her dark hair. "I've got you now, Katy."

Chapter 11

The police called it an unfortunate accident. After all, it was an old movie set about to be dismantled. Over the years the worn timbers had become loose and unsafe. Never mind the fact that numerous people and equipment had been up on the catwalk only days before without any "accidents."

They didn't believe C.J.'s statement that she'd been pushed. The bottom line was that when Sam got to her, she was alone on the catwalk, and no one saw anyone else up there.

She'd slept little after Sam brought her home. That made two nights she'd gotten the sum total of four hours sleep. To top it off, Sam wasn't too pleased with her either. One of the last on her list of people to question was Carl Cartwright, production manager for *Hard Country*. The opportunity to talk to him came unexpectedly that morning, and she hadn't felt the need or inclination to ask Sam's approval. Now she watched as he shoved his hand back through his hair, still damp from his shower. He stood at the window that looked out onto the beach, his back to her. Anger was written in every hardened line of his body.

"I just wish you'd have let me go with you to talk to Cartwright."

She let out a long, tired sigh. "There wasn't any point in both of us being dragged out at the crack of dawn. Neither one of us has had much sleep the last two days. He was on his way out of town for the Fourth of July weekend, and this was the only time he was willing to see me."

C.J.'s eyes narrowed as Redford, her orange tabby cat,

tentatively stretched out a paw toward her jelly doughnut. She scooped up the doughnut and took a huge bite out of it. Redford gave her what could be described only as a look of contempt. With an aggravated flick of his tail, he jumped down from her desk and sauntered out of the office.

It appeared she had a knack this morning for making the men around her angry. Newman hadn't been seen since dawn. After her office was ransacked, she had lectured him about his duties as watchdog and he was definitely offended. He was probably out on the beach somewhere, mooching food off the first of the sunbathers who were beginning to crowd the sand. She would undoubtedly have a call from the beach patrol to come pick up her wayward dog or they would cart him off to the A.S.P.C.A.

And then there was Sam.

"I don't suppose it occurred to you that Cartwright appeared awful fast last night, after your little "accident." He was the first one there," he reminded her with a long, penetrating look over his shoulder.

C.J. let out a sigh. She didn't bother telling him it was Cody who'd suggested she go up on the set scaffolding. Sam was fond of him, and she knew he would never consider Cody a likely suspect. But she had to. Right now, though, she had to deal with Sam's anger about Cartwright. She didn't like explaining herself, and she'd done more of it the last few days than in her entire life.

"All right, the truth is, I didn't take you with me because you intimidate him. You practically took his head off last night."

He whirled on her. "Dammit, Katy, you deliberately put yourself in danger going out there alone. Don't you see what's happening?" He punched a fist through the air for emphasis, almost as if he'd been aiming at some imaginary target.

"First someone takes your office apart, and no matter what little lie you told Lucy about some petty thief looking for money, you and I both know what they were after."

"I know," C.J. said in a small, exhausted voice.

"And now someone has tried to kill you," he said bluntly, making her wince.

"I can't prove that."

"Can't prove it!" He came across the office in long, angry strides, his fingers just itching to get a hold of her so that he could shake some sense into her. Instead, he grabbed the edge of the desk and braced his weight on it.

"You don't see it, do you? You're getting too close to something and someone is trying to stop you."

"Right!" C.J. came up out of her chair and glared at him across the desk. "And at this moment Gloria Ames is the most likely suspect. She had the strongest motive. Dan knew about her drug dealing on the set. Maybe he threatened to expose her. She has a very fancy life-style to maintain, and I get the definite impression she isn't about to give it up."

"She's half your size," Sam pointed out, "twice your age and not nearly as strong. I can't see her throwing you off that balcony."

"Catwalk," she flung back at him.

"Hi, you two. Sorry I'm late." Lucy breezed into the office, a whirlwind of flashing bracelets and crystal pendants. "After all the excitement last night, I overslept."

They both ignored her.

Lucy looked from Sam to C.J. "So, are we planning our usual July Fourth picnic on the beach?" she asked innocently, but got no response.

"All right!" C.J. slammed the desk drawer beside her as she rounded the desk, tired beyond reason, angry beyond caution. "You've been hedging around something ever since you started yelling at me. Out with it! What is your brilliant opinion on this case, Marshal Hackett?"

Lucy stared at them both wide-eyed. "I can see this is not the best time to discuss the picnic. Maybe I'll just go by the market and pick up a few things. We can discuss it later."

They both turned on her and said in angry unison.

"Fine!"

They were answered by a whirl of disappearing fuchsia silk as Lucy ducked out the door.

C.J. turned back to Sam. "Why don't you say what you really want to say?"

"All right!" Sam met her nose to nose, only the telephone and the answering machine separating them. "Traeger's the man you're after and you can't even see it."

"So we're back to that, ignoring the fact that Traeger has absolutely no motive!"

"It's there, Katy. I know it is. We just haven't found it yet."

C.J. threw up her hands in frustration. The phone rang. With several choice expletives on the tip of her tongue, she ignored it. It rang again, switching over to the message tape with her voice giving instructions about leaving name and number.

"Aren't you going to answer that damned thing?" Sam spat out.

"Sure!" she said from between clenched teeth. "Maybe it's Emmett Traeger making a death threat against me." That brought just the reaction she thought it would as Sam turned away from her in disgust. She picked up the phone, cutting off the recorded tape.

"Yes?" she said angrily, practically shouting into the hand set.

Sam stood, elbows cocked, hands resting on his hips. He needed a cigarette, and he needed a drink, but he couldn't decide which one he needed first. Christ! She had the ability, more than anyone he'd ever known, to infuriate him to the point where he wanted to smash something. He didn't like that feeling. Usually he controlled his anger. A Federal Marshal couldn't afford to lose control. Often times, it was the only thing that separated him from the man he was after—that thin line that distinguished law and order from violence, good from bad.

At least that was the way it was in his time. Now he wasn't so certain. That thin line seemed to have disappeared over the last hundred years. There was no longer a clear distinction between right and wrong, and he didn't like it. He didn't like it at all, and he didn't like it touching Katy.

As he heard her hang up the phone, he remembered the phone call he'd answered earlier when she'd gone over to Cartwright's without him. Lynn had called with an invitation for that evening.

"Who was that?" he asked, still wrestling with the anger over her refusal to see what was so painfully clear to him.

"It was Emmett. He was calling to see if I was all right."

"Very thoughtful of him," Sam snapped. "But the conversation was a little long just for a report on your health."

"He invited me out tonight to celebrate the holiday." She plunged recklessly ahead. "I'm having dinner with him."

The muscle at Sam's jaw clenched as he stared hard at her. He knew what she was doing and he wasn't about to bite. Two could play at this game.

"Good. That should suit you just fine."

"It does. Immensely."

C.J.'s chin rose one more notch to a stubborn angle. "Of course, that does mean you'll be here by yourself. I'll call and have a pizza delivered. They have a wonderful fireworks display on the beach. I'm certain you'll enjoy that. It should remind you of a gunfight."

"Don't bother," Sam said as he headed for the door and some fresh air, "I'm going out."

He stopped, his hand on the doorknob. Then, mimicking something he'd seen in one of those video movies that seemed especially appropriate at this moment, he said, "Don't wait up. I have no idea when I'll get in."

The door slammed and C.J. stared after him with cold fury. What did he mean by saying he was going out? Just who was he going out with?

"Damn," she muttered to herself, turning back to the desk. She glared at the answering machine, only now noticing the bright red number one illuminated on the message panel. A call must have come in earlier, when she was out questioning Cartwright.

She punched the button to recall the message and slumped down behind her desk. But as soon as she heard

the message, she sat up straight. It was from Lynn Delvecchio, and it wasn't for her at all. It was for Sam.

Lynn's sultry voice came over the tape, asking Sam to
call her. Then it abruptly stopped as Sam picked up the
phone. Because Sam wasn't familiar with the operation of
the machine, he hadn't turned off the recording tape. His
entire conversation with Lynn was on the tape. Lynn
wanted Sam to join her for the evening. Sam's reply had
been hesitant at first. His anger at being left behind by C.J.
came through loud and clear in his tight, clipped response.
But Lynn had a way about her, and as the conversation
ended, she insisted he just couldn't refuse. She would pick
him up.

C.J. slammed down the phone.

A friend who was a manicurist gave C.J. a manicure
and a pedicure. Then she borrowed a slinky outfit from
another friend who was a model. By the time she returned
it was a little past six o'clock. There was just enough time to
shower and blow-dry her hair before her date with Emmett.

She found Lucy and Cody in the kitchen, elbow deep
in potato salad, corn on the cob, and fried chicken. Lucy
looked up from the wicker picnic basket.

"I hope you don't mind our coming over, sweetie.
Cody has never seen the fireworks display on the beach.
We packed a picnic dinner." She wiggled her auburn brows
as she held up a bottle of wine. "There's plenty for
everyone. By the way, where's Sam?"

C.J. felt the knot in her stomach tighten—a sure sign
of an anxiety attack.

"You mean he's not here?" She tried to sound casual as
she stole several green cocktail olives. She loved the stupid
things—she liked to suck the pimientos out of the center.

Lucy frowned slightly. "No, I thought he was with
you."

"Not likely." C.J. shrugged as if she couldn't care less.
"He has a big date tonight." She almost choked as she said
it—and told herself it must be the tartness of the olives.

"A date?" Lucy's frown deepened. "Who with, for God's sake? He doesn't know anyone."

"He does now." C.J. stole a peek under the lid of the cake pan. Chocolate double fudge with fudge icing, her favorite. And there was sliced watermelon too. Lucy had thought of everything.

"Who on earth is Sam going out with?"

"Lynn Delvecchio," C.J. answered as she swung the dress over her shoulder and headed for her room.

Lucy followed her. "Lynn Delvecchio? Isn't she your agent?"

"*Was*, Mother," she said as she stripped out of her cutoffs and T-shirt and into a short terry robe.

"How could you let this happen?"

"I'm not Sam's keeper. He's free to do as he pleases. And so am I. Now, if you'll excuse me, I have a date too."

With that she went into the bathroom, closing the door firmly behind her.

Later, as she dressed and carefully applied her makeup, she couldn't stop thinking about Sam out there somewhere with Lynn. She wondered where Lynn would have taken him. L.A. was a big city and everyone would be celebrating tonight. They could be anywhere—an intimate little restaurant on the beach at Malibu, an exclusive private nightclub on the Sunset Strip, or, disturbing thought, in Lynn's overdecorated high-rise condo.

C.J. had been to a party there once, and had thought at the time that the whole place was designed for seduction. The lighting was soft and flattering, undoubtedly to hide Lynn's growing wrinkles; the sofas and chairs scattered throughout the huge high-ceilinged living room were over-stuffed and immensely comfortable; and there was even a sheepskin rug in front of the black marble fireplace.

She could just imagine Sam there, at Lynn's mercy. Only, as Lynn often said, her motto was "Show no mercy."

When the doorbell rang and C.J. went to answer it, she wasn't thinking about her date with Emmett Traeger. She was thinking about Sam and what he might be doing at that moment.

* * *

Dinner was all right, though Sam found the food a bit mushy for his taste. Lynn called it French cuisine. Whatever it was, everything was covered with sauces, and there wasn't much of it.

He'd been worried about how to talk to Lynn, but as it turned out that wasn't a problem. She talked enough for the two of them, mostly about her work and the people she knew. She acted like Sam should know the people she mentioned with an obviously phony casualness. So he simply said "Oh, really?" every time she dropped another name.

Halfway through dinner he realized the whole thing was a terrible mistake. He'd accepted Lynn's invitation only because he had been angry with Katy for leaving that morning without him. It was that damn stubborn, independent streak of hers, and it was going to get her into trouble.

He had wondered if all women of this time were like Katy. A couple of hours with Lynn answered that question beyond any doubt. She reminded him of women he knew who were too impressed with themselves. That much hadn't changed in the past hundred years. She put on one helluva act though, he had to give her credit for that. Only problem was, he found his thoughts drifting to Katy.

Didn't she realize the danger she was putting herself in? No, the truth was, she didn't know. Or she refused to know, just as she refused to accept that Traeger had to be behind it.

Damn, he thought. Katy irritated him more than any human being he'd ever come across, in his own time or this one. But he had to admit she was also warm and compassionate, strong, honest, and downright gutsy.

As he sat there listening to Lynn go on and on about herself and what she could do for him, he found he missed Katy. It was a feeling so deep it was almost painful, and it surprised him.

Even when they argued, even when she wasn't very perceptive when it came to Emmett Traeger, he would still rather be with her. He felt safe with her, as if he'd found a haven in a strange and uncertain new world. But it was more than that and he knew it. He'd met all kinds of women, and as he was finding out with Lynn tonight, the times might have changed, but human nature was pretty much the same. It was just that Katy was . . . well, she was Katy and he wanted to be with her.

It was a new feeling and caught him slightly off balance. He hadn't really wanted to be with anyone since Maria.

He was abruptly yanked out of his reverie when he realized that Lynn had just asked him a question. He hadn't been paying attention and didn't have the slightest idea what she had asked.

Leaning toward Sam, Lynn whispered, "Why waste time on small talk? Let's get down to business."

They were sitting on the couch in Lynn's house, or condo, as she called it, and Sam didn't have to ask what kind of business she meant. Though Lynn had made it perfectly clear from the very beginning that she was attracted to him, he wasn't prepared for her to start undressing at precisely that moment.

Her eyes had gone to soft smoke as her fingers trailed down the front of her blouse, loosening buttons along the way. When she reached the last one, she moistened her lips as she leaned toward Sam and took his large hand in hers. Her eyes never left his as she stroked his fingers and then slowly brought his hand to her breast. Her breath shuddered out of her at the contact.

The only times in his experience when women had been this matter-of-fact were in sportin' houses, and that was only *after* the negotiations for payment. Lynn hadn't said a word about being paid, and somehow Sam didn't think she was going to as she wrapped her long body around his.

This had nothing to do with money. And since they'd known each other for only a few hours, it certainly wasn't love. He knew only that Lynn had very efficiently unbuttoned his shirt and was now quickly unbuckling his belt as she pressed her high, full breasts against his chest. In a minute he'd be buck naked.

He felt his body respond to Lynn's touch, and the

wetness of her mouth against his neck. It had been a long time since he'd been with a woman. And this one wanted him. She wanted him bad.

Why not? he asked himself. It seemed to be the thing to do nowadays. For all he knew, Katy was doing the same thing at that very minute with Emmett Traeger.

He'd never been at a loss as to what to do with a woman. He knew there were times when love had nothing to do with it. Was that how Katy felt about Traeger? That seemed to be part of this new independence women enjoyed so much—the freedom to go to bed with whomever they wanted, whenever they wanted it.

The anger returned sharp and painful. Why not? he thought. Why not?

The club was one of the most exclusive in town. You had to be very wealthy or very famous, and preferably both, just to get in the door. The doorman waved C.J. and Emmett Traeger inside, at the same time holding back an impatient line of people who had for the moment been refused admittance. C.J. had to confess to herself, she was impressed. After all, she had recognized some fairly famous faces in that line, a couple of hot new television stars and a producer.

The maître d' led them straight to a small table in a corner. The room was dimly lit, intimate, romantic. It was the sort of place where inhibitions would begin to be shed, one by one, until the last one dissolved in a bedroom somewhere. She had no doubt that was exactly Traeger's intention. She would have been surprised if it was otherwise. And she had to admit she was flattered. The only question was whether or not she would go along with the carefully crafted seduction.

Through a delicious meal and champagne, Traeger kept up a wonderful conversation. She was pleasantly surprised to find he didn't talk about himself, or the business he played such a major role in. Instead, he asked her about herself, seeming genuinely interested, and touched on the hot topics of the day in politics, current events, philosophical discussions. In short, he was a wonderful dinner companion.

Any mention of the evening before was brief and solicitous. He even presented her with an exotic ginger blossom, especially ordered for the occasion, as his way of apologizing for what he termed another "unfortunate" accident.

C.J. gave him high marks for originality. If he'd been self-absorbed, like so many men she knew in the entertainment business, or uninteresting intellectually, it would have been easy to resist him. Instead, she found herself drawn to him. He was attractive, smart, interesting, and well read. And there was no denying she was attracted to his aura of power.

Her reserve thawed, her defense mechanism crumbled. She was having a terrific time and she didn't want it to end.

When the last of the champagne was emptied into her glass, and C.J. was feeling just high enough to be in a terrific mood, Traeger suggested they take a drive out to the beach. C.J. knew he wasn't just referring to parking along one of the public beaches. He had a fabulous beach house at Trancas, just north of Malibu.

She gave him a direct look, and replied in a voice slightly huskier than usual, "Sounds lovely."

His Ranger Rover was tough and utilitarian on the outside, but inside it was all glove-soft leather, intricate instrument panel, wood-grain dashboard, and state-of-the-art stereo system. Traeger slipped in an old Billie Holiday tape, and while the lady sang the blues as only she could, they sped along Pacific Coast Highway.

Neither C.J. nor Traeger spoke during the forty-five-minute drive. When they pulled into his driveway and he said, "Well, here we are," the sound of his voice startled her.

His house was on Heron Drive, a narrow road that branched off Pacific Coast Highway on the ocean side. Beach houses lined the road, but Traeger's stood apart from the rest. A two-story structure built of weathered redwood and glass, it was dramatic and impressive, both architecturally and in terms of the money C.J. knew it must have cost.

When they entered the house through a side door from the driveway, Traeger flicked a switch and immediately the living room was brightly lit. The dark, rough-hewn beams that spanned the cathedral ceiling contrasted sharply with the stark white of the walls. The wall facing the ocean was entirely floor-to-ceiling windows. Through those windows C.J. saw the ocean glistening silver and ebony in the moonlight.

The house had clearly been decorated by a top designer. The decor was masculine without being heavy-handed—ivory-colored-leather sofas and chairs, plump madras cushions, bold modern art on the walls. Evidence of Traeger's work was subtle, but nevertheless apparent—in the scripts piled casually on the marble coffee table, and framed photos of Traeger with top-name celebrities, directors, and producers in the business.

As C.J. glanced around, he moved to a built-in bar. "What would you like?"

"Something non-alcoholic," she answered with a smile. "I don't want to become comatose."

"I'm glad to see you know your limits." Traeger filled two glasses, slipped ice into the drinks, and came around the end of the bar. "Too many people don't know their limits, and then they get into trouble."

Her gaze came up to meet his with new interest. Had he meant something other than the obvious? C.J. chose her answer carefully. "Drunks are so boring," she said.

He agreed. "I have to put up with a lot of them, usually young actors, sometimes actresses, who've gotten too big too fast, and don't know how to deal with it."

It was the only reference to his business that he'd made all evening. And it revealed an objective view that C.J. liked.

As he handed her a glass of mineral water over ice, he went on. "So tell me, how is your investigation coming along? Turned up any guilty secrets yet?"

C.J. shrugged. "Only a few. But to be honest, nothing that would be a motive for murder. At least not yet."

His interest seemed casual. "Have you talked to everyone on your list?"

"Just about," she answered evasively.

Opening a sliding glass door onto a redwood deck, Traeger gestured for C.J. to follow him. Outside, he said, "And if all your investigating can't turn anything up? What then—will you finally admit Dan Prescott's death was an accident, not murder, and give it up?"

C.J. leaned against the redwood railing and stared out across the glistening thread of dark ocean beneath the moon. Her gaze wandered down the coastline in the direction of Venice. On a clear evening she might be able to see the fireworks later on. Then she remembered Sam and how she had originally assumed she would spend this evening with him. But then, things didn't always work out the way she thought they would.

Turning back to Traeger, she said, "I never give up."

He smiled slowly. "I suspected as much. But enough of the case—or the noncase, as I prefer to think of it. Look at that ocean. Isn't it lovely tonight?"

It was, indeed. Black. Limitless. Peaceful, and yet awesome.

Traeger had set his glass down on the railing and stepped closer to her. She smelled the subtle, musky scent he wore, and saw the desire in his dark eyes. Traeger's appeal, the romantic setting, and the fact that it had been a long time since she'd slept with anyone, all combined to bring a highly charged electricity to the moment.

Why not? she thought as his lips met hers.

When he pulled away briefly, she looked into his eyes. For an instant she had the undeniable sensation that something was wrong. With a sinking feeling she realized that she didn't want to be looking into Traeger's dark, enigmatic eyes at that moment. She wanted to be looking into Sam's.

When C.J. got home, she tiptoed as quietly as possible into the living room. But as she neared the sofa, she realized she shouldn't have bothered. Sam wasn't asleep on it.

A hard lump tightened in her throat and she had to fight back the sharp stiletto pain of realization that Sam must still be with Lynn. And since it was past eleven o'clock, and Lynn was a fast worker, that could mean only one thing.

Well, of course, she told herself bitterly, what else should she have expected? What did she think he would do? Was he supposed to say "Sorry, ma'am, this ain't my style." She was a fool. A total, complete, certifiable idiot. She deserved all the bad luck she'd ever had with men because she'd brought it on herself by being stupid, stubborn, gullible . . .

The thin sliver of light under the closed kitchen door caught her attention. She heard the soft murmur of voices. Surely he wouldn't dare bring Lynn back here to watch the fireworks.

With rising anger she thought, I'll show them some fireworks!

She pushed open the door, then stopped abruptly.

"Hello, sweetie," Lucy greeted her warmly, waving a forkful of chocolate cake at her. "Did you have fun? You're back awful early."

C.J. gave Cody and her mother a weak smile. "Sure, it was *swell*."

Lucy clearly wasn't fooled. "About as *swell* a time as Sam must have had."

"Sam? He's back?"

"Hmmm," Lucy answered with a smug expression. "I think he's around here someplace."

"Don't tease her, Lucy," Cody said with a grin. "He's takin' a walk along the beach. Said he wanted to look at the fireworks. See if you can catch up with him," he suggested with a wink.

C.J. tried to look as though she couldn't care less. She said casually, "Maybe I will. It's a little warm in here tonight anyway. It's bound to be cooler out by the water."

"That all depends on what kind of fireworks you find," Lucy said.

She gave her mother a dark look as she slipped off her satin heels and kicked them across the floor. Then she headed for the beach, questions churning through her thoughts. Why had Sam come home so early? Did that mean that Lynn had come on to him, or that she hadn't?

The usual Fourth of July crowd was nothing if not loyal. Even this late, the beach was packed. Bonfires dotted the sand. People sat huddled in blankets and beach towels, laughing, singing. Another volley of fireworks zipped aloft and burst in a rainbow of color overhead.

The Parks Department sponsored the fireworks each year and usually started around nine o'clock and finished sometime before midnight. In years past, people remained on the beach long after the last of the fireworks had exploded in a hail of bright light. Come morning the stragglers could be found huddled inside sleeping bags and blankets as the surf rolled in.

Couples strolled along arm in arm, children were running around, families shared late-night picnic meals. C.J. almost turned back. It was absurd thinking she could find Sam in this sea of humanity, more absurd when she tried to think what she would say to him. But she walked on, the sand pushing up through her toes. Out on the water all the colors of the exploding sky were reflected back on cresting waves. It was a beautiful sight.

Then she saw him. She would have known that dark silhouette anywhere. It was that lanky stance, his wide shoulders thrown back while he gazed overhead. The breeze off the ocean caught at his longish hair, whipping it around his head. His hands were on his hips, his weight shifted back on one leg. Looking at him now, she wondered why he was so different from all the other men who'd gone in and out of her life, leaving nothing more than a pleasant memory or a tiny emotional scar.

Was it simply that he was from another time? Was it an odd fascination for someone who was a little different? No, a *lot* different.

She didn't think so. At first she'd thought of him as a strange but interesting phenomenon, an incredible oddity of nature and circumstance. But in the past few days, with everything they'd been through together, she'd been forced to see him as a human being just like anyone else.

With feelings and emotions like anyone else. But a male human being. A *very* male human being.

What was it about him that appealed so strongly to her? What was it that she wanted in a man, that other men hadn't been able to fulfill? What did any woman want? God knows Freud had asked that question a hundred times in frustration.

After knowing Sam, C.J. thought she was beginning to have a clue. Maybe women wanted a man they could lean on when they needed to, but someone who would let them be strong too. Maybe women wanted a man who made them feel like they were all woman. Maybe women wanted simple kindness.

She'd found all those things in Sam.

He turned and caught her watching him. "Katy?"

He had a way of saying her name that slipped around her defenses.

"You're back." His eyes were inscrutable in the darkness broken only by the flickering light from nearby campfires.

She was at a loss for a moment. "Yes, I'm back. I guess we're both back." It was small talk of the worst kind and only made her all the more uncomfortable. The silence stretched out to a full minute, too, then three. She was dying to know how his date with Lynn had gone, but her pride wouldn't allow her to ask.

One big beach party surrounded them, but C.J. had never felt so lonely in all her life. Finally, when the silence was almost unbearable, Sam said, "That Lynn's really something."

It wasn't exactly what C.J. expected. Because she didn't know how to interpret it, she snapped back at him, "She's a barracuda. If you knew anything about modern women, you'd have seen that immediately." The minute it was out of her mouth, she could have kicked herself. The last thing she wanted was to sound like a nagging, possessive female.

The light from a nearby fire flickered across Sam's chiseled features. "Oh, I think I've learned a thing or two about modern women. I'm not quite certain what the word *barracuda* means, but I think I have a pretty good idea."

C.J. dug her toes into the sand. Get it all out, she told herself. Get it all out, in the open—don't hold back now.

"And another thing," she went on, unable to stop herself, "she just wants to use you, you know. Men are toys to Lynn. She doesn't give a rat's ass about anyone."

The corners of Sam's mouth quirked in the beginning of a smile. "I know."

C.J. stopped short. "What?"

"I said, I know."

She'd been prepared to argue with him. That seemed to be what they did best lately. With that remark, she didn't know what to say. "So . . . what happened . . . ?" She winced. God, she hated the way that sounded, as if Sam had to account to her for his evening. What was the matter with her anyway?

"So I thanked her politely for the dinner, even though I was still hungry afterward, and came home."

Home. That one small word affected her profoundly. He thought of her place as home.

"I see."

There was a wild hoot of excitement from down the beach. It appeared the organizers were ready to launch the final fireworks display of the evening. She jerked back around as Sam repeated his question.

"How was your evening with Traeger?"

She couldn't see the anger, but she could feel it in the way his words whipped out impatiently. The question was meant to be as casual as hers, but his voice hardened around Traeger's name.

"It was all right." She made circles in the sand with her toes. "He took me out to his beach house."

"And?"

C.J. shifted her shoulders, bare above the plunging neckline of the designer gown she'd borrowed.

"So I like the view from here better."

Sam nodded as he flicked his cigarette down into the wet sand and crushed it out. His eyes were thoughtful when he looked back up at her again. "Maybe now you realize I'm right about him." The words hissed out over the restless sound of the water and the explosive noise of the fireworks.

She squared her shoulders and raised her chin stubbornly. They were back to the same old argument.

"Maybe I was wrong about the view," she said stiffly, and turned to walk back to the house.

Sam reached out, stopping her with a hand on her arm. It was as if she'd been touched by fire.

Behind them, the last round of fireworks soared into the night sky. The air erupted in a series of loud explosions and brilliant lights. People cheered while pointing out the dazzling display in a midnight sky. It was like standing under a rainbow at night.

Sam took a step closer, bringing his hand up along her arm. For one timeless moment they stood there, facing each other. C.J. looked into those blue-green eyes, knew she was lost, and didn't care.

His fingers fanned across her cheek while his thumb caressed her lower lip. It was the most innocent of contacts, yet it sent shock waves through her. When he brought his other hand up to cradle her face, her breath shuddered in her throat. She should pull back and walk away from him. But she would be a liar if she tried to make anyone—least of all herself—believe she hadn't thought of this moment, hadn't wondered what it might be like and longed for it.

She thought she knew Sam, at least bits and pieces of him. He was a hard man, who had lived a hard, unforgiving life in his own time. He was used to living on the edge. Because of who and what he was, she'd prepared herself for untamed passion when he touched her. But nothing of what she thought she knew about Sam Hackett prepared her for this.

He slid his right hand behind her neck, clutching the soft waves of her hair in his fingers and pulling her head back. She brought her hands up against his hard-muscled chest. She'd always told herself that what she wanted from a man was tenderness, understanding, a connection of minds. But there was none of that in Sam at that moment.

There was just raw physical need and her response to that need.

She felt herself going under. He forced her to look him in the eye just before his mouth closed over hers. In that one moment the bright sky was blocked out and she was plunged into the darkest night.

His arm went around her, molding her against his body, leaving nothing to the imagination about the desire that spiraled through them both.

Once, when she was twelve, caught between childhood and young womanhood, rushing toward one, reluctant to leave the other behind, she had dreamed that a kiss would be like this. Somewhere along the way she'd reluctantly decided that this sort of consuming passion didn't exist.

It *did* exist.

His mouth was on hers, his tongue invading her, arousing her in a way she hadn't known she could be aroused, weakening her in ways she hadn't known she could be weakened.

Her hands were on his shoulders, holding on to him as the night exploded around them, and inside her. He tasted hot, of the salty ocean breeze and smoke from the crushed cigarette. The tastes mingled into something wild and dangerous. She twisted her fingers in his long, thick hair.

Sam had resisted challenges before, but he'd be damned if he'd resist this one. It had been coming a long time. Every time he looked at her, each time he turned and found those dark, whiskey-colored eyes fastened on him without the least bit of embarrassment or shyness, he'd known it would happen.

In spite of Traeger, and all the craziness of how he came to be there, or maybe because of it, he was powerless to stop what was happening now. He'd always been his own man, always taken what he wanted, then walked away, always been independent, in control, not hindered by emotions he didn't want to feel. Now he felt anger burn inside him. He had wanted to hurt her for going to Traeger tonight, wanted to punish her. But he was the one who was hurting, he was being punished.

C.J. moaned softly. Her arms were around his neck, pulling him closer, pulling him in. And her mouth . . . sweet Jesus, she *was* like whiskey, honeyed whiskey—wild, dark, and intoxicating. He wanted to drown himself in her. And like a drowning man, he struggled one last time to the surface, jerking her away from him.

"I guess you just wanted to find out how that might compare to Traeger," he said cruelly, his eyes glittering with the last of the exploding light in the sky.

C.J. stared at him, shaken, her thoughts refusing to come together. She moistened her slightly bruised lips.

"No, I . . . you don't understand . . . I wanted . . ." She started to say she'd wanted him to kiss her . . . wanted *him*. But his anger pulled him away.

Sam said tightly, "Well, now you know."

Chapter 12

Dan Prescott's ranch was a two-hour drive from Venice, tucked back in a rural area of the foothills called Canyon Country. A paved road ended abruptly at a wide steel gate and fence. On the other side of the gate a dirt road disappeared over a low rise.

It was just past ten o'clock in the morning and the day was already warm as C.J. and Sam came to a stop before the gate. It was a different heat than in the city. The air was clean and faintly pungent with the aroma of dry weeds and brush instead of concrete, asphalt, and exhaust fumes.

As C.J. looked beyond the gate, Sam asked with undisguised amusement, "Think this thing can make it over that road?"

It was the first time either of them had spoken during the entire drive from the city. They had sat next to each other in uncomfortable silence, both thinking about the night before, and neither willing to face it. C.J. hadn't gotten much sleep, and she suspected Sam hadn't either. Several times during the drive he stifled yawns, and there were dark circles under his eyes.

She was relieved that he finally broke the tension of their silence. She knew exactly what he was thinking now—under the circumstances, a horse would have been more reliable than her car.

She frowned. "I wonder if my roadside service covers damage from wagon trails full of cow patties."

Sam adjusted his hat lower over his eyes against the heat of the sun. "Roadside service?"

"Never mind. We won't need it. My car isn't going to

break down." There was more hope than conviction in her tone. She went on. "Will you get that gate, please?"

As he got out of the car and strode toward the gate, she thought how new everything was to Sam. Even the smallest or most mundane things seemed somehow special when she saw them through his eyes. It made her realize just how much she took for granted all the modern conveniences that made life in the late twentieth century bearable.

Sam swung open the gate and held it as C.J. drove past. Then, closing it, he got back into the car. "Cody said the ranch house is about ten miles along this road. How about if I drive?"

She gave him a startled look. "You?"

"Sure, Lucy's been teaching me in that little red contraption of hers."

He gave C.J. a sideways glance, his eyes shading darker green. Reaching across, he slipped his hand over hers on the gearshift.

"First gear, second, third, and fourth. Reverse is someplace else."

"It's in a different position on my car," C.J. explained as Sam's hand rested over hers with a slight pressure. She felt the scrape of callused skin, roughened by hard weather, hard work, and hard times. Yet the way his fingers curved gently over hers made her realize there was uncommon tenderness in those hands as well as strength. Somehow it made her feel reassured and protected.

She looked across at Sam, and for an instant her breath caught in her throat. It was just like last night on the beach, when his eyes had seemed to look right through her. It had been dark then, with only an occasional burst of light from the fireworks and bonfires, but she could see his eyes change color, the green overshadowing the blue as his mood changed.

He looked at her as if he saw something other men didn't see when they looked at her.

"What are you so skittish about, Katy?"

There it was again—that look in his eyes, the shift in the timbre of his voice. It was like a gift, something very special, just for her.

She couldn't handle it. Concentrating on driving down the rutted dirt road, she snapped, "I'm not skittish."

Sam's lips curved in a faint smile that somehow managed to turn itself down at one corner, as if he'd played a joke on someone. C.J. just wasn't sure if the joke was on her or him.

"Just drive, Katy, and try to keep this thing on the road, what there is of it."

She shoved the accelerator to the floor, and felt a thrill of satisfaction as the rear wheels of the Mustang dug into the soft dirt, churning up billowing clouds of dust in their wake. As the car fishtailed and bumped down the road, C.J. noted with satisfaction that Sam, bracing himself against the dashboard, was noticeably pale.

She knew Canyon Country fairly well. In recent years it had become the in place for actors who wanted to live within commuting distance of the studios but unconnected to the typical Hollywood life-style. Their "ranches" usually amounted to no more than five or ten acres. But Prescott's ranch was truly that—a hundred acres of fenced pasture and corrals, rolling foothills dotted with gnarled oak trees and scrub brush.

Cody had told her the house was over a hundred years old, and had neither electricity nor running water. Still, she was unprepared for the primitive level of the accommodations when they finally reached the house. She shook her head as she inspected the privy as Sam called it, an outhouse a hundred yards downwind of the house. Straight out of a western movie, it had a crescent moon cut into one wall, the circle of the sun into the one opposite.

The house was a true old-time ranch house with a wooden front porch that spanned the west side, looking out onto the barn and corrals beyond. There were three small rooms, and a pantry that adjoined the kitchen on the shady side of the house. C.J. was intrigued with what Sam told her was a "cooler," a large cupboard vented to the outside with mesh screen to keep it cool—in essence, an old-fashioned icebox.

The wood stove in the kitchen was clearly used to heat the entire house as well as to cook. The kitchen, dining area, and living room all blended into one room about fifteen feet wide by twenty feet long. Woven Mexican blankets covered the horsehair sofa and the rocking chair. One wall of the living room was covered by shelves of books and a large gun case.

There was one small bedroom upstairs.

For the next hour C.J. carefully inspected the house, rummaging through every drawer, reading every scrap of paper, and hurriedly skimming through the books to see if any papers were hidden in them. She checked the wooden floor for signs of a secret hiding place, and tore apart the bed.

Finally, dusty, exhausted, and frustrated, she gave up. There was nothing unusual here, no evidence or clues to explain Dan Prescott's murder.

She walked out onto the porch just as Sam came up from the nearest pasture, where he'd been tending to the livestock—two horses, several head of cattle, and a goat. As she watched him walk up the slight incline toward the house, she was struck by the strangest sensation. It was as if *she* were the time traveler, out of her own element and thrust suddenly into his.

Sam looked perfectly natural and at ease as he came toward her with his long-legged, easy stride, his hat pushed back on his head. He smiled at her. "Katy."

As always, it felt strange being called that. Not bad strange, just uncomfortable strange. And at the same time, kind of nice.

Unable to quite meet his look, she tucked unsteady hands in her jeans pockets and gazed out at the view.

Coming to stand beside her on the porch, he asked, "Find anything?"

"Nothing. How about you?"

He grinned as the late-morning sun cast strong shadows on his rugged features. "Some real hungry cattle and a right ornery buckskin gelding that needs to be ridden. I imagine the grazing gets a little slim during this part of the summer. I gave them some grain from the barn."

He seemed so perfectly at ease, in a way she'd never seen before. The wariness was gone, and his body was relaxed. She realized that out here, in the peace and quiet of the country, in a setting that must seem very much like home to him, he didn't have to be constantly braced for the next surprise.

"Do you miss your family's farm?" she asked.

She was relieved to see that the question didn't seem to bother him. He answered easily, "Farmin' and ranchin' aren't quite the same thing. I don't miss farmin'. Never could get any real interest in turning over a piece of dirt. But ranchin' is something else again. Especially if you can bring in some decent stock and start building something."

"The way Dan Prescott planned?"

"Maybe."

He was silent for a long moment, then said, "Sure is peaceful out here." Suddenly he looked alert. "Hear that?"

She listened intently but heard nothing. She was about to shrug her shoulders when she heard a soft hissing sound followed by a pop. "Is it a snake?" she asked nervously.

He grinned broadly. "There are probably snakes out here somewhere, but that, Katy, just happens to be quail. Cody said there was good hunting up here."

C.J. immediately conjured up images of adorable little feathered quails with topknots that kept falling in their faces as they scurried along in a line. "Why would anyone want to kill them?" she demanded.

"To eat, of course. Quail is mighty fine, roasted over an open fire or cooked slow in a stove."

C.J. couldn't imagine eating anything that didn't come wrapped in plastic on little Styrofoam trays. "I think I'll pass on the quail."

Amusement played across Sam's features. "Adapt and overcome, Katy."

"I couldn't eat anything that stared back at me accusingly."

"You prefer that plastic food we had at that place— what was it called? Mc-something?"

"The food wasn't plastic, the furniture was." Changing the subject, she went on. "Maybe we should search the barn. Prescott might have hidden something there."

Sam shook his head. "I already looked in the barn.

Nothing there but some harness and a couple of saddles."
He gave her a speculative look. "Cody said to make
ourselves at home. Think you could handle a real
mustang?"

C.J. tried to sound blasé, as if she went riding every
day of her life. "Sure."

"There's a gentle-looking mare who's probably about
your age. How about goin' for a ride?"

Determined not to be outdone by Sam, she said
blithely, "Why not? There's nothing more to do here."

Actually, the last time she'd ridden a horse was when
she was seven, during one of the rare times when her father
drifted back into her life. He took her to the fair, and she
rode around and around in a circle on a pony tied to another
pony in front of it.

Though she realized that Sam wouldn't consider that
riding, she told herself that the real thing couldn't be much
more difficult.

Over the next three hours she discovered just how
difficult it could be as she felt her backside getting more and
more sore. They rode the boundaries of Prescott's ranch,
crossing rolling foothills dotted with a few head of cattle and
some half-grown calves. A shallow creek meandered lazily
through a stand of spreading oaks.

In spite of her discomfort, C.J. was caught unaware by
the appeal of the country they were exploring. It was in
such stark contrast to L.A., or the beach at Venice. Heat
shimmered across the pristine blue sky and the dusty-dry
brown hills. A lone red-tailed hawk circled slowly overhead
on an updraft of wind.

There was nothing out there but a few cattle, an
occasional jackrabbit or coyote, and the two of them. They
might have been the only two people in the world.
Strangely enough, it was a pleasant feeling.

Sam seemed comfortable. When C.J. had first met
him, he'd been openly fearful. Then the fear had turned to
wariness. It was always there, as if he were constantly
looking over his shoulder, waiting for something to happen.

Of course, that was perfectly understandable under
the circumstances. Being transported over a hundred years

into the future was bound to make anyone a little anxious.

Now, for the first time, Sam seemed truly relaxed. She saw it in his smile, which came more readily, the ease with which he held the reins laced between his fingers, the easy sway of his body in tune with the rhythm of the buckskin's gait.

Sam was home—at least as close to home as he could get in this century.

He brought his horse to a halt. "We'd better rest the horses before heading back."

He dismounted beside the narrow creek. As he looked over his saddle at C.J., his mouth twisted into an easy smile. His eyes were shaded by the stained brim of his hat, making it impossible to see the expression in them. But it was all too obvious what he was feeling—sheer, unadulterated happiness.

He tied the buckskin to the low-hanging branch of an oak tree, then came around as she brought her mare to a halt by the same tree. "Need some help?"

"Of course not." Grabbing the pommel of the saddle as Sam had shown her back at the ranch house, she tried to swing her right leg over the mare's rump. It was an undignified position, made even worse by the fact that her legs trembled. She wasn't in shape for this. Her thigh muscles protested painfully, and her rear end was numb.

If she felt this bad now, she wondered, how would she feel by the time they got back to the house?

As she sat awkwardly, half in the saddle, half out of it, knowing that she looked like a fool, she felt the gentle pressure of Sam's fingers on her left thigh. "Sit back in the saddle," he ordered. "Now, lean back, bring your right leg across the front of the saddle at the same time you kick your left foot out of the stirrup, and just slide to the ground."

"Just like that, huh?" She was mortified beyond description. Thank God her mother wasn't around to witness this. Ever since Lucy had taken up body building, she'd been after C.J. to start exercising. C.J. had insisted that she got all the exercise she needed running around on her job. Now, every bone, muscle, and sinew from the waist down was predicting she'd never walk again.

Too exhausted, not to mention embarrassed, to argue, she followed Sam's instructions. Swinging her right leg across the front of the saddle wasn't too difficult. Then she freed her left foot from the stirrup and, as Sam had predicted, simply slid down the side of the horse to the ground.

Her legs were so shaky she would have crumpled in a pathetic heap if Sam's hands hadn't closed firmly around her waist. "It takes some getting used to," he said quietly.

Anyone else, including her mother, would have made some deprecating remark. But Sam simply stood there, holding her, taking her weight against his as she leaned into him for support.

"Yeah, well, it's been a while since I rode," she admitted in something of an understatement.

He had rolled up his shirt-sleeves on this warm day, and as her hands grasped his forearms she felt the soft hair on his arms and the hard muscles underneath the skin. She was steadier now, but instead of releasing her, Sam continued to hold her, his fingers clasping her waist.

Desire—as white-hot as the sun beating down—rocked her. Her senses filled with Sam—the strength as well as tenderness in those callused hands, his distinctly male scent mingled with the rich aroma of worn leather. With disturbing clarity she remembered the taste of him as they'd kissed last night.

She wanted to kiss him again here, now, in this place where he put up no barriers. The force of her sudden desire frightened her, and she pulled back from him.

Running her fingers through her tousled hair, she moistened her dry lips nervously and said, "I—I could use a drink of water."

Sam stared at her in absolute silence for a long moment, then said, "That creek looks safe enough. It moves pretty good."

C.J. laughed to break the tension she felt tightening every muscle taut as a cord in her body. "You don't know L.A. water. But I guess this must be okay. The cattle don't look like they're dropping dead."

Kneeling on a rock, she splashed water over her face and neck, then sipped water from her cupped hand.

"*Katy.*"

He'd felt it too. She could tell from the husky timbre of his voice.

But she couldn't handle it. A kiss on a public beach, with other people around, was one thing. This was something else again.

She said hurriedly, "The water tastes different out here. No chlorine."

Sam said nothing. He allowed her horse to drink, then tethered it to the oak tree. But he continued to look at her with a thoughtful expression.

Something in his look made her feel intensely uncomfortable. She'd never felt quite this way before with a man. It went beyond physical desire, and that frightened her.

Turning away from that disconcerting gaze, she found a place to sit on a sun-warmed rock at the edge of the creek. Picking up several pebbles, she tossed them, one after another, into the water.

Sam sat down beside her, idly chewing on a long shaft of golden grass, rolling it between his thumb and forefinger. He said slowly, "When I met Dan Prescott's grandfather, Rollie, he was living in town. Why would his family move all the way out here when he died?"

"His widow may not have been able to afford the place in town."

"But if she sold it, she should've gotten a lot of money for it. There was a lot of land."

Since C.J. had been raised by a divorced mother who struggled to support her without any help from C.J.'s father, she knew how tough it could be on a single mother. It hadn't been easy for her and Lucy, and it probably hadn't been easy on Rollie Prescott's widow and children.

"Maybe she thought it would be better to raise her children in the country, away from the city," C.J. said.

"She just had the one son. What was his name? Matthew. Now, why would she bring him all the way out here, to land that isn't good enough to farm? The best she could do was put a few head of cattle on it. And even at that, the way it dries up in the summer she'd have to buy feed. And that costs a lot."

He shook his head in frustration. "Doesn't make sense. Rollie's widow should've been able to do better for herself and her son."

"What are you suggesting?"

"I don't know," he admitted. He glanced at the sun, beginning its descent in the west. "We'd better get back to the house. It's getting late."

They rode back without speaking, both content to listen to the late afternoon silence dissolve into the early evening sounds of crickets, frogs, and birds. It was so peaceful and lovely out here, C.J. thought wistfully. The closer they got to the house, the more reluctant she felt to return to the city with its traffic, noise, and pollution.

But she had a case to solve. She had to get back.

At the house Sam unsaddled the horses, then put them in the corral and fed them. After stowing the saddles in the tack room in the barn, he walked toward C.J., who waited in the car. His long, lithe shadow mingled with the many shadows of evening falling gently over the landscape.

When he got in the car, she turned the key in the ignition. The starter ground slowly. She flicked it off, then tried again, making a mental note to add a new starter to the long list of things to be fixed on her car.

This time it slowed even more, and the lights on the instrument panel dulled to a faint glow. C.J. pumped the accelerator furiously, switched the ignition off again, then tried it once more. This time it ground to silence.

"Damn!"

Sam frowned. "What's wrong?"

C.J. gave him a withering glance. "Obviously, it won't start."

"Why not?"

She started to reply sarcastically, "Because it's dead," then stopped. *Why* was it dead? It had been working fine just a few hours earlier. There was no reason for it to do this.

Unless someone had tampered with it.

C.J. thought hard. She and Sam had been out riding

for several hours—more than enough time for someone to come here, tamper with the car, then leave.

Why?

Obviously, so she and Sam would be stranded in the middle of nowhere, with no telephone, no way to summon help. At that moment she would have given her collector's edition of *Sgt. Pepper's Lonely Hearts Club Band* for one phone call—just one.

"This is just great!" she snapped irritably. "No phone, no jumper cables, no other car even if I had a set of jumper cables."

She folded her arms across her chest in a gesture that was part helplessness and part frustration.

Who would do a thing like this to them?

Someone who knew they were coming out here. Someone who knew how isolated the ranch was, and that there was no telephone for miles.

Cody.

No, it couldn't be. Not Cody. Not that nice old cowboy. He was Dan Prescott's friend. He was dating Lucy. C.J. was just letting her imagination run away with her. Her car had died of natural causes. Period.

Sam said, "Looks like we're gonna be spending the night here. We'd better go inside and figure out what we're gonna do about dinner."

As C.J. went inside, she told herself not to be ridiculous. There was nothing to be afraid of.

But she couldn't help wondering if someone *had* tampered with the car. And, if so, was that person still close by, waiting, watching?

Chapter 13

As Sam watched Katy walk toward the house, he recognized that stubborn tilt to her chin. He'd come to know it quite well in the past week or so. He also recognized the expression in her eyes. She was scared, but she wasn't about to admit it.

One thing for sure, this wasn't a simple, uncomplicated woman. There were more twists and turns to her than a green-broke pony. He was beginning to discover that he liked some of those twists and turns. Like the shyness he'd seen in her eyes as they sat by the creek. For just a brief, fleeting moment, he recognized the same thing he'd seen in her eyes last night on the beach, when she'd wanted him to kiss her but was determined not to show it.

She'd wanted him to kiss her this afternoon too. He'd held back for reasons he didn't entirely understand. He knew only that he'd been shaken pretty badly last night when things seemed to move between them with all the sudden, unexpected force of an earthquake.

Katy could set everything and everyone at a distance one minute with just one of those looks of hers. At those times she kept her feelings all shut up inside. Then there were the other times when he knew exactly what she was feeling and thinking by the way she got all excited when she talked, waving her arms around, riding high on pure emotion.

As he followed her into the house, he decided he preferred the emotional times, volatile as they were. At those times she was completely honest, because she didn't have time to think about things, she just did them, acting from the heart.

Inside the house C.J. stopped and looked around at the rustic decor. "Maybe we could ride the horses to the nearest phone," she suggested half-heartedly.

Sam understood her reluctance in even making the suggestion. Her backside must be hurting real bad. Despite what she'd said, it had been immediately obvious to him that she wasn't an experienced rider.

"That's out of the question, at least for tonight," he replied.

"Why?"

"They're wore out from the ride today. We could try it in the morning, when they've rested up."

C.J. looked at him sharply. "You think I'm the one who needs to rest."

Ignoring the accusation, which was perfectly true, Sam went on. "How many miles would you say it is to the nearest town?"

"Forty or fifty miles."

Sam leaned against the wall, his booted feet crossed at the ankles, his arms folded. "Shouldn't take more than two or three days, then. Two, if we travel by night too. But that can be dangerous."

"What?"

"Sure. We can only go twenty to twenty-five miles a day without hurtin' the horses."

Frustration was apparent in her blazing eyes and tightly clenched fists. "This is why they invented the automobile! A far superior form of transportation."

"Except when it doesn't work," Sam pointed out.

C.J. collapsed on the sofa, flinging her head back and staring at the ceiling. "I don't believe this." She sighed heavily, then looked over at Sam. "Are you sure we can't ride out tonight? Maybe after the horses rest for an hour or two?"

"I'm not setting out in unfamiliar territory at night on horses that are winded. Any number of things could happen."

"This is 1989, Marshal. The Indians are not on the

warpath anymore. We're not likely to run into a raiding party."

"I'm not worried about Indians. Besides, they wouldn't be after me."

"Meaning?"

"They like white squaws. I'd just hand you over and be done with it." He went on matter-of-factly. "It's you or my scalp, and I'm pretty attached to it."

At her look of consternation, a slow grin spread across his face. "I'm just teasing, Katy."

She didn't crack a smile. "Very funny. Look, we've got to get back as soon as possible. I've got to give the police the information about Gloria Ames dealing drugs. If they can prove it, maybe they can pressure her into revealing what she knows about Prescott's murder. I'm convinced she's holding back something."

"I understand. I'm eager to get back on the case too. But we can't do anything about it tonight."

Suddenly he remembered something. "Wait a minute. Didn't Cody say he was coming out here tomorrow morning to check on the livestock?"

C.J.'s gloom lifted in an instant. "Yeah! Thank God. He can give us a ride into town."

"Okay, so that's settled, then. We've just got to get through tonight. It won't be so bad. This place is a sight more comfortable than sleeping on the ground."

She obviously didn't share his enthusiasm for Prescott's home. Sam continued reassuringly. "I'll build a fire in that stove and you rustle us up some grub."

"All right," she agreed reluctantly. As she rose and headed into the kitchen, she murmured, "I just hope there's something here besides beans."

Sam stood watching her thoughtfully for a moment. She was clearly very reluctant to spend the night here. Actually, it was more than mere reluctance. She was afraid. Why? he wondered. Sure, it was irritating that the car wouldn't start, but he had the impression that wasn't an unusual occurrence with cars, especially Katy's.

As he went outside to gather firewood for the stove, he

tried to figure out why Katy was so afraid and was trying so hard not to show it.

It was worse than C.J. could have imagined. True to his word, Sam built a fire in the wood stove. It belched out clouds of black smoke. Only then did she understand what Sam had meant when he told her to open the damper that vented the smoke out of the house.

Tears stung her eyes as she choked on the smoke. With an efficiency of movement that never failed to amaze her, Sam reached over and turned the lever at the side of the stovepipe. Smoke immediately stopped pouring out of the stove.

"Sorry," she gasped as she stood in the doorway open to the outside, gulping in deep breaths of fresh air.

"Didn't your mother teach you anything?" Sam asked as he threw open the windows in the kitchen and living room.

"Lucy? You must be kidding. She doesn't cook. She's into fruits and berries and grains. If it isn't right off the vine, the tree, or the natural foods shelf at the health food store, she won't touch it. She's a vegetarian."

"Vegetation?" Sam asked quizzically.

C.J. grinned. "*Vegetarian*. It's sort of like grazing instead of eating."

"But she made fried chicken last night."

"For Cody. She's no fool." Noticing that Sam seemed to be staring at her, she asked, "What's wrong?"

"It looks like we're going to need a lot of hot water tonight. I better fill that hot water chamber on the stove."

"Why?" C.J. crossed to the washroom at the back of the kitchen and looked in the small round mirror hanging above the washbowl. "Oh, my God, I look like a raccoon!"

Her face was covered with soot, except for white rings around her eyes and mouth.

"Do you always cook in disguise?" Sam quipped.

C.J. glared at him.

"I think I'll get that water now," he went on, fighting back a grin.

A half hour later he was pouring steaming water from

the stove into the tin tub in the washroom. "A hot bath feels real good when you're saddle sore," he said.

C.J. was too tired and sore to pretend any longer that she felt no aftereffects of their ride. "Sounds heavenly."

"What did you find in the pantry?" he asked as he set down the empty pail.

Sitting down on a chair, she grimaced as she pulled off her shoes. "Canned peaches and canned beans, and canned beans and canned peaches."

"That's quite a choice."

She looked up at him, standing in the doorway to the washroom, his wide-shouldered height filling the door frame. He did that, filled doorways and rooms just by being in them, as if they were somehow otherwise incomplete.

Sam said, "I need something a little more substantial, and I think you do too."

"There isn't anything else except some flour and sugar. And a little coffee."

"I'll take my rifle and see what I can do about improving the menu. Take your time and enjoy your bath."

The snap of the screen door swinging shut was followed by the heavy thump of his boots across the front porch. C.J. stripped off her jeans and shirt, then gently lowered herself into the tiny tub. She decided to take Sam's advice and enjoy this. There was certainly no reason to rush. They were stuck here until Cody showed up in the morning.

Nothing had ever felt as wonderful as that hot bath in the soft glow of light as the sunset edged down behind distant hills. Heat from the stove radiated through the open doorway of the washroom. Water lapped under her chin as she laid her head back against the rim and closed her eyes.

She didn't know how long she slept. Suddenly she jerked awake at the sound of a single rifle shot. A few minutes later Sam came into the kitchen, carrying something in a flour sack.

"What did you get?" she called out.

"You'll see. Take your time with your bath. This'll take a while to cook."

Leaning her head back against the rim of the tub, she

closed her eyes again. She heard Sam rummaging around the kitchen. There was the sharp metallic sound of the oven door being opened and closed. She wondered if Sam was heating more water so he could take a bath. The thought of Sam with his long legs partially submerged in this same tub was deliciously erotic. C.J. let herself go with the image, wondering if it was possible for two people to fit in the tub together . . .

Sensing a presence, she opened her eyes and found Sam standing in the doorway, watching her.

He said with a hint of humor in his low, husky voice, "You've been in there a long time. You'll get all wrinkled."

C.J.'s eyes widened as her lethargy abruptly left her. The water had cooled, but in spite of that she felt a heat that had nothing to do with water temperature. Feeling suddenly shy, she lowered her gaze.

To her complete surprise, Sam crossed the small room, leaned over the tub and, bracing his weight with one hand at the back of the tub, tilted her face up to his and gently brushed her lips with his.

She'd tasted fierce passion on those lips last night. It had been sudden, volatile, and spoke of needs that both excited and frightened her. This kiss was entirely different, slow, deliberate, gently teasing. Yet nonetheless dangerous in its own way.

Suddenly she felt awkward. Drawing back, she looked at Sam uncertainly. Until now she had set the boundaries and made the rules in her romantic encounters. It allowed her the freedom to end a relationship when she became disillusioned, as usually happened, and keep her pride intact if the man decided to end it.

But she knew Sam wouldn't allow her to play that game. And that scared her.

She wrapped her arms around her legs as she hugged them to her chest. "I'd better get out so you can have a turn."

Sam stood and held out a towel for her. As she took it, he turned and went back into the kitchen, saying over his shoulder, "I showered down at the well house."

C.J. was taken aback. *"Showered?"*

"Dan had a makeshift shower rigged up from the holding tank at the well. You got a better deal in that tub. It was damn cold at the well."

As C.J. watched Sam moving about the kitchen, she noticed telltale damp streaks in his hair and the way his shirt clung to his chest. Obviously he'd put his clothes back on without drying off.

When she padded barefoot into the kitchen, he asked, "Hungry?"

Breathing in a tantalizing aroma, she felt her stomach grumble in protest. She'd had nothing to eat aside from the jelly doughnut at breakfast. Whatever she was smelling wasn't beans.

"What smells so good?"

"I came up with something a little more substantial than peaches and beans." Smiling at her, he lifted the metal lid off a cast iron skillet. Inside, slowly turning a golden brown color, lay what looked like a small chicken.

C.J. couldn't believe it. Nothing had ever looked or smelled so good. "Where did you get chicken?" she asked in amazement.

"It isn't exactly chicken."

It was pheasant. She vaguely wondered if pheasant was in season. Sam, of course, knew nothing about hunting restrictions, and she decided not to tell him.

Whether it was legal or not, it was just about the best meal she had ever eaten. Sam made pan cornbread served with honey, beans with peppers from a small garden out back, and peaches with cinnamon. When they finished eating, Sam cleared the table and set the dishes to soak in hot water from the stove.

C.J. sat with her elbows propped on the rough wooden table, her chin resting on her clasped hands, watching Sam be surprisingly domestic. He moved around the kitchen with the same catlike grace with which he did everything. After putting several pieces of wood in the stove, he dried the dishes and put them away.

Then he joined her at the table, taking out a pack of cigarettes he'd found in the house, and inspecting it from end to end. "I always wondered when they'd get around to rolling 'em like they do cigars. Still, there's some pleasure to be had rolling your own after a good meal, or when you're sitting out on the porch, watching the day go down."

He lit up a cigarette, inhaled, then exhaled slowly. "Why don't we go out on the porch. There's something I want you to see."

She followed him out into the cool night air. Inside, kerosene lanterns hissed low and pooled soft light through the windows and open doorway onto the porch. In the distance loomed the dark outline of the barn. Beyond that lay nothing but darkness.

They sat down on the steps, side by side, and Sam said softly, "Listen to that—nothin' but night sounds—an owl, a coyote way off somewhere. It's nice, isn't it?"

C.J. nodded. It *was* nice. It had been so long since she'd gotten out of the city, she'd forgotten what peace and quiet were.

She glanced at Sam, who sat smoking, staring out into the night. "Are you sure you're a marshal?" she asked.

His eyes opened wide in surprise. "What do you mean?"

"It's just that tonight you don't fit the image. You know, someone who's tough, hard as nails, with a gun in his hand. A wanderer who doesn't want any ties and lives off the land. That doesn't fit with your skill in the kitchen."

Sam smiled. "You've been watching too many of those western movies. When you're on your own, like I've been, you get to be pretty good at managing some kind of grub for yourself. Out of necessity."

"So, you learned how to cook out of necessity?"

"Yeah," he chuckled, "the necessity of not getting my backside warmed when I was a kid at home. You see, my ma had a peculiar notion about things. It didn't matter whether it was boys or girls, or whether the chore was men's work or women's work. Everybody was expected to help out. I was the oldest, so naturally I was expected to help with the babies when they came along. That's how I learned how to cook and do laundry, along with hunting and some farming."

"*Some* farming?"

"As little as I could get away with," Sam confessed with a grin.

C.J. leaned back on her elbows and looked up at Sam. "I can't picture you washing clothes."

He laughed. "You have to, sometimes. Especially when you get to smelling worse than your horse."

He flicked his cigarette down into the dirt at the foot of the bottom step and crushed it beneath his boot heel. Then his left hand gently closed around hers as he pointed up into the night sky with his right.

"Look, Katy, that's what I wanted you to see."

She tilted her head back and looked up at the sky above them. It was huge, dark, and mysterious, like a black canopy blanketing the earth. Pinpoints of light twinkled overhead as stars emerged through wispy clouds. In the city the stars would be obscured by a blanket of smog. Here they could be seen clearly, and there seemed to be millions of them, more than C.J. had ever imagined. The vastness of space was soul-stirring.

"And to think man has actually walked on the moon," Sam said with all the wonder of a small boy. His voice was filled with such wistfulness that her skin tingled.

"You're cold," Sam remarked as his hand slid along her arm. "I'd better get you inside." His fingers laced briefly with hers as he got to his feet and pulled her along with him. "You take the bedroom upstairs. I'll bunk on the sofa."

Just like at home, C.J. thought as she undressed a few minutes later. She found an oversize nightshirt that must have belonged to Dan Prescott folded neatly on a chair by the bed. She curled up under a heavy quilt, then turned off the kerosene lamp she'd brought upstairs. As she lay in the darkness, she listened to Sam downstairs. She heard him kick off his boots and the sound of his weight on the worn sofa. Then there was only the night sounds and her own loneliness closing in on her.

As a modern woman she had learned that it was okay to express her sexuality, and necessary to take responsibility for it. She knew how to encourage sexual advances, or discourage them. If she wanted a man purely for physical reasons, she'd learned how to communicate that without embarrassment.

She had learned a lot. The only problem was that nothing of what she'd learned applied to Sam.

She was sure there were only two kinds of women in his eyes—the marrying kind and whores. While she wasn't ready to be the former, she couldn't bear it if Sam thought of her as the latter. The dreadful thing was that she wanted him. She wanted him in all the ways a woman could desire a man. But if she let him know it, he might think worse of her. She had come down to the foot of the stairs and stood just inside the opening into the living room, trying desperately to decide what to do. Finally, in sheer frustration, she turned to go back up the stairs.

"Katy?"

His voice coming from out of the darkness stopped her cold.

"Are you all right?" he went on, his tone concerned.

When she turned around, she found Sam standing so close she could reach out and touch him.

"I . . . it was a mistake . . ." Mortified beyond description, she started up the steps.

His hand reached out to close over hers, stopping her flight up the stairs. "Katy, what's wrong?"

There was such tenderness in his voice, and an implicit promise to take care of whatever was wrong, that she thought she would melt.

"Tell me," he coaxed her. His hand was warm against her cheek as he tilted her face toward his. The tip of his thumb caressed her bottom lip.

Her senses came alive. Every part of her was acutely aware of Sam's touch, his nearness. He had taken off his boots and shirt, and stood bare-chested, wearing only jeans. The muscles in his arms were lean and hard. His skin was tanned, except where a thick mat of dark hair covered his well-muscled chest.

She closed her eyes. God, how could she tell him? How could she explain that for the first time in her life she wished she wasn't worldly wise and experienced. She would give anything to be innocent so that she could experience love for the first time with Sam.

She felt tears welling up in her tightly shut eyes. Damn, she despised herself for crying, but she couldn't stop.

"What is it, Katy darlin', what's wrong?"

She opened her eyes and looked into his. "What I feel is wrong," she whispered, her throat aching.

He released her wrist and brought both hands to cradle her face, stroking away her tears with his thumbs. "What do you feel?"

Steeling herself to face his disapproval, she answered honestly, "I want you."

To her amazement he smiled gently, then his mouth lightly brushed hers, tasting the salt of her tears, giving unimaginable sweetness in return.

She closed her eyes again as Sam left her breathless with want, fascination, desire.

His hand slid around the back of her neck. With the gentlest of pressure he forced her to look at him.

"I know you must think I'm shameless—" she began.

"What's between us has nothing to do with shame."

His mouth was so close to hers now that she could feel his warm breath on her cheek.

"I know I'm probably not what you want a woman to be," she went on, her voice so low now it was barely audible.

"I didn't know what I wanted a woman to be until I met you."

And then his mouth was on hers in a soft, seeking kiss that seemed to go on forever. It ended, only to begin again. It was like riding the crest of a wave that kept getting better and better.

Sam ran his fingers through her hair. She looked at him with faint surprise and dawning innocence. Nothing she'd ever known of men applied to Sam. Where they rushed into sex, hoping to find desire, he built the desire first, patient enough to let it lead where it inevitably would.

His hands moved down to hers, then brought them to his chest, caressing her fingers with such rousing tenderness that her fingers curled into the soft mat of hair where his heart pounded against the palm of her hand.

Picking her up as easily as if she were a rag doll, he carried her upstairs to the big four-poster, then gently lay her down. Slowly he unbuttoned the nightshirt, then with exquisite care slid it off her body. C.J. shivered as she lay naked before him in the moonlight filtering through the window. She wasn't cold, however. Her skin was on fire.

Her arms closed around his neck as his hands explored her breasts . . . her waist . . . the curve of her hips. She molded her body to his, guided purely by desire, without calculation.

The words he murmured as his lips moved across her skin tumbled through her jagged thoughts. *Let me love you, Katy darlin'.*

He spoke her name over and over again, as if it were a magical incantation. When his mouth covered hers once more, she opened up to him completely, her tongue meeting his. She felt the jolt that went through his body the instant before he plunged back in, tasting, giving, taking.

Her skin burned where he touched her, ached where he hadn't yet touched. Even the cool night air wafting in through the open window couldn't dissipate the warmth spreading through her.

"Sam."

He pulled away for one brief moment to slip off his jeans, then lay down beside her. She reached for him, her hands eagerly following the contours of his hips and thighs. She felt his skin quiver beneath her touch, and she exulted in the response she could elicit within him.

Wanting more, she came up on her knees, raining soft moist kisses on the hard flat surface of his belly.

He groaned, then, taking her by the shoulders, lay her back on the bed. As he stared down at her, his face so very close to hers, she whispered, "Love me, Sam."

His hands tenderly stroked her hips, then moved slowly up the insides of her thighs. She arched against him, guiding his rough-skinned but gentle hands.

There was one breathless moment when he hovered

over her, skin barely touching skin, and then he was inside her.

He asked less of her than any man she'd ever known, and gave more than she'd ever believed possible. As she returned passion for passion, he reacted as if she were giving him a precious gift that he would treasure forever.

When, much later, she fell asleep in his arms, she felt as if she'd finally come home after a long, long journey.

Sometime before dawn she awoke to find Sam, dressed only in his jeans, squatting near the low window, peering out into the darkness.

"Sam?" she whispered uncertainly.

He motioned to her to be quiet. After a moment he said in a voice so low she could barely hear him, "Someone's out there."

She was immediately gripped by fear. "Oh, my God." It was true, then. Someone had purposefully disabled her car so she and Sam would be stranded here, alone, vulnerable.

Suddenly she heard the loud clattering sound of something being thrown against the house, and immediately afterward the sound of footsteps running away.

"Stay here!" Sam ordered before racing downstairs.

But she wasn't about to wait up there alone. Hurriedly pulling the nightshirt over her head, she followed him downstairs.

The porch was on fire.

And then there was the sickening stench of gasoline. It had been poured all around the outside of the house.

Grabbing a pail, Sam scooped water out of the tin bathtub and threw it over the rapidly growing flames. C.J. grabbed a large pitcher and did the same. Desperately, they raced back and forth, from the tub to the porch, dousing the flames. At first she didn't think they'd be able to contain them.

As they fought the fire, they heard the sound of a car starting up in the distance, on the other side of a low rise. Sam was clearly torn between grabbing his rifle and racing after their assailant and fighting the flames.

"We can't let this place burn!" C.J. shouted. The truth was, she didn't give a damn about Dan Prescott's house. She just didn't want Sam going out there, into the darkness, alone, after someone who had just tried to kill them.

Sam hesitated, then, muttering a curse, went back to throwing water on the flames.

It was all over so quickly, C.J. could barely believe it. One minute the flames seemed to be growing, licking the roof of the porch, and the next she and Sam had beaten them down to glowing embers. Relief flooded through her. But at the same time she felt a sick realization that if Sam hadn't awakened when he did, not only would the house have been lost, they would have been lost with it.

When he was sure the fire was out, Sam took his rifle, put on his boots, and set out in the direction the sound of the car had come from. C.J. knew it was hopeless, but she also knew that Sam had to find out for sure.

She went into the washroom and washed her face and hands in what little was left of the bathwater, then collapsed on the sofa, exhausted. A few minutes later Sam returned, looking frustrated.

"There were tire tracks, but he was long gone."

C.J. was silent. There was nothing to say.

After a moment Sam went on. "C'mon, let's go back to bed. It's almost dawn. He won't try anything more tonight."

But she noticed that he took his rifle and Colt upstairs with him. And when she finally fell into a fitful sleep, she knew he lay wide awake.

C.J. wasn't sure which was worse; the blinding glare of sunlight through the open window, or the rattle and backfire of Cody's old pickup. Both assaulted her senses and brought her rudely awake at a time of morning she usually considered indecent.

Looking around, she saw that Sam was gone. As Cody's pickup came to a halt in front of the house, she heard Sam's voice call out a greeting to him.

Dressing quickly, she went downstairs just as Sam was pouring a cup of coffee for Cody. The old wrangler looked grave, and C.J. assumed that Sam had already told him about the terrifying events of the night before.

Sam looked at C.J., then back at Cody. "Tell her," he said simply.

Cody pushed back his battered old Stetson and nodded his thanks as Sam handed him a cup of coffee. Then he let out a long, heavy sigh and said, "Gloria Ames is dead."

Chapter 14

They made the long ride back into Los Angeles in silence in Cody's battered old pickup. C.J. was wrestling with several new complications in her life. The news of Gloria Ames's death stunned her. It was the second death on the *Hard Country* production in only two weeks. The coincidence was too easy.

And then there was Sam.

As much as she tried to talk herself into believing that what happened between them should never have happened, the more she had to confront the fact that she had wanted it almost from the beginning. The problem here was Sam. He didn't belong in 1989. At the first chance, if it was possible, he would undoubtedly leave, like the other men in her life, only under slightly unusual circumstances—going back in time to 1882. It would have been so much easier if she had never gotten involved with him. But she had, and the fact that they had made love complicated it. Whether she wanted to admit it or not, the night with Sam was unlike anything she had ever experienced in her life.

He had the capacity to be strong yet tender, demanding yet giving. She'd expected urgency in their lovemaking. God knows she'd felt the need as much as he. Sensing it, he'd given them both what they wanted, but that had been only the beginning of what was to follow. They'd made love several times and each time she learned something new about Sam.

He treated her with a tenderness that filled her with a slowly building sense of urgency that was far more intense than that first quick rush of desire. He teased her, laughed with her, soothing her only to build her up again, until she begged him to take her. Only it wasn't begging with Sam, it was sharing, blending, losing herself in his strength only to feel renewed power when he filled her again and whispered his need of her. Sam made her feel things she'd never felt before—shadows, light and dark places deep inside that she never knew existed. It was wonderful and a little frightening.

Even now, as she sat in her office, the thought of what they had shared through the long hours of the night at the ranch heated her skin.

That disturbing thought was put aside as Lucy came in.

"Hi!" Lucy beamed as she threw her enormous woven straw shoulder bag over the back of a chair and dropped a ragged notebook down on the desk.

"I came by last night to see you, but you weren't here." She glanced pointedly at C.J. "I fed Redford and Newman. They were about to eat each other. You and Sam must have gotten back late last night."

C.J. looked up only briefly from the phone. "We spent the night out at Dan Prescott's ranch," she explained, then concentrated on her phone call.

Lucy's eyes widened at that enlightening piece of information. "Say, that is a good sign."

C.J. spoke briefly, jotted down some notes, then she hastily grabbed her purse as she headed for the door. "I'll be back later."

In her bedroom upstairs she put on clean clothes, then went into the bathroom and combed her hair and hastily fixed her makeup.

"C.J.? What's up?" Lucy stood in the doorway to the bathroom, eyeing her curiously.

"Can I use your car?" C.J. asked.

"Not Hello, Mother, it's good to see you, or Yes, Mother, we had a fantastic time and made love all night. What I get is Mother, can I use your car? Somehow I thought we left that all behind when you were sixteen and got your own car. Where's Sam and why are you wearing that boring suit? You look like a saleswoman for copy machines," Lucy grumbled as she followed C.J. from bathroom to closet, then to the bed, where C.J. sat down and slipped on conservative, low-heeled pumps. There was a bright flush of color on C.J.'s cheeks.

"I was right!" Lucy exclaimed excitedly. "You two did spend the night together!"

"I already told you that." C.J. sprang off the bed and went to her closet. Pulling a box off the top shelf, she took out thick glasses and shoved them into her purse.

Lucy's eyes were alight with curiosity. "What was it like?"

"Mother! I don't have time for this right now."

"I don't mean what was *it* like, I mean what was it *like*? You know, was it any different with a man who's over a hundred and thirty years old?"

C.J. gave her a withering look. "Where are your keys?"

"In the car," Lucy answered, "but . . ." Before she could continue, C.J. had turned and raced back down the outside stairs.

Lucy shook her head in exasperation as she followed C.J.

Just then Sam came walking up from the beach.

"Will somebody please explain what is going on?" Lucy demanded as Sam got into the MG.

Sam answered, "Gloria Ames is dead."

Lucy's eyes widened. "Dead?"

Sam glanced skeptically down at the MG.

"Do they make these things any smaller?" he asked sarcastically.

C.J. looked up at him with a faint smile as he pulled his long-legged frame into the passenger side. His knees were buckled between his chest and the dashboard. "This is about as small as it gets."

"Thank God."

He gave her a wry smile. "I suppose we don't have any other choice?"

"Not if you want to come with me."

"That's what I thought." He tried to get more comfortable in the seat. "Let's go."

She jammed the gearshift into reverse, grateful he didn't want to talk about last night.

"I need to talk to both of you," Lucy called out as she stepped back from the car. "I've found the answer—the way to get Sam back."

C.J. spun the MG out of the driveway.

"We'll talk later," she shouted back over her shoulder.

As the car leapt forward, Sam held on to his hat with one hand, the door handle with the other.

C.J. had never been to the coroner's office before. The interior of the building was spartan with countless doors, stark walls, and linoleum floors. The secretary at the front desk placed a quick call and then gave them instructions to go on back through the double doors to the adjoining examination rooms, laboratories, and the morgue storage area.

"The morgue?" Sam asked.

She nodded. "It's where they keep bodies. . . ."

"I know what a morgue is, Katy," Sam said. "I simply wondered if you really want to do this."

She nodded.

The assistant coroner was a qualified medical examiner. He was understaffed and overworked, undoubtedly dealt with far too many bureaucratic agencies, and wore a harassed expression when he greeted them.

"How can I help you?"

"I understand a woman by the name of Gloria Ames was brought here last night." C.J. swallowed back her uneasiness. "I'd like to see her."

"We've already had positive identification. Are you a member of the family?"

"Yes," C.J. lied, ignoring the surprised expression on Sam's face.

He led the way through a set of double doors. "Right this way."

C.J. took a deep breath and quickly followed before her courage evaporated. Sam was right behind her.

She had seen countless reruns of the old Jack Klugman series where he played an L.A. County coroner, and the comedy *Night Shift* that took place in a morgue. This was no comedy. Nothing on television or film could even come close to the feeling of walking into that cold, sterile room with white tile floors, and row upon row of steel refrigerator compartments recessed into the walls, each with a label.

C.J. swallowed hard as she and Sam followed the coroner to the far wall. Just like in the movies, he found the compartment with Gloria Ames's name on the end, released the latch, and pulled out the steel slab.

"We finished up on her this morning," the coroner explained quietly as he pulled back the stark white sheet. "She was pretty badly bruised up. There were multiple injuries."

As long as she lived, C.J. would never forget the sight of Gloria Ames on that cold steel rack. The gray pallor of her skin made the webbing of multiple bruises stand out in sharp contrast. Her bleached gold hair was matted around a bad gash on her head. The face that had once adorned posters for grade-B movies was devoid of all makeup, making her seem somehow younger. More bruises covered her shoulders. She looked like a broken doll that had been discarded.

Gloria had ended badly but somehow predictably. She was like so many other actresses who never quite made it and settled for whatever role kept the rent paid, even the role of drug pusher, or candy man. Ironic that the ending was anything but sweet.

"What was the cause of death?" C.J. asked shakily. Somehow in the back of her mind she had expected suicide when she first heard the news from Cody. It happened when people lived on the edge. But it wasn't suicide. It was murder.

"Katy?"

It was as if the walls and the ceiling had moved. Steel and the stark white tile all blurred in a flash of cold nausea that swept up from her stomach. Sam's voice seemed to come from very far away as the room began to close in on her.

Sam saw her face suddenly drain of all color and her eyes flutter uncertainly. Her hands were like ice when he took them in his, and she half turned, half collapsed against him as he pulled her against him.

"It's all right," he whispered against her forehead as he stroked her back. "Just breathe in slowly, it'll pass."

He led her out of the room, into the hallway. He was warm, incredibly warm and alive. She could feel the heat of his skin through his shirt seeping into her, filling all the cold places inside. He simply held her, his arms wrapped protectively around her.

"I'm sorry." She tried to pull back, expecting him to be embarrassed. Instead, she found only the steady scrutiny of those blue-green eyes that always seemed to see more of her than she was willing to allow. He smiled, a smile she remembered from the dark shadows of the ranch house after they'd first made love.

"No reason to be sorry," Sam answered softly. "It's never easy."

C.J. looked up at him as strength slowly warmed back through her veins, seeing yet another side of Sam.

"I would have thought that in your line of work you see a lot of death."

"I do," he remarked matter-of-factly as he held her and stroked her hair back from her pale cheek. "Too much sometimes. It goes with the job. But that doesn't mean it's ever easy. Especially when it's someone young."

"Like your partner." She saw a flicker of emotion in his eyes.

Sam nodded. "Even Rollie Prescott, Dan's grandfather. He was an outlaw, but I regretted him dyin'."

"What about Emmett Traeger?" she asked.

His voice hardened. "I won't regret that, Katy."

Not, I *don't regret it*, but I *won't regret it*. Nothing had changed. It didn't matter that he'd been brought forward in time over a hundred years, and that Emmett Traeger was long dead by now. There was a part of Sam that wouldn't let go, wouldn't give up.

"What did the coroner say about the cause of death?" she asked, desperate to change the subject. She didn't want to think about Sam leaving and going back. "I don't seem to remember that part of the conversation."

Sam smiled faintly. "You were a little unsteady on your feet." Then his expression shifted. His tone was speculative. "He said the police are calling it a hit-and-run—whatever the hell that is."

"It means she was struck by an automobile and they haven't found the person who did it. They hit her and then ran away from the accident," C.J. explained as she combed her fingers through her hair. "It doesn't fit," she said thoughtfully.

"What doesn't fit?"

"Coincidence. I wonder what the odds are that Gloria Ames would die so soon after Dan Prescott?"

He gave her a long, level look. "What are you trying to say?"

She looked up at him. "First Dan Prescott dies, supposedly an accidental shooting, only it's not an accident. Gloria Ames may have had a motive to kill him. She had access to the prop trailer just like everyone else and could have put the bullet in the gun. When we interviewed her, she lied. I'm sure of it. Now Gloria is dead. There's more to this than just mere coincidence." She looked up to find Sam watching her with a suspiciously pleased expression.

"Why are you looking at me like that?"

"I was wonderin' when you were goin' to figure that out."

"Is that right?"

"Yeah, that's right. Where do we start?" He was already on his feet, and pulling C.J. to hers.

"The police. I need to get a copy of the accident report and any follow-up investigation they're conducting. The problem is they don't hand that information out to the general public until the investigation is completed."

"So how do we go about getting that information?"

C.J. whipped the thick-rimmed glasses out of her purse and shoved them back on her nose.

"I didn't take all those acting classes for nothing." At his doubtful expression she explained. "I'm going to lie. I've seen it done dozens of times on TV. It's a piece of cake."

She laughed at Sam's confused expression. "Trust me." Then she became serious as she realized once more just how confusing the world must seem to Sam. Yet, he had dealt with being stranded at the ranch house, and he'd handled the fire. When she nearly fainted, he dealt with that. Once more C.J. was forced to confront something rather surprising. In spite of being thrown into a different time, Sam was strong and capable, like a cat who always landed on its feet. He was protective of her in a way she'd never experienced before. She admitted she liked being able to lean on someone else, liked being protected and feeling safe, which was absolutely contrary to everything she knew about herself. Sam had a way of doing that—making her look at herself and things around her differently.

As she rose she said, "Thank you," and lifted her mouth to his. It was a simple gesture. But there was nothing simple about the feelings that immediately rushed to the surface.

Sam's expression was a mixture of surprise and embarrassment when they pulled apart. She laughed softly. "Relax. It's all right."

"No, it's not, when I'd like to do a whole lot more with you, Katy." He ran the back of his fingers along her cheek, his callused thumb tracing her bottom lip with a rough tenderness.

It was the first time he had mentioned the night before. Surely it shouldn't have the effect on her that it did. After all, she was used to casual sex. But deep inside she knew there was nothing casual about what passed between them out at the ranch, or the way he was touching her now.

"We'd better go," she replied a little breathlessly.

With the thick glasses perched on her small nose, C.J. stepped up to the counter at the West Hollywood Police Station.

"I'll handle this," she whispered to Sam. "I played a character just like this once. It's easy. You just have to look the part."

"Piece of cake?" Sam asked with a quirk of a smile.

"Exactly." As the uniformed officer of the day came up to the counter, C.J. laid her leather notebook down with a confident gesture and fixed a very professional, slightly bored expression on her face.

"May I help you?" the officer asked.

"Yes, I'm with the district attorney's office." She paused for just the right effect, then went on.

"You had a hit-and-run last night," she said, flipping open her notebook as if checking a name. "Gloria Ames. I'd like to see the workup on that."

"Your name?"

C.J. moistened her lips. "Grant. Ms. C. J. Grant."

"Identification?" the officer asked.

She took a deep breath. "I explained, I'm with the district attorney's office."

"That may be, Ms. Grant, but I still need to see identification."

She allowed a trace of irritation to edge her voice. "Look, I called down earlier this morning and cleared it with the desk sergeant. He said I could pick up a copy of the file. Where is he, I want to talk to him."

"I am the desk sergeant, Ms. Grant. I don't know who you talked to, but it wasn't me. You're from the D.A.'s office, you know the rules. No identification, no file."

So much for acting class, C.J. thought. She'd been right to reevaluate her career options.

"Sergeant, I believe the lady asked for a copy of the file on Gloria Ames."

C.J.'s gaze snapped up to Sam, standing beside her.

"Right," the sergeant said irritably, "and as I explained to the lady, I need identification to release that information."

Sam leaned across the counter, slamming his hand down. His gaze bore into the sergeant's.

"Sam Hackett, Federal Marshal. I'm working with Ms. Grant and I'd like to see that information. Now!"

He pulled back his hand and C.J. stared down at the gleaming badge on the counter. The expression on the sergeant's face changed completely.

"Yessir, I'll get that right away, I didn't realize the lady was with you." He picked up a phone and put a call

through, instructing that a copy of the Ames file be brought
up immediately.

As they got into her car, C.J. turned to Sam. "I'll have
to learn to carry one of those. I can buy one at the toy
store."

"It wasn't the badge, Katy." He added with a hint of
amusement, "You have to look the part."

Ignoring him, C.J. turned her attention to the report.
"What does it say?"

She frowned. "Just as the coroner said, Gloria's death
is being listed as a hit-and-run. They tagged it as possibly
being involved with drugs. Evidently they knew about
Gloria's dealing. But there were no witnesses. That's not
surprising considering the area of town it happened in."
She frowned slightly at the address of the location.

"What are they doing about it?" Sam asked, legs
stretched over the open window frame of the topless MG.

"Nothing at the moment."

"These things happen all the time. The newspapers are
full of dozens of these kinds of accidents every year. With
all the crime in L.A., it's not a high-priority situation, which
means the police will get to it when they can, which
means . . ."

". . . that we're going to do it ourselves," Sam finished for her as he pulled his long legs into the car.

"Exactly."

"Where do we start?"

"We check out the same people we talked to before.
Find out if they have alibis for the time that Gloria was
killed."

Alan Denny and Lance Ford were the obvious first
choices.

There was a possibility Denny had found out Gloria
was dealing drugs on the set. It was impossible not to know
those things in the close-knit-family atmosphere that de-
veloped during a movie production. C.J. quickly discovered that both Denny and Lisa Kennedy had left for an
exclusive hotel up the coast in Santa Barbara immediately

after the wrap party. A phone conversation with the hotel manager confirmed that they were having a late dinner in the hotel restaurant when Gloria was killed.

At Sam's insistence she called Emmett Traeger. He was in a meeting, as usual. The studio was aware of Gloria's death, and Traeger's secretary was quite upset about it. When C.J. casually questioned her about Traeger's schedule the evening before, she said she was certain he'd worked late at the studios. He'd called her close to nine o'clock, looking for contracts she was supposed to have left out.

Carl Cartwright had an alibi as well. At the time Gloria was killed, he was in the screening room on the studio lot, going through the last of the dailies from the movie. The projectionist verified he was with Carl all evening.

That left Lance Ford. C.J. wondered how he was taking the fact that Lisa had gone off with Denny. Lance was in L.A. but was hard to find. His manager insisted he didn't know where to find him. Sam got on the phone and with quiet authority demanded to know where Lance was.

He'd been admitted to St. John's Hospital in Santa Monica under a different name. St. John's frequently dealt with celebrities involved with substance abuse. Lance was in the hospital drying out, and had been since the morning after the wrap party.

"We've got nothing!" C.J. paced around her office. "They all have alibis for the time the report says Gloria died."

"Except Traeger."

She looked up and glared across the desk at Sam.

"His secretary insists he worked late."

"Was she actually with him?"

"She said he called her from his office about some contracts."

"And you buy that?"

"At the moment I have no reason not to. Sam, we can't just keep coming back to Traeger because you have a gut feeling that comes from something that happened over one hundred years ago between you and his great-grandfather."

"Uh-huh."

"What is that supposed to mean?"

"It means we'll just have to dig up that proof that you want."

"I suppose you have a brilliant idea about all this."

"Nope," Sam said as he came up out of the chair behind the desk and grabbed his hat. "There's nothing brilliant about it." He grabbed the car keys the tow service had returned to her along with her car, which now had a brand-new one-hundred-and-twenty-five-dollar battery. In that aggravating, long-legged stride of his he sauntered out of the office.

"Oh, God." Conjuring up mental images of Sam trying to drive the Mustang, she grabbed her purse and ran after him.

C.J. slowly pulled the car around a corner in the warehouse district. She looked for the address indicated in the accident report but needed to look no further than the section of sidewalk that had been roped off. This was where Gloria Ames had died.

It was early evening. Most of the warehouses on this block were locked up for the night. One was open, and a large truck was backed up to the loading bay. A conveyor rattled under the weight of boxed CD and VCR units while workers packed them into the truck. A man, obviously the foreman, stood with clipboard in hand, chewing on a green cigar as he verified inventory. C.J. crossed the street, unbuttoning the top button of her blouse as she approached the foreman.

"Excuse me." She smiled flirtatiously. "I was wondering if you could help me with something."

He looked up, grinned with frank appreciation, then looked past her to Sam. The grin faded to a more careful expression.

"Yeah, what is it?"

"Were you working night before last?"

"Every night this week, three P.M. till midnight. That's when we close down for the night."

The police report said Gloria had died at night, between eight and ten o'clock.

"Then you must know about the woman who was killed near here."

"Yeah, one of my drivers found her."

"Did anyone see anything? Possibly the car that hit her?"

"You with the police?"

"No, I'm an . . . investigator. . . ." She hoped her performance was more convincing than her earlier one at the police station. "Insurance," she clarified.

"Insurance?" He hooted. "It's taken you long enough to get here."

C.J. ignored his remark. "We're just checking out the police report. The company wants to verify a few details. It would help if someone saw something."

"Can't help you." He cursed as a box shifted off the conveyor, stacking up several more boxes. CD units made in Korea piled up and crashed onto the floor.

"Maybe you would prefer to talk to the police," C.J. called after him as he shouted to stop the conveyor.

He turned around. "Is that a threat?" He started toward her.

Sam stepped between them. "If you have information, I suggest you tell the lady."

"Yeah? And what if I don't, cowboy?" The foreman blew cigar smoke in Sam's face.

For the first time C.J. felt afraid for Sam. She had no doubt he could take care of himself against the foreman, but there were the dozen or so employees who had stopped working and were slowly walking toward them. They were hard-looking men and Sam was unarmed. She'd insisted he leave his gun in the car.

"Gentlemen"—she laid a restraining hand on Sam's arm—"there's no need for this. All I want is some information. In exchange I won't tell Immigration about the illegal aliens working here."

It was a gamble and she knew it. But in L.A. any business that used unskilled labor stood a good chance of hiring at least some illegals.

The foreman let out a disgusted grunt, then waved his men back to work. Turning back to C.J., he said, "The driver gave the police all the information he had. There was nobody else around here last night except for old Stella."

That name wasn't in the accident report. "Who is Stella?" C.J. asked quickly while he was still cooperating with them.

The foreman jammed his cigar back in his mouth. "A crazy old lady who's always down here."

"What's her last name?"

"Damned if I know."

"Where does she live?"

He chewed on the cigar. "She don't live anywhere."

"What do you mean?"

The foreman glared at her. "She lives on the street. You know, one of them homeless people. She's always hangin' around here. The company across the way deals in fresh produce. That's where she does her grocery shopping. She's always around, pushin' that grocery cart and pilin' it high with whatever she can find on the streets." He turned and yelled something at one of his men.

"Where could I find Stella now?"

He shrugged. "Who knows? Pick a street around here. You can't miss her. She wears a bright pink straw hat and all kinds of clothes. But she can't give you any information."

"Why not? She might have seen something."

"It wouldn't matter if she did. The old biddy is wacko."

C.J. felt her initial excitement drain.

"What do you mean?"

"I mean certifiable. She's filthy rich, but she lives down here. Her son comes up here once a month in a big fancy car. He's taken her home lotsa times and she always comes right back. Says she don't want the money." He gestured to his head. "Wacko."

Three blocks over they found Stella with her neon-pink hat, pushing her grocery cart. She was humming to herself.

"What do you want to do?" Sam asked as the car slowed and pulled to the curb.

They watched Stella rummage through a dumpster. She found several cast-off pieces of trash to her liking and put them into her cart.

C.J. sighed. "She doesn't look like she'd be much help. Let's go get a hot shower and something to eat."

"Maybe she did see something. You might as well talk to her."

"She's certifiable," C.J. grumbled. At Sam's confused expression she explained.

"Crazy, mentally unbalanced, insane."

Sam gave that some thought. "Like somebody believin' he's a U.S. Federal Marshal from the year 1882?"

"That's different."

Sam shrugged.

"All right, I get the point. We're here anyway. It won't hurt to ask, unless, of course, she tries to run me down with that grocery cart."

Sam smiled. "Want me to bring my gun?"

"No, I think I can handle this one."

"Good, I think I'll just take a rest." He settled himself back into the bucket seat. "I didn't get much sleep last night."

He grinned at her from under the brim of his hat. That devilish grin turned her knees to jelly.

"You're not going to get much sleep tonight either, Sam Hackett." She felt a rush of satisfaction at the way his smile changed. She liked setting him off balance like that every once in a while.

Stella was no bigger than a minute, as Lucy would say. Her tiny frame was covered by an odd assortment of cotton dresses layered underneath a colorful array of threadbare sweaters. She had twinkling blue eyes and thinning blond hair that poked out from beneath a knit stocking cap. She was humming an odd little song as C.J. tentatively walked up to her.

"Stella? Hi, my name is C. J. Grant. I was wondering if I could talk to you."

"You are talking to me, aren't you?"

C.J. was taken aback at the woman's bluntness.

"Well, yes, I guess I am."

Stella didn't look up but continued picking through trash in the dumpster.

"You find a lot of good things around here, don't you?"

"Oh, yes, lotsa nice things. It was a good day today. Mondays are always good. A lot of the trucks come in from across the country." She gave C.J. a conspiratorial wink.

"I even found an electric fan." She gestured to the cart as she cackled with glee over her treasures. "It'll come in handy when those hot Santa Ana winds start up."

C.J. didn't think now was the time to point out that Stella didn't have a place to plug in the fan. Her heart sank. Obviously the woman had lost more than a few of her marbles. She started to turn back to the car.

"You look familiar," Stella remarked as she pushed the cart along. "I seem to remember seeing you before. Are you an actress by any chance?"

C.J. gaped at Stella. She couldn't believe it. After all the struggle, sacrifice, endless cattle calls, and meaningless, insignificant television roles, when she'd desperately wanted someone of importance to notice her and launch her meteoric film career, finally she was recognized—by a bag lady!

"You played a bit part in that movie *Nightmare on Elm Street*. I remember because you've got great legs. Besides, I like redheads."

C.J. remembered the role with a shudder. She lost her great legs to knife-wielding Freddy twenty minutes into the film and her name was lost somewhere in the credits.

"How do you remember that? My mother doesn't even remember that role."

"I remember all the movies. I see as many as I can. They certainly don't make 'em like they used to. The best ones were from the thirties and the forties. I can name all the big movies from those years, all the stars who played in them, and tell you which ones won the Academy Awards. I saw them all. The women had better legs back then, too, not these skinny, air-brained blondes they have nowadays."

Where was this woman when she was trying to build a career? C.J. wondered.

"I haven't seen you in anything lately," Stella observed as she drew back and took a long look at C.J.

"I gave it up. Too many skinny blondes to compete with."

"So what do you do now?"

C.J. almost laughed. It was like talking to anybody else she might meet on the street, except Stella was dressed like a reject from the Salvation Army thrift shop. "I'm a private investigator now."

"Oh, well, that sounds lovely, dear." Stella started to move past her, humming that melody again that sounded vaguely familiar. C.J. trailed along behind her.

"That's why I wanted to talk to you. I'm investigating a case."

Without responding, Stella continued walking down the street, stopping now and then to pick up a page from a discarded newspaper or an empty sack.

"It's about someone who was killed very near here. She was hit by a car." When there was no reply, she tried again. "She was an actress."

Stella stopped and slowly turned around, fixing C.J. with a narrow look. "She *was*?"

"Did you see the accident last night?"

Stella nodded. "I was just makin' my rounds over by Certified. I get my salads there."

"That's really great, Stella, but what about the accident?"

"I saw it. I thought it was a little strange for that woman to be standin' there all by herself." She leaned closer, as if sharing a secret. "This isn't the best neighborhood, you know. I keep threatening to move."

C.J. groaned. How could she possibly make heads or tails out of someone who spent half her time in the twilight zone? Still, it was all she had.

"What about the accident, Stella? Please, try to remember."

"This woman was standing by herself over by the warehouse. I thought about asking her for a cigarette. All I find out here are butts. She lit one up, but she put it out when she saw the car coming, like she was waiting for it."

C.J. frowned. A drug dealer maybe? Had Gloria set up a meeting with her supplier and then been killed?

"What happened?"

"The car speeded up when it got close. Then he hit her. Boom, just like that. Then he drove off."

"I know it was dark and the lighting probably isn't very good over there, but do you remember anything about the car?"

"Twelve, twenty-seven, thirty-nine."

C.J. looked up. She was hoping for a description, possibly the color of the car. But not this. "What did you say?"

"The license plate was twelve, twenty-seven, thirty-nine," Stella repeated with an exasperated shake of her head.

"How could you possibly remember the license number?"

"I saw it."

"But that's a lot of numbers. Maybe you mixed them up." She frowned as she looked down at the numbers she'd written. California license plates, at least newer ones, were a combination of a number, three letters, then three more numbers.

"I remember it because of the date."

"Date?"

"Don't you know anything. December 27, 1939. It was the date of the premier of *Gone With the Wind* in Los Angeles, at the Carthay Circle in the Wilshire district."

"Why didn't you tell the police?"

"They wouldn't believe me. They think I'm crazy." And with that, Stella strolled of, pushing her cart and humming to herself.

"Did she know anything about the accident?" Sam asked when C.J. got back to the car.

"Yeah, she saw it." C.J. started the car, and whipped it around in a U-turn.

"She *saw* it?" He stared at her. "What did she say?"

"She gave me the license plate number of the car that hit Gloria."

"And that means something?"

"It means we need to find a phone. Stella could be completely bonkers—crazy. But then again, she might not be." When Sam tried to grasp all this, she explained. "All automobiles are registered to the owners. All the information is kept in computers at the Department of Motor Vehicles. If you know a license number, you can find out who the owner of the car is. *If* you happen to know someone who is willing to give you that information."

"Do you know someone?"

"An old friend of Harry Carlucci's, if she hasn't retired from the DMV yet. They used to be quite an item. I'm hoping she has hot memories of Harry."

"There's a phone." Sam pointed across the street to a service station. C.J. wheeled the car into the lot.

It was close to five o'clock and she was put on hold three times. She finally located Harry's friend Cecile at the Department of Motor Vehicles in Santa Monica. She practically had to shout into the phone over the noise of traffic on the street.

"I need a favor, Cecile. I'm trying to trace a vehicle, but I don't think I have enough numbers." Cecile agreed to help, and C.J. repeated the numbers over the phone.

She was put on hold again while Cecile put the numbers into the computer. Finally, Cecile came back on the line.

"Yes, I'm still here. What did you find out?"

C.J.'s eyes widened. "Are you sure?" Then, "Yes, thank you, Cecile. I'm, very grateful." She slowly hung up the phone. Her troubled gaze met Sam's.

"What is it? Who did the car belong to?"

"The numbers are for a special CB license, that's why they were different."

Sam took hold of her by the arms. "Katy! Who does the car belong to?"

C.J. swallowed hard. She had been prepared for anything but this. She looked up at Sam.

"Emmett Traeger."

Chapter 15

"Sam, wait!"

C.J. had to run to keep up with his long stride. He slammed into the passenger seat as she reached the car.

"Sam . . ."

"Just get in and drive."

His voice stopped her. It was hard, edged with a raw anger she'd never heard before, even during some of their more colorful arguments. He'd shouted occasionally and she'd known when she was pushing a little too far. He wasn't shouting now. His voice was low, even, tightly controlled. Because she had a fiery temper she understood shouting. A person got it out, got it over with, and forgot it. But this was different, and she didn't quite know how to handle it. She tried the only thing that came to mind.

"We need to talk about this."

"Get in, Katy."

"All right." She got into the driver's seat, forcing herself to remain calm. "But we have to talk."

"Drive, Katy."

The command whipped out at her, cold and emotionless. C.J. swallowed back the tightness in her throat. He wouldn't even look at her. For the first time since she'd met Sam Hackett, he was a man she didn't want to know.

Silence drew out between them on that long drive back to Venice. She fully expected him to order her to drive him directly to the studio so that he could shoot Traeger, or arrest him, or whatever it was he intended. Maybe she would have felt better if he had. As it was, Sam said nothing, and that frightened her more.

She let out a long sigh of relief when they finally pulled into the driveway at her house. Maybe they could talk this out calmly, rationally. Before she could turn the car off, Sam was already out. Without a backward glance he strode into the front office and headed straight for her private office—and his rifle in the closet.

C.J. jumped out of the car and ran after him.

"Sam! Please, don't!"

He was in her office, pulling the Winchester down from a shelf.

She grabbed him by the arm. "Listen to me!"

Sam jerked his arm free of her hand and reached for the shells she'd put in a bag and thrown into the far corner. With cool efficiency he loaded the rifle.

Panic engulfed her. Horrible thoughts flashed through her mind at the repercussions of what he was contemplating.

"It can't be this way! This is 1989!"

He turned on her with an expression she'd never seen before, except in a reprint of an old, faded photograph in that book at the library. This wasn't the Sam she knew, or thought she knew. This was Sam Hackett, U.S. Federal Marshal, who had tracked countless outlaws and by his own admission brought them in more often dead than alive. It brought the reality of who and what he was crashing in on her.

"*My* way, Katy. It has to be *my* way. I've waited long enough."

Words such as *motive, probable cause, proof,* and *Miranda* flashed through her mind. She'd worked with the police on some cases, even dated a detective several times. She knew what would happen if Sam took the law into his own hands. Except as far as Sam was concerned, he *was* the law.

"This isn't the man you were after! This is a different man, a different case . . ." He shoved past her, not even listening. She ran after him, blocking his way out of the office.

"It's a different time!"

"Get out of my way."

Now that she momentarily had his attention, she had to make him understand.

"Sam, please. Just listen to me." She held on to his arms as if she could physically stop him.

"It's different now, the law is different. You can't just go after Traeger based on something an old woman told us."

"She's a witness, Katy."

The anger hadn't eased a bit. It was there in every cold word.

"And she's unreliable at best!" She dug her fingers in when he made a move to step past her.

"Just listen! Maybe it *was* his car. There's no other way she could've known those numbers. But the point is the police won't consider that enough. The woman is unbalanced. If you tried to use her as a witness, the defense attorneys would destroy her credibility, the case would be thrown out of court, and Traeger would go free. And believe me, he'll have slick attorneys."

"I'll settle this my way, like I should've in the first place," Sam bit off angrily. "I knew Traeger was at the bottom of this."

"*Your* way?" Her voice was shaky. "Can't you understand? Your way isn't how it's done anymore! Right or wrong, the legal system has changed. Whether I like it, or you like it, criminals have rights. You can't simply go after Traeger because you're certain he was involved with Gloria's death, or because of gut instinct. *You have to have proof that can stand up in a court of law or it means nothing!* It might have been someone else in his car."

"You know he did it and I know he did it."

"Yes," she answered quietly. "I believe now that he did have something to do with it."

Sam looked at her sharply.

"In many ways I wish this were 1882," C.J. admitted, "and you could just go after him. As a Federal Marshal, it would be enough. But the fact is, it's not enough today and the police would never accept who you are. Telling them the truth about you would make us both sound as crazy as Stella."

"I want him, Katy."

The anger had changed. It was controlled. She knew he would listen to her now.

"I know that. But we have to do this my way." He still held on to the rifle and she held on to him. "Please, trust me on this," she whispered.

Nothing had ever been so important to her. C.J. felt the last of the anger ease out of the hardened muscles in his arms. She'd relied on that keen intelligence of his to see that what she was saying was true, and she'd been right.

"All right," he conceded reluctantly, "we'll try it your way."

C.J. was so relieved, tears pooled in her eyes. She knew what this cost him. She laid her hand against his cheek. "Thank you."

His hand stopped hers. "But if this doesn't work, Katy, if you can't get Traeger your way, then I'll do it my way."

She stifled an automatic objection, knowing he wouldn't give her more than that, at least not right now. He was meeting her halfway. That was more than he'd ever given anyone before.

"All right."

Sam laid the rifle across her desk instead of putting it away, a subtle reminder he would let her take this only so far. His eyes were intense. "What's first?"

She breathed out slowly. "First I want to check Traeger's license number with the police to see if anyone else might have seen his car there. We need a reliable witness."

"Is there someone who can give you that information?"

"Yeah, there's a guy who's a detective with the L.A.P.D. I dated him a couple of times."

"Dated?"

"You know, go out, have some fun, neck in the car?" Realizing Sam didn't have the slightest idea what she was talking about, she tried again. "How about *courting*?"

"You were betrothed to this guy?"

"Betrothed?" C.J. laughed. Obviously failing to see the humor, Sam gave her a slightly wounded expression. She reassured him. "No, it was nothing like that. We just went out together a few times. But I will admit, he did have the hots for me." When Sam's expression darkened, she decided to let it go at that.

"Never mind. He's just a friend, but I think maybe he'll help me out on this. I'll call and see if I can get him at the precinct." She casually removed the rifle and put it back in the closet, then sat down at her desk. She felt Sam's steady gaze.

"I'm going to take a walk on the beach," he said as he turned toward the door. "C'mon, Newman," he called. Newman padded out the door, wagging his tail with excitement, followed closely by an anxious Redford.

C.J. put in a call to Tom Gates. She knew it might take a while to reach him because he worked undercover and kept crazy hours. There were times when he disappeared for weeks on an assignment. That was how she met him in the first place.

She had been investigating a case for a distraught father whose daughter had an unsavory boyfriend. The father wanted information on the guy, and C.J. spent long hours in her car trailing him, little realizing the police were doing exactly the same thing. The boyfriend was involved in a major drug ring.

There was a bust and C.J. ended up right in the middle of it. Afterward she was called in to give testimony on the boyfriend's activities. Tom was the detective in charge of the case. They dated several times and might have hit it off if their work and their hours hadn't made it difficult to find time for each other.

It was no different now. Tom was out and the desk officer didn't know when he'd be in, but he assured her Tom would get the message.

Sam blew out a long streamer of cigarette smoke as he walked the beach and tried to bring his anger under control. A full moon glistened off the water, curling silver fingers over the tops of waves as they rushed in endless rhythmic procession across the sand.

He walked barefoot. Everyone walked barefoot on the beach. It was something he had to learn about all over again. He hadn't done it since he was a kid on the farm and felt the hot, fertile earth during planting season push up through his toes.

The froth from the waves soaked his jeans at the ankles. He liked the feel of the water and the wind, different from the plains and deserts he'd known. It had its own timelessness.

There was an occasional campfire—bonfires, Katy had called them. Groups of people, young and old, clustered around them, laughing, talking, telling stories. It wasn't much different from evenings he remembered.

He passed a couple bundled in a blanket. At least he assumed it was a man and woman. He overheard the man say something and the woman's soft laughter in response. Their indistinct shapes changed beneath the blanket and they became quiet.

Sam thought of the time he and Katy spent out at the ranch. During those few hours he had almost felt as if he had his old world back again. Everything was familiar—everything except Katy. She was a constant surprise to him.

Katy was a fascinating combination of all the women he'd known in his life. Like his mother, she was resourceful, resilient, and unafraid. At the same time, damn if she couldn't be strong-willed and downright testy about things when she wanted her way. He'd known women like that too. But then he figured that's where they got their strength, by knowing they were right and not backing down.

He'd expected all those things when he first saw her wearing men's pants, with her hair cut short, and that stubborn tilt to her nose. What he hadn't expected were all the things he had discovered about her during the last few days.

Along with the strength was an openness that always caught him slightly off guard. She was honest about her feelings and free with her opinions. When she was angry, he knew it. And when she was sad, he knew that too. Like the unexpected tears when she'd asked him to trust her.

Then there was the sensuality. It was a new word he'd learned. Lucy had filled him in on it. In his time it would have been considered bawdy or wanton for a woman to make her desires known to a man. Only women who were paid did that. But this was a different time and Katy was a different woman. And he liked the difference.

The problem was, his feelings for her were all wrapped up in his feelings about Traeger, and he couldn't let that go.

He'd get him. He'd keep his promise to her; but one way or the other he'd get the son of a bitch.

He'd walked the entire stretch of beach and back. His last cigarette was smoked down to nothing. He tossed it toward the waves. It arced in the night air, sparks scattering like the burst of miniature fireworks. Sam looked across at C. J.'s beach house. The ground floor office was dark, as were the upstairs rooms.

He wanted to go to her. He wanted to climb those stairs, walk straight into her bedroom, and lose himself in her. That way maybe he could get back what they had shared at the ranch and find peace once more. But he was still angry that he couldn't go after Traeger his own way, and he wouldn't go to her with anger.

He slowly climbed the stairs. The door to the upstairs apartment was unlocked. Accustomed to the darkness, he left the lights off as he padded across to the sofa. He pulled off his boots, then stripped off his shirt and pants and lay down on the sofa.

C. J. heard him come in. The luminous numbers on the clock radio beside her bed read two o'clock in the morning. She hadn't slept since going to bed two hours earlier. Listening to Sam move around in the other room, she waited expectantly. But he didn't come into her room. Finally she got up and opened the door.

"Sam?"

"Any word from your friend?" he asked through the darkness.

She could just make out his silhouette in the darkness as he lay on the couch. A cigarette glowed between his fingers. She remembered the feel of those fingers on her skin.

"Not yet. Sam . . .?"

His voice was low in his throat. "Good night, Katy."

She longed to go to him but she couldn't. Nothing was the same between them. She had somehow gotten through to him and persuaded him to let her do this her way. But at what cost?

The jangling of the phone jarred her from sleep. With a muffled curse she looked at the clock—seven-thirty. Then she came fully awake and grabbed for the bedside phone.

When Sam came in a moment later she was just saying "Thanks, I really appreciate it" to Tom. As she hung up, she noticed that Sam's long, unruly hair was disheveled, as it has been the morning before when things had been so different between them. Now there was no lingering lovemaking, no gentle caresses, not his voice, thick with sleep and desire, speaking her name.

"What did your friend say?"

C.J. looked up. God, he was so achingly handsome, more than any man she'd ever known, with a rugged sensuality that made her want him in spite of the distance he'd put between them last night.

"Katy?"

She swallowed convulsively, wondering if he would still keep his promise about giving her a chance to handle this her way. She decided to plunge in. There was no other way with Sam.

"He ran that license number through the police computers." Knowing that wouldn't mean much to Sam, she went on to explain. "He found something on the car."

Sam leaned against the door frame. It was a deceptively casual stance that didn't fool her for a second. He was already dressed and he'd obviously showered and shaved. He was ready to leave, which meant if she didn't hurry, she'd be left behind.

"What did he find?"

"Traeger's car was stolen. The police found it yesterday. It had been stripped."

"Stripped?"

"Torn apart. He couldn't have been driving it when Gloria was killed."

"I don't believe it."

"It doesn't matter whether or not we believe it. He filed a police report. He claims the car was stolen from the parking lot at the studio hours before Gloria was killed. He told the police that if his car hit Gloria, someone else was driving it."

Sam simply stared at her, his expression hard. She knew what he was thinking and she was already ahead of him.

"The police are satisfied he had no involvement. But I'm not." She crawled out of bed, already pulling clothes on over the teddy as she made her way to the bathroom.

"Why not?"

She turned at the door, surprised at the question. She'd long since learned that Sam wasn't one to sit around analyzing feelings or why things were the way they were. He was a man of action, pure and simple. That was definitely part of his appeal.

But now he'd thrown her a curve, wanting to know *why*. She decided to throw one of her own.

"Because *you're* not satisfied."

"What is this place?" Sam asked as she pulled the car into the parking area near the downtown police station.

"The city impound yard. This is where they bring cars when they're brought in for evidence. Traeger's car is here."

Sam followed her up to the office. The attendant cleared them, thanks to an early telephone call from Tom. Another attendant directed them to Traeger's car.

She remembered the Range Rover from the evening of her date with Traeger. It had all the extras, including a citizens band radio, which explained the different combination of numbers Stella remembered from the license plate. As the report said, it had been stripped. The expensive wheel covers were gone, leaving exposed rims. The CD player, mobile phone, radio, and special cassette for dictation were also gone, as were the front and rear seats. Whoever stripped it had even taken the mobile antennae from the trunk lid. They had been thorough.

Sam looked at the car then shook his head. "I don't understand why anyone would do this."

"For money. It's a major industry. The cars are stolen, sometimes stripped down, and the items sold or exchanged for drugs. Sometimes the entire car is stolen, repainted, and sold intact. It's called black market, and it's big business."

Sam knelt in front of the Rover. He ran his fingers over the damaged grille with a slight dent, and broken headlight.

"That must have happened when Gloira was hit and killed," C.J. said with a faint shudder as she stared at the shattered headlight. "But how do we prove it?"

Sam said simply, "We backtrack and see if we can pick up something the police missed. We found Stella. Maybe there's something else."

He shoved his Stetson back on his forehead and gave her a long look. "We need proof."

"Very good, Marshal. You may just make it as an investigator yet. What would be your guess for our next step?"

Sam slowly circled the car. His intense gaze missed nothing as his hands slowly moved over it. He looked up when he came back around.

"The car is the link. There has to be some way to tie the accident back to Traeger."

"All right," C.J. conceded. "But that raises an important question. Why? What would be his reason to kill Gloria Ames?"

"Maybe she was supplying him with drugs and threatened to tell someone about it?"

Leaning back against the shell of a BMW 635 CSI, C.J. thought that better cars were junked than what she drove. "Not very likely."

"Why not?"

"Traeger is in a highly visible profession. If he was on drugs or allowing them to be distributed among the cast, it wouldn't be a secret very long. The scandal would really hurt the studio. In fact, U.F.S. backed a major campaign to keep drugs out of its productions. That's one of the reasons

Denny recently signed a three-picture deal with them. He's notoriously clean, and as far as drugs are concerned, Traeger is clean. I'd bet on it." She shook her head. "It has to be something else. Something important enough to kill two people for."

Sam asked, "Where was the car found?"

C.J. grinned. "Of course!" Impulsively she gave Sam a quick kiss. But there was nothing impulsive about the intense energy that leapt between them at that brief contact. Sam's arm went around her waist, and he pulled her into him. His mouth hovered a fraction of an inch above hers.

"That's where we have to begin," C.J. whispered a little breathlessly as she leaned full into Sam, luxuriating in the feel of his strong, hard body supporting hers. At that moment she cursed the uniformed attendant and the tow-truck operator backing a car in beside them.

"All right," Sam whispered. Then he grinned and gave her a quick kiss on the cheek. As easily as he pulled her against him, he set her back down.

"Let's get going, Ms. Grant. We've got an outlaw to catch."

"This area looks a little familiar," Sam remarked as they slowly cruised down the deserted street.

"It should. Gloria was killed not three blocks from here."

C.J. pulled the Mustang to a stop beside the curb at the vacant lot.

The residential area on the fringe of the warehouse district was known for teenage gang activity. Any car parked here for more than a few hours was bound to end up stripped.

"Nice neighborhood," Sam remarked dryly.

"It was once, about thirty years ago. Now it's just run-down." She gave him a sideways glance and saw the subtle transformation. The easy, relaxed angle of his long body curving into the bucket seat beside her had changed. His hat was still pulled low over his eyes as he slowly sat up. But his gaze quickly took in everything along the street.

C.J. saw him bring up the gleaming Colt and slide it inside his shirt at his waist. Her fingers tensed around the steering wheel.

"I don't think that will be necessary."

"It's too quiet."

She got out of the car, slamming the door a little harder than necessary.

"This isn't exactly block-party time. Of course it's quiet. Most of those houses are abandoned. Now"—she planted her hands on her hips—"are you coming with me or not?"

"I'm right with you, Katy." He swung his legs over the door. "Where did they find the car?"

She pulled out her notes as she walked onto the lot. "According to the police report"—she stopped and slowly looked around—"right about here. There are a lot of tire treads in the dirt."

C.J. slowly scanned that area of the lot. The car had been driven here, stripped, and abandoned. Obviously that sort of thing happened often here. There were numerous sets of tire tracks of varying widths. She didn't have to be a forensics expert to see that.

"I don't get it," she muttered to herself.

"What don't you get?"

"I wouldn't have expected to find the car here."

"Why not?"

She looked at him. "Gloria was killed only three blocks from here. If I were trying to cover up a murder, I'd dump it as far away as possible."

"Uh-uh."

"What do you mean by that?"

"I mean that is precisely the reason it was left here. Don't you see, Katy? Traeger wanted the car found. *After* he reported it stolen. It was his alibi. If it was stolen, he couldn't very well be the one driving it. My guess is he drove the car off the studio lot himself. Those guards question people who are coming in, not people leaving. He went after Gloria, then dumped the car. Except that he wanted it found. So he left it in an area where it would be too big a temptation to leave alone. He was relying on car thieves, as you call 'em, to do their best on the car. That would support his story that it was stolen."

"That might work, but you still have no proof. You need something to tie Traeger in—motive, a witness . . ."

Sam came to his feet. "How big do you want 'im?"

"What?"

"Will that one do?" He gestured past her. "He just might know something about what happened."

C.J. gave him an exasperated look. "What are you talking about?"

"I'm talking about the little fella tryin' to pry the wheels off your car."

"What?" She whirled around. "Oh, my God!"

"You want him?" Sam asked with a faint quirk of a smile.

"Yes!"

Sam ran toward the car. He'd almost reached it when the kid looked up and bolted.

"Hold it right there." Sam made a running leap, trying to bulldog the kid. He grunted as he landed painfully, his shoulder taking the blow as he landed on the asphalt.

"Aw, to hell with this," he cursed as he pulled the Colt from his belt.

"No!" C.J. screamed.

"You want him or not!" Sam shouted back at her.

"Yes! I mean no! Not dead! Stop this!"

A loud gunshot exploded in the warm afternoon air. It echoed off the abandoned buildings. C.J. screamed. The bullet popped off the pavement just in front of the boy. He stopped as if he'd hit a wall, his hands reaching high in the air.

"Hold it, Mister! I ain't goin' nowhere!"

C.J. pried her fingers away from her eyes, anger rising in her throat as she ran from the lot out into the street.

"Damn you, Sam Hackett!" she cried as she charged toward him.

He turned just as she got to him. A frightened Hispanic boy approximately twelve years old stared at them with wide-eyed fear.

"I didn't want you to kill him!"

"If I'd wanted to kill him, Katy, I would have. The fact is I'm not in the habit of killing children."

"Children!" the boy exploded. "I'm not a child. I'm old enough to take care of myself."

"Shut up, boy!" Sam turned on him, waving the Colt under his nose. The boy's eyes grew even wider.

"Hey man. It's cool. I'm not goin' nowhere until you say so."

C.J. glared at Sam. "I really think you could have handled this a little better."

He shifted with a grimace of pain. "At the time it seemed like the thing to do. I don't like chasin' after someone on foot."

For the first time she noticed his torn shirt and the raw flesh of his shoulder.

"You're hurt." She started toward him.

"It'll keep. Don't you think you should ask him if he knows anything."

Turning to the boy, she gave him a smile that was intended to be reassuring.

"I'd like to ask you some questions about a stolen car that was found here."

"I don't know nothin' about no stolen car, lady." The kid's face drained of all color as Sam cocked the hammer back on the Colt.

"Answer the lady," Sam ordered.

"Hey, man, you for real? Who you think you are, the Lone Ranger?"

Sam jammed the Colt in the kid's face.

"I'm a U.S. Federal Marshal and I want you to answer the lady's question."

"Right!" the kid bravely shot back. "And if I don't yer gonna run me in. Mi amigos, my gang, will have me out inside of one hour."

"I don't take anybody in." Sam's voice was deadly.

C.J. didn't believe Sam meant it, but she stepped between them. This was one tough street kid. He probably already had a criminal record. She decided to try a bluff.

"Look, I only want information. We're investigating a murder. We think a car that was found here might have been used to kill someone. It was a 1989 black Range Rover and it was loaded. It was picked up here yesterday."

The boy glared at her suspiciously and C.J. plunged on. "I don't give a damn about what you might have taken off the car." She saw the subtle shift in the boy's eyes and knew she'd hit home. "What I do want is information about where you got the car."

"You assumin' I took the car, lady?"

"I'm assuming you know a great deal more than you're telling us. Now, here's the deal. You give me the information I want and I'll get my friend here to leave you alone. And I'll give you twenty bucks. Otherwise . . ." She shrugged and said nothing, leaving it to the boy to guess what those repercussions might be.

"Twenty dollars? Just for information?"

"That's right."

"Get him to back off." The boy jerked his head toward Sam.

"Sam, please," C.J. begged, "trust me."

"All right, but if he moves, I shoot him."

The kid looked at him incredulously. "Man, you really got a problem. You better see someone about that."

"The information," C.J. reminded the boy.

"First the twenty dollars."

She handed it to him and he asked, "What do you want to know?"

"Did you see the car?"

He gave Sam a long look, as if considering the odds of getting across the street before Sam could shoot him.

"Yeah, I saw it. Two nights ago."

"Where did you find it?"

"Find it? Hell, lady, I didn't find it. It was delivered."

C.J. blinked. "Delivered?"

"Yeah, right onto the lot. This guy drives it up over the curb, just missed the power pole. Then he leaves it, doesn't even bother to lock it. I mean, it was easy."

"Who left it?"

"I don't know, lady, some guy in a suit, real uptown with one of those fancy haircuts. He just gets out and walks away."

"You saw him?"

"Yeah, real clear. Only he didn't see us on accounta we were over there workin' on another car."

C.J. took hold of him by the arms. "What did he look like?"

"I already told you." The kid drew back a little uncertainly.

"No, I mean his face. What color hair did he have? Did you see his eyes? You must remember something."

"Yeah, I remember. 'Cause I thought—*this guy is weird*. Leavin' a cherry car like that in a place like this. Anyway, he was a tall dude, dressed real nice, with dark hair. Maybe thirty or forty years old."

C.J. met Sam's look. "It was Traeger."

While Sam's attention was momentarily diverted, the kid seized his opportunity and ran.

"What the . . .?" Sam whirled around and raised his gun.

"No!" C.J. jerked his arm down. "Let him go!"

"He's our witness!"

"Not if you kill him."

"I was only going to scare him."

"It won't work. He isn't any more reliable than Stella. And there still is no motive. Why would Traeger want Gloria Ames dead?"

Sam shoved his gun back into his belt, wincing as pain shot through his shoulder. "Because she knew he killed Prescott."

C.J. knew he had to be right. At the time they interviewed Gloria, she thought Gloria knew more than she was telling. She wouldn't be at all surprised if Gloria tried to blackmail Traeger.

Suddenly she noticed that Sam was bleeding. Blood was seeping through the fabric of his shirt. "Come on. I need to find you a bandage. Julie lives nearby. We'll go there."

As Julie bandaged Sam's shoulder, she said, "I thought it was pretty odd when I heard about Gloria."

They all sat around the table in Julie's small kitchen.

Cody was there, helping her pack away some of Dan's things. Julie had decided to give Cody some of her grandfather's mementos from their days together in films. At the moment Cody was initiating Sam into the pleasures of ice-cold beer.

When she'd called and asked if they could come by, C.J. hadn't said anything about the connection to Emmett Traeger. For now she wanted to keep that to herself. After all, they still had no proof.

She looked up with a frown. "You shouldn't drink with an injury."

"I've had worse than this, Katy." He gently prodded the bandage at his shoulder. "And drunk stronger than this." As he lifted the frosty glass of beer, he kicked back in the chair, his weight supported on two legs with the back of the chair resting against the wall.

"I always kept iced glasses in the freezer for Cody and Granddad," Julie said. "When they got off work at the studio or came in from the ranch, they'd stop by here."

Cody gave Julie an affectionate wink. "My favorite waterin' hole."

C.J. sipped hers slowly. It was so hot this afternoon, she could almost develop a taste for beer. *Almost*.

"Julie, there has to be more. You said your grandfather mentioned something about things changing soon."

"Yes, but he never did say how that was going to happen."

"Did he mention anything about Gloria being involved?"

"No. He didn't approve of what she'd gotten herself into—with the drugs—but I think more than anything he just felt sorry for her."

C.J. tried another angle. "What if Dan threatened to go to the studio about her selling drugs?"

"He wouldn't do that to her."

Knowing this was difficult, she took Julie's hand. "What was his mood the day he died? Did he seem preoccupied about anything, or upset? Did he change his routine in any way?"

Julie shook her head. "No, in fact, I'd never seen him

happier. This was to be his last picture, and he was actually glad about it. That was unusual for him. He'd always worried before about what he'd do for money if he had to retire and lose his income from the studio."

"Did he do anything differently in the weeks before he died?"

"No—" Julie stopped. "Well, lately he'd started reading the Bible."

"The Bible? And he didn't before?"

Julie laughed softly. "Grandpa wasn't what you would call religious. But when I moved him in from the ranch he brought this old Bible with him. It was our family Bible going way back. I found it and packed it away. Grandpa unpacked all that stuff when he moved in with me. He was fascinated with it. I suppose because it had a lot of family history in it. He would sit for hours with it open on his lap, and talk about what he remembered of his grandmother and his parents. "

Sam thought of Rollie Prescott, Dan's grandfather and Traeger's partner. Most family Bibles had records of marriage, births, and deaths. He supposed Rollie's death was recorded there as well. It gave him a strange feeling to realize that for him those events had happened just a couple of weeks earlier. But for Dan and Julie, it was family history going back more than a hundred years.

He watched Katy as she got up and slowly paced the kitchen. She never failed to amaze him. One minute she was tough as hardtack defending that little kid they'd encountered, and the next she was gently questioning Julie. She had heart, lots of it, and she had guts.

Julie went on. "That morning was like any other morning. Granddad was excited about the scene they were going to be shooting that day. He always liked the action scenes. It gave him a chance to do his thing."

C.J. asked, "Did he say anything unusual? Did he mention a meeting with anyone? Or maybe a name you didn't recognize?"

Before Julie could answer, Cody said slowly, "Matthew."

C.J. looked at him. "What did you say?"

He sat staring down into his beer. Then he slowly raised his head. His eyes were red-rimmed and his voice broke a little. It had nothing to do with the beer.

"The last thing he said was 'Matthew.' I remember thinking it was strange, 'cause he didn't mention Julie's name, or nothing. Just 'Matthew.'"

Sam's chair thumped down onto all four legs.

"Rollie Prescott said exactly that same thing before he died."

Cody and Julie both looked at Sam as if they thought he might have had a little too much beer.

Cody said sharply, "Rollie Prescott?"

C.J. stared at Sam. Then she was across the kitchen and pulling him out of his chair. "We'll be right back," she threw over her shoulder as she dragged him into the living room beyond earshot of the kitchen.

"What did you say?"

Sam stared down at her.

"I was with Rollie Prescott when he died, before the earthquake. The last thing he said was 'Matthew.'"

"Matthew! Oh, Sam, if both of them said that name just before they died, it's got to mean something!"

"At the time I thought maybe it was his kid. The boy was right there in the house when I went out there. I just assumed he was callin' for his son."

"C.J.?" Julie called from the kitchen. "Is Sam all right?"

"He's just fine," she replied. She racked her brain desperately for a connection of some kind. It had to be there.

"What could the name Matthew possibly mean to two men, generations apart?"

They stood there thinking furiously. Then Sam said, "The Bible."

C.J. blinked, then her eyes widened. "The old family Bible!"

He gave her that slow, lazy grin that did strange things to her heart rhythm.

"Matthew, Mark, Luke, and John," he recited.

C.J. turned to the kitchen. "Julie, where is your family Bible?"

A moment later her hands shook as she took the Bible from Julie. What could the Book of Matthew possibly mean to both Dan and Rollie Prescott?

The Bible was huge and heavy, the leather binding dried and peeling away from the spine. Just as Sam predicted, there were entries in the front of the Bible, going back through six generations of Prescotts. The names of Rollie and Addie Prescott and the date of their marriage was the first entry. The second was the birth of their son—Matthew—Dan's father.

She didn't know where to begin to look through the huge volume for the Book of Matthew and looked up at Sam helplessly. Taking the Bible in his large, rough hands with something like reverence, he turned immediately to the appropriate place.

A piece of folded paper fluttered to the worn carpet at his feet.

Chapter 16

"What is it?"

C.J. scooped up the paper and carefully unfolded it. It was old and yellowed and very thick. She carefully read the hand lettering, frowning slightly.

"Katy?"

She looked up. "It's a deed."

Julie came around to peer over C.J.'s shoulder. Her eyes widened with fascination. "It's a deed from Rollie Prescott to Addie Jennings Prescott. Do you think it's real?"

"It looks real enough. It's certainly real old."

Julie read a legal description of property set out in legalese that was over one hundred years old. "Maybe it's the original deed to the ranch property."

"What's the date of the deed?" Sam asked as a thoughtful expression furrowed his brow.

"June 25, 1882." Julie read the date of the document. "And it was notarized on the same date."

"Two days before Rollie died," Sam mused thoughtfully out loud.

"What did you say?" Julie looked at him with a perplexed expression.

C.J. replied quickly, "Sam was just remembering the entries from the front of the Bible." She gave him a pointed look. "Weren't you, Sam?"

"Yeah, right."

Julie looked in the front of the Bible. "You're right. It says here that Rollie Prescott died on June 27, 1882."

She read through the other entries. "That goes back six generations. That would make Addie my great-great-grandmother. Seems like a strange place to keep a document."

C.J. was thinking exactly the same thing.

"Look, Julie, could I borrow this deed? I'd like to check it out—see if it's authentic."

Julie shrugged. "Sure, go ahead. I don't need it. The ranch property is in my name now. But I would like to have it back, as a keepsake. We Prescotts don't have much, but we do have a family history."

C.J. looked up at Julie as something she said clicked. "I'll take good care of it," she promised.

As they walked to the car, Sam asked, "What is it?"

She got behind the wheel. "Probably just grasping at straws."

"Come again?" Sam asked as he slid in beside her.

She talked while she drove. "A hunch." She smiled teasingly. "You know, one of those gut feelings."

"Such as?"

Her smile deepened as she glanced at Sam and saw him cringe as she wove through heavy traffic. It was almost noon, and everyone seemed to pour onto the freeways.

"There's got to be a connection, so let's try to find it." While she drove, C.J. went over what they knew so far about the deed. "Months before he died, Dan Prescott took to reading the Bible, something he wasn't in the habit of doing. My guess is he found the deed when Julie moved him from the ranch property."

"Which," Sam cut in, "the Prescott family had owned for several generations. So the deed is worthless."

"Dan Prescott obviously considered it important. He was trying to tell Cody that when he died."

"There's something else that bothers me about that deed," she went on, briefly glancing over her shoulder as she changed lanes at breakneck speed.

"What's that?"

"Well, I realize it undoubtedly doesn't mean anything to you, but that deed is in Addie Prescott's name, *alone*."

Sam failed to see what significance that held. "She was a widow after Traeger killed Rollie Prescott."

"Except that the deed was dated two days before Rollie

was killed," C.J. pointed out. "And while I applaud such a progressive decision for way back then, it's still a fact that most women didn't own property in their own names."

"That's true," Sam agreed thoughtfully.

She swerved, cut off a slow driver, and shot onto the off ramp. When the driver honked loudly she merely made a face in her rearview mirror.

"Will you slow this thing down?" Sam grumbled.

"Just trying to keep you on your toes." She grinned. Then she went on. "All right, why would Rollie put the title to the land in his wife's name?"

"Are you trying to make one of those *feminine* statements about all this?"

"The word is *feminist*, and no, that has nothing to do with it. But the reason Rollie executed that deed does. It was just before Traeger shot him."

"In the back," Sam reminded her, "his specialty."

"The question is, why did Traeger shoot his own partner in the back?"

Sam went on to speculate. "When Prescott left the gang, there was talk he took a lot of money with him— money stolen in various bank robberies. Maybe Traeger came after it."

"Did Traeger get what he came after?" C.J. crossed yet another lane to the exasperated honking of several drivers, then drove off the off ramp.

"I think it's safe to assume he did," Sam muttered, "since he obviously became a man of wealth and stature in the years following Rollie's death."

C.J. agreed with that as far as it went. "True enough, but you said Rollie had sunk every penny he owned into that farm property. In fact, he had just bought another section adjacent to it."

"Are we there yet? Wherever it is we're going?" There was a tinge of desperation in Sam's voice as C.J. cut in and out of traffic with a singular lack of caution.

"Almost," she assured him with a devilish grin as she cut through a yellow light at the next intersection, turned left, and shot across an overpass. Three more lights, a right turn, and she pulled into the parking lot of an ultramodern multistory concrete and bronze-glassed building. The Mustang lurched into a parking space.

"By the way, where was that farm located?" C.J. asked.

"How should I know?" Sam said as he swung out of the car. "Somewhere in town, but everything has changed now."

They cut across the parking lot and into the bronze-glassed office building.

"What is this place?"

C.J. explained. "If you want to know about a piece of property, you go to a title company. This place handled the transfer of the agency when Harry Carlucci died. They have access to all county records, even those recorded over a hundred years ago."

"May I help you?" the young woman at the Customer Service desk asked with a glowing smile aimed at Sam. C.J. immediately pegged her as a hopeful starlet. She was tall and long-legged with a breathy voice that spoke of seductive promises and very little gray matter.

She replied, "I'd like some information about a piece of property." She slid the deed across the counter.

The young woman frowned slightly, except that it came out more as a sensual little pout that C.J. had no doubt she practiced before a mirror for hours.

"It's very old. The property has undoubtedly been split up after all this time. Do you have a more recent description?"

"No, just that one."

The clerk turned toward a computer. "I'll give it a try, but it may take a while."

"Thanks, we'll wait."

To C.J.'s surprise, she was back in five minutes. "Silly me for not recognizing the description right away. The date of the deed threw me. But one of the other girls recognized it."

"You know this property?"

The young woman shrugged. "Sure, who doesn't, after all the publicity and everything."

"What publicity?"

The clerk looked from C.J. to Sam. "Just the single

biggest land transaction in Los Angeles County in the last
ten years. It'll be worth hundreds of millions of dollars
when the Japanese finally get through buying it. The first
phase is in escrow right now."

Sam asked, "What is this property?"

"U.F.S." She smiled up at him brilliantly.

"U.F.S.?" Sam asked.

"United Film Studios," C.J. slowly translated for him.

The young woman looked at her. "You got it. The last
major, privately held studio. There have been lots of
write-ups in the paper about it."

Her thoughts churned. "And you're certain this is the
same property description?"

"Of course I'm sure. Everyone knows the U.F.S.
property. You know, that deed might be a collector's item."

C.J. had a sudden idea and asked, "Could I get a copy
of the deed that originally transferred title of the property
to the Traeger family?"

The clerk gave her a cool look. "It's almost noon. There
wouldn't be time before I leave for lunch. Besides, that isn't
part of our customer service. You'd have to get a title search
for that."

C.J. remembered the weeks it had taken to get a title
search on Harry's property. She struggled to be patient.
"Look, we don't have time for a title report. I'd gladly pay
you for the copy. It shouldn't be that difficult. It's just one
document."

"Look, I really can't—" The young woman started to
object. She clearly had no intention of cooperating. Then
Sam leaned across the counter.

"Look, darlin'," he said with his lazy drawl as he took
the clerk's hand between his, "I would truly appreciate it if
you could help us out on this. It's real important."

The clerk melted. "Well, I suppose I could make an
exception—just for you."

"I won't forget it."

"All right, I'll be right back."

As the young woman left, Sam turned to C.J. with a
grin that could only be called devilish. Her knees turned to

mush as she remembered the last time she'd seen that same smile and what had followed afterward.

"A little charm never hurt, Katy," he reminded her.

A few minutes later the clerk returned with a copy of the deed from Prescott to Traeger. Sam thanked her and he and C.J. went out to her car.

As she quickly scanned the deed from Prescott to his wife, then compared it to the one from Prescott to Traeger, she whispered, "Oh, my God."

"What is it?" Sam asked.

She collapsed back against the seat. "This is unbelievable."

"Are you going to tell me what that says?" Sam demanded, turning in his seat to face her.

C.J. slowly looked up and whispered incredulously. "It was Traeger all along."

"What are you talking about? Which Traeger?"

"The original deed to the property was signed by Rollie Prescott to Emmett Traeger. Look at the dates."

Sam read the information on the copy of the document. "It says here it was signed and recorded on June 27, 1882." He looked up at her slowly. "Traeger must have forced Rollie to sign it the day he went out to the farm. Then he shot him."

She knew the most important part still hadn't clicked into place for Sam. He frowned as he stared down at the documents. Then he looked up and went on slowly. "Rollie Prescott signed over property to Traeger that wasn't even in his name."

"Exactly! It was already in his wife's name. But Traeger had no way of knowing that. That's why when you saw Prescott he tried to tell you where to find the deed."

"Only I didn't realize what he meant." Sam put the rest of the pieces of the puzzle together. "That deed wasn't filed, so no one knew that the property really belonged to Addie Prescott."

C.J. nodded. "That must have been when she moved out to the ranch with her son. She never knew the farm was still hers. But why didn't Rollie tell her he had transferred the property to her?"

"Traeger must have shot him before he got the chance to tell her," Sam reasoned, then went on. "Dan Prescott knew what this deed meant. He must have gone to Traeger, perhaps hoping for some sort of settlement. That's probably what he meant when he told Julie everything was going to change for them. Only Traeger didn't want to pay, or else was afraid that Dan might still try to get the property back. Then Traeger killed Dan Prescott and tried to make it look like an accident."

"And we know he probably killed Gloria Ames," C.J. added. "She was an opportunist. Her career was just about finished. My guess is, she saw Traeger go into the prop trailer that morning."

"Then, when Dan was killed, she went to Traeger and tried to make a deal."

C.J. nodded sadly. "For someone like Gloria, that would be the thing to do. Only she didn't realize how dangerous Traeger was."

"And it was Traeger who ransacked your office trying to find out just how close you were to the truth." Sam's voice hardened. "It was Traeger who pushed you off that catwalk and set the fire out at the ranch."

C.J. said, "And it was Traeger who tore Julie's place apart looking for the deed."

Sam thrust the papers back at C.J. "Now we go after Traeger, like I wanted to do in the first place."

"Sam, wait! It's not that simple."

"Katy, I let you handle this your way. Now we'll do it my way."

"No!"

He turned on her. "Don't push me on this, Katy."

"You can't simply go after Traeger because we *think* we know what happened. It's too big. There's too much at stake."

"What the hell are you talking about?"

"I'm talking about a right way and a wrong way to do this."

"*My* way, Katy."

They were back to that again. She wanted to scream. "The right way, in 1989. Listen to me. We need help."

"I want Traeger." The muscles in Sam's jaw worked as he stared hard-faced out across the parking lot.

"I know that. I want him too. But the truth is, we don't have any real evidence, even with the deed. We can't prove he knew about it." She laid her hand on his arm, feeling the anger in the hardened muscles beneath her fingers. "*Please*, Sam."

"You better be right about this, Katy." His voice was low and cold. "I lost his great-grandfather; I won't lose him." When he turned there was a look in his eyes she'd seen only once before—in that old photograph of Sam Hackett, U.S. Federal Marshal as he stood over the bodies of the men he'd hunted down and killed.

They drove back to Venice and C.J. put in a call to Tom Gates. When he got off duty he drove out to meet them.

When she explained everything and showed him the deed he exclaimed, "Jesus, C.J.! Do you have any idea what you're talking about with all this?" He looked from her to Sam.

"I have a pretty good idea."

"You've got nothing but circumstantial evidence," he informed her as he brushed back his shoulder-length hair which was all part of his undercover identity as a drug dealer.

"We know Traeger killed Gloria Ames," she shot back at him.

"You've got the word of a bag lady who does regular tours of duty at the psychiatric ward, and some chicano kid who probably turns fifty to a hundred thousand a year in high-class stolen automobiles. And you don't even know his name. I thought Harry Carlucci taught you better than that."

"That's why I came to you. How do we get Traeger?"

"You can't. You haven't got enough. You need a credible witness that the D.A.'s office could put on the stand. And even then there's the stolen-car report. Traeger could still beat it."

"You're saying it's hopeless."

"Pretty much so," Tom admitted. He came around the desk and took C.J. gently by the shoulders.

"Look, you've got the deed. Get it authenticated. Have your client get herself a good attorney and she could get a big settlement."

C.J. shrugged out of his grasp. "It's not enough."

"Why the hell not? Be practical, C.J."

She turned on him, aware that Sam sat quietly, too quietly, watching their exchange. He hadn't said one word since Tom arrived. "Because my client hired me to find out who killed her grandfather."

"So tell her, but explain the reality of things to her. She'll be thrilled when she finds out she's entitled to a chunk of U.F.S. Sometimes, sweetheart, you have to cut your losses."

She stubbornly shook her head. "No."

Tom paced across her office, jamming his hands into the pockets of his jeans. "Why can't you just collect a big fat fee and let it go?"

Her gaze locked with Sam's. "Because someone once told me that there are some things you just can't let go."

"C.J. . . ."

Sam came up out of his chair and moved on Tom. "You heard the lady."

Tom looked from Sam to C.J.

She stepped between them, leaning back against the solid strength of Sam's hard-muscled shoulder. "There has to be a way, Tom. You can come up with something."

Tom shook his head. "There is one way. But it's dangerous . . ."

"No! I won't let you do it!" Sam shouted at her.

"I thought you wanted to get Traeger."

"I do. But I'm not gonna let you risk your life."

She crossed the office and put her hands on his shoulders. "Sam, please. It's the only way we can prove Traeger's involvement. We need a confession."

His lean fingers closed over her arms as if he would shake some sense into her if all else failed. "Tom said it's dangerous. And he's right."

"Why, Sam Hackett," she said softly, reaching up to

stroke her fingers against his cheek, "to hear you, someone would think you actually care what happens to me."

"I do care, Katy. More than you know."

"I'll be perfectly safe. I'll be wearing a wire and I'll have a gun." She gave him an indignant look when he choked on that last statement.

"Yeah, if you don't shoot yourself."

"It'll be all right. Tom's the best."

Sam gave her a look that told her exactly what he thought of that assessment. "I don't trust any man who wears an earring." "It's just part of his disguise." That was a small lie, but she didn't want to get into the fact that a lot of men wore earrings. "I know his record, and I trust him. Tom and his men will be right there if I need any help."

"Help with what?"

They both turned around as Lucy burst in the door followed by Redford and Newman. The cat sauntered in and jumped on his favorite perch. Newman was the last in the door, dragging his paws, his tongue lolling out the side of his mouth.

"We jogged. Really, C.J., you must do something about that dog's diet. He's getting to be a real slug."

C.J. ignored Lucy's question. She didn't want to open herself up to any more criticism by explaining what they were planning.

"I need to talk to you two. You're so busy, I considered making an appointment, except you're never here to get your messages."

"We've been busy with the Prescott case. What did you want to talk to us about?"

"The date." Lucy removed Redford from his perch and snuggled into the chair, tucking her legs beneath her brilliant lime-green jogging outfit.

"What date? What are you talking about?"

"The date for Sam to go back."

C.J. was stunned. "Back?"

"Back in time, back to 1882. Ravi pinpointed the date and time of the next big aftershock."

"Mother, please." She was tired, they had a lot ahead of them tomorrow, and she wasn't in the mood to talk nonsense with Lucy.

"I know what you think about all this, C.J., but the fact is that Ravi has calculated everything precisely. It has to do with the time-space continuum when certain celestial bodies line up and a door in time opens. That's how Sam got here in the first place. Anyway, Ravi has been out at the Griffith Park Observatory every night for the last week, charting everything."

"And tomorrow night, at precisely nine-seventeen P.M. there will be an aftershock. Sam has to be in the identical spot he was in when the first earthquake hit."

"I don't believe that Ravi can predict the exact date and time of the next earthquake," C.J. insisted.

Sam spoke up quietly behind her. "So it's tomorrow night."

She whirled around. "You actually believe all this?"

"Well, I got here somehow. Maybe Lucy knows what she's talkin' about."

"You're both nuts." She stormed out of the office and up the stairs.

Sam looked at Lucy. For the first time in his life he felt helpless.

"You better go to her, Sam. There isn't much time."

He found her standing in the upstairs parlor. The lights were out, there was only the scattered light from the moon outside as it raced with the clouds over the ocean. The windows were open, the curtains lifting restlessly on a night wind that carried the heavy, tangy fragrance of a summer storm.

"Please don't turn on the lights," she whispered as she moved away from him, cursing as she collided with the coffee table.

"We need to talk."

"No. It's late. We've a big day ahead of us tomorrow. Let's just . . . go to sleep."

She moved toward the bedroom.

"Katy, wait." His hand stopped her. The first flash of

lightning lit up the night sky and reflected in her darkened eyes.

She looked at him helplessly. "If we talk about it, I'll feel like I'm as crazy as old Stella."

He saw the flash of anger and it surprised him. "But you don't believe in it."

"I don't need to. *You* believe in it." Something came and went in her face—the first shadow of real sorrow he'd ever seen there.

"You said yourself that I don't belong here."

She looked at him. "Do you want to go?"

Standing there, touching her, he realized that he already missed her. He wanted to choose the right words, say the right thing. Over and over the last few days, ever since Lucy came up with a way to get him back, he'd imagined what he would say to her, what he would do.

He thought he'd experienced bad times before. He'd been wrong. Pain tightened in his stomach like a fist with claws. Because it was unexpected, it was that much worse. She made him see things in new ways, made him feel things he'd never felt before.

It *was* late, much too late to pretend he didn't want her. Need her.

C.J. took his hand and placed his palm against her cheek. The contact was so simple, so tender, and yet it sent a jolt through them both. She turned her face so that her lips pressed into his palm. Then, reaching up on her toes, she pressed her open mouth to his.

She curled around him, her lips quick and urgent. She framed his face with her hands, tracing the planes and angles with her mouth.

His blood was hammering. Sam could feel it in his head, somewhere below his stomach, and in his fingertips.

Like the storm that raced the pounding surf outside, she was all flash and fire. His arms banded around her, holding her hard and close as he fought to maintain some control. But she was pushing him beyond the limits he always set for himself, away from reason, beyond time.

He heard his own breath come fast and uneven. His skin was moist and hot from need.

"Katy." His mouth was against her throat as he tasted, devoured. More . . . he could only think of having more. He would have absorbed her into him if he knew how so that she would always be there.

Quickly they tore off each other's clothes, then sank to the floor.

Rain, tossed by the restless wind, hit the open window, soaking the curtains and puddling on the floor.

There were no murmured promises, no whispered endearments. Neither were there tender caresses or gentle kisses. There were only sighs and shudders. Only demands and hunger.

There was no gentleness when they came together, only the need driving them. Lightning flashed, highlighting her face and hair. Her head was thrown back, her eyes clear and open when they finally came together with a violent urgency that bordered on desperation.

C.J. turned her face into his throat as they lay twined together. She didn't want him to see her tears.

He tilted her head back with a finger under her chin. Her eyes were wide and luminous. His were intense.

His lips met hers with such fragile tenderness that her breath became a helpless moan. Her eyes shuttered close at the sound. She was a strong woman, but she had no defense against his tenderness. She had never believed she would need a man to watch over her. But at that moment she didn't know how she could live without him.

Sam lifted her in his arms, her silken skin warm against his chest as she curled into him. She was delicate now as her bones seemed to dissolve into him, leaving her smaller, softer. The knowledge struck him; he'd waited a lifetime for her.

The knot tightened in his throat. If she asked it, he would stay. If she were another kind of woman, she would have. The woman he'd come to know wouldn't ask that of him.

"We have tonight, Katy," he whispered as he carried her to the bed.

Chapter 17

C.J. was up before dawn.

Sam remained asleep, his outstretched arm lying across the empty expanse of bed where C.J. had lain. His fingers curled slightly, as if even in sleep he wanted to hold on to her. The ache that had begun last night with Lucy's news intensified as she looked down at him.

C.J. had tried to soothe the ache by losing herself in Sam. They made love again and again. Each time it was new and different. There was so much to discover about him. Each time they came together, then lay spent, she wanted him more. She knew with absolute certainty she could never get enough of him.

That thought drove her from the warmth of his body out onto the beach in the cold grayness of early dawn. It had never been like this before with the other men she'd known. Those other men were only a prelude to this man, this time, this passion.

As she walked along the deserted beach, in the fragile moments between night and day, she realized that time was the key. She'd always believed in the importance of timing. Not luck, karma, predestination, fate, or any of the other concepts her mother embraced with such zealous devotion. But *timing*, when everything clicked into place easily, naturally.

Time had brought her and Sam together. If Lucy and Ravi were right for once in their harebrained lives—and C.J. had an awful sinking sensation that they might be—time would separate her and Sam forever.

Not that she would stop him from leaving even if she

could. She didn't believe in controlling another person, manipulating another person's life to suit her own wishes. Sam had the right to return to his own time.

His own time. C.J.'s smile was bittersweet as she dug her bare toes into the wet sand at the edge of the water and contemplated a phrase from the Bible.

To everything there is a time under heaven.

This had been their brief time under heaven. Now their time was running out.

There was always the possibility that Lucy and Ravi's theory wouldn't work and Sam wouldn't get back to 1882. Even Sam had said the idea seemed ridiculous. Any rational scientist would reject it.

Of course, any rational scientist would reject the whole notion of time travel too.

C.J. had decided that she wouldn't go with Sam and Lucy. She told herself it was pointless because she didn't believe in Lucy's silly theory anyway. But the truth was she was afraid Lucy might be right for once.

At any rate, she hated good-byes. In her own way she'd said good-bye to Sam last night. She couldn't bear to go through a formal, polite leave-taking.

Determined not to think of any of this any longer, she began to run down the beach, and continued running until her side ached and the muscles in her feet and calves screamed with exhaustion.

The sky was a pale blue-gray as she returned to the apartment. A cool breeze came in off the water. Other people began to appear on the beach—early morning surfers, an occasional jogger, a man walking a fat, plodding basset hound.

C.J. walked up the boardwalk from the beach to the road that ran between the houses and the sand. Looking up as she reached her house, she saw Sam standing nonchalantly, leaning against the door frame at the upstairs landing. Dressed only in jeans, he was barefoot. It struck her that he could have been any other contemporary man, right down to the cup of coffee he held in his hand.

But he wasn't any other man. He was the man she'd looked for over so many lonely years, and despaired of finding. *Where do you find a really terrific guy?* she'd asked herself repeatedly. The answer was simple—in another time.

Sam said quietly, "I woke up and you were gone." He searched her face. "Are you all right?"

She knew he referred to her emotional state rather than physical well-being. She never would have expected such a personal question from someone who kept his feelings to himself. Sam wasn't used to analyzing emotions. Because of who and what he was, as well as the time he came from, he just wasn't that kind of man. The fact that he asked such a question now showed how he had changed.

C.J. knew she had changed as well. Neither of them would ever be quite the same again.

She gazed out at the ocean, unable to meet Sam's look as she answered. "I couldn't sleep. I slipped out quietly so I wouldn't wake you."

He smiled rakishly. "That didn't seem to concern you when you woke me up at midnight, and again at three o'clock."

Her gaze snapped back to his. She melted inside. He was so damn sexy and sweet, and she wanted him so much. Suddenly she was intensely aware of her body—sweaty and sandy from the long run on the beach. She needed a shower badly.

Then a thought struck her. Bounding up the stairs, she took Sam's hand and pulled him inside. "Come on. I'm going to show you how to thoroughly enjoy a shower."

"I already had one," he protested.

"You haven't had one like this."

Neither had she, C.J. realized two hours later as she sat in her office, bringing her file on the Prescott case up to date. Sam had headed for the beach with Newman. Redford was curled up in C.J.'s in basket. It was just after eight o'clock, Lucy hadn't arrived yet, and C.J. was alone.

Taking advantage of the rare moment of privacy, she had called Tom Gates and together they had planned how they would set up Emmett Traeger for a big fall. Then she had called Traeger at home and arranged to meet him at his office later that afternoon. Knowing how Sam would feel about this, C.J. made a point of doing it before he got back.

Traeger's voice had sounded smooth, in control, yet with an undercurrent of surprise. After all, they hadn't parted on the best of terms after their date. C.J. told him she needed to see him to discuss a recent development in the Prescott case—which was certainly true, in a sense. He agreed to meet her at three o'clock—right after executive lunchtime.

At one o'clock she was to meet with Tom to be "wired." He would fit her with a tiny, concealed microphone and explain exactly what she was to say to Traeger. The crucial thing was to get Traeger to admit that he had killed Prescott and Gloria Ames. She wanted to get Traeger—wanted it as badly as Sam had wanted to get another Traeger.

Facing a murderer alone, pretending that she wanted to blackmail him, was the most challenging role C.J. had ever tackled as an actress. She just hoped she could pull it off. She'd always told herself she was good—now she would find out for sure.

Sam returned from his walk, holding Newman in his arms.

"My God, is he okay?" C.J. asked, rushing over to him.

Sam lay Newman down on the sofa in the reception area. "Damn fool dog nearly got me killed."

"What happened?" she asked, grabbing some tissues from a box and dabbing at some minor scratches on Newman's face.

"He had a run-in with a dog named Rambo."

C.J. knew Rambo well. He was eighty pounds of the meanest rottweiler on the beach—the muscle dog of Venice Beach.

"Newman never did have much sense. He won't back down."

"Is that right?" Sam asked wryly. "Then, after I stepped in and saved him, he refused to walk back. Just stood here, looking at me and wagging his tail."

C.J. giggled. "I can just see you two talking that one over."

"*That*"—Sam pointed to Newman—"is a worthless dog."

"Then why did you take him with you?" she asked with a smile.

Sam shrugged. "Aw, hell, he means well."

As C.J. sat beside Newman, who actually needed a little tender-loving-care more than actual medical care, she knew that she would have to tell Sam what she was going to do. She couldn't lie to him. He'd see right through her.

Taking a deep breath, she said point-blank, "I called Tom and I'm going after Traeger today."

Sam's expression sobered in an instant. "Why can't someone else do it?"

"I'm the only one who can set him up to get a confession out of him. It's the only way to nail him. There just isn't any hard evidence that would stand up in court. Tom is going to fit me with a hidden microphone."

At Sam's confused look, she explained. "That's a device that will allow Tom to listen to my conversation with Traeger from another location, and record the whole thing. I'm going to pretend I'm trying to blackmail Traeger, just as Gloria Ames did, and hopefully I'll get him to admit that he killed Gloria and Dan Prescott."

"I'm going with you."

She knew he would say that. His immediate reaction would always be to protect her. Unfortunately, this was one time she couldn't let him do that.

"Sam, listen to me, it won't work unless I'm alone with him. He won't admit anything if someone else, especially you, is there."

"But it's dangerous!"

She met his look. "Yes. But it's the only way to get him. If I don't do this, I'll fail in my job. I'll fail Julie, my client. And I'll fail myself."

"Why does it have to be this way?" he demanded.

"Because we can't bring the bad guys in dead or alive anymore. We need proof. And I'm the only one who can get it."

He was silent for a long moment, considering what she'd just said.

C.J. swallowed hard. Everything depended on how Sam dealt with this. If he chose to, he could prevent her from doing this—at least that day. But more important, it would destroy the fragile understanding they'd reached. He had to accept that her work was part of her, that it was every bit as important to her as his work was to him. If he couldn't accept that, then they were back where they'd started the day they met, a man and a woman who couldn't begin to understand each other.

Sam's inner struggle was evident in his eyes. A strong, proud man, it was difficult, maybe impossible, for him to back down from what he saw as his responsibility to protect the woman he loved. He'd changed profoundly in the brief time that C.J. had known him. The question was, had he changed enough?

Sam's mouth had set in a tight line. Now it relaxed. "All right."

C.J. stared at him. "What?"

"I know you're gonna do it whether I want you to or not."

"I have to, Sam."

"Just one thing—I'm gonna be as close as possible without actually being in Traeger's office with you."

She grinned. "I'd like that."

By one o'clock C.J. had devoured two candy bars in her nervousness. The caffeine in the chocolate had her almost as wired as the small electronics device nestled between her breasts.

The tiny microphone was taped against her chest, with a wire wrapped around her ribs and hooked into a small but powerful amplifier. The amp was necessary because of the distance her conversation with Traeger would have to travel—from his thirtieth-floor office to the unmarked police van on the street below.

As C.J., Tom, his partner, and Sam entered the elevator in the U.F.S. building, Tom said, "Now, remember, we'll be in the stairwell just down the hall from Traeger's office. We'll be monitoring the conversation along with the guys in the van. If anything goes wrong, we'll be in Traeger's office in a flash."

"How do you feel, Katy?" Sam asked in concern.

"A bit like Frankenstein with all these electrodes and wires."

She started to add a quick explanation of who Frankenstein was, but Sam interrupted. "It's okay, I read Mary Shelley's book."

Sam Hackett, you never cease to surprise me, C.J. thought.

The elevator reached the thirtieth floor and the chrome and smoked-glass doors opened. It belatedly occurred to her that for once Sam hadn't been frightened by the elevator ride. Tom and his partner headed for the stairwell just down the hall, but Sam hesitated. The faint lines at the corners of his eyes and his mouth that made his handsome face rugged rather than merely attractive had deepened with worry. C.J. realized how afraid for her he was.

She laid the palm of her hand against his cheek. "I'm okay. Don't worry."

"You don't have to go through with it. You could let someone else handle it."

"Could you do that?"

He sighed. "I just wish you weren't going in alone."

"I know."

"Remember what kind of man you're dealing with, Katy. Traeger's ruthless and cunning."

"Which Traeger are you referring to?" she asked with a hint of a smile.

"It doesn't matter. They're both the same. I knew it as soon as I saw the man. It's there, just like it was in his great-grandfather."

C.J. stood on tiptoe to kiss Sam. "Just promise me one thing," she whispered.

"What's that?"

"If I get in a jam, you send in the cavalry." She smiled at his perplexed expression. "Just get there as fast as you can."

"I'll be there," he promised.

Not until C.J. turned and began walking toward Traeger's office at the end of the hall did Sam head for the stairwell.

In the office Traeger's receptionist greeted her. "Good afternoon, Miss Grant. Mr. Traeger's expecting you. Go right in."

She took a deep breath, prayed that the microphone was still working, and entered Traeger's private office.

"C.J., how are you?" Traeger asked, coming forward to meet her.

As he reached for her, she sidestepped around him and moved toward the bank of floor-to-ceiling windows behind his desk. "You really have a magnificent view," she said in a voice that she hoped didn't betray her nervousness.

He frowned, clearly surprised by her coolness. "Would you like something to drink?" he asked politely, walking over to a bar built into one wall and concealed behind mirrored doors. At the touch of a button the doors opened, revealing the lavishly stocked bar.

"No, thank you." She swallowed back a tiny, hard knot of nervousness deep in her throat. Actually, a good, stiff drink sounded wonderful, but she needed to keep her wits about her.

"So tell me," Traeger asked as he poured Perrier into a crystal glass, "are you still running around questioning people about this alleged case?"

C.J. forced herself to turn and face him. "Actually, no."

"Decided to give it up, eh? That's probably for the best. You were just wasting your time anyway. Now you can go on to bigger and better things." He raised his glass in mocking salute before taking a sip of mineral water.

"I've been thinking, C.J.," he continued in that smooth, silky manner that was so successful at manipulating people, "you should consider reviving your acting career. I could speak to a few of the right people and see what sort of role we could come up with."

Was it intended to be a reward for dropping the case, C.J. wondered, or a bribe to insure that she not pursue it in the future? She gritted her teeth. Sam was right—

Traeger was slick, no, *slimy*, she thought with a clarity that hadn't been there when she was briefly dazzled by him.

"I'm through with acting," she replied. Except, of course, for the role she was playing at that moment. "I think the Prescott case will turn out to be so lucrative I won't have to work again."

His expression changed ever so subtly.

"Oh? How is that?"

"In the beginning I really didn't think there was a case," she admitted. "But as I investigated, I kept coming back to something you said."

He raised one dark eyebrow. "Me?"

C.J. slowly walked around the perimeter of the large office, never too close to Traeger, but never so far away that the mike wouldn't catch his voice. She ran her finger appraisingly over a Meissen vase, then continued. "You commented that Prescott's death had to be an accident."

"That's right. It was an accident."

"That statement didn't make sense. Prescott was, by all accounts, very careful with guns. He always checked them before a scene. If the propman had made a mistake, Prescott would have caught it. Since he didn't catch it, that meant someone substituted a real bullet for the blank right before the scene. That couldn't be an accident. It had to be deliberate."

Did she imagine it, C.J. wondered, or had Traeger's hand tightened around the crystal glass?

She went on. "Then other things happened."

"Such as?"

"Someone ransacked my office. I had nothing worth stealing, and the burglar didn't take anything anyway. I think he was looking for my file on the Prescott case. Then there was the incident at the wrap party."

"An accident," Traeger insisted.

"*Another* accident? That's quite a coincidence. I think someone was trying to discourage me."

"Go on." Traeger's voice had changed. There was a sharp edge that hadn't been there before.

"I talked to Gloria Ames. I felt that she had either

killed Prescott or knew who had. Then Gloria was killed by a hit-and-run driver. Another *accident*."

Staring intently at Traeger, C.J. added, "There was a witness the night Gloria was killed."

"I find that hard to believe. According to the police report, there weren't any witnesses."

"The police missed this witness. She gave a full description of the car and the license number—twelve, twenty-seven, thirty-nine."

She saw him stiffen, and she began to relax and enjoy herself.

"My car was stolen early that evening," Traeger insisted. "Hours before Gloria died. I filed a police report."

"That was very clever of you, Emmett. But your car wasn't stolen, was it? You drove it that night."

She saw the subtle shift of his gaze toward a door that led to the adjoining office suite. Briefly, she worried that he might be thinking of making a break for it. But it didn't matter, she told herself. Sam was out there, and there was no way Traeger would get past him.

She went on with growing confidence. "Witnesses saw you abandon your car just three blocks from where Gloria was killed."

His eyes darkened dangerously as he slammed the glass down on his desk. The water sloshed over the rim and onto the highly polished granite. "Just who are these supposed witnesses?"

Refusing to answer the question, C.J. continued. "I knew there had to be a motive. I assumed you killed Gloria because she was blackmailing you over Prescott's death. But why would you kill Prescott? As you said, he was a washed-up old bit player, a nobody."

"I don't have time for a ridiculous conversation like this." Traeger moved toward the intercom on his desk.

C.J. wasn't about to let him call a security guard to remove her. Leaning across the desk, she stopped his hand with hers. Staring into his face, only inches from hers, she said, "I found the deed, Emmett."

In an instant his pretense of mild irritation vanished. "Where is it?" he demanded harshly.

She pulled back. "Incredible, isn't it? When your great-grandfather forced Rollie Prescott to deed this land to him, it was illegal. Prescott had already deeded the land to his wife, but he didn't have time to tell her before your great-grandfather killed him."

Gesturing out the window, toward the studio in the background, C.J. said, "All of this—some of the most valuable property in L.A.—belongs to the Prescott family. Not the Traegers."

"That would never stand up in court!"

"Wouldn't it? Then why did you kill Prescott when he confronted you?" When Traeger didn't answer, C.J. went on relentlessly. "Gloria saw you go into the prop trailer that morning, didn't she? And she tried to blackmail you."

"She tried to," Traeger spat out. "And not just for money. The stupid bitch actually wanted me to give her a major role. Can you imagine?"

C.J. could imagine it, all right. Poor Gloria must have had fantasies of a renewed career that would put her in the spotlight once more. It was a pathetic fantasy—and a fatal one.

"So you killed her," she said quietly.

"I killed her. With both her and Prescott dead, there shouldn't have been a problem." He shook his head slowly. "But you wouldn't give up." He asked in a voice as cold as ice, "What do you want?"

"I want you to fry."

C.J. didn't know whether Tom, his partner, and Sam burst through the door or simply walked in. One moment she and Traeger were facing each other, the truth exposed at last, and the next moment Sam was beside her and Tom was reading Traeger his rights.

"Emmett Traeger, you're under arrest for the murders of Gloria Ames and Dan Prescott. You have the right to remain silent. Anything you say can and will be used against you in a court of law."

C.J. looked at Sam. "You heard it all?"

He nodded.

She grinned up at him. "We did it."

"No," he corrected her, "*you* did it."

Chapter 18

The six o'clock news carried a full story on Emmett Traeger's arrest for murder. The revelation that the scion of a film industry dynasty was accused of murdering two people stunned the film community. But C.J. knew that even murder couldn't match the media blitz that would explode the very next day when Julie Prescott filed a lawsuit claiming to be the rightful owner of all the U.F.S. property.

When she had explained everything to Julie, the young woman's immediate response was one of complete incomprehension. Finally, C.J. made her understand that not only had they caught her grandfather's murderer, she was now an heiress to a vast fortune. When the dust settled in the inevitable court battle, Julie would control U.F.S. and all its property.

At C.J.'s urging, Julie put herself in the hands of a good attorney. Late that afternoon she drove Julie to his office, located, ironically, in Century City, only a block from U.F.S. In the lavishly appointed reception area of the office, decorated with expensive English antiques, Julie came out of her daze long enough to say in her sweet, fragile voice, "Thank you, Miss Grant. For everything."

C.J.'s last vision of Julie was a punk waif being escorted into the attorney's private office, desperately clutching the hundred-year-old deed that had caused so much tragedy. As she left, she couldn't help smiling at the thought that this young woman would someday be running a major studio.

Back home, C.J. took her phone off the hook, to avoid

the hordes of news organizations that wanted to interview her, locked up the office, and went for a long walk on the beach with Sam.

Neither of them spoke. They simply walked hand in hand, each lost in their own thoughts, watching the sun set over the horizon in a vivid palette of red-gold, burnt orange, and lavender.

Looking at Sam now, C.J. tried to imprint his image on her memory—those faint lines at his eyes, his mouth slightly turned down under the curve of his mustache. How many times had she seen him just like this, beside her in the car as they chased after some clue, at the ranch when he opened up and revealed so much about himself, when they made love.

She'd once thought him a simple man with uncomplicated values, a clear-cut sense of right and wrong, truth, and justice. But she'd seen him in a new light yesterday when he stood by her even though she insisted on doing something he didn't want her to do.

He was the most giving, caring, tender man she'd ever known. He wasn't intimidated by her, wasn't afraid to let her be all that she could be. But he'd taught her that in addition to being strong and independent, it was all right to be vulnerable and need to be protected sometimes.

In the process he'd learned a few things himself, and changed in ways she wouldn't have believed possible only a few days earlier.

She swallowed hard. Looking at him walking beside her, she whispered, "You've come a long way, baby."

He glanced at her. "What?"

She forced herself to smile casually. "Nothing. How about some dinner? I'm starving."

A nice, intimate, candlelit dinner would have been nice, C.J. thought, but there wasn't time. It was already eight o'clock by the time they got back to the apartment and packed Sam's few possessions in an old duffel bag of hers. On the way to Century City, they ordered some food from the drive-through window at a Taco Bell. But neither had much appetite all of a sudden, and the food remained untouched.

In Century City, Lucy, Ravi and, to C.J.'s surprise, Cody, waited at the exact spot where Sam had first appeared. Because it was night, the parking lot was nearly empty and there were no people around.

When C.J. saw Cody, she turned to Lucy in dismay. "You told him!"

"Don't worry," Lucy insisted. "He won't tell anyone else."

C.J. said to Cody, "You believe her?"

Cody grinned. "Not really. But I thought I'd come along anyway—just in case." Looking at Sam, Cody added, "If it is true, it would sure explain a lot of things about you."

Sam smiled at him. "It's been good knowin' you."

Cody shook his hand vigorously. "Same here, Marshal."

Lucy noticed Sam and C.J. exchange a poignant look. She said quickly, "We've still got a few minutes yet. Let's go wait in Ravi's van."

As they walked over to Ravi's ancient, battered Volkswagen van, Sam turned to C.J. Looking down into her eyes glistening with unshed tears, he began uncertainly. "I'm not very good at talking about my feelings."

Her throat ached as she replied, "You don't have to say anything, Sam."

"*Katy.*" He whispered his special name for her, his tone almost unbearably intimate. She knew no one would ever call her that again.

She reached up and laid her hand against his cheek. He kissed her deeply, pouring everything he couldn't say in words into that tender contact. She breathed him in, tasted the sweet, masculine essence of him.

Tearing herself away, she looked at him one last time, then turned and walked quickly to her car.

When she got home, C.J. couldn't bear the thought of sitting around the apartment, waiting to see if Lucy's crazy theory worked, so she went downstairs to her office. It was all ridiculous, of course, she told herself. Stopping at the door to the office, she glanced up at the clear, star-laden sky, and frowned. Lucy and Ravi didn't know what they were talking about, with their half-baked notions of time and space and stars lining up. Sam would return in a while, looking slightly chagrined, and Lucy would be full of some nonsense as to why Ravi's theory failed.

Then she felt it.

First came the telltale rumble deep underground, the sound building inexorably. The ground began to tremble, then shudder uncontrollably. C.J. ran out to the middle of the beach, away from the swaying buildings and falling debris. Unable to stand on the shifting ground, she fell down and watched buildings swaying slightly.

All around her, people streamed out of the houses and apartments lining the beach and stumbled toward safety. Children cried and some women screamed as the nightmare they'd experienced less than two weeks earlier repeated itself.

It didn't have the intensity of the original quake, but it wasn't just another minor aftershock either. This was the real thing, just as Ravi had predicted. At that moment C.J. knew that Sam was gone forever. And her fear of the earthquake was nothing compared to the terrible sense of loss that engulfed her.

It ended as abruptly as it began. Standing up on legs that felt like jelly, she surveyed the scene. Fortunately, there had been little damage, at least to the exterior of buildings—a few broken windows and cracks in cement. Inside, C.J. knew from experience, everyone would find broken dishes and lamps, and cracks in walls and ceilings.

But as she dusted sand from her jeans and walked slowly back toward her place, she wasn't thinking about the inevitable mess to be cleaned up. She was thinking about Sam, and the fact that she would live out the rest of her life without ever seeing him again.

Inside the office things weren't as bad as she had expected. A couple of pictures had fallen from the walls, and files that Lucy had left in a stack on her desk were strewn all over the floor, but that was all. Leaving all this for Lucy to deal with in the morning, C.J. went into her office.

The pen and desk calendar that always sat on her desk had fallen to the floor. Bending down to pick them up, C.J. found a handwritten note. She quickly scanned it. It read: *Sam and C.J., please meet me at the studio in front of the administration building at ten o'clock*. It was signed, *Julie*.

C.J. wondered why Julie would want to meet at the studio so late. Then she realized that Julie had probably spent hours with the attorney, and this was the first free moment she'd had all evening. Glancing at her watch, she saw that it was already a quarter to ten. She would have to hurry.

Grabbing her purse and car keys, she drove quickly to the studio. Because it was so late, there were few cars on the streets. From what C.J. could see, there had been little damage from the quake. Unlike the aftermath of the previous quake, there were few ambulances and fire engines racing down the streets. She just hoped that Julie, waiting at the studio, had survived the quake okay.

It was a quarter past ten when C.J. drove up to the gate. A drive-on pass was waiting for her and the guard waved her on.

The lot was nearly deserted. Taking advantage of all the empty spaces, C.J. parked in front of the administration building in Emmett Traeger's old space. She got out of her car and looked around. There was absolutely no sign of Julie, and C.J. worried that she might have been injured in the quake.

She was trying to decide if she should wait for a while or go home and call Julie, when a long black limousine pulled up next to her car. Wondering what some studio bigwig was doing here this late, she glanced curiously at the tinted windows. To her surprise, one of them rolled down slowly and a voice called from inside, "Miss Grant."

Walking closer, C.J. peered into the dark interior. "Yes?"

Behind her, she vaguely noted the sound of a car door opening, then footsteps. But her attention was fixed on trying to see the occupant of the car.

The next thing she knew someone had grabbed her, pressing a thick handkerchief, damp with chloroform, against her face. She didn't even have time to struggle before oblivion overcame her.

"Wake up, Miss Grant." The male voice jolted her into consciousness. Opening bleary eyes, C.J. gazed in bewilderment at a short, stooped figure standing alone in a pool of dim light in the center of a soundstage. At the same time, she realized that she was lying in a crumpled heap on the cold cement floor. Her throat burned from the chloroform, and her body was sore from being dumped unceremoniously on the floor.

"So good of you to join us," the weak, gravelly voice continued.

C.J. had only a moment to wonder who on earth this wizened little man could possible be, when suddenly her arms were pinned behind her so forcefully she thought they would break. She screamed once, and a rough voice ordered, "Shut up, or I'll gag you."

It wouldn't do any good to scream anyway, she knew. There was no one around to hear her.

Despite being weak from the chloroform, she tried to free herself from her attacker, using all the moves she'd learned in self-defense class. But it was no good. Though she couldn't see him clearly because he remained behind her, it was obvious the man holding her was very large and very strong. Nothing she tried fazed him, and she was quickly tired out from the effort.

"It's no use," the elderly man in the center of the stage said calmly. "Give up, Miss Grant."

She stood there, breathing heavily, trying to gather both her strength and her wits.

The man ordered sharply, "Bring her here, Bruno."

Bruno pulled her to her feet, then forced her to walk toward the man, stopping just a few feet away. He was incredibly ancient, his body thin and bent. The outline of his skull was evident beneath the thin, parchmentlike skin and sunken eyes.

C.J.'s eyes widened in surprise as she recognized him

from the portrait outside Traeger's office. "Charles Traeger," she whispered.

"Very good, my dear. But then, you've proven yourself quite clever at making correct deductions. You and your partner, Mr. Hackett. Where is he, by the way?"

She hesitated, unwilling to admit to Traeger that she was alone and helpless. "He'll be coming soon," she lied.

His dark eyes surveyed her critically. "No . . . no, I don't think so. You're a good enough actress to fool my grandson, my dear, but not quite good enough to fool me."

He paused, then went on in a slightly baffled tone. "Odd, isn't it? A man by the same name killed my father."

C.J. stared at him incredulously. "But—your father lived long enough to found this studio."

"True. However, he was in a gunfight with a U.S. Marshal by the name of Sam Hackett. He took a bullet in his back, near his spine. It didn't kill him then, but it did so slowly over the next twenty years. Now another Sam Hackett has helped you destroy my family and everything we own."

So that was what all this was about, C.J. realized—revenge. She had brought down the Traeger family and their empire. Now the last Traeger remaining free would make her pay. Panic seized her as she realized the full seriousness of her position. She had no doubt at all that Charles Traeger meant to kill her. Her only consolation was that Sam was forever beyond the reach of Traeger's vengeance.

Thinking desperately, she knew that her only chance lay in keeping Traeger talking until she could figure out someway—anyway—to escape. "Your grandson killed two people," she said in a voice not nearly as strong as she would have liked.

Traeger frowned. "He was merely the instrument of my strategy. *I* planned Prescott's death. It would have been perfect if that fool grandson of mine hadn't allowed himself to be seen entering the prop trailer. I planned the Ames woman's death as well. But once again my grandson failed me."

C.J. stared at him in amazement. This elderly man,

barely holding on to life, controlled everything. Emmett Traeger was merely a figurehead, waiting for the day when the real power would finally be passed on to him.

"You planned my 'accident' at the wrap party too."

"Of course. That was the first time my grandson failed me." Traeger shook his head in frustration. "I don't know what's happened to this family. We used to produce more capable offspring."

"I don't imagine you would have made his mistakes," C.J. went on, her mind racing, discarding plan after plan, searching desperately for something that might give her a chance at escape.

"He's a damned fool! He could have beaten you at your own game. You didn't have any *real* proof. But when you confronted him, he panicked and gave you what you needed—a confession."

Then C.J. knew. "You were there—in the office next to his yesterday afternoon."

"That's right. I listened to the entire conversation. Not that it did any good." He thumped the cane down hard on the wooden floor, fury coursing through his thin, fragile body. "My father should have killed Rollie Prescott's wife, and their brat as well. Then none of this would ever have happened."

C.J. swallowed hard. "It will look awfully suspicious when I turn up dead here at the studio. The police will come after you. With your grandson in jail, you're the logical suspect."

"I don't think so." His rheumy eyes glistened unnaturally. "Let me explain exactly what will happen. This soundstage is one of the original ones my father built before World War I. I think it only fitting that if it all has to end, then it should do so here. These old soundstages are made entirely of wood, Miss Grant. It's old and dry and brittle."

He smiled grimly. "Rather like myself. At any rate, one little spark and it will all go up in flames in a matter of minutes."

Terror gripped her at the thought of burning to death. She couldn't envision any death more agonizing.

Traeger shuffled across the set, stopping at a panel box

of electrical switches and a circuit breaker that controlled the lights on the set. "I dedicated my life to this studio. I know everything there is to know about this business, from gaffer to sound mixing to special effects. This box controls the entire electrical system in this soundstage."

He slammed down the handle of the circuit breaker. It sparked as metal hit metal, sending a live current flowing between.

"Just one little spark, Miss Grant," Traeger repeated as he thrust his hand into a nearby packing crate and came up with a fistful of shredded straw packing material.

C.J. tried to moisten her dry mouth. She knew exactly what he intended. If a spark ignited some of that straw, it would instantly start a fire. In a matter of minutes the entire soundstage would be engulfed in flames.

"Your body will be found and, eventually, identified," Traeger went on. "It will be viewed as a tragic accident. Your charred remains won't show that you had been hit on the head and knocked unconscious. And there will be nothing to connect me to it."

She tried to blink back her tears, but it was no good. She felt them trickle down her cheeks.

"Tears, Miss Grant? I wouldn't have expected it of you. You've been so very determined and resourceful up to now."

C.J. fought then with all the desperation of a trapped animal. She bit and clawed and kicked, but it was useless. Bruno simply stood there, as massive and implacable as a mountain. When her energy was spent, his grip on her was as tight as ever.

Traeger shook his head slowly. "Really, Miss Grant. Don't be such a fool."

Turning back to the electrical panel, he stuffed some straw around the circuit breaker. Then he lifted the metal handle and slammed it down. It sparked, the straw caught fire, smoldering at first, then bursting into flames. The fire spread over the control panel until it was engulfed.

She glanced helplessly in the direction of the door.

Following her look, Traeger smiled. "Forget it, Miss

Grant. There's no one to rescue you this time. Don't you know there are no more heroes?"

When C.J. had driven away from Century City, Sam stood watching her until she was out of sight. As long as he lived he knew he would remember the look in her eyes just before she kissed him. He knew that with every fiber of her being she longed to ask him to stay. But she didn't.

He'd always thought he preferred long hair on women. Hell, all the women he'd known had long hair. But with C.J.'s short, cropped hairstyle, he could stroke the curve at the back of her neck as he had done early this morning when they made love for the last time.

He'd thought himself sated after this morning. But it was still there, that gnawing need that sharpened at the mere thought of her.

He'd thought her irritating when they first met. Then he'd come to appreciate her strength and courage. Only after making love to her had he realized how vulnerable she was beneath that facade of self-sufficiency. That vulnerability had touched him as nothing else had done—not even with Maria.

"Sam, we have to get ready," Lucy said gently, touching his arm.

He looked at her, then looked away. C.J. was just a memory now. One that would haunt him for the rest of his life.

"All right," he said heavily. "Let's go."

A minute later Sam was in position. Lucy asked excitedly, "You're sure this is where you were standing when you saw the car heading toward the little boy?"

Sam nodded. "One minute I was running toward a boy in a dusty street, with a water wagon comin' right at us, then the next minute I saw a different little boy and an automobile. I didn't know what it was, but it was pretty clear it was going to hit him, so I kept running."

Cody came up to them. Motioning to Ravi sitting in his van, he said, "That fella says it's just about time."

Lucy's eyes glinted with excitement. "All right!"

Sam took her hand. "Thanks for everything, Lucy. I

don't know what I would've done if you hadn't been there."

Lucy grinned. "You're a good man, Marshal. Far better than most I've met in my lifetime."

Cody said, "If Lucy's right about all this, I hope you have a safe journey, or whatever it is. I'd trade places with you if I could."

Sam smiled warmly at him. "Looks to me like you've got your hands full with Lucy here."

Cody took his hand and shook it vigorously. "Dan Prescott would've been pleased that you had a hand in catchin' his murderer." He sniffed loudly, then finished in embarrassment, "Damn smog must be gettin' to me."

Sam turned to Lucy. "Look after Katy. She isn't nearly as independent as she pretends to be."

"I know," Lucy whispered.

In the background Ravi jumped out of the van, waving his arms from the deep folds of his flowing white robe. He cried out, "Eeet's time, everybodeee!"

Sam felt a rolling motion begin deep beneath his feet. The minor aftershocks he'd been through after the big quake were nothing like this. This was like the original, a powerful force that buckled and heaved the earth beneath them.

"Sam, look!" Lucy shouted, pointing behind him.

Sam turned to see a brilliant white light, so intense it was almost painful to look into.

"That is eeet!" Ravi yelled, his robe billowing around him as he struggled to stay on his feet.

For the first time since Lucy had told him of her wild theory, Sam truly believed it. He *could* get back to his own time. Back to his own life. Living from one day to the next, never setting down roots, not caring what lay ahead. And never seeing Katy again.

"Hurry," Lucy urged him, "you'll miss it!"

He grabbed her as she was about to fall down. "I can't go, Lucy. I can't leave her."

"But this chance may never come again!"

"I know."

Looking back at Ravi, Lucy shouted above the roar of

the earthquake, "What would happen if someone else stepped through there?"

Ravi, who was hanging on to the van for dear life, said, "Eeet is a portal to the past. Anyone can step through eeet." He added uncertainly, "Theoretically, of course."

"I'm going," Lucy announced. "Tell C.J. good-bye," she said to Sam. "I know she's in good hands."

"Lucy, wait!" he shouted. "You don't know what you're getting into."

She threw back her head and laughed. "No. But it'll be one hell of an adventure!"

Cody said abruptly, "I'm goin' with you. Just think of it, no more smog, no more taxes." He took her hand. "Let's go, Lucy."

Together, they staggered toward the light . . .

Ravi gave Sam a ride back to C.J.'s. As Sam raced up the steps, taking them two at a time, he didn't know how he was going to explain Lucy's absence. But at the moment all he could think of was seeing C.J. again.

Finding the door locked and the apartment dark and silent, Sam hurried back downstairs to the office. That door, too, was locked. But Sam knew where she hid the extra key—under a potted plant beside the door.

A moment later he found the note that C.J. had dropped back on her desk. He frowned—why would Julie want to meet them at the studio tonight? He sat on the edge of the desk, pondering this, when the phone rang.

Sam picked it up gingerly. He had used a telephone only once before, and still wasn't used to the strange contraption. Holding the receiver some distance from his face, he spoke into it hesitantly. "Hello?"

"Hi, Sam, it's Julie. I'm sorry for calling so late, but I need to ask C.J. something."

"Wait a minute—isn't she with you?"

"I haven't seen her since she dropped me off at the attorney's office. You wouldn't believe all the things he said. It's so rad!"

Interrupting Julie, Sam asked, "Did you leave a note

here at the office asking C.J. and me to meet you at the studio?"

"No, of course not."

"I've gotta go, Julie," Sam said quickly, then slammed down the phone.

Something was very wrong. The only question was how to deal with it. He knew what Katy would say—go to the police, let them handle it. Well, to hell with that. He'd done things her way, but now she was in danger, he could feel it, and he was going to handle this the only way he knew how. *His* way.

Obviously, Katy had gone to the studio. But how was he to get there?

Then he remembered Lucy's car parked out on the street. He remembered she usually left her keys in the car. Sure enough, they were there. As he started the car, he felt a sudden jolt of nervousness. Driving along this street a couple of times with Lucy was one thing. Heading out onto the freeways and major thoroughfares of L.A. was another.

He told himself he could handle it. He had to. Katy's life might very well be at stake.

Sam had been back and forth to the studio so many times with C.J. that he had no trouble finding it. The problem was getting inside. He knew the guard wouldn't admit him without a pass, and he had no way of getting one. He would just have to sneak in.

Parking the car near a poorly lit section of fence, he left his rifle in it but tucked the Colt snugly in his waistband. Then he climbed over the fence.

He raced to the administration building and found her car. But there was no sign of her. Looking around desperately, he saw nothing that indicated where she might have gone. The administration building, like the rest of the studio, was dark and locked up for the night.

Katy could be anywhere. She might even have left the lot entirely. Sam had no idea what to do, where to start looking. He couldn't ask the guard, because the man would immediately throw him off the lot.

Unable to stand there one more minute, he simply started walking around the lot, searching desperately for some sign of Katy. As the minutes passed his desperation grew. He had decided he would have to go to the guard after all, and, if necessary, demand his help at gunpoint, when he noticed a red light revolving over a door to a soundstage. Something Katy had said came back to him—that light was on only when the soundstage was in use, as a warning that nobody was to go inside. But the lot was deserted, no one was working this late. Why would the warning light be on?

Sam opened the door quietly. The smell was of old wood, faintly musty, like a hundred old buildings out of his past. Stepping inside, he caught another smell—smoke.

And then he saw them—a man holding Katy, and another, incredibly old, man standing nearby.

"Katy!"

At the sound of Sam's voice the man holding her dropped her arms and whirled around, pulling a gun out of a shoulder holster. He fired first, barely missing Sam, who had dropped to the floor and whipped his Colt out of his waistband. Sam took him out with a single shot. The man slumped to the floor, a red stain spreading quickly across the front of his white shirt.

The fire was growing rapidly and smoke filled the soundstage. Coughing and choking, C.J. ran over to Sam. "It's Charles Traeger," she said hoarsely. "He planned everything."

Sam looked over at the old man, staggering toward a far door, leaning heavily on a cane, trying to find his way through the billowing smoke.

"We've got to get out of here," Sam shouted to C.J., "or we'll burn to death."

"We can't just leave him," she insisted.

He didn't have time to argue with her. Grabbing her hand, he pulled her toward the exit. As they stumbled toward the door, a loud roar exploded behind them.

Looking back, Sam saw that most of the soundstage was completely engulfed in flames. Traeger lay in the center of the building, crushed by a fallen beam. He was very clearly dead.

"C'mon, we're getting out of here," Sam shouted, then

dragged her through the door and out into the fresh air as the roof of the soundstage collapsed in a fiery mass of falling timbers.

Outside, he held her to him tightly, as if he would never let her go.

"I felt the earthquake and knew you were gone," she sobbed into his shirtfront.

"I couldn't leave you," he whispered. "Not now. Not ever."

She hiccuped and Sam gently wiped her tear-stained cheeks, leaving a streak of white in the soot. She looked so funny, he couldn't help smiling at her. "Let this be a lesson to you," he said with mock gruffness. "You *need* me, lady."

Her smile warmed his heart. "I know."

Epilogue

C.J. sat at the desk in her office, drinking coffee and reading the paper. But her mind wasn't on the story of the fire at Soundstage 24 or the amazing transformation of Julie from starving would-be actress to wealthy studio mogul. She was thinking about Sam.

She smiled to herself. They were going away for a while. The Mustang was all packed and ready to head out of town. C.J. was just waiting for Sam to come downstairs. For someone who had very little to pack, he sure was taking a long time, she thought, glancing at her watch.

While she waited, she considered their destination. Maybe they would head south to Mexico or north to Mendocino. Not that it mattered where they went, as long as they were together. She needed time with Sam, time to come to terms with this whirlwind relationship that had turned her life upside down. She wasn't at all sure Lucy could handle the business all by herself for a while, but she would just have to risk it.

Thinking about her mother reminded her that it was nearly nine and Lucy hadn't shown up for work yet. That was the problem with hiring your mother, C.J. thought with a long sigh. You couldn't fire her.

Sam same in, stepping over Redford, then nearly tripping as the cat abruptly decided to get up.

"Damn cat," Sam muttered. He set down a book in front of C.J., then perched on the corner of the desk, facing her.

"What's this?" she asked.

"It's one of the library books your mother got for me.

Katy, there's something I've gotta tell you, but first I wanted to check out an idea I had."

She leaned back in her chair and smiled up at him. "Okay, what do you want me to look at in this book?"

"Before I show you, I've gotta tell you something that might be kind of a shock." He took her hands in his, holding them gently, and said, "When I changed my mind about going back, Lucy and Cody decided to try it themselves. She asked me to look after you and to tell you she loves you, then they went back together."

C.J. was stunned. *"What?"*

Sam hurried on. "It's okay, they weren't hurt."

She didn't know whether to be furious or sad. Pulling her hands away from Sam, she shot up from the chair and glared at him. "God knows, my mother has done a lot of crazy things in her life, but how could she do something like this? How could she leave her only child? Didn't she care about me? She could be a royal pain in the ass, but she *was* my mother, and mothers are supposed to be there for their children. They aren't supposed to go gallivanting through time, doing God knows what, ending up God knows where."

Her tirade came to a sudden stop as Sam opened the book to a full-page photograph and held it directly before her eyes.

"Oh, my God," C.J. exclaimed. "It can't be!" There in front of her, in glorious black and white, was a photograph of a famed saloon owner, Miss Lucy, wearing a gaudy silk gown with plumed feathers in her Gibson girl hairdo. Standing beside her in the photograph was her husband, one Cody Wilkerson, looking debonair in an embroidered satin waistcoat.

"They made it back, Katy," Sam went on gently.

C.J.'s voice was small and helpless. "But . . . do you think I'll ever see her again?"

Sam grinned. "Knowing Lucy, I'd bet on it." He set down the book and took her in his arms. "And in the meantime I intend to keep my promise to her. I'm going to look after you very, very well."

They were just about to kiss when—

"Ah-hem. Excuse me."

C.J. looked up to see a gray-haired man in his midsixties standing in the doorway of her office. Short and balding, with a pronounced paunch, he reminded her of her fifth-grade teacher, Mr. Avery, whom she had adored.

"I hope you'll forgive me for barging in, but the door was open."

"Can I help you?" C.J. asked, trying to inject a professional note in her shaky voice.

"You *are* Miss C. J. Grant?"

"Yes."

"The same C. J. Grant who solved the Prescott murder case?"

She nodded, then said quickly, "But I'm afraid I'm leaving on vacation, so if you could possibly come back in a few days." She glanced at Sam. "Er, make that a few weeks."

He hurried forward, his expression anxious. "But I don't have a few weeks. It's been much too long already."

He sat down in the chair facing the desk, then laid an old photo album in front of C.J. "I need you to find this woman. It's vitally important. I'll pay anything."

Sam interrupted firmly. "Miss Grant is going away on her honeymoon. She can't take on any new clients right now."

C.J. looked up in surprise. She and Sam hadn't discussed marriage.

Turning back to the client, she saw a stricken expression on his face that went right to her heart.

"Perhaps, if you could quickly explain your problem, Mr.—"

"Spencer. Charles Spencer. I first saw her in 1944. I was stationed in England, getting ready for D-Day. She came with a USO troop and put on a show at my base. Her name was Jeanne Randolph. She sang like an angel and danced as if her feet had wings."

C.J. was touched by the poetic flight of fancy. Mr. Spencer, she realized, must have had a dreadful crush on this girl.

He went on. "After the war, I saw her first movie,

Dream a Little Dream. She was wonderful in it. After that I saw every movie she made, and kept every article that was written about her. It's all in here—the story of her career and her life."

C.J. didn't recognize the name, or the photos in the album. Jeanne Randolph must not have progressed beyond B-movie roles.

Spencer added sadly, "Her last movie came out in 1957. After that she retired to Carmel."

"Mr. Spencer, I don't quite see . . ."

"Miss Grant, I fell in love with her when I was just a boy. An adolescent infatuation, you might say, but I continued to love her for the next forty-five years. I love her still. I promised myself that someday, somehow, I would meet her. I've accumulated a certain amount of money, and I'm willing to spend every penny of it to find her."

"But if you know she lives in Carmel, why not simply go up there?" C.J. asked.

"I did. She hasn't been there in months. And no one knows where she went."

C.J. glanced helplessly at Sam, who stood beside her, shaking his head.

"I'm sorry, Mr. Spencer, but—"

He interrupted gently. "Miss Grant, I'm no longer young. I don't want to die without meeting the woman I've loved all my life."

In spite of herself, C.J. was hooked. "All right, Mr. Spencer, I'll see what I can do. A case like this, involving a public person, shouldn't be too difficult." At Sam's look of irritation, she went on quickly. "I'm sure it will take only a few days. I can take my vacation afterward."

"Thank you, Miss Grant," Spencer said with tears in his eyes.

"May I keep the album for the time being?"

"Of course. Just—be careful with it. It means a great deal to me."

She smiled. "I understand, Mr. Spencer. If you'll give me your address and phone number, I'll get back to you as soon as possible."

When Spencer left a few minutes later, Sam frowned at her "*Katy.*"

"Oh, Sam, how could I turn him down? It won't take long, then we can leave on our vacation."

"Honeymoon."

"*Vacation,*" she insisted as she grabbed her purse and headed outside. As they got into her car, she said, "We haven't discussed marriage yet. I'm not sure about it."

"I'm sure. Can't you just let this case go?" he asked as she backed the car out of the garage.

"No, I can't let it go."

"All right," he gave in grudgingly, "we'll find this Randolph woman. But as soon as we do, we're gettin' married. And once the kids start comin', I'll handle the agency and you can stay home."

"Wait just a minute," C.J. said with growing irritation. "I'm not giving up my career. And I'm not at all sure I want kids."

"Of course you do. Five or six would be nice. I like big families."

As she turned onto Pacific Coast Highway, she said, "Let's get one thing straight right now, Sam Hackett. You are *not* going to tell me what I do or do not want. Understand?"

He pulled his hat down low over his eyes to shade them from the morning sun. "All right, I'll compromise on the kids. We'll have four. But that's my final say on the matter."

"Oh, it is, is it?"

"Yup."

With that, C.J. gunned the engine, throwing Sam back against the seat. "We'll just see who has the final say, Marshal," she said as the Mustang shot down the highway.

DON'T MISS
THESE CURRENT
Bantam Bestsellers

☐	28390	**THE AMATEUR** Robert Littell	$4.95
☐	28525	**THE DEBRIEFING** Robert Littell	$4.95
☐	28362	**COREY LANE** Norman Zollinger	$4.50
☐	27636	**PASSAGE TO QUIVIRA** Norman Zollinger	$4.50
☐	27759	**RIDER TO CIBOLA** Norman Zollinger	$3.95
☐	27814	**THIS FAR FROM PARADISE** Philip Shelby	$4.95
☐	27811	**DOCTORS** Erich Segal	$5.95
☐	28179	**TREVAYNE** Robert Ludlum	$5.95
☐	27807	**PARTNERS** John Martel	$4.95
☐	28058	**EVA LUNA** Isabel Allende	$4.95
☐	27597	**THE BONFIRE OF THE VANITIES** Tom Wolfe	$5.95
☐	27510	**THE BUTCHER'S THEATER** Jonathan Kellerman	$4.95
☐	27800	**THE ICARUS AGENDA** Robert Ludlum	$5.95
☐	27891	**PEOPLE LIKE US** Dominick Dunne	$4.95
☐	27953	**TO BE THE BEST** Barbara Taylor Bradford	$5.95
☐	26892	**THE GREAT SANTINI** Pat Conroy	$4.95
☐	26574	**SACRED SINS** Nora Roberts	$3.95

Buy them at your local bookstore or use this page to order.

Bantam Books, Dept. FB, 414 East Golf Road, Des Plaines, IL 60016

Please send me the items I have checked above. I am enclosing $_____
(please add $2.00 to cover postage and handling). Send check or money
order, no cash or C.O.D.s please.

Mr/Ms _____

Address _____

City/State_____ Zip_____

FB–4/90

Please allow four to six weeks for delivery.
Prices and availability subject to change without notice.